P9-CRV-052

Masters of Fantasy

BAEN BOOKS also edited by BILL FAWCETT:

The Warmasters

Masters of Fantasy

edited by

Bill Fawcett

&

Brian Thomsen

MASTERS OF FANTASY

This is a work of fiction. All the characters and events portrayed in this book are fictional, and any resemblance to real people or incidents is purely coincidental.

Copyright © 2004 by Bill Fawcett & Associates; all stories copyright © 2004 to the authors thereof.

All rights reserved, including the right to reproduce this book or portions thereof in any form.

A Baen Books Original

Baen Publishing Enterprises
P.O. Box 1403
Riverdale, NY 10471
www.baen.com

ISBN: 0-7434-8822-9

Cover art by Jeff Easley

First printing, July 2004

Library of Congress Cataloging-in-Publication Data

Masters of fantasy / edited by Bill Fawcett & Brian Thomsen.
   p. cm.
"A Baen Books original"—T.p. verso.
   ISBN 0-7434-8822-9 (hc)
   1. Fantasy fiction, American. I. Fawcett, Bill. II. Thomsen, Brian.

PS648.F3M37 2004
813'.0876608—dc22

2004005565

Distributed by Simon & Schuster
1230 Avenue of the Americas
New York, NY 10020

Production by Windhaven Press, Auburn, NH
Typeset by Bell Road Press, Sherwood, OR
Printed in the United States of America

10 9 8 7 6 5 4 3 2 1

Contents

Introduction
   Brian Thomsen 1
Out of the Deep
   A *Valdemar* story, Mercedes Lackey 5
Earthborne
   A *Witchworld* story, Andre Norton 29
Mything in Dreamland
   A *Myth Adventures in Dreamland* story,
   Robert Asprin and Jody Lynn Nye 47
Race for the Sky
   A *Bifrost* story, Mickey Zucker Reichert 69
Shadamehr and the Old Wive's Tale
   A *Shadamehr* story, Margaret Weis and Don Perrin 95
Serenade
   A *Spellsinger* story, Alan Dean Foster 115
Child of Prophecy
   A *War of Light and Shadow* story, Janny Wurts 145
The Afterlife of St. Vidicon of Cathode
   A *Warlock* story, Christopher Stasheff 169
The Elf House
   An *Isles* story, David Drake 197
Gifts
   A *World of Paksenarrion* story, Elizabeth Moon 211
The Amorous Broom
   A *John Justin Mallory* story, Mike Resnick 233
Web of Deception
   A *Bahzell* story, David Weber 245

From Category to Genre in a Bookselling Sense

Or
When Sales and Popularity Begin to Command Respect

We all have friends who might look at our reading tastes as being a bit eccentric.

You know who I mean—those who call it "sword and sorcery stuff" and seem to think that every fantasy needs a Frazetta or Boris cover that will appeal primarily to adolescent boys in search of cheap thrills.

There was a time when their point of view was in the majority and fantasy titles were relegated to the same level of respect afforded to other "category" fiction titles.

"Category" is a pejorative. For example, in category terms, westerns were "horse operas" or "shoot 'em ups," romances were "bodice rippers," and fantasies were "that Conan stuff." And the principal venues for sales were drugstore and gas station wire racks next to this month's issue of *Good Housekeeping*, *Popular Mechanics*, or *Playboy*. Category books were sold at the bottom of the list and engendered little respect from either the publisher or the bookseller.

Then, a funny thing happened.

Category books began to break out and sell like hotcakes, and not just at the truck stops but in the book stores as well.

Louis L'Amour became a topselling author of western fiction (notice "western fiction"; that's a *genre* designation, not just a category), romances became either "historical romances," "regency romances" or "contemporary romances" (again, with genre-specific designations) and fantasies, well . . . let me tell you what happened.

First, the powers that be began to split hairs.

Tolkien wasn't really fantasy; it was fiction, just like Richard Adams's talking rabbit novel, *Watership Down*, and John Gardner's *Grendel*. Any new book that commanded an equal amount of respect like, say, *The Mists of Avalon*, was also obviously fiction, and therefore not like those category fantasy titles that appeared in paperback and usually were part of some large series like Conan (you know, just like Mack Bolan except without the guns and gadgets).

They were considered a flavor-of-the-month sort of thing where the authors didn't really matter except to a small but rabid fandom.

The truth was, however, that the fandom wasn't that small, and in no time at all their buying power became more noticeable.

In 1982, *Ogre, Ogre* by Piers Anthony made the *New York Times* paperback bestseller list, something category books were not expected to do.

Now, *Ogre, Ogre* was a paperback original (no hardcover edition), part of an ongoing series, with no special movie tie-in (à la *Star Wars*) or critical prestige.

It made the list solely because it sold or, more specifically, because enough people wanted to purchase it as soon as it was available—and subsequent books in the series followed the same pattern.

Soon, other authors' works followed suit with successful paperback series making the list, such as Foster's Spellsinger books, Weis and Hickman's Dragonlance and Dark Sword series and Lackey's Valdemar books. And in no time at all every publishing house realized that a commercially successful fantasy series was every bit as significant as a bestselling mystery or historical romance. Such books no longer received a "category" treatment because there was the potential for even greater sales.

Such books became treated like "fiction" titles and, from a bookselling standpoint, fantasy went from being a category to a genre.

As a result of these new sales and the attention they engendered in-house, science fiction and fantasy lines sprang up everywhere, with independent new publishers specializing in the genre beginning to command respect. Books that were formerly paperback originals became hardcovers.

Fantasy had become a force to be reckoned with.

It had gained the respect of booksellers and publishers alike, the same respect that its fans had had for years.

This book contains brand new stories set in some of the series that were part of the bestselling phenomenon that brought this about, written by the authors who earned their now well-deserved respect.

Enjoy!

—Brian Thomsen

Out of the Deep

A Valdemar Story

Mercedes Lackey

Now *this* was a forest!

Trees crowded the road, overshadowing it, overhanging it. You didn't need a hat even at midday; you almost needed a torch instead to see by. Herald-Intern Alain still couldn't get used to all of the *wilderness* around him—trees that weren't pruned into symmetrical and pleasing shapes, wildflowers that were really wild, ragged, and insect-nibbled. All of his life—except for the brief course in Wilderness Survival—he'd never seen a *weed*, much less a wilderness. He kept expecting to wake up and find that all of this was a fever-dream.

By all rights, he shouldn't be out here, league upon league away from Haven on his Internship Circuit. He was a Prince, after all, and Princes of Valdemar had *never* gone out of Haven for their Internships, much less out into the furthermost West of the Kingdom, where there were no Guardsmen to rescue you if you got into trouble, and often nowhere to shelter if nature decided to have a bash at you. He *should* have been serving his Internship beside one of the Heralds who helped the City Guard, the Watch, and the city judges.

There was just one teeny, tiny problem with that.

:Actually,: his Companion Vedalia observed, *:There are seven rather tall and vigorous problems with that. And four slender and attractive ones as well.:*

Alain sighed. It wasn't the easiest thing in the world, being the youngest of twelve royal children who had *all* been Chosen.

:*It wasn't the easiest thing in the world trying to find things for all of those young and eager Heralds to do,*: Vedalia pointed out. :*It wouldn't take more than a candlemark for any of you to figure out that he'd been set make-work. As it was—*:

As it was, it was just bad luck that Alain was not only the youngest of his sibs, he was the youngest by less than a candlemark. Queen Felice was not only the most fecund Consort in the history of Valdemar, she had the habit of having her children in lots. Three sets of twins and two sets of triplets, to be precise. The Heir, whose real name was Tanivel but who they all called Vel for short, was the eldest of his set of twins. Alain was the youngest of his. And in between—

:*It is rather a good thing that your mother was never Chosen,*: Vedalia observed. :*I'm not sure her poor Companion would have gotten much exercise, much less attention. . . .*:

It was true enough that until after Alain had been born, no one in the Court could remember her in any state other than expecting. The fact that she actually possessed a waist had come as a complete surprise to everyone except the King. Everyone wanted to know—and no one dared ask—both the "why" and the "how" of it.

The "how" was easy; multiples ran in her family. Felice was one of a set of twins, and not one of her sisters had ever given birth to less than twins. Her family history held that it had something to do with a blessing placed on them, but by what—well, there were several versions.

The real question was "why"—having had Vel and Vixen (his twin's name was Lavenna, but no one ever called her that) she could have stopped with the traditional "heir and a spare." Certainly most women would have called a halt at the next lot, which were triplets. Not Felice. Rumor had it that she was trying to fill all the extra rooms in the newly rebuilt Heralds' Collegium with her own offspring.

Only Alain had dared to ask his mother what no one else would. She'd hugged him then looked him straight in the eye and said, "Marriages of state. You're *Heralds,* all of you. You don't need a spouse to be loved."

Now, Alain knew his blunt-spoken mother well enough to read between the lines. Shockingly blunt in this case . . . except . . . well Felice had not made a love-match with King Chalinel; she cared deeply for him, but theirs had been a marriage made in the Council chamber. She knew very well that the way to cement the loyalty of a powerful noble house was to marry into it; the way to ensure a foreign alliance was to send (or send for) a bride or groom. Neither she nor the King would force one of their children into a marriage he or she did not want; they would consent to *any* marriage, even to a beggar, where love was. But this way . . . if an alliance had to be made, there would be someone available to make it at the altar.

Vanyel Ashkevron had made his terrible sacrifice decades ago; Queen Elspeth was Alain's great-great-grandmother. Valdemar's borders had expanded as more and more independent nobles sought to come under the banner of those who had defeated the Karsites. Those nobles—some no better than robber-barons—had no traditional ties to the Valdemaran throne, and no real understanding of what Heralds (the backbone of Valdemaran authority) were and did. One of the obvious solutions was Felice's. After all, it had worked for her family. Her father had gone from an uneasy ally to a doting grandfather who would no more dream of a disloyal thought than jump off the top of his own manor.

And all of his grandchildren—Chosen. That truly brought it home to him and every one of his people what Heralds were and what they did. The lesson was painless and thorough, and the Baron soon was accustomed to having white-clad Heralds coming and going on his lands.

Both Heralds' Collegium and Valdemar had benefited by the arranged marriage with Felice—for now eleven other Heralds, whose skills would be useful outside the capitol, would be freed up by Felice's brood for those other duties while the Princes and Princesses took over.

All of the ten eldest had done well in their classes. Alain and his twin sister Alara had run through the Collegium curriculum like a hot needle through ice. How not? They'd listened to ten siblings as they recited their lessons, they'd practiced weapons-work and archery with ten older siblings, watched and listened with ten siblings. King Chalinel often said that intelligence in the family just kept increasing with each set of children and culminated with Alain and Alara. Alain didn't know about *that*—all of his sibs were clever . . .

:But you and Alara made it through a year early, and Kristen, Kole, and Katen lagged behind because they lost a year to the scarlet fever. With five of you going into Internship at once, there was

something of a problem, since we don't like to Intern relatives with relatives,: said Vedalia.

Which was, of course, why *he* was out on Circuit in the wilderness. No one wanted to risk the health of the triplets after that near-miss with fever, which meant they *had* to stay within the confines of Haven.

And there were only four Haven Internships available. The four Haven Internships had gone to his other siblings, yes, because of the triplets' uncertain health, but also because they all had Gifts that were useful in those internships. To create a new position just for Alain would have been wrong—

:Yes, well my so-called Gift probably had something to do with why I'm out here, on the edge of the Kingdom, and not somewhere else,: Alain observed.

Vedalia's tone turned sharp. *:There is nothing wrong with your Gift,:* he said. *:It's as strong as anyone in the Collegium has got, and stronger than your sister's.:*

:And a fat lot of good Animal Mindspeech would have been, Interning with the Lord-Martial's Herald,: he retorted. *:What would I do, interrogate the Cavalry horses? What else can I do? Nothing that a weakly Gifted Herald can't. I don't even have enough ordinary Mindspeech to talk to Herald Stedrel—and he's got the strongest Mindspeech of any Herald anyone's ever heard of!:* He couldn't help it; a certain amount of bitterness crept into his thoughts. He hated not being able to MindSpeak other Heralds—when he could Hear a tree-hare chattering at ten leagues away.

Vedalia was silent so long that Alain thought the conversation was over.

:Look around you,: Vedalia said. *:Listen to the birdsong in the trees. Feel that free wind in your hair. Take a deep breath of air that no human has been breathing but you. Think about all you're learning from the wild things. Are you really so unhappy that your Gift brought you here?:*

Well, put that way. . . .

:Hmm. I suppose not.:

:And admit it; it's a relief to be away from Alara for the first time in your life.:

Alain laughed aloud; Herald Stedrel looked back over his shoulder and smiled at him, then turned his attention back to the trail ahead.

It *was* a relief to be away from Alara, who thought she had to have the last word in everything they did, who bossed him as if she was five years, not half a candlemark, older than he. It was a relief to be away from all of his siblings, and from the Court, and all the burdens of royal birth. And so far, although no one could call circuit-riding in the hinterlands a pleasure-jaunt, he'd been enjoying it. He would probably change his mind as soon as winter set in and they were riding with snow up to Vedalia's hocks, but right now, he was enjoying it.

Out here, no one knew he was a Prince. He could flirt with pretty village girls, he could swim naked by moonlight, he could dance at fairs and sing rude songs and no one would make a face or take him aside to remind him that he must act with more decorum. Stedrel actually encouraged him to kick up his heels within reason. He might even try the experiment some time of getting really and truly *drunk,* though he'd have to wait until he was pretty sure he wouldn't be needed.

:*You'll regret it,*: Vedalia laughed.

:*Probably. But at least I'll have tried it. And maybe I'll try a few more things, too—*:

:*Tch. Sixteen, and delusions of immortality,*: Vedalia teased.

:*Doesn't that go with being sixteen?*: he retorted.

No, on second consideration, he wouldn't trade being out here for any of the Internships his sibs had. He wished Alara joy of the Lord Martial, who thought that women in general were useless and good only as decoration, and female Heralds in particular were a nuisance. She wouldn't get around *him* by speaking in a slightly higher, more breathy voice and acting hurt, or by turning bossy either.

Maybe that was the point. Internships were supposed to teach you about really *being* a Herald.

He wondered just what *he* was supposed to learn out here.

:*A good question. Now find the answer to it.*: Vedalia tossed his head and Alain smiled.

Then he asked Vedalia to move up alongside of Stedrel's Lovell. "Is there anything I should know about the next village, sir?" he asked respectfully, drawing a smile from the taciturn Herald.

"This'll be our first fishing village, Alain," Stedrel told him. "Do you remember your classes about the Lake Evendim fisher-folk?"

Alain nodded, but not because he recalled his classes as such; one of his yearmates had been from Lake Evendim, and had regaled them all with stories about "home." "Not exactly Holderkin, are they, sir," he responded tentatively.

Sted just snorted. "Not exactly, no. But at least if one of the girls sneaks you off into the water-caves you won't find yourself facing a father, a priest, and a wedding next day." He grinned when Alain blushed. "And unless you have the stamina of a he-goat," the older Herald continued wickedly, as Alain's flushes deepened, "You won't flirt the way you have been with more than one girl at a time."

"They—wouldn't!" Alain choked.

"They would, both together," Sted replied. "Or even three—if you're monumentally stupid enough to put that to the test. With the men out on the boats so much, and fishing being the hazardous occupation that it is, the girls get—"

"Lonely?" Alain said, tactfully.

Sted laughed.

:Thinking of another experiment to try, Chosen?: Vedalia asked innocently.

Alain spluttered, but held his tongue—not the least because he was thinking that very thing. And none of his sibs would be around to tease him and cross-examine him about it afterwards, either.

But when they finally came out of the woods—abruptly, for the trail ended on a rocky cliff-face that dropped steeply down to the gray-green waters the lake—any tentative plans he might have been making vanished abruptly.

The little village that they were making for was built in a river-valley cutting through the cliff, making a narrow and gravel-strewn perch for the Evendim longhouses he'd heard so much about, and a harbor for the fishing boats. The boats should have been out this time of day; instead, they were pulled up on the gravel beach, and the place was in an uproar. They must have been expected, because the moment they came into view, someone spotted them and set up a shout.

Shortly the two Companions were surrounded by what seemed to be every ambulatory person in the entire village. The anxiety in the air was as thick as the smoke from the fires where great racks of fish were being smoked and preserved. Alain hung back, sensing that someone a great deal senior to *him* was who was called for at this moment, but he needn't have bothered with such diffidence. It was clear that the villagers knew the senior Herald here, and two of the more prosperous-looking men fastened themselves to Companion Lovell's reins and began babbling a confused tale of raiders. . . .

Alain couldn't make head or tail of it, but Sted seemed to have no trouble. Then again, this *was* his circuit, and he knew these people. To Alain's ears, their accent, thick enough at the best of times, rendered excited speech incomprehensible.

Then Vedalia came to the rescue.

:Some sort of bandits or raiders have destroyed the next village up the coast,: Vedalia supplied. *:The indications are that the bandits came in by water rather than overland, which is something new, and did so while the men were out fishing. The men returned to find their houses burned out, their women and children gone, and anyone older than forty or younger than four dead in the ashes.:*

Alain felt the blood drain from his face. This was over and above a mere raid. This was an atrocity. And *why* kill anyone they didn't take? Unless it was to prevent the survivors from telling something?

:The folk here just got warning from the men, who took their boats up and down the coast to warn everyone else. They're afraid to go out fishing now.:

But if they didn't, it wouldn't be long before they were all starving. Without fish, there was nothing to eat and nothing to trade to the farmers farther inland.

:Exactly so—: Vedalia shut up, as Stedrel began speaking calmly, confidently, and his manner soothed some of the agitation. Alain paid close attention; this was a master at work.

"This happened yesterday? Is there any attempt at pursuit?" he asked.

"Half the men—but it's a big lake—" said one of the men at Lovell's reins, waving at the water.

Big lake? *That* was an understatement. Even from the top of the cliff it had been impossible to see the other side, and the curve of the shore was imperceptible.

"Defenses first, then," Sted said firmly—turning attention to that without making it obvious that he felt the captives were beyond help.

:They are. There's nothing we can do for them,: Vedalia said glumly. Alain bit his lip; his heart wanted to launch some sort of rescue, but how? With no troops, and no ships—out on a trackless expanse of water—

:The only way to track them might be to FarSee—neither of you have that Gift.:

So they would have to wait until a Herald with that Gift could reach them.

"I wouldn't think that this village is very defensible," Sted began, giving orders—cleverly phrased as suggestions—to safeguard the people of this place.

:*Solenbay,*: Vedalia supplied.

"Have you anywhere that people can go to hide if raiders appear?" he wanted to know. "These raiders won't know the lay of the land, they won't know where to look, and I doubt if they would linger very long to search."

The babbling died to whispers, and anxious eyes were locked on Sted's face.

"The water-caves," suggested one girl promptly, from the back of the crowd, and blushed.

"Good. If there are any that are particularly hard to find?" Stedrel prompted.

The girl giggled nervously, and Alain had a shrewd notion that she knew the location of every water-cave within walking distance of the village. "Reckon I know some that no one else does," she offered, turning such a deep crimson that she looked sunburnt.

"That be why we can't find you, half nights, Savvy?" asked an older woman—not unkindly, but knowingly.

"Perhaps if you moved all your valuables and stores there *now,* you'd have only yourselves to get into hiding," Sted suggested, and got nods, some reluctant, all around. "Obviously the main thing is to save *you,* but I doubt these raiders are going to appear over the horizon within the next day or two, and we should save as much as we can from them."

"I can't see us fighting them off," said one of the other men (who seemed to be one of the village leaders) with a defeated air. "We're fisherfolk, not fighters."

"So save everything that you can in the caves," Sted agreed.

"The ones farthest from here?" Alain ventured. "That way the ones nearest wouldn't be crammed so full people wouldn't fit."

"Good thought," Sted seconded. "Now, I suppose there's no reason why you couldn't spare the young women and children with the swiftest feet and keenest sight to keep watch along the coast?"

"With a horn for each—or something to build a signal fire?" added Alain, and got another approving glance from Sted.

"But the chores—" objected one of the men. "The cleaning, the cooking—"

But the ones who were at risk here were nodding vigorously. "No reason why we can't eat common out of the big fish-kettle 'till this is over," pointed out one old man. "Only takes *one* set of hands for fish-stew, cooking all day." "And if the choice is dirty floors and unmade beds or being carried off, dirty floors we'll have, Matt Runyan," said another woman sharply. "As for the rest—well, we'll barrel up the fish as it's finished smoking and move it into hiding. *Let 'em have a few racks of fish, I say. Better fish than our children.*"

"And when they come, find no one, and burn the place out?" the same man objected.

"They'd do that anyway!" shouted a haggard-looking fellow who Alain realized must be one of the now-bereft fisherfolk from the village that had been destroyed. "What's more important, your *things* or your people? You can rebuild *housen.* You tell me how to bring back your wives and kiddies!"

"I'll be sending word of this to Haven anyway," Stedrel pointed out. "As soon as I've got a moment of quiet."

That quieted some of the agitation, as they all recalled that Stedrel was so powerful a Mindspeaker he could send directly to Haven itself, and every receptive mind along the way. Help would not be far off—two or three fortnights at most.

"The King will send troops, and when *they* get here, you'll be able to go back to life as usual. And we'll be able to scour the coast for the missing." That last as a sop to the men from the destroyed village. They surely knew it was an offer unlikely to bear fruit, but they looked hopeful anyway.

"Soonest begun's soonest done," one of the women said briskly. "We've only got two wagons for the whole village. Let's get our traps moved before sunset!" Within moments, the women, young and old, were heading purposefully towards their family longhouses, followed a little reluctantly by the men.

"Savvy!" Sted called after the girl who had confessed to knowing where most of the water-caves were. She turned back abruptly.

"Sir?" she responded.

"Go to that longhouse over there—" Sted pointed at one where a bevy of women were already moving bundles, barrels, and boxes out briskly to be piled beside the door. "When they're ready to take a load out, guide them to the farthest cave you know of—"

"I'll take her up behind, pillion," Alain offered quickly. "That way we can come back for the next load while the first is still unloading."

"Good. I want you to keep each longhouse's goods in a separate cave, that way when this is over there won't be any quarrels over what belongs to who." Sted smiled encouragingly at her, and the girl returned his smile shyly.

There was some objection to the choice of cave as the wagon-load

Masters of Fantasy

set off: "We're ready *first*," grumbled the oldest dame, "Don't see why *we* should be goin' the farthest."

"But milady, the farther away the cave is, the less likely it will be that it will be discovered," Alain pointed out, thinking quickly. "You're getting the *choice* spot, not the worst one." The old woman gave him a quick look, but nodded with reluctant satisfaction, and made no further complaints.

He would never have believed it, but the longhouses were stripped of every portable object—and some he wouldn't have considered portable—by twilight. The two village mules were ready to drop before it was over, but they were made much of and given an extra ration. The village was substantially deserted now, with only a handful of the very old and the very young remaining behind. In order to get everything moved, the wagons had simply been unloaded at the flat spot nearest to each family's cave before returning for another load. Now all of the able-bodied were lowering their goods down the cliff walls to be stored; they would work all night, if necessary.

As darkness fell, Sted looked around the empty street down the middle of the village. "I'm going to go somewhere quiet and contact Haven," he told Alain. "See what you can do to make yourself useful."

Sted and his Companion drifted off in the twilight. As gloom descended on the street, it occurred to Alain that the most immediately useful thing he could do would be to light the village lamps, so that the returning villagers would have lights beckoning them homeward. There were lamps outside the door of each longhouse, lamps with fat wicks and large reservoirs of oil that by the smell could only come from fish. He got a spill and ventured into the first of the longhouses.

He had never seen anything like it; there was a central hearth with a cone-shaped metal hood over it, and a metal chimney reaching up to the roof. For the rest, it seemed to be one enormous room with cupboards lining all four walls. There were no windows, only slits covered with something that wasn't glass just under the eaves, like clerestory windows, but smaller.

It must be very dark in here during the day.

He knew why there weren't any windows, and why, as much as possible, the Evendim folk spent their time out-of-doors. When winter storms closed in, the coast was hellish; storms swept in over the water with fangs of ice and claws of snow. During the five Winter Moons it was hardly possible to set foot outside these houses, and it would have been folly to give the wind that the fisherfolk called "the Ice-Drake" any way to tear into the shelter of their homes.

But winter was moons away, and the present danger was not from nature but from man. Alain lit the spill at the remains of the fire, and went out to light the lanterns.

When he had done the last of them, he found a couple of old men, limbs knotted with age, slowly stacking wood in a firepit at the center of the village and he ran to help.

From that moment until late that night he worked, as hard as he had ever worked in his life, and despite being a Prince, he was no stranger to physical labor. He carried wood and water, the enormous iron kettle, and all the ingredients for the great pot of fish-stew that would be cooking night and day for as long as this crisis lasted. He took a torch out to the drying racks for an old woman, rolled up empty barrels and brought a keg of salt and a bag of herbs, and helped her stack smoked fish in layers with salt and herbs. There were no fresh fish to spread upon the racks, but he helped her layer the fires for the next day, when the men *would* go out. With aching muscles and sore feet he put babies and toddlers to bed, persuaded them to *stay* there, then helped their grandmothers and grandfathers to their beds when old bodies could do no more. Then he waited, getting off his feet at last, with Vedalia beside him, watching the stew to see that it didn't burn. He'd taken Vedalia's tack and packs off him, but had no idea where he should be stabled or where the two Heralds should stay. So he heaped tack and packs beside the fire and used them as props for his back. As full as that kettle was, it would be a long time cooking, and he needn't actually *watch* it, just stir it from time to time to keep what was on the bottom from sticking and burning. He wished he could have a bath; even his hair felt full of smoke, and his eyes gritty.

Slowly, slowly, the folk of the village began trickling back in, weary, too weary to think past the next footstep. They didn't seem to notice him sitting by the fire; they trudged into their houses to seek what they'd left of their beds, leaving him standing guard beside tomorrow's dinner.

And *he* could hardly keep his eyes open.

:*You sleep,*: Vedalia said. :*I'll wake you if it needs stirring—or anything comes.*:

"No—I'm still on duty," Alain protested.

:*Just close your eyes then to rest them,*: Vedalia suggested. It seemed a sensible suggestion; they were sore, irritated by all the smoke he'd been standing in. He let his lids fall for just a moment.

When he opened them again, it was because there was a rooster crowing in his ear. He jerked awake and startled it and the two chickens scratching around his feet into flight.

It was dawn, and there was a young girl stirring the pot with a great wooden paddle. Someone had draped a cloak over him, and he had curled up with Vedalia's saddle as a pillow. His packs were nowhere to be seen, but Vedalia dozed hip-shot beside him.

The Companion snorted and stirred as Alain sat up, opening his brilliant blue eyes. :*Stedrel was here and took our packs, but he didn't see any reason to wake you. There's a Waystation just outside of the village. If you'll just drape my saddle on me, we'll go wake him.*:

They didn't have to; they hadn't gotten past the last longhouse when he and his Companion appeared on the road before them. "You might as well turn back around," Sted called cheerfully. "We have to organize the coast-watch now, and we'll both be a part of it."

Wishing mightily for more sleep, and trying not to feel disgruntled at Sted's announcement, Alain sighed and did as he was told. At least there was food waiting—a communal kitchen set up by all the grannies to dole out cold smoked fish and bread to anyone who stuck out a hand. The men, trusting blindly that Sted would see to the protection of their families and village, took to the boats with their breakfasts in their pockets and more of the same for eating later.

Before a candlemark was out, the village resembled a ghosttown. One set of elderly women minded children and babies—but Sted had cunningly assigned every child too small to run to someone big enough to pick it up and carry it. Several of the adult women were to carry babies—and were put to fashioning slings that let them have one slung on the back, one on the front, and one on each hip. That left the older children and some of the adult women—and a few of the grannies and granthers that were still spry enough to sprint—on coast-watch.

And now came the shock for Alain. This was not the only village at risk—

Which, when the men returned, Sted made very plain.

"We've done what we can for you," he told the villagers, once the men returned with holds full of fish and the catch was distributed on the smoking racks. "Help is coming, and it will come *here* first, in three days' time. I reached a Herald riding with a troop of the Guard no farther away than that. Now Alain and I have to do the same for the rest of the villages."

He'd chosen his moment well; in the first flush of success, or perhaps because of exhaustion, no one objected.

"I will go north along the coast; Alain will go south and west," Sted announced. "We'll do for them what we've done for you. If you can hold out for three days, all will be well."

Alain had gone quite still with shock. *He* would be going out alone? He looked at Sted in silent appeal, but the older Herald was already mounting and preparing to ride to the next village. "Herald Stedrel?" he faltered.

The Herald just gave him a sobering look, and he shut his mouth on any objections.

:*Let's go,*: Vedalia said. :*If we push, we can make the next village by sundown.*:

They pushed—and found that place in as much of an uproar as the first, and having had a full day to stew over the warnings, people were ready to greet *anything* that looked like help with full cooperation. Either they were not necessarily expecting Stedrel, or they were so grateful to see the uniform that they were willing to overlook the youthful face. In either case, no one objected to a single aspect of the plan.

The water-caves here were nearer and larger; evacuation of goods and stores took place by torch- and moonlight, and this village had a leader in the form of one indomitable old woman. Once given a plan, she was perfectly prepared to see it carried out. Conscious of the passing of time, Alain decided to move on that very night. He'd always understood that it was possible for a Herald to sleep in the saddle; now he found out the truth of it. It wasn't exactly *sleep*, but it was no worse than his night beside the kettle. He reached the third village at dawn, finding it in as desperate a state as the previous two.

And in coming closer to hysteria. So much so that he decided to organize the coast-watchers *first*. And it was a good thing that he did.

For it was no more than a candlemark after the youngsters had set off than wild horn-calls sounded in the middle distance, and all the careful plans fell to pieces.

After the first moment of blank incomprehension, while people, interrupted in mid-task, stared silently at the west, someone screamed.

Then all hell broke loose. No one seemed to know where to go, or what to do, despite Alain's instructions only two candlemarks ago. They dashed in all directions, some to their homes, some to the woods, some to snatch up belongings, and some dropping them. Five people managed to keep their heads: Alain, Vedalia, and three of the village elders.

"Get them to the caves!" Alain shouted over the screaming, the weeping, as people milled in panic around him. "We have to get them to the caves!"

The elders began picking up children, shoving them into random arms, shouting at those who had frozen with fear to rouse them, and shoving them in the right direction. Once little groups were moving towards safety, Vedalia encouraged them by charging at them with lashing hooves and bared teeth, looking utterly demonic.

Alain headed off those going in the opposite direction, screaming at them, even going so far as to swat a couple of those lagging behind with the flat of his blade until they disappeared into the trees in the direction of the caves—

Then he returned to chivvy another group into safety.

He had not a moment to spare to look for the enemy—as they sailed swiftly into the harbor he got nothing more than a glimpse of ships, long, lean, fast-looking to his land-accustomed eyes. He sensed, more than heard or saw, the moment when the raiders came ashore. Vedalia was hot on the heels of another group of stragglers; he went back to chase a few more away from a chest they were trying to haul off.

He never realized how close the raiders were, that they were charging up the street at a run, until it was too late. He never even got a chance to defend himself. There was just a shout behind him, and he half-turned, and then—

—he woke in darkness, head reeling, stomach heaving, pain shooting through his skull; his hands were tied in front of him, and his ankles bound together. He'd been tossed on a pile of what felt like rope, and he was just about to lose what little he had in his stomach. He managed to roll over to the side before throwing up, and managed to roll away from the mess he'd made. The floor beneath the ropes on which he lay was moving.

From the way his head hurt, someone had coshed him, and done so with enthusiasm and some expertise. Enthusiasm, because they'd given him a concussion for certain—given the way that his stomach churned and the deck (it must be a ship's deck) beneath him felt as if it was spinning as well as rising and falling. Expertise, because he wasn't dead.

He was trussed up, but hastily; evidently his captors trusted to the hit on the head to keep him quiet. And he was in darkness, because it was night, but he was also under a tarp draped between two bulky objects. Around him were foreign noises, the rushing and splashing of water, sounds of creaking, the groaning of wood, men shouting. The air was damp and cool and smelled of open water.

At least they hadn't shoved him into the hold.

Well, perhaps there wasn't any room in the hold. *He* was probably the least valuable object the raiders had taken.

Right. I'm on a ship, a captive, and—

Only then did he realize that there was a conspicuous *absence* in his thoughts.

—in trouble. I can't hear Vedalia.

He must be leagues away from the village, if he couldn't hear his Companion. Leagues away, and no way for anyone to track him.

"—and I don' know what th' *hell* ye wanted with the Herald!" someone said, just coming into earshot. "He's no good to us—a woman or a kiddie we could use, but him?"

"Look, if we kill him, we get more trouble than we can handle," said a second voice. "Kill one of them white-coats, and the rest *never* give up comin' after you!"

You've got that right, Alain thought—though what good that would do him if he was dead—

"If we left him, gods only know what he'd manage to do—him or that horse. And gods know how close *their* people are. I thought, we take him, though, *they* won't dare come after us with everything they've got. Even if they got ships ready to sail, you bet they'd hang back. They won't risk our killing him. If we held him till we were safe out of reach, I figured we *stayed* safe."

His heart plummeted and his spirit went cold. *Gods help me. Bandits who think.*

"So now what?" asked the first voice, sounding a little mollified.

"We sail a little farther, we make sure there's nothing chasing us, then we dump him." The second voice sounded utterly indifferent. "We could probably get a ransom for him, but that'd put us in *their* reach again."

Alain felt his heart falter, and the panic he had been holding off until that moment rise up and seize him. He wanted to scream, but he could only whimper a little, a pathetic whine lost in the sounds the ship made. And inside, he began screaming silently—and futilely—for help. He couldn't *help* himself—it was an automatic reaction.

But he even as he shrieked at the top of his mental voice, some part of him despaired and *knew* it was useless. Maybe in the woods, even if there was no human with Mindspeech near enough to help, he could have summoned elk, a mountain-cat, wolves to his aid. But this was the vast water, with nothing in it but fish. Still his mind yammered as if anything that *could* help him was likely to hear him. . . .

:?:

The response, faint as it was, stopped his mental gibbering in its tracks. :*What*?: he called back.

:??: came the return—stronger! There was a sense of something he hadn't expected; behind that startled query was intelligence. Maybe enough to help him?

He fought back pain and nausea and focused all of his strength behind something more coherent.

:*Help me! Please!*: he Sent, and added overtones of his situation; easy enough to do since it was all very physical.

The response was not a single voice, but a chorus.

:*Landwalker? Yes, Landwalker!*:

:*Landwalker. Net-bound.*:

:*Brother to Weeps-On-Shore.*:

:*Captive to——*: What followed was emotion, and senses, rather than words—a sense of something destructive, a taste of blood, and anger on the part of the speaker. Whatever these creatures were, they knew his captors, and they had *no* love for them.

:*Yes.* They *must not have him.*:

:*Enough.* They *must be stopped.*:

:*Call the Deep One.*:

:*Yes! The Deep One will know! The Deep One will rid the face of the waters of them!*:

:*Call the Deep One!*:

Well, it was very nice that they saw his enemies as their own, but they hadn't answered *him*. He chose this moment to insert his own plea.

:*Please? Help me?*:

But at that moment, the tarp was ripped aside. He blinked up at four shadowed faces interposed between him and a star-filled sky.

Someone else, just out of sight, spoke. "Right. We're safe enough. Over the side with him."

Fear and nausea warred within him, but he had no time to react—four sets of hands seized shoulders and ankles, there was a moment of futile struggle as they heaved him up—

Then flying weightless through the air—just enough time for a last gulp of air—

Then he hit the water like a stone.

He managed to keep his breath, and he sank for a moment, the cold water hitting him a blow that made him choke back a gasp that would have lost him that precious breath. With bound hands and feet, disoriented in the black water, he thrashed, trying to find the surface, the air, the precious air, and not knowing where it was.

:We come, Walker!:

Miraculously he was surrounded by large, fleshy bodies, warm, slick bodies that bore him suddenly up to the surface and held him there as he gasped for breath.

He couldn't see them—the moon must have set—so he had only the sense that they were larger than he was, slick and not scaly like a fish. As they thrust under his arms with oblong heads and long snouts, they used those rounded, bulbous heads to keep him afloat. Others went to work on the ropes tying his hands and feet. They had sharp teeth, too, in those snouts—they took it in turns to slice at his bonds, slicing into his hands, though he sensed apology every time tooth met flesh and he gasped with pain.

:It's all right,: he managed, and conveyed the sense that he would rather be free and wounded than bound and whole. He got amused concurrence and a renewed assault on his bonds. They must be the terror of the fish, these creatures; veritable wolves of the water.

Just as the final rope parted on his hands, there was a stirring among his rescuers, a rush of excitement.

:The Deep One comes!: cried one voice, and then another—

And suddenly he was alone in the water, paddling frantically. *:Wait!:* he called after them. *:Wait, I don't—I can't—:*

:Peace, little Walker.:

The Mindvoice was like none he had ever heard before; *huge,* deep, with a kind of echo. It swept through his mind and made him shiver and catch his breath, knowing in his bones he was in the presence of something—monumental.

:Peace. Be still. I come.: He felt something, a pressure in the water beneath him, and then—

Then something bigger than the biggest ship he had ever seen rose up beneath him like a floor. And he felt himself in a Presence.

:Yes, little Walker. I uphold you. Well for you that you cannot see me, else your fear would make a dumb beast of you, and render you lawful prey. . . . :

It had the same sort of slick, resilient hide as the others had, this creature whose back held him, supported him, in just a few thumb-breadths of water. He couldn't *see* anything of it, but the sense of something so huge he couldn't even imagine it held him silent.

:So, tell me, Walker-On-Land, what is it that should cause the Bright Leapers to come to your aid and call upon me?:

:*I don't know, my lord,*: Alain said humbly. :*I just—asked for help.*:

:Just asked for help. Never has a Walker asked help of *us*. Perhaps that is reason enough. But what of these others?: The Mindvoice lost its sense of amusement, and Alain shivered again. :The Leapers say that they must be stopped. Their tree-float tastes of blood and pain, their minds of ravening. I know what they have done to the Leapers—but what else have they done to their own kind?:

As briefly as possible, Alain outlined to the vast creature beneath his hands just what it was that the raiders had done, and he felt an anger as enormous as creature itself slowly rousing.

:So. Bad enough to make war, but those who make it upon the infant and the aged . . . the wisdom of the people and the hope. . . . : A pause. :Yes. I can see. But this is between you and your kind, and although I wish to follow the wishes of the Leapers, I must have a price from you.:

:*A price?:* It didn't matter; whatever it wanted, it could have, if it would put an end to these marauding bandits. :*Is it—*: he gulped. :*—me you want, oh Lord of the Deep?:*

The surface beneath his hands vibrated; in a moment, he recognized it as laughter. :No, little Walker, be you ever so tasty, you are too noble for my eating. Besides, I would not cause the Weeper-On-The-Shore, your White Spirit-Brother, to dissolve in grief. No. Before I act in the affairs of Walkers . . . a vow from you, Walker, brother to the White Spirit. That you reveal me to no one. Ever.:

:*You have it,*: he promised, not entirely sure why this creature wanted it, nor what he was exchanging the vow *for*, but willing enough to give it. :*None shall know. Not even my Companion.*:

:Then I shall act.:

He felt the great bulk beneath him begin to move, felt it rise until he was completely out of the water. He balanced on this hill of flesh, and the air of its passing flowed around him, chilling him so that he shivered. The resilient flesh beneath him undulated slowly.

Lights appeared on the horizon, lights too yellow and unwinking to be stars.

They were lanterns, lanterns hung on the rail of the ship that had taken him and on its sister-ships in the raiding fleet. Swiftly as these ships sailed, the creature beneath Alain was faster.

Now he sensed other minds around him, the minds of the smaller creatures that had initially been his rescuers. They exchanged no words, only feelings of excitement and some of the same anger that the greater creature felt. And with that came glimpses of the cause of that anger—the wanton slaughter of these creatures by the men of the swift, agile ships.

:Stay with the Leapers, Walker, and observe.:

The bulk that supported him slipped from beneath him, plunging him into the water again as it disappeared. But before he could panic, the others were around him, one under each outstretched arm. And before the ship sailed away from where they waited in the water, something black and terrible surged up out of the waves beside it—

—and crashed down on it before the few sailors manning the sails and tiller had a chance to do more than register the presence of something beside them.

The ship disintegrated with a horrible sound of shattering timber and the screams of the men aboard.

The men on the other ships had that much warning—enough to know their doom, not enough to avoid it. Again and again, the huge bulk leapt from the waves and smashed down on their ships, splintered them as a wanton child would splinter a toy, but with anger no child could ever feel.

How many died instantly, how many were left to flounder in the water he would never find out, for the smaller swimmers left him again and the huge one rose beneath him and carried him quickly away.

:There are more of them yet, clinging to bits of their tree-floater, but I will hunt tonight, Walker,; said the voice with grim satisfaction. :When you are safe I shall return, and oh, I shall dine well . . . so remember your vow.:

:I will,: he pledged fervently, with a shudder, and felt the creature's amusement.

:Come. I hunger. The sooner the Leapers can take you ashore, the sooner I may feed.:

Again the huge bulk rose out of the water with him atop it, and sped—in what direction? He could not tell. He could only cling to it as best he could, exhausted, cold, shivering, aching in head and limb, and hope this *thing* that had spoken of dining on men would take him home.

And yet—and yet—

He was afraid of it—but it was more respect than fear.

:Speak with me, Walker. Tell me of your life. I have never met one who could Speak to my thoughts, and I have lived long . . . long.:

So throughout that long night, that strange journey, he spoke with the unseen creature that bore him. It was not ignorant of the ways of humans, but Heralds and Companions were new and fascinating to it. He came to understand that it was his despised Gift of Animal Mindspeech that had saved him; the creature could *hear* the strong thoughts of others, but imperfectly. Only Alain had ever been able to converse with it, and with the ones called the Bright Leapers.

Gradually, respect entirely replaced fear—

Though he did not forget what it intended to do when it returned to the shattered wrecks to hunt. And he was torn; the men were guilty of murder, robbery, rapine—and certainly their lives would have been forfeit had their fate come upon them from the hands of Selenay's Guard. But to be devoured after candlemarks of terror, floating on the face of the water—

:Their fate is what it will be. Perhaps they will drown before I return; drowned or living, they will serve me well. It is neither you, nor I, to whom they must answer for their deeds. I do but send them quickly to that judgment.:

There was nothing he could say to that; and in the end, perhaps this was no worse than imprisonment, perhaps a trial, and in the end, the axe or rope. . . .

:But the dawn is near, and so is the shore,: the creature continued. :No Walker has yet seen me, nor shall they—not those who I let live, at least. I go to hunt; the Leapers will see you to your friends.: There was a sense of a smile in its Mindvoice. :Begin to call when I leave you, so that your Spirit-Brother will cease to lament. His weeping tears at my heart even now.:

The creature slowed and stopped, and slowly submerged, dropping him again into the water. A moment later, it was gone—it could probably swim faster under the water than above it, and had only kept to the surface for his benefit. The water felt warm after the chill of wet garments in rushing air; the Bright Leapers were soon around him, holding him up.

:Move your limb from out the dead-skin you wear, so we can take it in our mouths and pull you,: said one. After a moment he puzzled out that they meant him to pull his hands and arms up into his sleeves so they could take the ends in their mouths. He did as they asked, and soon they were towing him between two of them, with the others swimming alongside, occasionally leaping into the air, apparently just for the sheer exuberance of living. Remembering what the Deep One had said, he began to MindCall Vedalia. And as the sky before them grew light, and the water reflected it back in dull silver, he heard Vedalia answer.

What passed between them was too deep for words, and he was glad to be towed and not swimming, for he couldn't have swum and wept at the same time.

And as the sun itself appeared on the horizon, it seemed that the Leapers were not going to have to take him to shore after all, for there were boats coming to meet them—and although Vedalia could not have fit in them, Sted was in the prow of the foremost, his white uniform shining in the early light.

The Leapers—he saw now that they *looked* like fish, but with sleek, brown hides, merry eyes, and mouths frozen into a perpetual grin—now made good their name, for all those who surrounded the two who towed him flung themselves into the air in graceful arcs. From the distant boats a cheer arose, made faint by distance—and by the water in his ears, perhaps.

He grayed-out for a moment—it was a good thing that his caretakers were competent and kept him from drowning—for when he came to himself, there were two bright-eyed heads holding him up, with his arms across what might have been their necks if they'd had such a thing. And the foremost boat was coming alongside. Many hands reached down to haul him aboard, which was a good thing, because now that he was safe, the last of his energy ran out, and he felt as weak as a newborn kitten.

But he was not so exhausted that he didn't notice the fishermen bowing to the Bright Leapers, and calling out their thanks as he was hauled aboard. "You know these creatures?" he said, surprised.

"They are the Wave-Wise," said one of the fishermen, wrapping a rough woolen blanket about his shoulders. "Some say they are the spirits of those of us who drowned and never came home to be buried on land. We *never* molest them, and if one should be tangled in a net, we cut the net to let him free. Better to lose a catch than drown a brother."

:Deep-Speaker!: one called, bobbing with its head above the water, making a chattering sound and nodding as it MindSpoke. *:Tell your friends that we know where the Netted Ones are, and we will guide them there!:*

The Netted Ones? The *kidnapped women?*

:Yes! Yes! And now the Deep One feeds, there are none to keep them netted!:

"Dear gods—" he grabbed the fisherman by the collar. "Listen— your Wave-Wise are wiser than you guess! They say they know where the women and children are that were stolen away, and will guide you there!"

Pandemonium broke out among the boats, as the Bright Leapers cavorted and word passed from vessel to vessel. *All* wanted to go, but the crew of the boat that held Sted and Alain reluctantly agreed to turn back with them.

Then, and only then, did Alain lie back, his shivering easing, a flask of some herb cordial that Sted had pressed into his hand, sheer exhaustion flattening him against the support of rope and blankets that Sted had rigged for him.

Sted, who spoke but seldom, had been babbling ever since he was brought aboard out of sheer relief. Since most of what he was saying had been variations on "Thank the gods you're safe!" Alain hadn't paid a lot of attention.

Now, though— "Vedalia said you were rescued by those fish— or whatever they are," Sted was saying.

"Not fish—I s'ppose they must be something like a Pelagiris-creature, a *kyree* or whatever," Alain replied, hoping he sounded as exhausted as he felt. "They said the only reason they could hear me, and I could hear *them,* was my Gift."

"But how did you get away?" Sted asked.

Alain tried to laugh and coughed instead, taking a sip of the cordial. "I didn't. The bastards only kept me long enough to be sure you weren't chasing them with boats full of Guards. Then they tossed me overboard. But I'd been yelling like a scared baby, and the—they call themselves Bright Leapers—the Bright Leapers heard me." He held out his wrists so Sted could see the cuts from their teeth. "Got the ropes off, then towed me back. I suppose I was rescued for the novelty of listening to me talk while I was brought back as much as anything else. I got the impression that these water-creatures, the intelligent ones, spend a lot of their time just—

playing, learning, being curious. So much for the honor and glory of being a Herald! My real value seems to have been that I could tell a good story!"

He might be exhausted, but he was choosing his words very carefully. He was telling the exact truth, just not all of it . . . and as long as he stuck to the exact truth, Sted was not likely to wonder what he was trying to hide.

Sted chuckled, and so did the fisherman nearest them, the man at the tiller. "We've always honored the Wave-Wise, but if they bring us to the captives, they'll be getting a share of our catches from now on," the fisherman said. "As for stories, I expect you'll be tired of telling this one long before anyone gets tired of hearing it. There've been other tales of the Wave-Wise rescuing fisherfolk, but never like this one."

"And I fervently hope there never is again," Alain said emphatically. "I pray that no one *ever* meets the sort of things I did last night."

He closed his eyes and Sted's urging, and felt consciousness rapidly slipping away. But—did he hear the far-off echo of an appreciative—and sated—chuckle at that last?

:No, of course not.:

:*Of course not,*: he agreed, and slept.

⟨⟩ Earthborne ⟨⟩

A Witchworld Story

Andre Norton

Mereth drew a deep breath. Breezes here were still ice kissed, though this cup of land was well beneath those mountain walls, which formed its confines. She pulled her heavy cloak closer and secured its throatlatch before freeing Mage Ruther's experimental distance see-all. Mereth never ceased to wonder at its ability to draw into her vision things that lay far away.

If this tool had only been available in the days of the invasion— It seemed, she thought, that nowadays minds were proving sharper. Knowledge, either long forgotten or newly discovered, advanced steadily from one sunrise to another. It was almost as if the constant alerts, necessary before the Warding, having now vanished, had opened the way for the flouring of learning. Mereth did not, of course, accept the suggestion that a Golden Age had come to Estcarp and her own High Hallack. No, when the Gates, known or secret, had drawn captives from many far sources to people this long-mixed world—Estcarp, Arvon, High Hallack, Karstan, Escore— evil had come, nonetheless, twinned with good.

Gone were the Gates—yes—but though the Dark might not feed its forces here now, it had not yet shrunk to nothingness. Behind her now, within the near-repaired walls of Lormt, more than a score of scholars engaged in research, eager to recover any hint of what might rise to threaten again. Towers, brought low by the Dance of the Mountains, were now near restored. However,

beneath the ancient floors of those venerable storehouses of knowledge, long-hidden rooms had burst open to be explored by the
then few, reclusive inhabitants. Newcomers, sages of high learning, had flocked in. The efforts of at least three quarters of the
Lormt dwellers were now bent toward this exploration and were
being repaid—mainly with—

She lifted again the far-seer, held it to her right eye and turned
it down slope. There appeared movement now, which in this near-
deserted country might herald a visitor—one of those seeking to
trace war-tossed kin, raider scout, or homeless wanderer?

Peering so through her new tool, Mereth saw straightly
enough. What leapt into instant view was a gaunt villager garbed
in rags. It was the shepherdess she had observed warding a tiny
flock of bedraggled sheep a day gone. To the woman's eye, skilled
through years in merchanting, the pitifully thin mottled creatures
rated of the poorest quality. Such faded, ragged wool would bring
scarcely half a glance in the past from the factors at Ferndale
Warehouse.

The distant village girl rounded a rock and then half stumbled
against the stone as if unable to stand erect. Mereth gained her
feet with the aid of her long staff, thrust the far-seer into a belt
loop and headed down the hill. She had made no mistake in
reading the expression of abject horror that had grimaced that
narrow face.

Being a mute, Mereth could not call out, nor did she appear
to possess any of the Old Talent of mind-touch. Suddenly her feet
struck something slick in the sprouting grass and she dug in her
staff just in time to prevent herself from falling.

The shepherdess's head jerked up and she looked directly at
Mereth, terror still etched on her features. She screamed and
lurched away from the rock, running, not toward Mereth, but away.

Mereth was not close enough to bar the girl's way with her
staff and had to steady herself, once more unsure of her own
footing. Just as she reached the upstanding spur of rock, the girl
had reached the far side—no chance to stop her now.

Leaning heavily on her staff for support, the woman of Lormt
doggedly followed the frightened girl; however, now a strange
awareness broke upon her so sharply that she almost staggered.
Clutching the rod of polished wood with all her might, she met
such an odor that she held her breath for amoment. Death's foul
stench—Death with the sickening effluvia of an ancient evil.

A battle ground might well poison the rising wind so, but even during the years of the war, Mereth had only once met with such a stomach-twisting smell—it filled the nostrils, but—it also reached deep within her and awakened a nameless fear. Perhaps the loss of one ability, that of speech, stirred and sharpened all her senses. It posed a question for the likes of Maid Mouse, whose visits she cherished. Mouse was renowned for her magic talent and the gift of discerning the balance of things.

As the woman continued to plod persistently along the track the girl had taken, her thoughts were rudely interrupted—

Looking down, she was met with a strange sight indeed. At her feet in the spring-green meadow grass lay a fleece, rent and be-splotched with great gouts of blood. Among the young blades of recently nibbled grass there showed rough patches of blood-soaked mud.

Mereth carefully inserted the ground tip of her staff under the edge of the hide and flipped back a part of it to examine the flesh side. With so much blood about, this must be a fresh kill, but how could this be with no sign of paw-, claw- or footprint? Furthermore, there was not one scrap of flesh adhering to the underside of the sheepskin. No animal could kill and clean its prey and leave the hide thus. And where were the bones? There was no sign of any remains—nothing but blood and hide!

There were feral hunters in plenty in these mountains—borsebear, val-lops, snow cats. But sites of their feasting bore no resemblance to this. The very look and feel here shouted danger in the Lormt woman's mind.

Wessel—he might know. Lormt and its grounds had been his charge for years. He was truly both Lord Duratan's right and left hand and the first to be queried about land or towers. She had seen him an hour earlier supervising the finishing of the crenellations of a new tower in the outer wall.

But, the herder—Mereth turned slowly to scan the reaches of the meadow. Of course there was no sight of the girl. She might have traced the child by the sound of her running, but the sight of the strange kill had lost her that advantage and she probably could not have kept pace long enough to catch her. Many heavy boulders thrust up along the fringes of the pasturage like ill-socketed teeth. Any one of them offered an ample hiding place.

Perhaps later she might borrow one of the tough little ponies and ride down to the village to inquire about the girl, though the prospect of success was dim. There was no great friendship between the village and Lormt, for many of those living there now were

Karsten survivors of the Mountain Dance and deeply bitter against those with Talents.

No, to learn what she could from Wessel was her best move at present. Again planting her sturdy staff with care, Mereth turned to retrace her steps.

She found Wessel leaning on an overturned cart, happily engulfing, with obvious hunger, a huge round of herb bread wrapped about a fat chunk of cheese. The filling looked about to escape his hold, but he adroitly stuffed the last of it into his generous mouth. Mereth hesitated; to call a man from his midday meats simply to observe a puzzle lying down-mountain was hardly fair. But—time was crucial. The evidence must be seen immediately or be of no value.

The bailiff swallowed again as she came up.

"Trouble, M'Lady?"

Mereth steadied her slate and carefully printed, the easier for him to read.

"Down slope—look—something curious to see—"

He rolled what remained of his meal into a square of coarse linen and tucked it into the front of his jerkin. Then he hesitated for a moment and looked closely at her.

Instinctively catching his unspoken question, she shook her head and he forbore to pick up the only possible weapon at hand, a mattock that leaned against the wall behind him.

This time she took more careful account of her footing. At the nooning it was warmer now and her hearing, always acute, caught the drone of buzzing insects. As they approached the site of the kill, it seemed that the stench had intensified; however, the near-palpable evil she had sensed clouding the spot was now dissipated. Wessel practically vaulted the last few paces down to stand beside the blood-clotted fleece and after a moment squatted, his hand over his nose.

" 'Pears something took one o' Fuser's ewes," he had half advanced a hand near but not quite touching the befouled wool.

Again Mereth's writing tool was busy. "Mot-wolf, bear— Snow cat—?"

He shook his head in response to her list. "Not as any mountain hunter was this done, M'Lady. Where be the paw prints, bones and the like? Best we put Lord Duratan on this—he was ranger trained. Now," Wessel rose to his feet, "I'll just go and tell him."

Mereth withdrew. The cloud of blue flies and the pervasive stench were more than she could bear any longer. Even when she reached Lormt again, she avoided visiting the buttery for a while.

Instead she went to the tiny chamber that opened off her well-appointed living space and sat down at her desk, which was thickly spread with documents and a couple of wood-covered books so heavily fashioned to protect the ancient parchment pages.

There was the Larweeth case—this was her duty at Lormt; she must keep to it. The great war behind them, the massacres of the old race in Karsten, the Moving of the Mountains had stirred up her entire world as one stirs the stiff batter for a feast cake. Families and clans had been brutally rent apart.

Now Lormt was devoted to gathering and cataloging of news of such losses, ready to offer aid to any who came seeking news of kin. Sometimes one had to sift through very old records for needed clues. Accustomed to keeping accounts of business on land and sea for her trading family, Mereth had found this a suitable occupation in her old age, one she could ply with skill.

Only—she closed her eyes for a moment and saw only bloody wool. Clapping her hand to her lips, she swallowed firmly and reached for a book of armorial bearings. This she opened with determination and forced herself to locate a particular mark.

At last able for a time to push the disturbing scene out of her mind and settle down to pursue her research, Mereth became shortly so engrossed that it almost startled her when a message from Lord Duratan arrived to ask, if it were no trouble, could she attend upon him?

It was near twilight when Mereth trudged through the halls, aided by her staff in making cautious descent into the bowels of Lormt. There she knocked on the door of Lord Duratan's quarters from whence he ordered the affairs governing the safety of the ancient seat of knowledge. Once of the Borderers, he kept his chamber well lighted and when the woman knocked and entered at his invitation, she immediately caught a sound that betrayed his mood—a random clicking.

He had swept a space clear of paper, pens and folios on the ancient wood surface of the table before him. Above this his hands rose and fell as his fingers gathered a partial palmful of colored crystals, only to toss them in a scattered pattern, which he studied after each throw. So, he gauged this matter serious indeed! Mereth stared down in turn at the results of his last pitch—one shaped by chance and his particular Talent. The crystals lay about the cleared place in a discernable array.

Most of the darker colors had fallen well away from the central core, where appeared different shades of green from that of new spring grass to the darkest bramble leaf hue. However, these were lightened by a sprinkling of pale yellow, lying randomly. After one long stare, the Marshal of Lormt raised his head to look directly at Mereth and begin to recite as if reading from some report drawn from Wessel's account book, ending:

"Lady Mereth, in the days before the Warding the ships of your house sailed far. Have you ever heard report of such a foulness as you discovered today?

The woman's slate and stylus were at the ready. "No." A terse enough answer, but none further was needed.

"There are beasts enough in these heights to be feared." He was sweeping up the crystals to pour them back into a double bag of lizard skin. "At this season of the year such are well hungered from the sparseness of winter game. Yet none known to be at large hereabouts gorges to the point of leaving naught but an empty hide. Wessel is now asking questions—"

Duratan's next word was drowned by a sound, which instantly brought them both to their feet and swinging toward one of the narrow windows in the guardian's chamber. The man reached it in two strides, but Mereth was not about to be left behind and crowded against him to see—

The last vestiges of twilight dimmed the slope that walled the valley. Some distance below small blazes bobbed up and down— torches, by the look of it, Mereth opined. These seemed not to be approaching Lormt, rather milling around at a remove.

Duratan pushed the woman aside as he strode across the room, pausing only to snatch a cloak draped over a chair back. Uncaring that she was many passages away from her own covering, Mereth followed him through the door, though he was running now. Even with the aid of her staff, she could not keep pace and by the time she reached the center court, a small company of armed guards was assembling, while two at the gate were grunting as they opened the massive portal with straining muscles. They carefully limited the space to just enough to let a single armsman pass.

Though the torches were not visible from this level, a shout came from a wall sentry two levels above.

"Still there!"

"M'Lady—this be a cold night! Here, get you into this." Mistress Bethelie, housekeeper for Lormt, had whipped off her own cloak to wrap it around Mereth's shoulders. Mage Lights swayed above them—brighter than any torch. Clearly Lady Nalor's powers were at work.

Mereth gave hasty thanks, for Duratan had, by then, slipped
through the narrow opening of the gate and the porter was preparing to shut it when she squeezed by. He made as if to stop her
but she paid no heed. Only as the darkness closed around her
outside did she pause. The mage globes did not extend to this place.
A misstep would surely mean a painful fall. Ahead came the sounds
of the armsmen and she bit her lip in irritation. She had no choice
but to stumble along at a crawling pace, exerting her waning
strength to dig in her staff for support at each step.

Cries rose from the huddle of torch bearers and a shrill scream,
suddenly cut off, as if by a blow. When Mereth finally reached the
point of action, the flickering torchlight, though poor, was enough
to reveal much of the struggle that surrounded her.

No armsman had drawn steel, but all were fighting with short,
thick wooden staffs, not unlike her own longer one. Their opponents were men from the village who shouted raucously as they
fought.

Mereth could make out raw oaths mingled with cries of "Ye
Dark Ones! Begone! Leave us be!" Historically the researchers of
ancient lore in Lormt had little contact with the villagers, save for
the troublous times when they had opened the great depository
of knowledge to shelter those fleeing for their lives. The landsmen
and their families had been grateful enough then, but after the
vast disaster of the Turning, distrust had arisen and communication was limited to dealing for supplies. However, she had never
heard of such trouble as she now witnessed.

Mereth had scarce time to ponder the matter, for as she pivoted about her staff, she barely escaped a killing blow aimed at
her head. As it was, it landed crookedly and painfully against her
shoulder.

Rober! Why, only that morning the carter's son had greeted
her civilly with proper respect, but now his reddened face was
drawn into a twisted mask like a blood-mad raider. Mereth shuddered. It was as if the old days had come again. Instinctively she
retaliated, swinging her stout staff with practiced force and caught
the youth at knee level. He screeched and went down.

Holding his knee, he rolled over. He had not landed on bare
ground but on another body. Naked flesh revealed by torchlight
writhed frantically. The shepherdess, so small and withered-seeming
without her rags, had been roped into a bundle. Raw weals across
her arms gave evidence of earlier abuse.

Mereth moved to stand over her, ready to defend the pitiful

girl and herself, but Rober had dragged himself away, still clutching his knee and howling continuously. The core of conflict had moved away from them and shadows enclosed the two females as torches were either snuffed or carried distant.

However there was just enough light for a few moments for Mereth to spy a refuge of sorts—another of the upstanding rocks. She could not carry the girl but she might perhaps roll her. She leaned over and grasped the girl's hair, greasy and dust clotted. She could tell by a brief gleam that the shepherdess's eyes were upon her. The older woman made a hand motion to indicate rolling and pointed toward the stone, hoping the girl would understand.

There was no answer, but push Mereth did with what strength she had left and the small body did seem to undulate into a roll until together they came up against the harsh surface of the boulder. The woman dropped to the ground, near exhausted, with the helpless girl lying against her. Mereth was shivering—no, rather what she felt was wrenching shudders that shook the girl's so-thin body.

Mereth had no blade with her to cut the small captive's bindings, but loosing the throatlatch of Bethelie's cloak, the woman drew the trembling girl into her arms and did what she could to pull the sturdy length of tightly woven wool about them both.

As she attempted to draw the girl higher in her grasp, the edge of her cloak tangled about one of the thin arms so strictly bound. The villager lurched forward as best she could but was unable to free herself. Twisting in Mereth's tightened hold, she screamed again and managed to near face her captor squarely.

"Evil— Make kill—quick!"

Mereth was in no position to write either question or answer. But at that moment one of the torch bearers, a supporter on either side, retreated near enough that the woman saw— Across the shepherdess's tightly bound arm, stretching as a ghastly fringe along the shoulder was rough, raw flesh—lacking any skin. Immediately Mereth swung the girl from close contact, the better to see the bony back riddled with more vicious patches of exposed flesh, in which was seen embedded bits of torn leaf or dark broken stem.

There was evidence of, not a heavy flogging, but something far more frightening. Mereth shuddered. She must get the victim to Lormt, where Nalor could employ her healer's skill to ease the child's torment.

The girl writhed, trying to pull herself away from Mereth, though even the slightest movement brought harsh cries of pain from her. While the woman's attempts to hold her closer to prevent further self-inflicted torture only made her screech louder. Without the ability to communicate, Mereth was near as helpless as the bound one. No! No! NO! Her mind battled against the gag nature had laid upon her as she had once before in her life when her younger sister had been cut down before her eyes by an Alisonian during the Kolder War.

"M'Lady!"

The light was stronger. Wessel stood nursing his left arm against his chest as Master Forbie, with whom she had exchanged greetings that morning, lowered closer a torch—

"What have we here?" Duratan joined them. "Lady Mereth, how came you here?"

She looked down at the trembling girl who seemed to have suddenly shrunk to little more than a tiny armful of abraded flesh. As Mereth leaned back against the rock, the torchlight pitilessly revealed more of the blood-oozing body. Wessel uttered a blistering oath while the commander of Lormt's garrison turned to shout, "AID!" over the field where the battling guards and villagers could no longer be seen.

Back at last at Lormt, at a gesture from Nalor, two of the elderly scholars had pushed a table closer to the high blazing fire of the chamber where dried herbs swung on cords anchored well above. Mereth crouched on a stool within close reach of the flames' warmth, nursing a mug of cordial hot enough to be a blessing to her frosted hands.

She watched Nalor whisk a length of bed sheet across the table and Duratan, aided by a guard, stretch the village girl thereupon, face down, the herb mistress at the last moment turning the youngling's head gently to one side. A low swung lamp chained to a beam above the table revealed the child's abused flesh.

To Mereth's astonishment, the ghastly skinless wounds now in full view did not continue clear across the back as would signs of a severe lashing. Instead they could be seen on left shoulder, left arm and left hip; the rest of the skin was bruised but untorn—

Mistress Bethelie, bringing with her a small steaming kettle, folded cloths in a pack under one arm, appeared beside Lady Nalor as the men left.

Her face was contorted, flushed with anger. "What manner of brutes are these village louts?" she demanded.

Lady Nalor made no answer, but she had opened one of her medicine pouches to take out slender tweezers. Mereth guessed her intention, pulled herself up, setting aside her drink, and twitched one of the cloths from the housekeeper's grasp.

Stretching this flat on her palms, Mereth pushed Bethelie aside to stand at the Herb Mistress's side as, with obvious care, yet swiftly, Nalor began to free the wounds of the bits of stem, matted leaves and portions of blossoms, which clung so tightly to the raw flesh that they seemed to be embedded.

Once she had cleared these all away, she nodded to Mereth, who had immediately clapped one side of the waiting cloth over the other, that nothing escape.

"Feel it?" Nalor asked.

Mereth nodded, the cloth pressed tightly between her hands. Feel it, she did. Perhaps not as strongly as did Nalor, who was of the Old Race and had some of the Talent: rage, blistering, concentrated rage—such an emotion as might drive a man into battle with no thought of himself, simply to slay and slay until he, in turn, would be slain.

And, though there was no possible physical cause, the emotion was rooted in the folded cloth she held.

She must continue to hold; she could not reach for her slate to write any of the questions churning in her mind. Thus Mereth stood and watched Nalor go about her healing work, while keeping half her attention on the wadded cloth into which her nails burrowed.

At length Mistress Bethelie supervised two of her own staff as they carried away the girl, heavily swathed in bandages. But there was no time, even then, for questions and answers—not when one of them could not speak them freely. Either Mereth had become accustomed to the burning of the strange rage, or else much of that had subsided. She still clasped the cloth tightly, however as cudgel-battered men began to be either carried in or aided by comrades. There came both defenders of Lormt and villagers, bloody, bruised and somehow scarcely aware of their surroundings.

Lady Nalor paused to snatch up a glass bowl and curl a summoning finger at Mereth. "In." She had opened a hinged lid. Mereth pushed in the crumpled fabric and the Herb Mistress snapped the lid back down instantly and made it secure.

The housekeeper appeared, holding Mereth's staff and drew the cramped and wrinkled hand of the older woman into the crook of her sturdy elbow. "Come, M'Lady—'tis near sunup. We do not wish any fever, now do we? Bed for you now—"

Nalor had not only relieved her of that burden that had hammered against her strength, but it seemed that she had drawn on Mereth's energy, draining her as well. She allowed herself to be half guided, half carried to her own chamber and the soft comfort of her waiting bed.

It was light again—the clear gloss of very early sunlight touched the undrawn curtain of the bed as she roused. Mereth sat up among the pillows and drew her hand across her forehead, a gesture which brought no relief to her aching head. She looked around twice to reassure herself that no evil shadow had followed her out of the dreams that had imprisoned and tormented her.

Slowly she washed in the tepid water she found in her bowl. Its warmth suggested that someone had looked in at her not long before. Shivering, she drew a heavy gown of quiet violet from her chest and a gray shawl formed into lace by knitting. Mereth continued to battle the pain, which had established itself behind her eyes and, leaning on her staff much more heavily than usual, she sought out company.

This she found in one of the common rooms. The chamber was more crowded than she had ever seen it, and voices rose more loudly than usual. As Mereth entered, partly unnoticed, she was near deafened by fragments of news that were being passed around the room.

Lord Duratan had sent for the nearest Wise Woman—no, he had ridden off to seek her—he was going to appeal to Lord Koris who ruled in Es these days—the villagers had been dabbling in ancient and forbidden things—they had actually brought a girl child as a sacrifice to some devilish thing—and on it went!

Mereth lingered near the door, wanting to escape the din. If she could only cover her ears—but she dared not lose the support of her staff and perhaps end up on the floor for her trouble.

"Lady Mereth!"

Mage Faggold, one of the oldest scholars, suddenly appeared beside her. Though he had counted a vast tally of years, he had not retired as far from the world of the present time as most of his age group, and he was credited with being perhaps the finest historian of those now at Lormt.

He raised his voice more strongly to overcome the din. "This is indeed fortunate, finding you so. We are about to sit in council." He offered her his arm with the grace of a courtier.

Thus those, who might this day be considered the new defenders
of their world, gathered. Lord Duratan was not present. In his place
sat Nalor, his lady, and lying before her on the table, around which
their chairs had been gathered, was the cloth Mereth knew well.
There sat Wessel and another former Borderer, three of the sages,
and Faggold.

When Mereth was comfortably seated, her slate to hand, Lady
Nalor, using the point of a pen as an indicator, raised the edge
of the cloth and flipped it out flat. Next she pointed to indicate
brown splotches, sticking to its length, which was now far from
white.

"You have seen what lies here as it appears beneath the enlarging
glass. You have felt—" she paused, looking from one face to another.

From the moment her eyes had touched that cloth, Mereth's
head moved from side to side. She strove to repel what had followed her out of her feverish dreams. Without her conscious mind's
order, she was writing on her slate.

"It lives—it eats—eats the living—"

The horror of that thought shook her write-stick from her
hand. Faggold caught it before it fell to the floor. Lady Nalor
nodded.

"Yes." Tapping her pen on the table, as if to center their attention to her, with its tip the healer separated one of the dark twigs.
"This is not a thing of the sun or of the Light. It lives beneath.
Though it seems a plant, yet it is not as we know plants, for its food
is flesh and blood." She gazed from one to another of the council
members.

Mereth picked up her writing stick from beside her slate where
Faggold had placed it. She had regained her control and shaped
her words firmly.

"Is this one of the ancient evils awakened again? Or—is there
a gate undiscovered—unsealed? Do we dig to tear it up by the
roots?" She lingered a moment, supplied a final sentence, her
memory awake. Of course there in the past the crew had been
fighting a lesser peril on the strange island to the far south,
however their improvised weapon had worked very well. "There
is fire to cleanse, weed killing potions to poison—" she listed
on her slate.

Faggold and Lady Nalor had both been following her writing
closely.

"Acid of Safall," Nalor nodded vigorously.

"Hot coals held tongs of bale iron," the Mage added his suggestion as quickly. "We must make the villagers aid—"

Mereth leaned back a little. Those in the council were all talking
at once again. She felt as if a cloud hung above her head. This
was all too simple somehow.

She picked up the slate and stick to stow them into the bag
fastened to her girdle. Those about her were planning now; sometimes they seemed of two minds as to what method to use, but
all were united on the fact that the task must be done with all
possible haste, before the monstrous ground-creeping scourge could
spread farther.

Mereth chewed her lower lip. There was more, of that she was
sure. Was a villager, one with some Dark learning, backing this?

With the aid of her staff she got to her feet. Lady Nalor looked
up and Mereth made a small gesture with her right hand. Over
the years she had been at Lormt she had developed hand signals,
easily understood by her daily companions. Now she also gave a
slight nod.

However, Mereth did not return to her chamber when she left
the council, rather she went but a short distance down the hall,
into a small side orom. A kitchen maid sat nodding in a chair
beside an occupied bed. She quickly slipped out of the chair,
rubbing her eyes and yawning. Mereth smiled and gestured to the
door. The maid disappeared gratefully, leaving the chair for the
old woman.

Mereth settled there gingerly, her attention all for the occupant
of the bed. She was entirely alert now, as more and more her suspicions grew firm. The village girl lay with her well-padded back
up-turned, the bandages giving forth an herbal scent. However, her
head was turned toward the elderly woman and now her eyes opened
abruptly.

Speech being denied her, and perhaps even all communication,
if the girl could not read—how could she—?

Mereth's head jerked. It was as if she had heard—sly laughter.

"What would you have of me, old woman?"

This creature could surely not be one with the Power Women—

"Right," the word struck into Mereth's aching head like the point
of a spear. "Power sweeps in both ways. All things balance. What
would you have of me—I ask it again. And I am not patient—
Think what you would ask—scraping around on a slate wastes
time. If we deal together, something must be done about that."

Mereth clasped her hands tightly together. She had walked daily with fear in the war days, but this was something else—she might be chained in some cell while a flood of filth rose about her. Only she must force herself to discover what monster had been brought into Lormt.

"Who are you?" She shaped the thought with difficulty—painfully.

"I am Vorsla, Starqua, Deden, Karn—" Smooth flow of thought paused. Mereth's eyes were on her own tightly clasped hands. She refused to meet those other gray ones.

The voice spoke again in her mind. "Ufora."

Involuntarily a short guttural sound escaped Mereth's throat.

"Yes, oh, yes! When you were little did your dam never strive to threaten you with that name? Ufora of the darkest woods, she could make you one with a tree chosen by a logger, or with a jumper already entangled with the Skinner, the Eater?"

Mereth forced herself upright in the chair. Could this creature read more thought than that intended for communication? Quickly she readied another question.

"What do I do here?" The woods demon continued, "Well, I emerged from the Long Sleep as you see me—a small one easily abused by others, a throw-away of the war. It has taken me too long to become truly myself." The girl touched the crushed linen covering her breast. "Only now after the letting of blood do I fully remember. These dolts of upper dwellers believe they won the ancient war at last by closing the Gates to the worlds of another level. We remain, we, who were sleeping away the flooding of endless years. So, again we were free to fold time. There have been openings left for those unguessed, in which to build their nests anew. So will Ufora do!"

The slight body on the bed moved, pulled up to its knees and slewed around. It plucked at the thick, odorous bandages until it was free. Smooth skin, shown much more darkly against the bedclothes, covered a body in which bones were no longer visible.

Mereth fought desperately against the pain in her head, throbbing as if words were beating a drum within her skull.

The seeming girl snatched up the uppermost sheet and was winding it about herself. She tied two ends together and knotted them, patting the knot when finished.

"Now—" She had spoken only the one word aloud. Standing with her head tilted a little to one side, as if listening, she remained quiet for a moment or two. Then her face twisted into a mask of rage. "So—" she spoke at last. "They would—" She started toward the door but her bulky covering slowed her. Mereth made a determined effort. Her staff, wielded as a spear, thudded home on the other's ribs. The girl screamed, caught at the bed for support, then collapsed to the floor. At once the door flew open with such force it crashed against the wall. Mistress Bethelie gave one glance at Mereth and then centered her attention on the girl, who was snarling at the old woman and visibly working her fingers in a pattern between them.

Bethelie caught at the heavy bunch of keys swinging from her own girdle, snapped it loose and crashed the jangling ball against the girl's hands with good aim. Mereth sat back weakly in her chair. She was finding it very difficult to breathe and her head pain seemed to draw a veil, clouding her vision; however, she could still hear Mistress Bethelie's precise voice:

"Iron, cold iron, to you, evil slut—iron!"

The ringing words followed Mereth into darkness.

Never, since her venture with the Magestone, had Mereth felt herself so removed from real and daily life. There was no sense of transition from the small room, of rising from the chair and making her way through the halls and the great courtyard into the open. A will, which she did not claim as her own, possessed her. Nor did she see anyone on that misty journey. In the huge edifice of Lormt, she might have been totally alone.

Then, with no warning, the walls and restored towers vanished. Mereth was no longer alone, though those about her had a tenuous look. Before her now stretched the sharply sloping, rock-studded land where the skirmish with the villagers had been fought. The sod had been torn away and, not too far away, more of it was yielding to rakes not meant for a farm laborer's cultivation. They were larger than customary and the prongs wider, scratching up clods of earth with vicious points more like weapons than farming implements.

It was near to this activity that the major part of a large assembly was to be found. Mereth blinked once and again, trying to rid her eyes of the cloying mist. Lord Duratan stood there with Wessel and two other one-time Borderers whom she knew to be expert archers. A step or so beyond stood Lady Nalor holding a drawn sword whose weight was obviously burdening her.

And—

That force, which had brought Mereth here, thrust her forward at a quicker pace. Fear like one of the sudden mountain ice showers, struck her full faced. A bundle, resting on the ground between Nalor and the yet undisturbed turf, stirred. She who claimed to be Ufora got to her feet. Her face was like a mask carved from greenish ice of the higher mountain slopes. She tried hard to raise her arms, but her wrists were drawn tightly together. Though there was no strong light, the day being gray, yet flashes glittered. The captive was in irons—

Iron, cold iron—

Nalor was chanting. Now and again Duratan tossed at Ufora a fistful of crushed herbs. Once, twice Ufora tried again to raise her hands. The lips of her masklike face twisted. She might have been seeking to utter words of some dark ritual of her own.

Then—the seeming girl lifted her head a fraction and the dark eyes in her oddly green face fastened on Mereth, meeting those of the elder woman—

Ufora was instantly before her, fettered arms inching out to her. She could see them—impossibly reflected in the creature's eyes. If one pressed there—and there—the bonds would loosen. Mereth knew what the other strained to force her to do.

Three times her own hands came up and out toward the iron-encircled wrists. Three times her own will prevailed and they fell again, but she grew weaker, her head filled with such pain as she was sure would overcome her.

There was no hesitation in Nalor's chant. Her words held no meaning for Mereth. Only there were others!

"Anchor's up, ye sons of Gry—
To the sails—let us fly!"

A man's voice, deep from the throat, armed with courage, about to sail on a final voyage.

Deep in her resonated the words she could not voice—

"Wind and sail
Cannot fail
Men with the Light.
Not even—"

The song she could not voice aloud was fading within her. Rolf, he—. She shut away that memory fiercely. But—but—he had freed her! The staff, her ever-ready companion, lifted. She could no longer sense those dark eyes holding her in thrall. They were light—oddly flat.

Nalor's words were lifting upward in a single, final trumpet-voiced phrase.

The strange girl retreated, still facing Mereth and Nalor. Her foot caught as a noose of roots suddenly snaked out. She screamed, stooping to batter thin green stems ending in yellow flowers with petals that had the shape of sword blades.

Before the watchers could move the land did so. A great crevice gaped and from it arose a thin netting of fine roots to close ominously about the girl. Again the ground shook, preparing to close its doom-crack. Nalor moved; into that heaving growth she tossed a ball, only to snatch a second one—then a third, which Duratan held out to her. Close, the earth did at last! Mereth shuddered as shrill screams slowly faded away—death cries of that which should never have lived.

Thus passed the Latter Battle of Lormt, fought and won, and though the sages housed there sought often to find record of its like in the chronicles they prized, they did so in vain. However, Mereth related the tale to Maid Mouse of the Learned Ones and what she heard in reply, she never told, save that talk by thought became a gift to which she fiercely clung, so dearly was it won.

⋙ Mything in Dreamland ⋘

A Myth Adventures in Dreamland Story

Robert Asprin and Jody Lynn Nye

The dark green roof of the forest stretched out endlessly in every direction. To most, it would look like an idylic paradise. To me, it was a major problem.

I gazed out over the massed pine trees, wondering what kind of wilderness we'd gotten stuck in. A few bare crests, like the one I was sitting on, protruded above the treeline, but they were miles away. None of it looked familiar, but no reason why it should. There were thousands of dimensions in existence, and I'd only been to a few.

At the very least, it was an embarassment. Here I was, considered publicly to be a hotshot magician, the great Skeeve, utterly lost because I'd tripped and fallen through a magic mirror.

I went through my belt pouch for the D-hopper. I was sure it was there somewhere. I wasn't alone, of course. Behind me, my partner and teacher, Aahz, paced up and down impatiently.

"I told you not to touch anything in Bezel's shop," the Pervect snarled. When a native of the dimension called Perv snarls, other species blanch. The expression shows off a mouth full of four-inch razor-honed fangs set in a scaly green face that even dragons consider terrifying. I was used to it, and besides, I was pretty much to blame for his bad mood.

"Who'd have thought anybody could fall through a looking glass?" I tried to defend myself, but my partner wasn't listening.

"If you had paid attention to a single thing I've said over the last however many years it's been . . ." Aahz held up a scaly palm in my direction. "No, don't tell me. I don't want to know. Garkin at least should have warned you."

"I know," I said. "It's my fault."

"It's just basic common sense when it comes to magik. Don't eat anything that says 'Eat me.' Don't drink anything that says 'Drink me.' And don't touch Klahdforsaken magik mirrors with barriers around them that say 'Don't touch!' . . . What did you say?" Aahz spun around on his heel.

"I said I know it's my fault. I was just trying to keep Gleep from eating the frame," I explained sheepishly.

"Gleep!" the dragon added brightly, beside me.

"So why didn't you tie him up before we went in?" Aahz said.

"I did tie him up!" I protested. "You know I did. You saw me knot the leash around a post." But we could both make an educated guess as to what had happened.

My dragon was not allowed in most reputable places or what passed for reputable at the Bazaar at Deva, the largest trading area anywhere in the multitude of dimensions. It often happened that unscrupulous Deveel shop proprietors ridded themselves of unwanted merchandise at a profit, by arranging for accidents to occur. Such as having a convenient fire during for which time the owners have an unshakeable alibi. Such as leaving the door ajar while they just run next door to borrow a cup of sugar. Such as loosening the tether on a baby dragon whose reputation for clumsiness is almost as impressive as its master's reputation for magical skill and deep pockets. Said dragon would go charging after its beloved owner. Merchandise would start to hit the tent floor as soon as it entered. More goods, not even close to being in range of said rampaging dragon, would shatter into pieces. Outraged shopkeeper would appear demanding reimbursement at rates inflated four or five times the true worth. Unlucky customer would be forced to shell out or risk expulsion (or worse) from the Bazaar. All genuine valuables would have been removed from the shop ahead of time, of course.

"Maybe one of Bezel's rivals let him loose," I suggested hopefully, not liking my skills at tying knots to be called into question.

"What were you doing looking at that mirror anyhow?"

I felt a little silly admitting the truth, but it had been my curiosity that had gotten us stranded out here. "Massha told me about it. She said this was a really great item. It shows the looker his fondest dream. . . . Naturally, I wanted to see if it was anything we could use in our business. You know, to scope out our clients, find out what it is they really want . . ."

"And what did you see?" Aahz asked quickly.

"Only my own dreams," I said, wondering why Aahz was so touchy. "Daydreams, really. Me, surrounded by our friends, rich, happy, with a beautiful girl . . ." Although the mirror had been a little sketchy about the actual physical details I remembered vivid impressions of pulchritude and sex appeal.

A slow smile spread over Aahz's scaly features. "You know those dream girls, partner. They never turn out like you hope they will."

I frowned. "Yes, but if it's your own dream, wouldn't she be exactly what you want? How about yours? What did you see?"

"Nothing," Aahz said flatly. "I didn't look."

"But you did," I insisted, grabbing on to a fleeting memory of Aahz with an astonished expression on his face. "What did you see?"

"Forget it, apprentice! It was a big fake. Bezel probably had a self-delusion spell put on the mirror to spur someone stupid like you into buying it. When you got home you'd have seen nothing reflected in it but Bezel's fantasy of a genuine sucker."

"No, I'm sure the mirror was real," I said thoughtfully. I knew what I'd daydreamed over the years, but those wishes had been piecemeal, little things now and again. I'd never had such a coherent and complete vision of my fantasies. "Come on, Aahz, what did you see?"

"None of your business!"

But I wasn't going to be put off that easily.

"C'mon. I told you mine," I wheedled. Aahz's wishes were bound to be interesting. He had seen dozens of dimensions, and been around a lot more than I had. "You probably have some sophisticated plan about an empire with you at the top of the heap, in charge. Hundreds of people begging for your services. Wine! Women! Song!"

"Shut up!" Aahz commanded. But by now, my curiosity was an unignorable itch.

"There's no one around here for miles," I said, and it was the truth. "Nobody could get up here in hearing range. They'd have to build a bridge to that next peak, and it's miles away. There's no one here but us. I'm your best friend, right?"

"I doubt that!"

"Hey!" I exclaimed, hurt.

Aahz relented, looking around. "Sorry. You didn't deserve that, even if you did make a boneheaded move by touching that mirror. Well, since it's just us . . . Yeah, I saw something. That's why I think it's a delusion spell. I saw things the way they used to be, me doing magik—big magik—impressing the heck out of thousands—no, millions! I got respect. I miss that."

I was astonished. "You have respect. We respect you. And people in the Bazaar, they definitely respect you. The Great Aahz! You're feared in a hundred dimensions. You know that."

"It's not like in the old days," Aahz insisted, his gaze fixed on the distance, and I knew he wasn't seeing the endless trees. "Time was we'd never have been stuck up here on a bare mountaintop like two cats on a refrigerator . . ."

I opened my mouth to ask what a refrigerator was, then decided I didn't want to interrupt the flow. Aahz seldom opened up his private thoughts to me. If he felt like he wanted to unload, I considered it a privilege to listen.

" . . . I mean, it ain't nothing showy, but time was I could have just flicked my wrist, and a bridge would've appeared, like that!"

He flicked his wrist.

I gawked. A suspension bridge stretched out from the peak on which we were standing all the way to the next mountain. It was made completely out of playing cards, from its high arches down the cables to the spans and pylons that disappeared down into the trees. We stared at each other and gulped.

"That wasn't there before," I ventured. But Aahz was no longer looking at the bridge or at me. He was staring at his finger as if it had gone off, which in a sense it had.

"After all these years," he said softly. "It's impossible." He raised his head, feeling around for force lines. I did the same.

The place was full of them. I don't mean full, I mean FULL. Running through the ground like powerful subterranean rivers, and overhead like highly charged rainbows, lines of force were everywhere. Whatever dimension we'd stepped into was chockablock with magik. Aahz threw back his head and laughed. A pretty little yellow songbird flew overhead, twittering. He pointed a finger at it. The bird, now the size of a mature dragon, emitted a basso profundo chirp. It looked surprised.

It had nothing on me. For years I had thought only my late magik teacher Garkin could have removed the spell that robbed Aahz of his abilities. I didn't know a dimension existed where the laws of magik as I had learned them didn't apply. It seems I was wrong.

Aahz took off running toward the bridge.

"Hey, Skeeve, watch this!" he shouted. His hands darted out. Thick, fragrant snow began to fall, melting into a perfumed mist before it touched me. Rainbows darted through the sky. Rivers of jewels sprang up, rolling between hills of gold. I tripped over one and ended up in a pool of rubies.

"Aahz, wait!" I cried, galloping after him as fast as I could. Gleep lolloped along with me, but we couldn't catch him. As soon as Aahz's foot hit the bridge, it began to shrink away from the mountainside, carrying him with it. He was so excited he didn't notice. Once when I hadn't really been listening he had told me about contract bridge. This must be what he meant. This bridge was contracting before my eyes.

"Aahz! Come back!" I called. There was nothing I could do. Gleep and I would have to jump for it. I grabbed his collar, and we leaped into space.

I was pushing with every lick of magik in my body, but we missed the end of the bridge by a hand's length. A card peeled itself up off the rear of the span. It was a joker. The motley figure put its thumbs in its ears and stuck out its tongue at me, just before the bridge receded out of sight. I didn't have time to be offended by its audacity, since I was too busy falling.

"Gleeeeep!" my dragon wailed, as he thudded onto the steep slope beside me. "Gle-ee-ee-eep!"

"Gr-ra-ab so-ome-thi-ing," I stuttered, as we rolled helplessly down the hill. Where had all those force lines gone? I should have been able to anchor myself to the earth with a bolt of magik. We tumbled a good long way until my pet, showing the resourcefulness I knew was in him, snaked his long neck around a passing tree-stump, and his tail around my leg. We jerked to an abrupt halt. I hung upside down with my head resting on a shallow ledge that overlooked a deep ravine. We'd only just missed falling into it. As soon as I caught my breath, I crawled up the slope to praise Gleep. He shot out his long tongue and affectionately planted a line of slime across my face. I didn't flinch as I usually did. I figured he deserved to lick me if he wanted to. He'd saved both of us.

I studied my surroundings. If there was a middle to Nowhere, I had unerringly managed to locate it. The remote scraps of blue visible through the forest roof were all that was left of the sky. Once my heart had slowed from its frantic "That's it, we're all going to die now" pounding to its normal "Well, maybe not yet" pace I realized that the ledge we almost fell off was wide enough to walk on. I had no idea where it led, but sitting there wasn't going to help me find Aahz or the jokers who had carried him off.

"You lost, friend?" a male voice asked.

I jumped up, looking around for its source. I could see nothing but underbrush around me. Out of reflex I threw a disguise spell on me and Gleep, covering my strawberry-blond hair with sleeked-back black and throwing my normally round and innocent-looking blue eyes into slanted, sinister pits. Gleep became a gigantic red dragon, flames licking out from underneath every scale.

"No! I'm just . . . getting my bearings."

A clump of trees stood up and turned around. I couldn't help but stare. On the other side of the mobile copse was the form of a man.

"Well, you sure look lost to me," said the man, squinting at me in a friendly fashion. He was dressed in a fringed jacket and trousers, with a striped fur cap perched on his head and matching boots on his feet. His skin was as rough as bark, and his small, dark eyes peered at me out of crevices. Hair and eyebrows alike were twiglike thickets. The eyebrows climbed high on his craggy forehead. "Say, that's pretty good illusion-making, friend! You an artist?"

"Huh?" I goggled, taken aback. How could he have spotted it so readily? "No. I'm a master magician. I am . . . the Great Skeeve."

The man stuck out a huge hand and clenched my fingers. I withdrew them and counted them carefully to make sure none had broken off in his solid grip. "Pleased to meet you. Name's Alder. I'm a backwoodsman. I live around these parts. I only ask because illusion's a major art form around here. You're pretty good."

"Thanks," I said dejectedly. An illusion was no good if it was obvious. I let it drop. "I only use it because I don't look very impressive in person."

Alder tutted and waved a hand. "It don't matter what you look like. It's only your personality anybody pays attention to. Things change around here so often." He lifted his old face, sniffed and squinted one eye. He raised a crooked finger. "Like now, for example."

Alder was right. While I watched, his leathery skin smoothed out a little and grew paler. Instead of resembling a gnarled old oak he looked like a silver-haired birch instead. I was alarmed to discover the transformation was happening to me, too. Some force curled around my legs, winding its way up my body. The sensation wasn't unpleasant, but I couldn't escape from it. I didn't struggle, but something was happening to my body, my face.

"Gleep!" exclaimed my dragon. I glanced over at him. Instead of a green dragon with vestigal wings, a large, brown fluffy dog sat looking at me with huge blue eyes. Once I got past the shock I realized the transformation really rather suited him. I pulled a knife out of my pocket and looked at my reflection in the shiny blade. The face looking back at me was tawny skinned with topaz-yellow eyes like a snake and a crest of bright-red hair. I shuddered.

"What if I don't like the changes?" I asked Alder.

Meditatively, he peeled a strip of bark off the back of one arm and began to shred it between his fingers. "Well, there are those who can't do anything about it, but I'm betting you can, friend. Seeing as how you have a lot of influence."

"Who with?" I demanded. "What's the name of this dimension? I've never been here before."

"It ain't a dimension. This is the Dreamland. It's common to all people in all dimensions. Every mind in the Waking World comes here, every time they go to sleep. You don't recognize it consciously, but you already know how to behave here. It's instinctive for you. You're bending dreamstuff, exerting influence, just as if you lived here all the time. You must have pretty vivid dreams."

"This is a dream? But it all seems so real."

"It don't mean it ain't real, sonny," Alder whistled through his teeth. "Look, there's rules. The smarter you are, the more focused, the better you get on in this world. Lots of people are subject to the whims of others, particularly of the Sleepers themselves, but the better you know your own mind, the more control over your own destiny you've got. Me, I know what I like and what I don't. I like it out in the wilderness. Whenever the space I'm in turns into a city, I just move on until I find me a space where there ain't no people. Pretty soon it quiets down and I have things my own way again. Now, if I didn't know what I wanted, I'd be stuck in a big Frustration dream all the time."

"I just had a Frustration dream," I said, staring off in the general direction in which Aahz had disappeared. "How is it that if I have so much power here I couldn't catch up with my friend?"

"He's gone off on a toot," Alder said knowingly. "It happens a lot to you Waking Worlders. You get here and you go a little crazy. He got a taste of what he wants, and he's gone after more of it."

"He doesn't need anything," I insisted. "He's got everything back at home." But I paused.

"There's got to be something," Alder smiled. "Everyone wants one thing they can't get at home. So what does your friend want?"

That was easy: Aahz had told me himself. "Respect."

Alder shook his head. "Respect, eh? Well, I don't have a lot of respect for someone who abandons his partner like he did."

I leaped immediately to Aahz's defense. "He didn't abandon me on purpose."

"You call a fifty-mile bridge an accident?"

I tried to explain. "He was excited. I mean, who wouldn't be? He had his powers back. It was like . . . magik."

"Been without influence a long time, has he?" Alder asked, with squint-eyed sympathy.

"Well, not exactly. He's very powerful where we come from," I insisted, wondering why I was unburdening myself to a strange old coot in the wilderness, but it was either that or talk to myself. "But he hasn't been able to do magik in years. Not since my old mentor, er, put a curse on him. But I guess that doesn't apply here."

"It wouldn't," Alder assured me, grinning. "Your friend seems to have a strong personality, and that's what matters. So we're likely to find your friend in a place he'd get what he wanted. Come on. We'll find him."

"Thanks," I said dubiously. "I'm sure I'll be able to find him. I know him pretty well. Thanks."

"Don't you want me to come along?"

I didn't want him to know how helpless I felt. Aahz and I had been in worse situations than this. Besides, I had Gleep, my trusty . . . dog . . . with me. "No, thanks," I said, brightly. "I'm such a powerful wizard I don't really need your help."

"Okay, friend, whatever you want," Alder said. He stood up and turned around. Suddenly, I was alone, completely surrounded by trees. I couldn't even see the sky.

"Hey!" I yelled. I sought about vainly. Not only couldn't I see the backwoodsman, but I'd lost sight of the cliffside path, the hillside, and even what remained of the sky. I gave in. "Well, maybe I need a little help," I admitted sheepishly. A clearing appeared around me, and Alder stood beside me with a big grin on his face. "Come on, then, youngster. We've got a trail to pick up."

Alder talked all the way through the woods. Normally the hum of sound would have helped me to focus my mind on the problem at hand, but I just could not concentrate. I'm happiest in the middle of a town, not out in the wilderness. Back when I was an apprentice magician and opportunistic but largely unsuccessful thief, the bigger the population into which I could disappear after grabbing the valuables out of someone's bedroom, the better to escape detection. Alder's rural accent reminded me of my parents' farm which I had run away from to work for Garkin. I hated it. I forced myself to remember he was a nice guy who was helping us find Aahz.

"Now, looky-look here," he said, glancing down as we came to a place where six or seven paths crossed in a knot of confusion. I couldn't tell which one Aahz and his moving bridge had taken, but I was about to bolt down the nearest turning, just out of sheer frustration. "Isn't this the most interesting thing? . . . What's the matter?" he asked, noticing the dumb suffering on my face. "I'm talking too much, am I?"

"Sorry," I said, hiding my expression too late. "I'm worrying about my partner. He was so excited about getting his powers back that he didn't notice he was getting carried away—literally. I'm concerned that when he notices he's going to try to come back and find me."

"If what you say is true it's going to take him a little time to get used to wielding influence again," Alder said. I started to correct him, but if this was the way the locals referred to magik, I wouldn't argue. "Right now we're on the trail of that bridge. Something that big doesn't pass through without leaving its marks, and it didn't. He lifted a handful of chocolate-colored pebbles from the convergence, and went on lecturing me.

"Now, this here trail mix is a clear blind. Those jokers must have strewn it to try and confuse us, but I'm too old a hand for that. I'm guessing that bridge is on its way to the capital, but I'd rather trust following the signs than my guesses. We have to hurry to see them before the winds of change blow through and mess up the tracks. I don't have enough strength myself to keep them back."

"Can I help?" I asked. "I'm pretty good at ma— I mean influence. And if my partner packs a kick here, I should, too."

Alder's branchlike eyebrows rose. "Maybe you could, at that. Let's give it a try!"

Let's just say I wasn't an unqualified success to start. Dreamish influence behaved like magik in that one concentrated hard picturing what one wanted to achieve, used the force lines to shape it, then hoped the committee running the place let one's plans pass. Like any committee they made some changes, the eventual result resembling but not being completely like my original intention, but close enough. Over the several days it took us to walk out of the forest, I attained a certain amount of mastery over my surroundings, but never enough to pop us to the capital city of Celestia or locate Aahz. I did learn to tell when the winds of change were coming through. They felt like the gentle alteration that had hit me and Gleep the first day, but far stronger. They were difficult to resist, and I had to protect the entire path we were following. This I did by picturing it, even the parts we couldn't see, as a long rope stretched out in front of us. It could have knots in it, but we didn't want it breaking off unexpectedly. I might never find Aahz if we lost this trail. I did other little tasks around the campground, just to learn the skill of doing two things at once. Alder was a great help. He was a gentler teacher than either Garkin or Aahz. For someone who had little influence of his own, he sure knew how to bring out the best in other magicians.

"Control's the most important thing," he said, as I struggled to contain a thicket fire I had started by accident when I tried to make a campfire one night. "Consider yourself at a distance from the action, and think smaller. What you can do with just a suggestion is more than most people can with their best whole efforts. Pull back and concentrate on getting the job done. A little effort sometimes pays off better than a whole parade with a brass band."

I chuckled. "You sound like Aahz."

"What?" Alder shouted.

"I said . . ." But my words were drowned out by deafening noise. The trees around us were suddenly thrust apart by hordes of men in colorful uniforms. I shouldn't say "horde," though they were dressed in red, black and gold, because they marched in orderly ranks, shoving me and Alder a dozen yards apart. Each of them carried a musical instrument from which blared music the likes of which I hadn't heard since halftime at the Big Game on the world of Jahk.

I picked myself up off the ground. "What," I asked as soon as my hearing returned, "was that?"

"That was a nuisance," Alder said, getting to his feet and brushing confetti off his clothes.

"No kidding," I agreed, "but what was it?"

"A nuisance," Alder repeated. "That's what it's called. It's one of the perils of the Dreamland. Oh, they're not really dangerous. They're mostly harmless, but they waste your time. They're a big pain in the sitter. Sometimes I think the Sleepers send them to get us to let go of ourselves so they can change us the way they want. Other people just plain attract them, especially those they most irk."

I frowned. "I don't want to run into any more of them myself," I said. "They could slow us down finding Aahz."

Alder pointed a finger directly at my nose. "That's exactly what they might do. Stick with me, friend, and I'll see you around the worst of them, or I won't call myself the finest backwoodsman in the Dreamland."

Using the virtually infinite reservoir of power available to me, I concentrated on keeping the trail intact so that Alder could find it. I found that the less influence I used, the fewer nuisances troubled us. So long as I kept my power consumption low, we had pretty easy going. It would have been a pleasant journey if I hadn't been concerned.

It was taking so long to locate Aahz that I began to worry about him. What if the contracted bridge had trapped him somewhere? What if he had the same problems I did with influence? He might have trouble finding enough food, or even enough air! He wasn't as fortunate as I had been, to locate a friendly native guide like Alder. Visions of Aahz in dire straits began to haunt my dreams, and drew my attention away from admiring the handsome though sometimes bizarre landscape. Gleep, knowing my moods, tried to cheer me up by romping along and cutting foolish capers, but I could tell that even he was worried.

One day Alder stopped short in the middle of a huge forest glade, causing me and Gleep to pile up against the trees growing out of his back.

"Ow!" I said, rubbing my bruises.

"Gleep!" declared my dragon.

"We're here," Alder said. He plucked a handful of grass from the ground and held it out to me. It didn't look any different from the grass we'd been trudging over for the last three days. "We're in Celestia."

"Are you sure?" I demanded.

"Sure as the sun coming up in the morning, sonny," Alder said.

"All this forest in the midst of the capital city?"

"This is the Dreamland. Things change a lot. Why not a capital made of trees?"

I glanced around. I had to admit the trees themselves were more magnificent than I'd seen anywhere else, and more densely placed.

The paths were regular in shape, meeting at square intersections. Elegant, slender trees with light coming out of the top must be the streetlights. Alder was right: it looked like a city, but all made of trees!

"Now, this is my kind of place," Alder said, pleased, rubbing his hands together. "Can't wait to see the palace. I bet the whole thing's one big treehouse."

Within a few hundred paces he pointed it out to me. What a structure! At least a thousand paces long, it was put together out of boards and balanced like a top on the single stem of one enormous oak tree. The vast door was accessible only by way of a rope ladder hung from the gate. A crudely painted sign on the door was readable from the path: KLUBHSE—EVERYWUN WELCM. THE KING. In spite of its rough-hewn appearance there was still something regal about it.

"No matter what shape it takes, it's still a palace," Alder said. "You ought to meet the king. Nice guy, they tell me. He'd like to know an influential man like you. Your friend has to be close by. I can feel it."

A powerful gale of changes prickled at the edge of my magikal sense. I fought with all my might to hold it back as Alder knelt and sniffed at the path.

"This way," he said, not troubling to rise. Unable to help himself, he became an enormous, rangy, blood-red dog that kept its nose to the path. Overjoyed to have a new friend, Gleep romped around Alder, then helped him follow the tracks. The scent led them directly to two vast tree-trunks in the middle of a very crowded copse. Alder rose to his feet, transforming back into a man as he did.

"We're here," he said.

"But these are a couple of trees!" I exclaimed. Then I began to examine them more closely. The bark, though arrayed in long vertical folds, was smooth, almost as smooth as cloth. Then I spotted the roots peeking out from the ground. They were green. Scaly green. Like Aahz's feet. I looked up.

"Yup," said Alder with satisfaction. "We've found your buddy, all right."

A vast statue of Aahz scratched the sky. Standing with hands on its hips, the statue had a huge smile that beamed out over the landscape, Aahz's array of knife-sharp teeth looking more terrifying than ever in twenty-times scale. I was so surprised I let go of the control I was holding over the winds of change. A whirlwind, more a state of mind than an actual wind, came rushing through. Trees melted away, leaving a smooth black road under my feet. White pathways appeared on each side of the pavement. People rushing back and forth on foot and in vehicles. Across the way the palace was now undisputedly a white marble building of exquisite beauty. But the statue of Aahz remained, looming over the landscape, grinning. I realized to my surprise that it was an office building. The eyes were windows.

With Alder's help I located a door in the leg and entered. People bustled busily around. Unlike the rest of the Dreamland where I had seen mostly Klahds, here there were also Deveels, Imps, Gremlins and others, burdened down with file folders and boxes or worried expressions. Just as I had thought, given infinite resources Aahz would have a sophisticated setup with half of everybody working for him, and the other half bringing him problems to solve. And as for riches, the walls were polished mahogany and ivory, inlaid with gold and precious stones. Not flashy—definitely stylish and screaming very loudly of money. I'd always wondered what Aahz could do with infinite resources, and now I was seeing it. A small cubicle at one end of the foot corridor swept me up all the way to the floor marked HEAD-QUARTERS.

A shapely woman who could have been Tananda's twin with pink skin sat at a curved wooden desk near the cubicle door. She spoke into a curved black stick poking out of her ear. She poked buttons as buzzers sounded. "Aahz Unlimited. May I help you? I'm sorry. Can you hold? Aahz Unlimited. May I help you? I'm sorry. Can you hold?"

I gazed into the room, at the fanciest office suite I could imagine. I knew Aahz was a snazzy dresser, but I never realized what good taste he had in furniture. Every item was meant to impress. The beautifully paneled walls were full of framed letters and testimonials, and every object looked as though it cost a very quiet fortune. All kinds of people hurried back and forth among the small rooms. I found a woman in a trim suit-dress who looked like she knew what she was doing and asked to see Aahz.

"Ah, yes, Mr. Skeeve," she said, peering at me over her pince-nez eyeglasses. "You are expected."

"Gleep?" added my dragon, interrogatively.

"Yes, Mr. Gleep," the woman smiled. "You, too."

"Partner!" Aahz called as I entered. He swung his feet off the black marble-topped desk and came to slap me on the back.

"Glad to see you're okay. No one I sent out has been able to locate you."

"I had a guide . . ." I said, looking around for Alder. He must have turned his back and blended in with the paneling. I brought my attention back to Aahz. After all the worrying I had done over the last many days I was relieved to see that Aahz seemed to be in the very best of health and spirits. "I was worried about you, too."

"Sorry about that," Aahz said, looking concerned and a little sheepish. "I figured it was no good for both of us to wander blindly around a new dimension searching for one another. I decided to sit tight and wait for you to find me. I made it as easy as I possibly could. I knew once you spotted the building you'd find me. How do you like it?"

"It's great," I said firmly. "A good resemblance. Almost uncanny. It doesn't . . . put people off, does it?" I asked, thinking of the seven-foot fangs.

"No," Aahz said, puzzled. "Why should it?"

"Oh, Mr. Aahz!"

A small thin man hurried into the office with the efficient-looking woman behind him with a clipboard. "Please, Mr. Aahz, you have to help me," the man said. "I'm being stalked by night-mares."

Aahz threw himself into the big chair behind the desk and gestured me to sit down. The little man poured out a pathetic story of being haunted by the most horrible monsters that came to him at night.

"I'm so terrified I haven't been able to sleep for weeks. I heard about your marvelous talent for getting rid of problems, I thought . . . "

"What?" Aahz roared, sitting up and showing his teeth. "I've never heard such bunkum in my life," Aahz said, his voice filling the room. The little man looked apprehensive. "Pal, you've got to come to me when you really need me, not for something minor like this."

"What? What?" the little man sputtered.

"Miss Teddybear," Aahz gestured to the efficient woman, who hustled closer. "Get this guy set up with Fazil the Mirrormaster. Have him surround this guy's bed with reflectors that reflect out. That'll scotch the nightmares. If they see themselves the way you've been seeing them they'll scare the heck out of themselves. You'll never see them again. Guaranteed. And I'll only take a . . . thirty percent commission on the job. Got that?"

"Of course, Mr. Aahz." The efficient woman bowed herself out.

"Oh, thank you, Mr. Aahz!" the little man said. "I'm sorry. You're just like everyone said. You are absolutely amazing! Thank you, thank you!"

Aahz grinned, showing an acre or so of sharp teeth. "You're welcome. Stop by the receptionist's desk on the way out. She'll give you the bill."

The little man scurried out, still spouting thanks. As soon as the door closed another testimonial popped into existence on the already crowded wall. Aahz threw himself back into his chair and lit a cigar.

"This is the life, eh, partner?"

"What was that about?" I asked, outraged. "The guy was frightened out of his life. You gave him a solution without leaving your office. You could have gone to see what was really going on. He could have someone stalking him, someone with a contract out on him . . ."

Aahz waved the cigar and smoke wove itself into a complicated knot. "Psychology, partner, I keep telling you! Let him worry that he's wasting my time. He'll spread the word, so only people with real troubles will come looking for me. In the meantime, Fazil's an operative of mine. He'll check out the scene. If the guy just has some closet monsters that are getting above themselves, the mirrors will do the trick. If it's something worse, Fazil will take care of it." He pounded a hand down on a brown box on the desktop. "Miss Teddybear, would you send in some refreshments?" Aahz gestured at the wall. "Your invisible friend can have some, too. I owe him for getting you here safely."

"It's nothing, friend," the backwoodsman said. He had been disguised as a section of ornamental veneer. He turned around and waddled over to shake hands. "You've made yourself right at home here."

"You bet I have," Aahz said, looking around him with satisfaction. "I've been busy nonstop since I got here, making connections and doing jobs for people."

The efficient aide returned pushing a tray of dishes. She set before Gleep a bowl of something that looked disgusting but was evidently what every dragon wishes he was served every day. My pet lolloped over and began to slurp his way through the wriggling contents. My stomach lurched, but it was soon soothed by the fantastic food that Aahz's assistant served me.

"This is absolutely terrific," I said. "With all the information you've gathered, have you figured out a way to get us back to Deva?"

Aahz shook his head.

"I'm not going back."

"We'll tell everyone about this place, and . . . what?" I stopped short to stare at him. "What do you mean you're not going back?"

"For what?" Aahz asked, sneering. "So I can be the magic-free Pervert again?"

"You've always been Pervect without them," I said, hopefully trying to raise his spirits with a bad joke.

It didn't work. Aahz's expression was grim. "You don't have a clue how humiliating it is when I can't do the smallest thing. I relied on those abilities for centuries. It's been like having my arm cut off to be without them. I don't blame Garkin. I'd have done the same thing to him for a joke. It was just my bad luck that Isstvan's assassin happened to have picked that day to put in the hit. But now I've found a place I can do everything I used to."

"Except D-hop," I pointed out, slyly, I hoped. "You're stuck in one dimension for good."

"So what?" Aahz demanded. "Most people live out their whole lives in one dimension."

" . . . Or hang out with your old buddies."

Aahz made a sour face. "They know me the way I was before I went through the mirror. Powerless." He straightened his back. "I won't miss 'em."

I could tell he was lying. I pushed. "You won't? What about Tanda and Chumley? And Massha? What about the other people who'll miss you? Like me?"

"You can visit me in here," Aahz said. "Get the mirror from Bezel, and don't let anyone else know you've got it."

"You'll get bored."

"Maybe. Maybe not. I've got a long time to get over being powerless. I can't do anything out there without magikal devices or help from apprentices. I'm tired of having people feel sorry for me. Here no one pities me. They respect what I can do."

"But you don't belong here. This is the world of dreams."

"My dream, as you pointed out, apprentice!"

"Partner," I said stiffly. "Unless you're breaking up the partnership."

Aahz looked a little hurt for the moment. "This can be a new branch office," he suggested. "You can run the one on Deva. You already do, for all practical purposes."

"Well, sure, we can do that, but you won't get much outside business," I said. "Only customers with access to Bezel's mirror will ever come looking for you, and you already said not to let anyone know we've got it."

"I can stand it," Aahz assured me. "I'm pretty busy already. I'm important here. I like it. The king and I—we're buddies." Aahz grinned, tipping me a wink. "He said I was an asset to the community. I solve a few little problems for him now and then." The efficient aide leaned in the door. "'Scuse me, partner." He picked up a curved horn made of metal and held it to his ear. "Hey, your majesty! How's it going?"

If there was ever a Frustration dream, I was living it. For every reason I presented as to why Aahz should return to Deva, Aahz had a counterargument. I didn't believe for a moment he didn't care about the people he would be leaving behind, but I did understand how he felt about having his powers restored to him. He'd get over the novelty in time.

Or would he? He'd been a powerful magician for centuries before Garkin's unluckily timed gag. Would I be able to stand the thought of losing my talents twice? He did seem so happy here. He was talking with the local royalty like an old friend. Could I pull him away from that? But I had to. This was wrong.

"I'd better leave, sonny," Alder said, standing up. "This sounds like an argument between friends."

"No, don't go," I pleaded, following him out into the hallway. "This isn't the Aahz I know. I have got to get him through the portal again, but I don't know how to find it."

Alder cocked his shaggy head at me. "If he's half the investigator he seems to be, he already knows where it is, friend. The problem you're going to have is not getting him to the water, but making him drink. Right now, things are too cushy for him. He's got no reason to leave."

I felt as though a light had come on. "You mean, he hasn't had enough nuisances?"

Alder's rough-skinned face creased a million times in a sly grin. "I think that's just what I do mean, youngster. Best of luck to you." He turned his back and vanished.

"Thanks!" I called out. Using every bit of influence that was in me, I sent roots down into the deepest wells of magikal force I could find, spreading them out all over the Dreamland. I didn't try to dampen Aahz's light. I brightened it. I made every scale on the building gleam with power, both actual and perceived. Anyone with a problem to solve would know that this was the guy to come to. Aahz would be inundated with cases, important, unimportant and trivially banal. There would be people looking for lost keychains. There'd be little girls with kittens up trees. There'd be old ladies coming to Aahz to help them find the eye of a needle they were trying to thread.

Most important, unless I had missed something on my journey here, with that much influence flying around, every nuisance in the kingdom would converge on the building. If there was one thing my partner hated, and had lectured me on over and over again, it was wasting time. If I couldn't persuade Aahz to leave the Dreamland, maybe nuisances could.

My gigantic injection of magik took effect almost immediately. While I watched, things started to go wrong with the running of Aahz, Unlimited. The files the efficient employees were carrying to and fro grew so top-heavy that they collapsed on the floor, growing into haystacks of paper. Some of the employees got buried in the mass. Others ran for shovels to get them out, and ended up tangled with dozens of other people who came in to help. Framed letters began to pop off the wall, falling to the floor in a crash of glass.

Then the entire building seemed to sway slightly to the right.

"What's going on here?" I could hear Aahz bellow. He emerged from his office, and clutched the door frame as the building took a mighty lurch to the left. I grabbed for the nearest support, which happened to be Gleep. He had become a giant green bird with a striped head and a flat beak and curved talons which he drove deep into the wooden parquet floor. "Why is everything swaying?"

Miss Teddybear flew to the eye-windows and looked down.

"Sir, giant beavers are eating the leg of the building!"

"What?" Aahz ran to join her, with Gleep and me in close pursuit. We stared down out of the huge yellow oval.

Sure enough, enormous brown-black creatures with flat tails and huge square front teeth were gnawing away at the left leg of Aahz Unlimited. As each support in the pylon snapped, the building teetered further.

Aahz leaned out of the window. "*Scram!*" he shouted. The attackers ignored him.

"Everyone get down there and stop them!" Aahz commanded. Miss Teddybear hurried away, following the flood of employees into the moving-box chamber.

As Aahz and I watched, his people poured out of the building.

They climbed the leg, clinging to it in an effort to keep the monsters from burrowing any further. The beavers turned, and swatted them off with flips of their flat tails. Wailing, the employees whirled out of sight like playing cards on the wind. The monsters went on chewing. I felt bad about the people, though Alder has assured me that Dreamlanders were not easily hurt or killed.

"Call for reinforcements!" Aahz bellowed. I stared in amazement as white circles whirled out of the air, plastering themselves all over the leg, but the beavers chewed right through them. In no time they'd whittled the leg down to a green stick. The building was going to fall. Aahz's empire was crumbling before our eyes. Gleep seized each of us in one mighty claw and flew with us to the elevator. The floor split under us as we crowded into the small cabinet.

The ride down seemed to take forever and ever. Aahz paced up and back in irritation, dying to get out there and do something to stop the destruction. I could tell he was trying to focus his magik on driving the monsters away and keeping his newfounded empire intact. I concentrated all my magik on keeping us from getting hurt. The forces I had stirred up scared me. I didn't know if I'd get us killed trying to bring Aahz home.

"Come on," he snarled, leaping out of the chamber as it ground to a stop. "We've got to hurry."

It was too late. Just as we emerged from the front door, the enormous Aahz-shaped structure wobbled back and forth, and crashed to lie flat in the park. I gulped. One second sooner, and we'd have been inside when it fell. Aahz stared at the wreckage in dismay.

"Oh, well," I said, trying to look innocent. "Easy come, easy go."

"Yeah," Aahz said, with a heavy sigh. "It was just a dream. There's always more where that came from."

A boy in a tight-fitting uniform with a pillbox hat strapped to his head came rushing up. He handed Aahz a small package the size of his hand. Aahz gave the boy a coin and tore open the paper. Inside was a small mirror. I recognized the frame. "It's the portal back to Deva," I said in surprise. "You were looking for it after all."

"This was supposed to be for you," Aahz mumbled, not meeting my eyes. "If you had wanted to use it. If you had wanted to stay, I wouldn't be upset about it."

The change of tense made me hopeful. "But now you want to go back?" I asked encouragingly.

"I don't need to be bashed over the head with it," Aahz said, then looked at the fallen building, which was already beginning to be overgrown with vines. "But I almost was. I can take a hint. Come on." He took hold of the edges of the mirror. With a grunt of effort, he stretched the frame until the mirror was big enough for all of us.

Through it, instead of the reflection of our dreams, I could see Massha, my apprentice, my bodyguards Nunzio and Guido, and Tananda, our friend all surrounding the hapless Bezel. The Deveel, scared pale pink instead of his usual deep red, held his hands up to his shoulders, and his face was the picture of denial. Terrified denial. He might not be guilty for setting us off on this little adventure after all.

Aahz grinned, fearsomely.

"C'mon. Let's let him off the hook." He took a deep breath and stepped through the mirror.

"Hey, what's all this?" Aahz asked, very casually. "You trying to raise the roof?" He lifted a hand. In the Dreamland the gesture would have sent the tent flying. In this case, it was merely a dramatic flourish. Aahz looked disappointed for less than a second before recovering his composure. I experienced the loss he must have felt, and I was upset on his behalf, but relieved to have gotten him home. He didn't belong in the world of dreams. Some day we'd find a way to undo Garkin's spell.

"Aahz!" Tananda squealed, throwing herself into his arms. "You've been gone for days! We were worried about you."

"You, too, big-timer," Massha said, putting a meaty arm around me and squeezing just as hard. The embrace was a lot more thorough coming from her.

"Thanks," I gasped out.

"Gleep!" my pet exclaimed, wiggling through behind us. The trip through the mirror restored him to dragon-shape. In his joy he slimed all of us, including the trembling Bezel, who was being prevented from decamping by the firm grip Nunzio had on the back of his neck.

"Honest, I swear, Aahz," Bezel stammered. "It wasn't my fault. I didn't do anything."

"Altabarak across the way let the dragon loose, boss," Guido said, peering at me from under his fedora brim.

"Okay, Bezel," I said, nodding to my bodyguard. If he was positive I was positive. "I believe you. No hard feelings. Ready to go get a drink, partner?" I said. "Everyone want to join me for a strawberry milkshake?"

"Now you're talking," Aahz said, rubbing his hands together. "A guy can have too much dream food." Bezel tottered after us toward the door flap.

"I don't suppose, honored persons," the Deveel said hopefully, the pale pink coloring slightly as he dared to bring business back to usual, "that you would like to purchase the mirror. Seeing as you have already used it once?"

"What?" I demanded, turning on my heel.

"They ought to get a discount," Massha said.

"Throw him through it," Guido advised. Bezel paled to shell-pink and almost passed out.

"Smash the mirror," Aahz barked, showing every tooth. Then he paused. "No. On second thought, buy it. A guy can dream a little, can't he?"

He stalked out of the tent. My friends looked puzzled. I smiled at Bezel and reached for my belt pouch.

⋙ Race for the Sky ⋘

A Bifrost Story

Mickey Zucker Reichert

The warm, green fragrance of spring filled Al Larson's nose, a smell he had not appreciated for what seemed to him like decades; but, through the quirk of a time loop, was actually no time at all. A desperate year of combat in Vietnam haunted his memory yet did not exist in the annals of his family or the records of the United States Army. Dragged from death by a god, he subsequently spent at least a year in an elven body in a warped version of ancient Europe. Little remained from that time: just a lot of hairy recollections, his strikingly beautiful fiancée, Silme, and his best friend, Taziar Medakan the Shadow Climber.

Glad to be back in New York, as well as April of 1969, Larson savored the fresh, earthy aroma, even tainted by car exhaust. A Frisbee thunked against his skull, smacking pain through his right ear and driving him a step sideways. Unable to escape his war training, he hurled himself flat to the ground.

Taziar's not-quite German accent followed, "No fun play ambush-Frisbee when you make it so easy."

Larson clambered to his feet and turned toward the voice. Taziar peered at him from between the branches of a twisted maple. Its spattering of leaves did not conceal even his small form. He was dressed in his usual black, a habit from his days living on the brutal streets of an archaic, anti-historical Germany; though now his wardrobe consisted mostly of jeans and t-shirts.

Blue eyes peered out from behind a scraggle of overlong ebony hair that well-suited the sixties style. Fine-boned and barely five feet tall, he tipped the scales at nearly a hundred pounds. He had grown to love American fast food, Ovaltine, and Milky Ways; but he remained as active as a squirrel, a tiny bundle of sinew without a visible ounce of fat.

Without a word in return, Larson headed after the Frisbee. A recent haircut kept his own blond locks in check, parted on the left and perched atop his baby-round face. Daily workouts at the gym kept him as muscular at twenty-one as in his soccer-playing teens. Deliberately active, a foot taller than his little companion, he, too, could eat as he wished without worrying about his weight—a constant consternation to his sister and fiancée.

Larson snatched up the Frisbee, then flung it at the tree in the same motion. The plastic disk flew true, smacking the branch where Taziar had crouched moments earlier. Now on the ground, the little Climber watched it rebound from the branches amid a shower of leaves and plummet in an awkward arc. Displaying the stagnant calm of a man who had never moved, he said, "Good shot."

Standing on a concrete walkway near a line of grass, Larson's nine-year-old brother, Tim, laughed.

Larson dove for the Frisbee, planning to wing it toward the kid. Taziar's small hand darted out to claim the Frisbee first, and Larson's came up empty.

Tim laughed harder.

"Very funny, Shadow." Larson planted his blue gaze on Taziar. "Now what you going to do?"

Taziar shrugged, tucking the toy under his arm. "Wait you get daydreamy again, then . . . " He slapped the heel of his empty palm against his forehead. "Smack you in head."

"You just want to give me a concussion," Larson grumped.

"You pick game."

Tim howled until he grew breathless, strangers staring at him as they passed.

Larson glanced at his doubled up brother. Sandy hair tousled around features that had finally lost their baby softness. Bell-bottom jeans flared around his ankles, hiding all but a glimpse of his filthy black and white sneakers. "Timmy's incapacitated. Why not bean him for a change?"

Warned by a faint whistle of plastic cutting air, Larson flung up an arm just in time to rescue his forehead from another attack. The Frisbee stung his inner forearm, then caromed toward Tim.

"More easy to surprise you." Taziar grinned at the boy and winked. "More fun, too."

Larson could not help smiling. He liked the camaraderie that had developed between his brother and his best friend, though he occasionally felt a twinge of jealousy. Once the sole object of Timmy's hero worship, he now had to share the limelight with the Mets, the Giants, the '76ers, and a quick, dexterous little irritation he had inflicted upon himself.

When Taziar made no move for the Frisbee, Larson headed toward it. He had taken only a step, when a pressure touched his mind. He froze. Only one person could contact him in that manner. Forced to surrender her sorceress's powers to stay in twentieth-century America, Silme still maintained her ability to touch the surface thoughts of anyone without mind barriers. Since those evolved only in worlds with magic, no one born of Larson's era had them, the very reason Frey had rescued him from a firefight in Vietnam and thrust him into the body of an elf.

Silme. Larson concentrated on his fiancée's name.

Allerum. Silme resorted to what she had called him in his elf-form, though she now knew it had come from a stammered introduction. *Don't panic.*

Few words could so suddenly and certainly achieve the very opposite of what they intended. Larson stiffened, the Frisbee forgotten. He cast his gaze on the blue expanse of sky, heart rate quickening to fretful pounding. *Silme, what's wrong? What's happening? Is everyone all right?* She, his sister, Pam, and his mother had planned to spend the day sightseeing and wedding shopping. Car accident, he guessed, wondering why cabbies seemed to feel this compulsive need to drive like maniacs. *If anyone's hurt, I'll kill him.*

Everyone's all right, Silme sent back, a touch of terror filling her sending. *For the moment.*

The Frisbee bonked hollowly against Larson's head. He barely noticed. *What's going on, Silme? Tell me.*

Apparently struck by the oddity of Larson's reaction, Taziar approached, Frisbee in hand. "What you do?"

Larson held up a finger, a plea for a few moments of silent truce.

We're on the eighty-sixth floor of the Empire State Building. The first observation deck.

Larson nodded, then remembered she could not see gestures. *All right.* The information seemed to come far too slowly. He doubted this had anything to do with a simple fear of heights. The emotion behind the sending seemed far too urgent.

There're men.

Men?

With guns.

Larson's heart seemed to stop in mid-beat. For a moment, he hovered in a startled oblivion that precluded thought.

They won't let us leave.

Something tugged at Larson's shirt. He looked down to Tim and Taziar, the Frisbee tucked under the climber's arm. "Is it Silme?"

"It's Silme," Larson confirmed. "Big trouble." He returned to the internal conversation. *Silme, we'll be right there. I'll take the details on the way.*

Be careful, please, they thought in unison.

The taxi ride passed in a blur of mental communication broken only by pauses to explain the situation to Taziar and Tim.

They call themselves the Vietnam Peace Liberation Army.

A "peace" army. Too concerned to appreciate the irony, Larson pressed. *What do they want?*

As far as I can tell, they want the government to pull out of the war.

"They want us out of the war," Larson explained aloud, queasy from the mingled odors of stale cigarette smoke and exhaust.

"Sounds worthy," Taziar said, staring out the window at the skyscrapers zipping past.

"Worthy," Larson repeated, battling down his own memories of Vietnam. Once, flashbacks had plagued him mercilessly; and every stressful situation sent him plunging back into hellish and vivid memory. Silme and a god had reconnected the frayed and looped pathways of Larson's remembrances, returning control. He snorted. "Worthy indeed . . . if you totally ignore the fact that they're making their point by holding innocents at gun point." His own words sent him back into silent communication. *Can you tell what they're planning?*

I can only read surface thoughts, Silme reminded. *Anything else would take magic.*

Larson tried to radiate encouragement. She should be capable of extrapolating some long-term intentions from their current focus.

The leader . . . they call him Banqo.

Banqo.

In their language, that means "spiritual guide."

It sounded somewhat Spanish to Larson, though the word did

not translate into anything he understood. Though a related tongue, his high school French added little. *What language is that?*

Made-up one, Silme sent. *As far as I can tell, it only consists of a few key words.* Her presence disappeared abruptly.

Alarmed, Larson chased her. *Silme. Silme!* "Damn it all to hell, I've lost her." *Silme!* He shifted wildly in his seat. *Silme!!*

Taziar caught Larson's arm. "Easy. What happened?"

The question seemed like moronic delay. "I lost her! I lost Silme."

Taziar's voice remained quiet and level, a starkly nonchalant contrast to Larson's desperation. "How?"

"How?" Larson repeated. "I don't know how! One moment she's there; the next she's not." *Silme! Damn it, where are you?* Hopeless frustration fueled his anger. He had no way to contact her and could only wait for her to come to him again, if ever.

Al. Silme's touch carried none of the desperation that had tainted Larson's since her disappearance.

Larson froze. Silme? *What happened? Are you all right?*

As "all right" as anyone held at gun point, I suppose.

Larson rolled his eyes. Less than a year in America, and she's already learned New Yorker sarcasm.

Unaware that Larson had reestablished contact, Taziar continued in the ancient language they had shared in the other world. "Calm down, Al. She probably has something she has to do there. Appease a zealot. Soothe another captive."

Larson raised a hand to stay Silme, though she could not appreciate the gesture. "I've got her back."

Taziar waved broadly to indicate that he had proved his point.

How many are there?

Silme addressed the ambiguous question with both answers. *Three maniacs. Seventeen hostages.*

That's it?

You wanted more?

Larson hurried to correct a misconception that might make him appear callous. *Of course not. But I'd heard something like ten thousand visitors come every day. Pretty much all of them go to the observation deck.*

There was a scramble when the guns came out. Smashed into every elevator. Rushed down the stairs. I'm guessing the gunmen stranded a couple hundred people when they disabled the elevators.

Disabled. Another surprise. *Aren't there like a hundred of them?*

More like sixty. Seventy, maybe. They did something on the roof that took out all of them at once, I think.

Silme's uncertainty forced Larson to remember she only read surface thoughts. He fidgeted, willing the cab faster through the milling cars. Everyone seemed in a hurry, yet they still managed to block one another from moving anywhere quickly.

Tim tugged at his brother's sleeve. "Is Mom all right?"

The question jarred Larson back to the present. It was an important point that he should have asked long ago. A warm flush of embarrassment crept over his features. *Silme. Pam? My mom? How are they . . . handling this?*

A lot better now that they know I'm in contact with you.

Taziar was right again . . . damn it. "Mom's fine," Larson told his little brother. "Pam and Silme, too. But we've got to do what we can to help them." *Can you tell if they're capable of hurting anyone?*

Silme did not reply. At first, Larson thought he had lost her again, but a trickle of discomfort seeped through their contact. She was still there.

Silme.

They shot two men they believed were security guards.

Dread stabbed through Larson's gut. He tried to hold it from his thoughts, to force a calm rationality that would show Silme he had the matter in hand when, in fact, he stood spare inches from a blithering panic. *Shot,* was all he trusted himself to send.

One's dead. The other's not yet, but it's only a matter of time. Remorse tainted Silme's sending. *If only I still had my magic, I could heal him.*

If you still had your magic, Silme, the gods would have taken you back to your world and time. You wouldn't be here to help anyone, and I'd have killed myself long ago.

Don't say that.

It's true. Larson refused to lie. *I couldn't live without you, so keep yourself safe.*

The cabby's gruff voice startled Larson. "This's as close we get."

Larson glanced at the street signs: Broadway and Fourth, two blocks short.

"Something's going on. Never seen a crowd like this here. Usually just a few gawking tourists—from Ioway or Idaho or some such."

Larson craned his neck. A hovering mass of humanity filled the streets, all centered on his goal. The Empire State Building towered over the crowd like a massive rocket, its antenna disappearing into the clouds.

"Thanks." He leapt from the car, leaving Taziar to pay the tab.

The little man made a good living, along with Silme, with their sleight-of-hand/mind-reading act. It seemed a strange pairing, given that Taziar, with his mind barriers, was the one person whose thoughts Silme could not access. Somehow, they made it work.

Without a backward glance, Larson strode into the throng. Taziar and Tim caught up to him in a few paces. "So what's the deal?" his brother asked.

Larson softly detailed the information Silme had given him, skipping the part about the dead and dying men. It would only worry and upset Tim, and it would change nothing that Taziar did.

"Excuse me. Pardon me. Excuse me," Larson said mechanically as he shoved through the seething clot of people. He tried to keep his manner businesslike and his voice an authoritative monotone. Most edged aside, assuming him a professional of some kind. Some shot him dirty looks that questioned his right to progress while they remained pinned in place. A few times, he weathered shoves or elbows that barely budged his solid, weight-trained frame. No one directly challenged him, mercifully, for he would not have hesitated to deck anyone who dared to delay him.

Taziar and Tim managed to keep up, though Larson did not worry how they did so. He trusted the little climber to pace or exceed him in any endeavor that involved movement, though Taziar more often used dexterity, stealth, crawling, and climbing than the more direct and physical course Larson usually chose. Tim, apparently, simply slid into his brother's wake.

Tell me anything you can about these gunmen. Larson appreciated that the matter-of-fact, composed manner he adopted to sweep him through the crowd translated to his communication with Silme. It might soothe her to believe him in control.

Silme obliged. *Their names are Bob Hendricks, that's Banqo, Steve Heston, and Mike Pevrin. They call Steve "Hyron," which to them means "soldier in the cause." Mike is "Taybar" or "adviser."*

Great, a bunch of grown men with guns who think they're playing clubhouse. Have you tried to communicate with them?

Only verbally. Haven't spoken in their heads yet. Silme anticipated Larson's next question. *They seem unstable.*

Duh.

I don't know how they might react to an intruder in their minds. Thought I'd save it as a surprise maneuver or if things get desperate.

Good thinking. Larson tripped over someone's leg and jostled into an enormous man wearing fringed jeans and a Grateful Dead t-shirt. He whirled, jowly face locked in a dangerous scowl, dark eyes sizing up Larson.

Reflexively, Larson curled his hands into fists and screwed his features into his best boxing face. The other man muttered something Larson could not decipher, then turned back toward the Empire State Building. Larson continued to excuse and pardon himself through the crowd.

I can't do anything more than exchange information.

Larson realized that, if the men figured out what Silme could do, they would probably kill her to protect their plans from her invasion. He tried to hide that concern from his surface thoughts. No need to further alarm Silme. *You're right. Don't tip your hand until absolutely necessary.*

If Silme picked up on Larson's underlying concern, she gave no hint of her knowledge. *All right.*

As Larson shoved his way toward the front of the crowd, he saw police hurriedly cordoning off the area with poles and yellow tape while others kept the mob at bay with shouts and gestures. Taziar caught at Larson's shirt. "Al, I'll need a distraction."

Larson quickly filled Taziar in on the rest of the conversation, then added, "What are you planning to do?"

Taziar studied the building momentarily, then retreated back into the crowd. "You don't want to know."

Larson did, but he did not get the opportunity to press. He glanced to his left, where Tim silently studied the situation. "You stay here," he told his younger brother. "Don't go anywhere with anyone unless it's the police or a member of our family."

Tim nodded. "Be careful."

It was not a promise Larson could fairly make, so he chose no reply instead. Thrusting out his chest and squaring his shoulders, he stepped over the police tape. A sudden hush fell over the crowd in his quarter.

A harried-looking policeman with sweat-plastered brown hair dangling from beneath his cap lunged for Larson, whistle blowing.

Ignoring him, Larson strode boldly toward the Broadway entrance.

"Hey," the policeman called. "Hey! Where do you think you're going?"

Larson jabbed a thumb toward the tallest building in the world. "My fiancée, my mother, and my sister are in there."

Another policeman joined the first, a red-faced, heavy-set man who looked irritated to have to deal with one rabble-rouser amid a crisis and an unruly mob. "Join the club, man. Lots of people got relatives in there. We're doing everything we can."

Larson attempted to step around the larger man. "Look. There're only seventeen hostages, and three of them are my fiancée, my mother, and my sister. So, at most, there're thirteen people in the same boat as me. And your best just isn't good enough."

The red-faced man turned purple and sidestepped back into Larson's path. The other officer looked stunned. "How could you possibly know that?"

"Let's just say I served a stint in Vietnam but you won't find any record of it." For the first time, Larson tried to use the contradiction to his advantage by implying that he had served as part of a clandestine force. "You won't find any record of any kind on my fiancée. And we have a 'special' form of communication."

The larger man rolled his eyes and looped a finger near his temple.

But the smaller man ignored his comrade, clearly impressed by Larson knowing the exact count of hostages. Likely, they had discussed the Vietnamese Peace Army's demands and details by telephone and not with the press or public. "What else do you know?"

Larson recited what Silme had told him: "Bob Hendricks, Steve Heston, and Mike Pevrin."

The larger policeman shifted impatiently from foot to foot. "You're wasting time we could be spending rescuing your relatives and the others. Who do you think you are? Maxwell Smart and 99?" He made a throwaway gesture. "Get back behind the tape."

When the smaller cop returned only a blank look, Larson tried another tack. "Banqo, Hyron, and Taybar. Those were the real names of the hostage-takers and their aliases."

Now, even the heavy man's eyes widened, then narrowed suddenly in clear suspicion. "How do you . . . know that?"

En masse, the crowd went suddenly quiet and seemed to gasp in a collective breath. Knowing it probably had something to do with Taziar, Larson resisted the urge to look and draw the cops' attention, though that proved far more difficult than he expected. He dreaded the thought that the desperate kidnappers might have thrown someone from the building.

Silme's voice echoed through Larson's head. *They're angry the police won't provide a helicopter.*

They won't? It was a pointless question asked from distracted instinct.

They say it's too windy right now.

Wondering if this was a ruse, Larson asked, *Is it?*

Silme returned to sarcasm, a sure sign that she was more stressed than she was letting on to those around her, *Last time I flew a helicopter . . .*

Is it windy?

Well, yeah.

The conversation gained Larson nothing. He imagined a variety of air currents swept the Empire State Building at the calmest of times, but he thought he remembered talk of building a helipad on the top. Or maybe it was a dirigible mast. He shook the thought aside.

Larson looked up to find the policeman still glaring down at him, dark brows beetled. "So, how do you know so much?"

"I just told you." Growing impatient, Larson hoped Taziar had done whatever had required his stalling. "My fiancée and I—"

"I heard that," the large man growled, "and I'm not buying. How do I know you're not just another member of the gang?"

Larson could think of several ways but saw no reason to bother. Neither of them had time for it. "Look, my mother, sister, and my fiancee are up there, held at gun point. I don't have to prove anything to you."

The bigger cop glanced at his companion, who had gone silent, studying Larson intently. The look spoke of irritation and withering disdain. "Oh, you do have to prove it. You have to get past me to enter that building, and I have orders not to let anyone through."

Larson forced his tone to a deadly and serious calm. "Shoot me, if you have to. I'm going in."

Quick as a cat, Larson dodged around the larger man and strode toward the fire stairs.

The mob cheered, and Larson pretended not to hear the policeman's shouts over the tumult. The walkie-talkie on his belt blasted a strong round of static, followed by clear words: " . . . climbing the building!"

The cop scurried after Larson, who quickened his pace. He glanced upward. The sun sheened from the chrome-nickel steel mullions and into his eyes, but he could make out a small, dark shape huddled against the spandrels. *Taziar.*

Apparently believing the thought for her, Silme responded. *What about him?*

He's climbing the freaking building!

A shock of clear surprise radiated from Silme. *Does he know we're eighty-six floors up?*

Of course. I told him. Did you think that would discourage him? They both knew Taziar had a fatal attraction for anything anyone deemed impossible.

What if he falls?

Larson did not bother to send the obvious answer. Already, the little climber had clambered over the five-story base to the main portion of the tower, some seven floors above street level, enough to threaten life and limb, undeterred by a frantic group of policemen shouting at him through a bull horn.

"Let him go," Larson heard the smaller cop say behind him.

The larger one snarled in response. "Let him go. Let him go? Why?"

" 'Cause even if he makes it past the others, even if he makes it up the one thousand five hundred and seventy-five stairs—and I doubt it—he ain't going to be in any condition to do anything once he gets there."

"If he gets there."

The rest disappeared beneath the blather of the crowd, the shouts of the policemen, and the crackle of static and voices through radios. Larson reached the outer fire stairs, their usually locked door propped open by another pair of policemen.

Larson ran toward them.

Al! Silme's sudden return startled Larson, and he nearly fell on his face. *Where are you?*

Heading for the stairs.

The stairs? But there's like two thousand of them.

Great. Fifteen hundred wasn't enough. She has to throw bigger numbers at me. He shielded the thought from his sending. *What do you want me to do? Make like Shadow?*

Of course not. I want you to stay there and help the police. I'll send information.

Oh, yeah. That's worked great so far. Again, Larson guarded his sending.

The policemen blocked the stairwell. "No one allowed in there, sonny," one said.

Larson stopped. Too vexed to discuss the matter again, he pretended to turn away, spun completely around, and crashed a fist against one's shoulder. Impact drove the man sideways with a gasp, opening the way just long enough for Larson to dash through it. He sprinted up the stairs.

"Hey! Hey!" Their voices chased him, followed by slamming footfalls. "Hey! You can't go up there. It's dangerous. Hey!"

Larson thundered upward, paying the men no heed.

The policemen stationed every few landings had more important matters to attend than one lunatic hero wannabe attempting to defy the gravity of a greater than a thousand-foot climb. Even in his excellent athletic shape, Larson found himself panting by level ten, breathless by twenty. *Oh, great, Larson. Maybe you can crawl out the top in a wheezing frenzy and demand their surrender.*

The thought sparked a realization that desperate concern for his family had not allowed him to consider. *How am I going to handle these crazies?* Larson shook aside the thought, focusing fully on simply making it to the top. *Crazy, yes; but these guys aren't dumb.* He slowed his pace, continuing his climb.

Where are you? Silme sent, with a clear hint of suspicion.

Larson borrowed Taziar's line. *You don't want to know.*

Probably not, but I need to.

Larson did not oblige. *What's happening up there?*

The three are spending a lot of time together. They're not sure they believe it's too windy for helicopters.

Larson did not like the sound of that. He focussed intently on the mental conversation, attempting to use it as a distraction for his aching legs and lungs as he forced himself upward. *Can you convince them?*

Not without taking a big risk. Don't know how they'll react to a mind intrusion.

Can't you just make some comment about how it's so much windier today than the last few times you came?

They've demanded silence. Threatened to throw a scared young boy over the rail. Tossed an old man's wheelchair off.

Larson's heart seemed to slam against his chest, driven by worry as much as exertion. At least, they seem to be avoiding actually harming civilians. He added to himself, *Except whoever on the ground got smashed by wheelchair wreckage.* He did not long concern himself with the bystanders massed beyond danger by the police.

Silme's discomfort radiated clearly, even unaccompanied by words.

What?

What what? Silme sent, too innocently.

Irritable from the growing pain of his ascent, Larson refused to give quarter. *You know something you're not telling me.*

Many things, I'd warrant. Though a good joke at his expense, Silme took no joy from it, a clear sign that he had hit on or near the truth.

Larson kept climbing at a swift, steady pace, no longer finding policemen on the landings. *What are you hiding?*

I told you about the security guards.

Larson winced. He had not forgotten. *Is the second one . . .*

Still alive, Silme confirmed. *But not conscious.* She added uncomfortably, *Al, they're contemplating some . . . evil things.*

Air wheezed through Larson's lungs. *Go on.* He appreciated the ephemeral quality of their conversation. In his current state, he could not have spoken.

The security men go first, then they plan to work their way down by age.

Distracted by his body, it took Larson's mind inordinately long to grasp the meaning of Silme's description. "Go first" as in—

Thrown over the side.

My god!

One by one over a certain period of time. Until their demands are met.

My god! Larson repeated, no other words coming to mind.

They figure they're already murderers, so they have nothing to lose.

Aside from the lives of innocent people.

A sliver of fear slipped through Silme's carefully controlled facade. *They feel their cause is more important.*

Oh, yeah. That makes sense. Kill innocents to protest the killing of innocents. Knowing better than to seek logic in the actions of fanatical true-believers, Larson glanced at a door to discover he had reached the forty-ninth floor. He groaned. *Still thirty-seven to go.*

Apparently, Larson sent that last thought, because Silme replied to it. *Huh?*

Larson tried to reverse the sentiment. *Only thirty-seven more floors.*

You're climbing! I told you not to come up.

You never listen to me, either.

Silme would not be distracted. *You'll be exhausted by the time you get here. How can that help?*

Can't hurt. Larson deliberately avoided looking at the numbers, not wanting to know how far he had come until he had gone significantly beyond his last look.

Yes, it can hurt! It can get you killed!

Larson refused to argue the point. *Have you seen Shadow?*

Not yet, Silme returned. *I'm peeking over when I can, but they have us closely watched. Tend to keep us bunched so they can see everyone at once.*

Keep looking. Larson doubted even the Shadow Climber could make it up the outside of the Empire State Building without climbing aids, but he had to hope. His tiny companion had done many things deemed impossible, often for that very reason. Then, suddenly, something Silme had said returned to haunt him. *Oldest to youngest!*

Though not the words she had used, Silme caught the reference. *They're telling the police their plan right now. One person every half hour until . . . oh my god!* The contact abruptly cut off.

Silme. Silme!

When Larson did not get an immediate answer, he stopped the concentration. Without training like Silme's from the Dragonrank school, he could not reach her. He could only wait. He found himself staring at the number on the landing: 53. Above him, he heard voices. He slowed, moving as quietly as possible and straining to hear.

The talking stopped, but Larson could hear the occasional scrape of a shoe against concrete. Cautiously, he rounded the fifty-fourth landing and looked up to two uniformed men. Static hissed from one's belt. Cops. Confidently, with the look of a man who belonged, he continued upward.

The policemen spotted Larson and leaped to attention. Both were young, of average height and build; but the similarities ended there. One had red hair peeking from beneath his cap, while the other had no visible hair at all. The redhead sported blue eyes to his companion's brown, and a deluge of orange freckles. Both seemed in reasonably good shape, though neither seemed eager to continue the climb.

"Who are you?" the red-haired cop demanded.

Larson took advantage of the limitations of the walkie-talkies. If they could carry this far, these men would have known him, like the others. "Al Larson. Special team, FBI."

Both men looked him over top to bottom. "Got a badge?" the second asked.

"Yes," Larson lied. "But not the time to show it." He added harshly, "again." With the air of someone in authority and a hurry, he pushed past them and jogged up the stairs.

Larson heard the words "arrogant jerk" behind him but did not

bother to slow. He wanted them to believe that he had demonstrated his bona fides to those lower down the stairway, the most
likely way to explain his presence here and now.

Apparently, the ruse worked because he heard no signs of
pursuit. *That or they're too tired or lazy to follow me.* The reason
did not matter. The increase in speed dragged agony through
Larson's legs, but he scurried upward until he had gone high
enough that the others would not notice a change in pace.

Air rasped through Larson's lungs, raw agony; and the close
stuffiness seemed suffocating. He wiped sweat from his brow with
the back of his hand.

Silme appeared in his head. *Al, they've dropped the security
guards!*

What? Larson's reply was startled from him, without thought.
Even if the method of communication allowed for mishearing, he
did not want her to repeat that particular information. *Both at
once?*

They think it shows the police they mean business.

*As opposed to shoving just one guy off the Empire State Build-
ing.*

One was already dead.

The cops and the crowd didn't know that. Larson quickened his
pace, though his legs felt as if he had bolted bowling balls to his
thighs, and he seemed to have gasped the last of the stairwell air
into his lungs.

Silme's contact turned irritable. *You're arguing with me? They're
crazy, Al. Just get up here right away!*

Oh, so now you want me up there. Larson wisely kept that to
himself. *I'm coming as fast as I can. I'm a decent runner but no pro,
and going up isn't the same as on a track or even rugged terrain.*

Silme returned nothing for several moments. Larson concentrated on steady rhythmical motion, watching the patterned
marble stairs unscroll beneath his sneakers. By now, even his legs
appeared to remember the design: eighteen stairs to each landing. *Why not an even twenty?* Larson abandoned the idle thought,
glad for the 160-step reprieve.

A sudden thought brought a second, desperate wind. *Silme, my
mother?*

Scared but fine. Like the rest of us.

Larson was pretty sure Silme understood the deeper intent of
his question. *Oldest to youngest,* he reminded.

Y-ess. This time, Silme surely knew, but she feigned ignorance.

Pain and the battle for breath contributed to Larson's irritability. *Come on, Silme. Where does my mother fit on that spectrum?*

Silme dodged the question. *She's still a young woman.*

Silme...

Don't you think you'd be happier not knowing?

Probably, Larson admitted, rounding the sixtieth landing. *But tell me anyway.*

Silme waited inordinately long to continue. *After the guy in the wheelchair...*

Yes. Larson deliberately injected impatience into the sending.

He looks about a thousand years old. His caretakers says he's eighty-nine, but he acts more like an infant...

Silme... Larson chastised her clear delay, then guessed, *She's next. After the old man. Isn't she?*

Al, just hurry.

Though Silme gave no direct answer, Larson knew he had discovered the truth. He refused to let the news paralyze him. If he did, all was lost. *I'm hurrying,* he said. *But I'm going to need your help.*

After a crossover at the sixty-fifth floor, Larson charged toward the top with nothing to stand in his way but his own human frailty. He felt like he had run for hours, lungs burning, legs aching, sweat stinging his eyes. He longed for a companion, some bunkmate with eternal stamina to challenge him when he felt like giving up. But, as he gulped scant air into his lungs, he felt thankful that his only partner chose a different route to the top. There did not seem enough air for two in the cramped, stagnant stairwell. *Almost there. Almost there.* Larson drove himself forward, his legs numb, moving only from habit. He looked at the number on the landing door: 84. Excitement thrilled through him, chilling the sweat that covered every part. He dragged up the stairs, buoyed by the energy that comes of impending success.

Larson nearly crashed into a pair of policemen lounging on the landing. He froze, panting savagely, unable to speak.

The men did not press. Though their breath came more easily, they seemed noticeably fatigued, their uniforms askew and their faces pink-cheeked. Relatively young and sinewy, they had clearly been chosen for their ability to make the climb. One was black, round-faced with a well-tamed afro, the other sandy blond with quick, green eyes. "What's the buzz, cuz?" one asked, a far cry from the personal challenges Larson had, thus far, received.

Larson froze, too tired to move, too wracked with nervous energy to sit. "How much..," he panted, " ... do ... you know?"

The black man gestured toward himself. "Name's Carter. Yours?"

Uncertain whether the man had just given his first or last name, Larson gasped out, "Al."

"Mahan," the other man said. "Jimmy Mahan." He studied Larson with a knowing wince. "Take a load off for a bit."

Larson grasped his knees, seeking the best position to gulp air into his lungs. "Can't. Got ... to ... move ... fast."

Carter huffed out a laugh. "How you going to do that when you're gasping like a landed fish? Ain't doing no one no good in that state."

Larson had to agree. He lowered himself to the landing in a crouch, still too driven to fully sit. "They're ... tossing hostages. No time ..." *My mom!*

The cops exchanged glances, smiles wilting in an instant. "Tossing?" Carter repeated. "You mean over the side?"

"Eighty-six stories down," Larson confirmed, the concept, now spoken, staggering.

"Shit." Mahan wiped his brow, picked his cap up from the floor, and plastered it on his head. "What's the plan?"

Larson thought fast. Ideally, he would get one of the men to give him a gun; but he could not think of a way to request such a thing without raising ruinous suspicions. "To get up there, of course. What's blocking the way?"

Silme's presence returned in a wild flurry. *Al! The old man! They're carrying him to the rail.*

Mom's next. Larson knew he should feel callous about worrying more for what might happen than the fate of one at risk now, but he could not help it. The old man had lived a long life and probably had little understanding of his fate. *Silme, what's blocking the stairwell door?*

Which one?

Stumped by a simple and obvious question, Larson went quiet. Any ... one he tried.

Silme did not question. *They're locked.*

Of course.

Two guarded by armed men—usually. If there are more, I don't know about them. Anticipating Larson's question, she added. *I can only read surface thoughts, not everything they know.*

"Locks, for one thing," Carter said in answer to a query Larson had forgotten in the hailstorm of his and Silme's exchange. "We've got the key, of course, but it's not much use from inside the stair-well."

Larson pursed his lips, breathing gradually coming easier, though his legs still ached. He thought of Taziar, hoping the little climber would have the sense not to rush in alone. Taziar possessed nei-ther the ability nor the mentality to kill. Taziar. That gave Larson an idea. "Are there any windows on this floor?"

Mahan shrugged. "It's an office building. Practically made of windows." He added doubtfully, "Why?"

Larson did not even want to waste time saying "No time to explain." Instead, he charged for the heavy door, slammed in the handle, and dashed into the hallway. He charged down the high-ceilinged corridor, noticing nothing but the first office door. He turned the knob and struck it with his shoulder simultaneously. He hit solid wood frame, clearly locked, but the force of the blow shattered the opaque glass front. Shards stabbed his shoulder, and rained, further broken by the green marble floor. He sprang through the gap, dislodging the remaining, clinging pieces and crushing the glass beneath his sneakers to powder.

Eyes on the window, Larson stumbled into a desk, sending a chair careening to the floor and dashing pain through his hip. Ignoring it, he floundered through the wreckage, still unable to take his eyes from the window. Bumped and bruised, leaving a wake of askew furniture, he made it to a pane that stood more than a half-foot taller than his six-foot frame. He slammed the heels of his hands against the glass. It barely budged. Larson hammered his fists against the window, howling with rage.

Silme's voice entered Larson's head with an eerie quiet. *Al, they threw him over. He's gone.*

Oh god. Larson stifled the image of the old man tumbling through the air, eyes wide with terror, mouth wrenched open in scream after scream. He wondered how long the man would have to contemplate his fate before it ended with a flash of excruciat-ing pain, then nothing. *Silme, I'm coming.*

Hurry, she sent, bare understatement. *Please hurry.*

Larson hurled himself at the safety glass, vision suddenly filled with clouds, the buildings around seeming distant and small. The glass did not give, but Larson's rational mind did. *What the hell am I doing? If this breaks, I'm going down.* He backed up, reas-sessing the situation. Seeing a latch on the window, he smacked himself in the forehead, feeling like a royal fool. *Of course, they're made not to break. Can't have people accidentally falling, but no reason not to let some fresh air in now and then.* Working the catch, he easily opened the window. *Now what? I'm not Shadow.* Larson clambered to the sill, deliberately looking only up. A downward glance might paralyze him.

Groping along the rail-like mullions, Indiana limestone, and sandblasted spandrels, Larson discovered solid hooks placed as if for climbing. He nestled his hands into them, a million thoughts distracting him from the job ahead. *If these go the length of the building, Shadow probably figures this skyscraping monstrosity for the easiest thing he's ever climbed.* Larson recalled that Taziar's friends had bragged he could climb a straight pane of glass, and Larson had seem him scramble up brick buildings without a moment's hesitation. He also realized that the hooks had to serve as tie-ons for window washers and, possibly, maintenance workers.

Sunlight reflected from the steel, its glow shattering into a blinding array that forced Larson to squint. He worked his way to one of the enormous stainless steel pylons that braced the observatory tower, only one floor above him.

Al.

Larson stiffened, gouging the hooks into his hands. *Don't do that!*

Don't do what? It was a right and innocent question.

Larson realized that his own keyed-up terror had caused him to startle, not Silme. She had contacted him with an appropriate slow gentleness he should have appreciated. *Stay with me, will you? I'm going to need you.*

Sorry. I was just comforting a scared little boy. Where are you?

Larson shored up his leg and right-hand holds before groping over the observatory ledge with his left. *I'm coming over the side, like Shadow. Watch for my hand.* His fingers banged against cold metal. Only then, he remembered the fencing that surrounded the open-air terrace, constructed to frustrate suicides. *Wait a second,* he thought to himself and Silme simultaneously. *How did the gunmen get the old man past the fence?*

They cut a hole, Silme explained. *Pushed them through.* An emotion accompanied the sending like a mental shiver. *Made us all look through. Let us know what's in store for us if the police don't give in to their demands soon. Then, they placed some of the more terrified ones on the phone.*

Larson gripped the fence. *Peace Army, indeed. Bunch of crazy sadistic bastards.*

Abruptly, Larson's description sunk in. Silme's contact wafted terror. *You're where?*

Larson felt along the metal, defining diamond-shaped mesh that would admit the head of someone who wanted the dizzying experience of looking down. He knew from his one visit there, as a young child, that the bars curved toward the building at the top to thwart a more determined jumper from simply climbing over the security rail. *I'm at the outer edge of the terrace, touching the fence. Watch for my hands. Direct me toward the hole they cut, and distract anyone who might see me.*

All right, Silme returned. *I'm watching for Shadow there, too; but I can't communicate with him.*

Larson remembered Taziar's mind barriers. Choosing a direction at random, he worked his way along the edge, using pylons as steps. Movement proved easier than he had expected, though one wrong weight-shift would send him plunging to his death.

Al, I see you. You'll get there a lot faster if you go clockwise.

Larson repositioned, switching direction and heading back the way he had come. A trek that had seemed surprisingly simple, at first, rapidly became a discomfort. His muscles, already aching from the climb, cramped from the unnatural position; and his nerves wound them to tight coils. Wind pounded his face, threatening his grip. Granite scraped the skin from his arms, and the fencing bit into his fingers.

Almost there. Almost there. Silme's cautious pronouncement fell on welcome ears. Then, her tone changed drastically. *Wait! Al, one of them's headed toward you!*

Larson's heart pounded. He could imagine himself struggling to get up while a stranger tore off his hold and sent him into a long and fatal plunge, filled with evil laughter. *Distract him!*

I'll try. Silme's contact disappeared from Larson's mind.

Now completely disoriented, Larson made a desperate choice. He had to assume the worst, that Silme's interference would fail. He could freeze and hope the other man did not see him, but that did not suit him. A man of action, Larson found himself incapable of just remaining in place, blindly hoping a ruthless killer did not notice him. Instead, he increased his pace, the wind whipping though his ears making hearing all but impossible.

Jaggedly cut metal sliced Larson's palm, and pain shocked through him. Biting his lip, he maintained his grip, easing into position in front of the hole.

Al! Silme's presence jabbed into his mind like a hot spear. *He's right at the opening!*

Larson jerked his head up and found himself staring into the cold dark eyes of a killer. Shaggy black hair fell around a rugged Caucasian face a few years older than his own. He wore a V-neck shirt, a leather backpack, and a hand-hammered peace sign swinging from a gold chain. The eyes went wide with clear shock.

Push him, Silme! Feet wedged, one hand winched onto the shattered fencing, Larson wound his free fingers around one strap of the man's pack and pulled with all his considerable strength.

The man slid toward Larson, as if on a dolly. As most of his weight tipped forward, he screamed, grabbing wildly. Larson flinched. If those flailing hands caught him, they would both go tumbling. His own balance thrown backward, he seized a death grip on metal and strap. For an instant, they remained in a strange balance, hovering between life and death, while time seemed to stand still. Then, the man toppled toward oblivion, shrieking in mindless terror. The abrupt shift of weight tore free Larson's toeholds. Suddenly supporting the full mass of two, every tendon in his right arm seemed to snap at once, a stabbing explosion of burning pain. His fingers jerked open. *I'm dead.* The calm realization seemed savagely out of place. Then, the backpack straps slipped free. The weight of the killer disappeared. A scream swirled on the wind, and something steady clamped onto Larson's wrist, arresting his own fall. Battling rising panic, he sought and found his toeholds on the pylons.

Hold on, Silme sent. *I won't let you fall.*

Larson gulped down bile. He swung his left hand over the ledge, still gripping the killer's backpack. Only then he realized that he could have saved himself some serious injury if he had only let go instead of clinging to the backpack. At the time, the idea of loosing any solid grip had seemed madness. He looked up to Silme's worried features, both hands clamped around his left wrist.

Hurry, Silme sent, glancing wildly behind her.

Larson scrambled up the ledge and through the hole, the pain in his right arm a constant, screaming blessing. It reminded him he was alive. *But not for long if we don't do something quickly.*

Larson jerked up the pack and pawed through the contents. He found clothing, food, and spare magazines. *Damn it, no gun.* The irony became a burning bitterness. *I nearly died for no gun.* He glanced at Silme. *Get back with the others. Let them know I'm on your side. To help me if they can.*

Silme nodded, turning. She headed for the central gift shop.

At that moment, a huge man with long, greasy blond hair

crashed through the door. "Hey!" He seized Silme by the wrist, spinning her through the door, then slammed it behind her.

Though enraged by the manhandling, Larson kept his head. He dove aside, just as the man raised a .45 automatic. Larson skittered around the loop, pressing against the gift shop wall. Then, another man burst through a door to his left, sandwiching him between them.

Shit! Surrounded, Larson tried for desperate unpredictability. He sprinted for the fence and dashed up the diamond mesh, only then noticing another man just reaching the incurving spires at the top. *Shadow!* Brutal realization dawned. *And I just gave him away.*

"Holy fuck!" the blond shouted. Ducking, he fired at the figure over Larson's head.

Blood splashed Larson's cheek. "NO!" Without thought for his own safety, he hurled himself at the shooter. He struck the blond with a force that hurled them both to the floor. A bullet ricocheted wildly, and the hostages screamed, running toward the opposite side of the store. Both men slid, crashing into the glass storefront, pain jarring through Larson's left side. He caught the man's gunhand with his left, then slammed his aching right arm downward. He heard something crack, accompanied by a rush of pain through his strained muscles. The gun clattered to the terrace.

Shadow! Silme screamed in Larson's head.

Larson scooped up the gun, whirling. The other man fired at Taziar. The little climber dodged, then lost his footing on the fencing.

"No!" Larson shrieked, charging to save his friend, though he knew he could never arrive in time. The killer whirled on Larson, shooting. Fire tore through Larson's thigh, dropping him to a spinning crouch. He watched, helplessly, as Taziar pitched from the fencing into empty air. "No!" he screamed again. "No! No!" Rage overtook him. He trained the blond's gun on the second man, who was now hurriedly reloading. Larson pulled the trigger again and again, until the slide locked back on empty.

Al!

Nothing could stop Larson now. "Shadow!" he howled. "Shadow! NO!" Only then, he remembered the blond. The man lay unconscious by the gift shop, a horde of hostages swarming over him. Some attempted to tie him with souvenir King Kong airplanes and anything else with laces or strings. Others pelted him with metal statuettes.

Larson dropped the gun and fell to his knees. He clamped his face in his hands, his own blood warm and sticky on his cheeks. "No! No! No!" *It was all my fault! If I hadn't picked that spot, they wouldn't have seen him. Shadow would still be alive.*

Mrs. Larson rushed to her son, cradling him in her arms like an enormous baby. "Al." Tears dripped down her cheeks as she looked at the blood. "Al, say something." Pam knelt beside them and took Larson's aching hand.

"I'm all right, Mom," Larson croaked out, though he could not even convince himself.

Finally, Silme appeared, and she had clearly read the spirit of Larson's thoughts, if not the exact words. *Stop beating yourself up. You couldn't have known he was there.*

Larson wasn't so sure. Accidentally or on purpose, he had betrayed a buddy, had caused his very death. In 'Nam, he had learned to keep an eye on each and every companion, to do whatever it took to keep all of them safe. They relied on him, and he knew he could rely on them. Except, this time, he had made a mistake, and his best friend had paid with his life.

Silme's delay had, apparently, come from obtaining the key to the stairwell. Now, the police came to survey the scene, herding most of the hostages toward the safety of the stairwell.

"What happened?" Carter asked, opening the flood gates. Most of the hostages began talking at once.

Mahan made his way to Larson. "What really happened?"

Mrs. Larson answered first, hugging Larson to her, though it smeared blood onto her arms, face, and dress. "They shot my boy. Can't you see, they shot my boy."

"I'm all right," Larson said again. His arm ached, and his thigh felt like a bowling ball; but these faded beneath the terrible agony in his soul.

Carter called over the hubbub. "Mahan!"

"Yeah!"

"I'm going to take these folks down and get some backup. You okay up here?"

Mahan looked at Larson.

"Enemy's all down. Third one went over the side," Larson assured. The words ached through Larson. *And Shadow, too.*

"Yeah!" Mahan called back, barely missing a beat. He looked at Silme, Pam, and Mrs. Larson. "You three need to go with the others."

Mrs. Larson did not look up. "I'm not leaving my son."

Mahan looked at Pam.

"My brother," she said.

"My fiancé," Silme added before the policeman could even ask.

Mahan sighed, then clapped Larson's shoulder. "Guess I know now why you did what you did. You're not really FBI, are you?"

Larson smiled weakly. "Wouldn't tell you if I was."

Mahan laughed. "Carter'll have the paramedics up here soon. You going to make it till then?"

"I've been hurt worse."

"Really?" Mahan brushed hair from his forehead. "I better rethink that FBI question."

A voice wafted from the gift shop. "I hurt, too. Why no pretty lady hold me?"

Everyone whirled at once. Even Larson struggled to a painful stand, recognizing the voice. *Shadow? It can't be!*

Taziar dragged himself from the stairwell, smearing blood across the marble floor. Dirt covered every part, and scarlet splotches decorated his tattered clothing.

Silme at least managed to start the question Larson could not. "How did you . . . ? How . . . ?"

"Don't move." Mahan approached Taziar, hand raised, attention on the climber's every move. "Who are you?"

Silme brushed past the policeman to assist Taziar. "That's Taziar Medakan. He's our friend."

Pam just shook her head. "You . . . you fell off the eighty-sixth floor of the Empire State Building! How . . . how?"

Taziar smiled weakly. "Falling off, that easy. Climb up from ground, that hard." When no one laughed, he gave the explanation they all needed. "Just fall two floor. Land on ledge. Go through open window." He threw up a hand, as if stating the obvious. "Come here."

"A miracle," Mrs. Larson breathed.

Mahan scratched his head. "Actually, been about a dozen attempted suicides before that fence got up. I don't think any of them made it all the way to the ground."

"Really?" Mrs. Larson finally pried her gaze from her son, which pleased Al Larson. He did not think he could handle another moment of her pained scrutiny.

"Believe I even remember some old fellow landing on that very same ledge as this guy here. Broke a bone or two but otherwise all right. Wind currents tend to blow everything back toward the building. Probably got a fortune in pennies on every ledge."

Larson had always believed that a coin dropped from the

observatory would crush anyone or thing it hit. Now, he knew why he had never actually heard of anyone killed in such a manner despite the open eighty-sixth-floor terraces and the building's many windows.

The *ping* of the arriving elevator brought an unexpected rush of relief. Taziar was here, alive. The paramedics had come.

Larson closed his eyes, clutching his sister's hand, enjoying the music of a gurney rolling across the marble floor.

⊰≫ Shadamehr ≪⊱
and the Old Wive's Tale
A Shadamehr Story

Margaret Weis & Don Perrin
(Based on the world and characters created by Larry Elmore)

"Begging your pardon, good sir," said the barkeep deferentially, "but this note is for you."

"For me?" The man thus addressed was considerably amazed. "But I am a stranger in these parts! I am merely passing through on my way east. Surely you have made a mistake." He waved the note away. "This must be for someone else."

"I do not think I could be mistaken, sir," said the barkeep with a cunning look. "You have graced my tavern with your presence these three days now, being kind enough to say that my mead is the best in the area—"

"And so it is," said the man, interrupting.

The barkeep bowed and continued. "And thus I have come to know you, sir, very well, as have many of my patrons, for you have been most generous in buying rounds for the house."

The man smiled in a self-deprecating manner and smoothed the ends of a very long and very black mustache. He winked at his companion, a young woman with thick red curly hair, bound up in a coil at the base of her neck. She wore the plain brown robes of one who practices earth magic.

"Therefore," said the barkeep, "when a note is delivered to me to be given to a person of a certain description that matches you most wonderfully, sir, I am left with no doubts."

"What would that description be?" the man asked, his eyes glinting with amusement. "Let us hear it."

"This is what I was told: 'He is a human male of middle years with a nose like an hawk's beak, a chin like an ax-blade, eyes blue as the skies above New Vinnengael and a long black mustache of which he is very proud and is constantly smoothing or twirling. In addition, he has long black hair, which he wears bound in a tail at the back of his head, in the manner of the elves.' "

"Bah! That could be anyone," said the man.

"He is very handsome—" continued the barkeep solemnly.

"Oh, then, you are right. That *is* me," said the man calmly and he plucked the message from the barkeep's hand.

"You are insufferable, Shadamehr," said his companion in a low voice.

"You are only jealous, Alise," Shadamehr said as he broke the seal and unfolded the note. The two spoke in Elven, a language which no one in the Karnuan city was likely to understand. "Jealous that no one sent the beautiful human female with the red hair a mysterious missive."

His companion rolled her eyes and shook her head.

"I trust this note means that our generous hospitality has finally paid off," Shadamehr said. "At last we are about to receive some information. I don't mind telling you that I am growing sick to death of mead."

Reading the note, he appeared puzzled, then gratified. "Here now! I never expected this." He handed the note to his companion.

> Doubtless you do not remember me, my lord, but we were companions in our youth. I was an acolyte with the Revered Magi at the time you were in training as a knight. We met through the unfortunate circumstance of our each falling in love with the same woman at the same time. I shall never forget the tricks we played on each other as rivals, tricks that turned out to be for naught, when she married a third man neither of us had known about. Our rivalry became friendship, a friendship that was severed when you left Vinnengael in anger over the policies of the Emperor and I left to return to my homeland to take up my duties for the Church.
>
> I have followed the tales of your exploits with the deepest pleasure and, although you travel under another name, when I heard from a traveler of a generous stranger with hair as black as midnight, a nose like a hawk and a laugh that booms

like a mountain slide, I knew there could only be one. I am certain the gods have sent you. I believe that you come in answer to my prayers.

You will recall that I was particularly sensitive to the evil magic of the Void. I dare not write more in this note, for fear it will be waylaid. I live in the town of Cunac, about twenty miles north. I beg you to come with all possible haste.

Your friend,
Revered Brother Ulien.

Alise frowned. "How could he possibly have known it was you? Hundreds of miles from our homeland. I don't like this." She handed the missive back.

"Bah!" said Shadamehr with a grin. He tucked the note in his boot and beckoned the barkeep. "Our tab, please. We are leaving your fair city. Of course, Ulien would know it was me, Alise," he added, giving his mustache a twirl. "Everyone for a twenty-mile radius must be talking of the handsome and generous stranger, by now. And his lovely red-haired companion," he included teasingly.

He paid the bill, throwing in enough extra to cause the barkeep to sing his praises for days, and left the bar with Alise.

She snorted. "Your ego will be the death of you, Shadamehr."

"Nonsense, my dear," Shadamehr said, assisting her to mount her horse. "I will cheat death for the simple reason that all the wonderful things people say about me are true. Which is why you adore me."

He whistled to his own black steed, a horse of a vicious temperament who so terrified the stable boys that they would not come close to him. The horse whinnied in delight at the sight of his master and draped his head over Shadamehr's shoulder, almost purring with pleasure when Shadamehr rubbed the horse's muzzle.

"I don't adore you. I don't even like you," Alise said coldly. "I don't know why I put up with you. You will get me killed someday. Get yourself killed, too, in some hare-brained scheme to set the world right when it doesn't want to go right."

Shadamehr leaned over, kissed her on the cheek before she could push him away. Then he was off at a gallop, exhibiting his riding skills to the admiring populace, who took off their hats to wave good-bye.

"I should turn around now and go back home." Alise muttered as she kicked her horse in the flanks. She was forced to ride hard and fast to catch up.

Twilight had fallen by the time the two arrived in Cunac, a small town located near the border of the human kingdoms of Karnu and Dunkarga. Once a united kingdom, the two had split apart in a civil war two hundred years earlier. As much as humans of Karnu and Dunkarga hated all those of other races in the world of Loerem, they hated each other more. The town of Cunac was notable for only one thing—it was the site of a large military outpost, built to deter the Dunkargans from crossing the border.

Strangers were not normally welcomed into Karnuan towns, but Shadamehr, with his glib tongue and his charming manner, was never a stranger anywhere long. The guard who had begun by brusquely refusing them admittance ended by embracing Shadamehr with tears in his eyes. He gave them directions to the Revered Brother's dwelling and added an invitation to come drinking in the tavern when the guard was off-duty.

"What did you tell that man?" Alise demanded. She did not speak Karna. "I thought he was going to throw us out on our ears. What was all that hugging and kissing?"

"A Karnuan tradition when family members meet," Shadamehr said solemnly. "He is my second cousin once removed on my mother's side."

Alise stared at him. "I don't believe you!"

"Ah, but it's true, nonetheless. Someday I will explain. Let us make haste, before Revered Brother Ulien retires."

They secured rooms in the only inn in Cunac and stabled their horses. This done, they left in search of Shadamehr's childhood friend.

Brother Ulien's dwelling was a small house attached to the local temple. The brother was awake and very glad to see them.

"I would have known you anywhere, my lord," said Ulien, regarding his friend with pleasure.

"And I you," said Shadamehr with such heartiness that Alise knew he was lying.

"I could have walked past him in the street and never known it," he confided to her when Ulien had left to bring them food and water. "He used to be a tall, good-looking youth with curly black hair. Now he is gaunt and haggard and gone completely gray."

"He's probably saying the same thing about you," Alise said teasingly. "Especially the part about the gray."

"I am not!" Shadamehr protested. He drew forth the long black tail of hair that fell down his back and studied it by candlelight.

"Am I?" His search for gray hairs was interrupted by the return of their host, who told them of his concerns over dinner.

"About a week ago, I first noticed the presence of Void magic." Ulien spoke in hushed tones, his red-rimmed eyes glancing furtively at the window as if he feared they might be overheard. "The feeling was overwhelming. I've known nothing like it. It was as if a black and noxious cloud had settled over the town. I cannot draw breath. I feel as if I am being smothered."

In truth, he gasped for breath constantly. His thin body jerked and twitched nervously at every sound.

"And you say that two strangers arrived in town at the same time?" Shadamehr asked.

"One of them a dwarf, my lord. A Fire Mage," said Ulien.

Shadamehr frowned. "I have never known a dwarf to have dealings with the Void."

Ulien gave him a sad glance, as if pitying such naïveté. "He is one of the Unhorsed, almost certainly, most likely cast out of his clan for some terrible crime. He might well be a follower of the Void."

"Possibly," said Shadamehr, but he appeared unconvinced. "And the other?"

"A newly appointed commander of the fortress. Since Karnu is a military state," he added for Alise's benefit, "the military commander is also the leading government agent in Cunac. He is an ordinary enough fellow, not especially bright, but he carries a most remarkable sword. The hilt is set with black and red jewels, as is the scabbard. Such a valuable sword might be worn by the Emperor of Vinnengael. What is a captain in the Karnuan army doing with it?"

"Is it tainted with Void magic?" Alise asked with interest.

"I do not know for certain, Revered Sister," Ulien answered with a shiver. "I have not been able to get close enough to find out."

"If so—and I must say that it sounds very much like a Void artifact—this would explain the sensation you are feeling," Alise said.

Ulien shook his head. "I am sorry to have to disagree with you, Sister, but I have been around powerful Void artifacts before and I experienced nothing like this. I have been physically ill over it. I am frightened all the time. I cannot eat. I cannot sleep." He held out his hands. The long fingers trembled and shook. "You see how it is?"

"Then what do you think is causing this, Ulien?" Shadamehr demanded.

"I think . . ." Ulien paused, then said in a whisper, "I think we are dealing with a . . . with a vrykyl."

Ulien waited tensely for their reaction. Alise looked at Shadamehr, who hid his smile by smoothing his mustache. Ulien gave a great sigh and closed his eyes.

"I feared you would laugh at me, my lord!" he said, almost weeping.

"No, no," Shadamehr said, soothingly.

"What are vrykyl, after all, but tales made up by old women? That's what they said in the Temple in Vinnengael. That's what any sane person would say."

"Old women are wise," said Alise with a reproving glance for Shadamehr. "And the truths they keep burning bright through the years are oftentimes the only light we have to guide our footsteps when the darkness comes upon us."

"I say this to you, Ulien, for your ears alone," Shadamehr added, "but we have come to Karnu because I received information relating to the return of the vrykyl to this world."

Ulien gazed at Shadamehr in awe. "Then certainly the gods have brought us together!"

"Perhaps. Perhaps not," Shadamehr said dryly. "What is it you expect me to do?"

"Why, rid the town of this evil, of course," Ulien said.

Shadamehr shook his head. "If this is truly a vrykyl, that is a foe beyond my ability to fight. According to the old wives tales, that is."

"It is said that perhaps a Dominion Lord could slay them," Alise remarked. "That has not been proven, however."

"But, sir, you *are* a Dominion Lord!" Ulien protested. "You served under a different name, but—"

Shadamehr smiled and again shook his head. "You are mistaken. I am not a Dominion Lord. I never underwent the Transfiguration."

Ulien regarded him with narrowed eyes. "The counsel voted to approve you. It was unanimous. The Emperor himself—"

"It is a long story," Shadamehr said, abruptly ending the topic of conversation. "As to the vrykyl, if they do walk this world"— he quirked an eyebrow—"they walk it safe from me. I came to gather information on them. Nothing more."

"Then we are lost," Ulien said in despair.

Shadamehr placed a kindly hand on the trembling hand of his friend. "You are weary. You have not slept in days. Alise will give you a potion to help you find rest."

Alise was already removing a small potion bottle from a belt she wore around her waist. She handed the potion to Ulien, explained the directions for its use.

"We will return in the morning," Shadamehr said, rising to his feet. "I would like to meet this dwarf and the commander, at least. You will point them out to me. Good-night, Ulien. Rest well."

"I will try, my lord," Ulien said unhappily. He held tightly to the potion.

"Vrykyl!" Alise repeated the word accusingly, as soon as they were well away from Ulien's house. "So this is why you brought me!"

"And you thought it was for your red hair," said Shadamehr.

Alise gave a little sigh, which he did not hear, for he was humming a dance tune to himself. The town's streets were empty. Windows in the houses were dark and shuttered. All the inhabitants were decently abed. Or perhaps not all.

"After all, you are the acknowledged expert— What was that?" Shadamehr asked suddenly, stopping and turning his head.

"What was what?" Alise said. She had been walking the street abstracted, absorbed in her own thoughts.

"Someone passed us," said Shadamehr. "He was keeping to the shadows, but I caught a glimpse of him in the moonlight."

"A vrykyl?" Alise asked with a slight curl of her lip.

"No," said Shadamehr, continuing to stare behind him. "A dwarf. And he was headed in the direction of Ulien's house."

"Which is the same direction as the city gate," said Alise in exasperation. "And the barracks. And the six ale houses we passed on our way. You know how restless dwarves are. He might be out for a nightly stroll."

"That's true," said Shadamehr, but he did not move.

"If you want to traipse after him, do so," Alise said in exasperation. "But I am bone-tired. I mean to sleep until noon."

"He's gone. I don't see him." Shadamehr turned back and fell into step beside her. "You are probably right. Now, tell me all you know about vrykyl."

"I gave you my report in writing, my lord," Alise returned.

"Ah, but you know that I am no great reader," Shadamehr said with a laugh. "I glanced at it. I read enough to know that I want nothing to do with these fiends—or the old wives who made them up, for that matter. Tell me again. Just the main points."

Alise sighed, this time loudly, so that he would hear. "Very well, my lord. The vrykyl are creatures of the Void. Perhaps they date back to ancient times. We do not know for certain. All we do know is that when Prince Dagnarus turned to evil and became Lord of the Void, he received a most powerful artifact of Void magic known as the Dagger of the Vrykyl. With this dagger, he killed a living man and brought him back to life, granting him a horrible immortality. The vrykyl must continue to kill to maintain his life, feeding upon the souls of mortal beings. Lord Dagnarus created many vrykyl, who were constrained to serve him alone. Vrykyl wear magical armor that gives them strength and prowess in battle and immense power in Void magic."

"If the Lord of the Void had the ability to create beings of such power, I am surprised the world is not overrun with vrykyl," Shadamehr observed.

"Ah, but there is a catch," Alise replied, ignoring his bantering tone. "The man or woman who becomes a vrykyl must give free consent. He must be willing to choose death over life. And he dies with the knowledge that the magic may not work."

"All this happened two hundred years ago, you say, when Dagnarus was alive. And no reports of anyone seeing vrykyl since?"

"But there have been reports of mysterious deaths during those two hundred years, my lord," Alise said. "Entire families slain, their faces frozen in terror as if the last sight they saw was a horrible one. And every death the same—a single, small puncture wound to the heart. The mark of the soul-stealer dagger. Thus the vrykyl have remained alive, waiting—some believe—for their lord to return."

"Which, according to what we hear from the Dunkargans, he has. Well, well, this is all very interesting." He yawned widely. "Poor Brother Ulien. He was always a bit moonstruck. I think it must have whalloped him a good one this time."

The inn was dark. The landlord had gone to bed but had left them a candle to light their way to the not overly clean rooms.

"Good-night, Alise," said Shadamehr, handing her the candle. "My room is next door to yours. You know the code. Knock three times if you need me."

He entered his room and shut the door.

Alise spread out her bedroll on the floor, not trusting the bed, which was already occupied by at least one cockroach, who came out to glare at the light.

She put her hand to the wall, tempted to knock three times. But she withdrew her hand, after a moment. She closed her eyes and resolutely tried to banish the touch of his sensual lips, the glittering blue eyes and that ridiculous mustache.

A thunderous knock on her door woke Alise from a sound sleep. She could hear the sounds of crashing furniture and cries coming from the room next door. Roused and alert, she was on her feet, the words of a magical spell on her lips, when the door burst open and three armed guards entered her room. They were prepared to face an earth mage, for one immediately knocked the requisite spell component—a bit of earth—from her hand, while another clapped his hand over her mouth.

Once she was pinned, the guards removed the belt which contained her potions and vials of holy earth. They even had the temerity to pat their hands all over her body, searching for hidden objects, a task they enjoyed, by the leering grins. This done, they dragged her out into the hallway.

Shadamehr was neatly trussed and bleeding from a cut over one eyebrow. Two guards had tight hold of him. One of the guards was rubbing a swollen jaw and another nursing a cut lip. Looking past him, into his room, Alise saw another guard stretched out unconscious on the floor.

"Good morning, my dear," said Shadamehr. "Sorry about the early cock-crow. I told these banty-legged louts you wanted to sleep late but they wouldn't listen."

"I was having a bad dream anyway," Alise said. "What is all this about?"

Shadamehr shrugged and shook his head. There was no more time for talk. The two guards dragged them down the stairs, where the innkeeper stood pleading with a man in uniform, frantically disavowing all knowledge of them. A glance outside showed the sky just starting to grow pinkish gold with the dawn.

The uniformed man was tall and brawny, with the black curly hair and swarthy complexion of the people of Karnu. He wore trappings of a commander in the Karnuan military and he carried at his side a most uncommon sword.

Alise looked intently at the weapon. The hilt and the scabbard were encrusted with rubies and jet, set in a fanciful design. Since she could not touch it with her hands, she stretched forth her other senses to try to touch the magic. The taint of Void was palpable. She almost gagged with the corrupt odor. She shifted her gaze from the sword to its owner.

The dark eyes were flat and cold, small and mean. He had the sort of mouth that rarely smiled and then only at the sight of someone being hurt. But was he a vrykyl? Could she tell by sight? From what little she had read, she could not. Not unless he was wearing his magical black armor. For the vrykyl could take on the appearance of any mortal they chose and their victims would never know until the soul-stealing blade pierced the heart.

The sword, though. That was definitely of the Void. When Shadamehr looked at her with a question in his eyes, Alise nodded her answer.

"Take them to the prison," ordered the commander, the first words he had spoken.

"Excuse me, sir, but I wouldn't mind knowing why we are being arrested," Shadamehr said, his tone mild, as if this little misunderstanding could be easily rectified.

"You are under arrest for murder," said the commander.

"Murder?" Shadamehr was understandably confused. "We have murdered no one. We are newly arrived in town. We are friends of Brother Ulien. We were with him last night. You can ask him—"

Shadamehr's voice faltered and faded. For the first time in the months she had known him, Alise saw Shadamehr shaken.

The commander was eyeing him grimly. "So you admit it. You were with him last night. The last to be with him last night, it seems. He was found dead in his bed this morning. An empty vial, a vial that matches those vials"—he pointed to Alise's belt, now in the hands of a guard—"was by his bed. Proof enough that an earth mage was there."

"He did not die of what was in the vial, though, did he?" Alise asked.

The commander sneered. "You know well enough how he died, witch."

"Yes, I think I do. He died of a single, small stab wound to the heart," Alise said. "If you will look at the weapons we carry, you will find none that could have caused such a wound."

Shadamehr was silent, probably berating himself for having left his friend to die.

"Such a weapon is easily discarded," the commander replied scornfully. "And I have a witness."

"Of course, you do," Shadamehr murmured.

The commander rested his hand on the hilt of his jeweled sword. "A dwarf. We found him with the body, so at first we figured he was the killer. But then he told us he saw you two leaving the house and heard you speaking of the murder you had just committed."

"And so we were," said Shadamehr. "My companion and I were shouting it to the rooftops. We wanted everyone in town to know that we had murdered a man. I take that back. In fact, we were singing. My companion has a lovely soprano voice and I—"

"Shut him up," the commander growled. "It doesn't much matter who killed the brother. Maybe you and the dwarf are in it together. We have him in jail, as well. I'll have the truth eventually. I enjoy questioning people."

Grinning, the commander made a jerking motion with his thumb. The guard holding Shadamehr gave him a clout on the head that reopened the wound over his eyebrow, started the blood flowing.

"And so, my lord," Alise said in an undertone, as the guards marched them off, "we have just been arrested for murder by the murderer. How are we going to get out of this one?"

"I got us out of the last one, my dear," Shadamehr said, grinning through a mask of blood. "Now it's your turn."

The prison cellblock was located beneath the military command post, a massive stone structure surrounded by high walls, containing a barracks, stables, a headquarters building, and a parade grounds. Lit by torches that sputtered in iron sconces, the underground jail also housed the "interrogation rooms" replete with various instruments of torture and, next door, the morgue.

"How convenient," said Shadamehr.

The body of Brother Ulien lay on a stone slab inside the small, cold room. The corpse had not been attended yet. He was still wearing the brown robes in which he had died. There was little blood, Alise noted with professional interest. A wound such as the one Shadamehr had described—small, penetrating straight to the heart—might not bleed much. The skin of Ulien's face was grayish white, the lips and nails of the hands starting to turn blue. The eyes were open wide. The face was hideously twisted into an expression of extreme terror.

"Stop!" Shadamehr ordered, as he was being marched past the morgue.

Such was Shadamehr's presence that the guards halted at his command. He shook off the guards and stood looking intently at the body of his friend.

"I am sorry, Ulien," Shadamehr said quietly. "This is my fault. Forgive me. Very well, gentlemen," he added magnanimously, "you may proceed."

Realizing that they had just obeyed an order given to them by their prisoner, the guards looked guiltily to see whether the commander had noticed, then quickly seized hold of Shadamehr and hustled him off.

The cells were located along opposite sides of a long, dark and narrow corridor. Large iron keys hung from hooks on the wall. The commander lifted a set of keys in passing and took down a torch to light their way.

"To the cell at the end of the hall," he ordered.

A peasant was in the corridor, cleaning the floor with a large broom, sweeping a pile of foul-smelling straw out of one of the cells. The stench was horrible.

The other prison cells appeared to be empty. The prison was eerily quiet. The only sound Alise could hear was that of running water. She was wondering what this might be when the floor suddenly dropped out from under her.

Alise cried out in alarm. Off-balance, she wavered on the edge of a gaping chasm, terrified that she would fall. Her guards let her teeter one heart-stopping moment, then hauled her back to safety, laughing at her fear. Below her, a rushing stream ran black and turgid. A sewer, to judge by the smell. The peasant plodded past her, swept his load of muck into the hole. Tugging on a rope that hung from the ceiling, a rope attached to what Alise now saw was a wooden door set in the floor, he pulled the door closed.

"There are grates at either end," the commander announced. "Just in case you were thinking that this might make a good escape route."

The guards pushed Alise forward. Her footsteps echoed hollowly as she walked across the wooden door. She passed the cell occupied by the dwarf, who was dark-eyed and dour, unkempt, disheveled and dirty. He was shackled hand and foot, the manacles attached to the stone wall and he glowered as they passed him. In response to Shadamehr's polite greeting in dwarven, the dwarf made a rude gesture with a manacled hand.

The guards hauled Alise and Shadamehr into the same cell, stood them against a wall and clamped manacles over their wrists and ankles. The commander looked on with approval as the guards locked the manacles in place with the keys, which they then returned to the commander. He slammed shut the iron barred door of the cell and locked it.

"I demand—" Shadamehr began, but he was talking to himself. The commander had left, taking the torch with him.

The cell was pitch dark. Alise could not see Shadamehr at all, though he was chained only a few feet from her.

"Shadamehr?" she said softly, needing to hear his voice.

"Here," he replied. He was silent a moment, then said quietly, "Did you see Brother Ulien's face, Alise?"

"Yes, I saw." Alise decided it would be best to handle this dispassionately. Shadamehr would not appreciate maudlin sympathy. "His expression fits the description of a vrykyl's victims. Don't blame yourself, my lord. There is nothing you could have done. You yourself said that you could not fight a vrykyl."

"Especially not chained to a wall." His voice in the darkness was bitter. He shook his manacles in frustration.

"I've never known you defeated before," she said. Her hands were manacled to the wall attached by a short length of chain on either side of her head. She twisted her head experimentally to see whether she could reach her thick coil of hair. "I find it rather endearing."

"Yes, well, I hope you find it so when the vrykyl comes. What are you doing?" He could not see her, but he could hear her chains rattling in the darkness.

"You told me it was my turn to get us out of a situation," she said, her hands busy. "I have a vial of earth hidden in my braid. Do you have your lockpick?"

"I did bring you for your red hair, after all!" Shadamehr stated. "Yes, I have lockpick, but I can't reach it."

"I believe I can remedy that."

Her searching fingers discovered the small vial she habitually kept tucked into the thick coil of red hair for just such an emergency.

"Now, pray I don't drop it," she muttered.

"I'm praying," said Shadamehr fervently.

Alise forced herself to make each movement deliberate. Moving slowly and carefully, she pried loose the stopper on the vial and shook a pinch of earth into her hand. She concentrated her thoughts on the stone wall to which she was chained, especially the portion of the wall to which the manacles were attached, and closed her eyes to better focus her thoughts.

"Stone, split!" she commanded and sifted the bit of earth through her fingers, letting it fall to the ground.

The sound of rock cracking was extraordinarily loud, or so it seemed to Alise, who cringed and looked apprehensively at the cell door, expecting that the commander would return at any moment. No one came.

Alise tugged on the chain and the heavy manacles pulled free and fell to the floor with a crash. She grit her teeth and continued her concentration on the spell. The fissures spread down the wall and the manacles on her feet pulled out of the stonework.

Unable to lift her arms due to the weight of the iron manacles, barely able to move her feet, she dragged herself across the cell, groping along the broken wall to find her way. Finding Shadamehr, she clutched hold of him thankfully.

"What did you do?" he asked. "Knock the wall down?"

"In a way," she replied. "Don't talk to me. You'll break my concentration."

"Not talking," he said and shut his mouth.

Taking another pinch of earth, Alise repeated the spell. Again the loud cracking sound. Surely the commander must have heard that! Shadamehr dropped from the wall. He ripped open one of the seams of the leather jerkin he wore, removed the lockpick which had been sewn into the seam.

"I could use some light," he muttered beneath his breath, fumbling to try to find the keyhole in the darkness.

As if on command, light flared.

"Shadamehr!" Alise gasped. "We're on fire!"

The floor of the cellblock in front of the iron-barred door had burst into flame, a magical flame that consumed stone, apparently, for the fire had no other fuel. Not until the flames reached the dry straw that covered the floor on which they stood.

"Ah, that helps!" said Shadamehr. He thrust the lockpick into the keyhole of the manacle on her right hand.

"Hurry!" Alise urged, coughing in the acrid smoke.

"A dwarf Fire Mage, Ulien said," Shadamehr recalled, removing the other manacle from Alise's hand and starting on the manacles on her ankles. He cast a glance toward the cell where the dwarf was chained.

Alise covered her mouth with her hand to avoid breathing the superheated air.

The flames shot high into the air, forming a wall of fire between them and the cell door.

"I take that for yes." Shadamehr was working on the manacles on his ankles with one eye on the flames and the other on the keyhole. A click and he was free. He looked at the manacles on his wrists, eyed the fire, and shook his head. "We'll have to run for it. The flames are magical. Can we escape through that?"

"I don't see we have much choice!" Alise cried. "It's either that or burn to death where we are."

"Then here we go!" Shadamehr leapt into the fire.

Alise closed her eyes, covered her face with the sleeve of her robes, and plunged into the wall of flame.

She was through, gasping and slammed into the cell door. A few sparks clung to her robes, but she patted them out. Shadamehr had his arm thrust through the iron bars, turning the lockpick in the lock. An expert twist and the lock gave. The cell doors swung open.

"How are you?" he asked her, regarding her worriedly.

"A little weak," she replied. "The spell casting saps my energy. But I'll be all right. What about the commander?"

All was quiet in the cellblock. No sign that anyone had heard or seen anything.

"I don't know. I can't see anything for the smoke. I'll keep watch. You check on our neighbor the fire bug."

The flames in the cell had already starting to die out. Perhaps that is what gave Alise the clue. She knew before she went to look for the dwarf what she would find.

He hung from the wall, head and hands and feet dangling limp and lifeless. She could not see the hole in his heart from here, but she had no doubt it was there.

She caught hold of Shadamehr. He had managed to free one of his wrists from the manacles and was working on the second.

"The dwarf's dead," she said, her voice catching in her throat. She coughed. "Blasted smoke! My guess is that he didn't set the fire."

"One suspect gone. How much earth do you have left?

"Enough for one more spell."

"Excellent."

"Shadamehr, compared to a vrykyl, my magical power is that of a child!"

"I wasn't thinking of taking on the vrykyl. I was thinking more about removing grates. Can you swim?" he asked, working on the lock and not having much luck. "This one's stuck!"

"Swim! Shadamehr," she protested. "You're not serious! You didn't see what it was like down in that sewer!"

"Call it a hunch, but I don't think they're going to let us walk out the front door— Look out!" Shadamehr grabbed Alise bodily, swung her behind him.

A figure loomed out of the smoky darkness. Rubies sparkled blood red in the light of the dying flames. Fire light flashed on a steel blade.

Shadamehr ducked. The blade hissed through the air just above his head, sending the smoke swirling. Alise tried to see the person—or the creature—wielding the blade. The smoke was too thick. Her eyes burned and stung. She fell back against the wall.

Shadamehr scrambled backward to avoid the return stroke. He had no room to maneuver. The ruby-hilted sword slashed again and this time drew blood. He cried out in pain and staggered backward, clutching at his upper arm. Alise caught hold of him, pulled him into a dark corner.

The smoke whirled and eddied around them. The commander had lost them and was slashing blindly, coughing and peering through the smoke.

"Zounds!" Shadamehr gasped, leaning against her. "It feels like I've been stung by a thousand wasps!"

"That's the Void magic. It can work like poison. Can you stand?"

"Yes, but I don't know for how long. Here he comes again!"

Shadamehr's only weapon was the manacle, still attached to his wrist, and the short length of chain that dangled from it. He dashed forward, swinging the chain, trying to entangle the sword.

Alise took her last pinch of earth and flung it into the air. She focused her thoughts on the ruby-bejeweled sword and spoke a single word. "Brittle!"

The commander evaded the swinging chain. He lunged at Shadamehr, who was too weak to dodge the stabbing blade. The sword struck Shadamehr in the breast. He shut his eyes involuntarily, expecting his death blow.

The blade snapped in two.

The commander stared at his sword in an astonishment that changed rapidly to rage. Flinging aside the useless weapon, he leapt to grapple with his prisoner.

Shadamehr swept his manacled arm and the flying chain caught the commander in the jaw, snapping his head to one side. He fell backward, landed on the stone floor, and lay still.

Neither Shadamehr nor Alise moved. Both held perfectly still, not even breathing, waiting for the vrykyl to rise again. The commander was out cold. He didn't so much as twitch.

Shadamehr sank back against the wall. "The old wives' tales were wrong. I've known pecwae to put up more of a fight."

Alise knelt gingerly beside the commander. She put her hand to his neck. "Shadamehr," she said, "this isn't a vrykyl. He has a pulse."

"What are you saying? He *has* to be the vrykyl! Brother Ulien—" Shadamehr sucked in a breath. "Brother Ulien! What a fool I've been! We have to get out of here!" he said in a low, urgent voice.

But they had only taken a few steps when a blast of wind as chill as death blasted through the corridor. The smoke vanished, torn apart in shreds. The flames flared up behind them. The corpse of Brother Ulien strode purposefully down the corridor.

"*He's* the vrykyl!" Alise whispered.

The power of the Void magic crashed over her, an immense wave of soulless empty darkness which struck her an almost physical blow. Alise's hands went numb and limp. She dropped the vial of holy earth. Not that it would matter. Her own magical power was being sucked into the maw of the Void. Beside her, leaning against the stone wall, Shadamehr let his breath out in a long sigh.

"A trap," he said softly. "It was all a trap. You said my ego would be the death of me. I walked into it as blind as a mole in a snare."

"Indeed you did, Lord Shadamehr," said the vrykyl. The face was pale and gaunt in death, yet the lifeless mouth moved, the unseeing eyes saw. "My master has watched you long. He knows you to be a threat. He heard you were searching for information about us. We had orders to answer all your questions, provided we could find you. Imagine my joy when I discovered, after feeding upon the soul of Brother Ulien, that he was once your friend. The rest was simple, after that. Now you will see me for what I am."

The illusion of Brother Ulien vanished. In its place stood a hideous knight in shining armor, black as the carapace of some huge, malevolent insect. His hands were covered with metal gloves adorned with sharp, hooked black talons. In his right hand he wielded a small poinard that glowed with an eerie, empty white light.

Terror gripped Alise. She felt her face starting to contort into that look of horror which would freeze upon it when she died. She could not think. She could not scream. She shrank closer to Shadamehr and felt him move. His left arm was creeping slowly up the stone wall against which he leaned. She glanced above them and saw a length of rope, running across the ceiling.

Swiftly, Alise lowered her eyes, lest the vrykyl follow her gaze and guess Shadamehr's desperate plan.

"I wouldn't advise feeding on my soul," said Shadamehr, watching the vrykyl advance and hoping to keep his attention. Just a few more steps. A few more. "I'm likely to give you indigestion."

The vrykyl said no word. He walked toward them, his booted footfalls echoing loudly on the stone.

And then the footfalls struck wood.

Shadamehr grabbed hold of the rope and pulled hard. The

wooden trapdoor flew open, booming against the side of the stone wall below it.

The vrykyl vanished, plunging down into the darkness. They heard his roar of anger and a splash as he hit the water.

"What do we now?" Alise cried.

"We run!" Shadamehr said grimly.

He caught hold of her hand and together they dashed down the corridor, making wide detour around the hole in the floor. Neither took time to look for their enemy, who could be heard raging and thrashing about in the foaming water.

They ran up the stairs to the ground floor and out the front door of the military command post. They paid no heed to the startled guards, who yelled after them and began to give chase.

"Keep going!" Shadamehr panted.

Alise needed no urging. She could feel the pent-up rage and fury of the thwarted vrykyl rumbling beneath them like molten hot lava. The ground began to shake and the guards halted in alarm. Alise glanced back and saw blinding white flame engulf the fortress. A concussive blast tore the fortress apart.

Alise dove under a large wagon standing in the roadway and covered her head with her arms. Shadamehr flung his body down beside her and put his arms around her. Rock rained around them, crashing off the wagon and bounding into the street.

And then it was over. The night was eerily quiet, for an instant, until screams and shouts and the sounds of people running toward the burning fortress shattered the stillness.

Shadamehr crawled out from under the wagon, turned to help Alise. "Are you all right?" he asked.

She nodded. She was bleeding from cuts on her hands and face where she'd slid along the ground, but otherwise she was unhurt. "You?" she asked.

"Aside from being singed by magical fire and poisoned by the Void, I am fine," he said. "A lot finer than I thought I was going to be there for a moment."

"Do you suppose the vrykyl's dead?" Alise asked, shivering at the memory.

"No, I don't suppose it," Shadamehr answered. "But it's going to take him a while to crawl out from the under the ruins of the fortress. In the meanwhile, I suggest that we take our leave. My questions have been answered. We now know the nature of the foe the people of Loerem must eventually face. And we know that neither of *us* has the power now to face it."

"But who does have the power, Shadamehr?" Alise asked, helping him to his feet. She looked back at the burning, blackened fortress. "Is there anyone who can fight them?"

"Not even the Dominion Lords are prepared to face this, Alise," Shadamehr said. "I don't know anyone who is."

He shook his head and, putting his arm around Alise, he drew her close. "But remind me to apologize to the first old wife I meet."

⋖⋗ Serenade ⋖⋗

A Spellsinger Story

Alan Dean Foster

The young woman was beautiful, her male companion was shy, and the hat was surreptitious. This feathered chapeau of uncertain parentage bobbed along innocently enough behind the stone wall on which the two young paramours sat whispering sweet nothings to one another. The hat dipped out of sight an instant before the girl's lips parted in shock. Reacting swiftly to the perceived offense, she whirled and struck the startled young man seated beside her hard enough to knock him backwards off the wall. But by that time the hat had hastened beyond sight, sound, and possible indictment.

Beneath the hat as it emerged from behind the wall, having strewn amorous chaos in its wake, was a five-foot-tall otter clad (in addition to the aforementioned feathered cap) in short pants, long vest, and a self-satisfied smirk. Ignoring the occasional glances that came his way, the hirsute, bewhiskered, and thoroughly disreputable Mudge wended his way through the streets of downtown Timswitty. Eventually his sharp eyes caught sight of his friend, companion, and frequent irritant from another world leaning against the wall of a dry-goods shop while soaking up the sun. Dodging a single lizard-drawn wagon festooned with clanging pots and pans for sale, he hailed his companion with a cheery early morning obscenity.

Arms crossed over his chest, duar slung across his back, scabbard flanking his right leg, Jon-Tom opened one eye to regard his much shorter friend. In this world of undersized humans and loquacious animals, the unwilling six-foot-tall visitor stood out in any crowd. Except for his unusual height, however, he was not an especially impressive specimen of humankind.

"Back already? Let me guess—you've been making mischief again."

"Wot, me, guv'nor? You strike me to the quick! Why, I didn't even know the lass."

Jon-Tom frowned. "What lass?"

The otter mustered a look of innocence, at which self-defense mechanism he had enjoyed much practice. "Why, Miss Chief, o' course."

"One of these days I'll strike you for real." Pushing away from the wall, Jon-Tom nearly stepped into the path of a goat hauling firewood. Apologizing to the annoyed billy, he started up Pikk Street, only to find his path blocked by a lean human little taller than Mudge. Older than the two travelers together, the well-dressed graybeard wore a colorful cloak and trousers of some soft red and blue material. An integrated cowl covered his head and he carried a simple wooden staff topped by a polished globe. Mudge eyed the latter with cursory interest. This flagged the instant he identified the opaque vitriosity as ordinary glass not worth pilfering

"Excuse me, good sirs." Though he addressed them both, it was Jon-Tom's face that drew the bulk of the visitor's interest. Jon-Tom had spent enough time in this world to be wary of strangers: even those who were elderly, polite, well dressed, and to all intents and purposes, harmless.

"Is there something we can do for you, sir?"

"I am called Wolfram. I am in need of assistance of an uncommon kind." With a nod of his head he indicated a nearby doorway. Swaying from an iron rod above the portal was a sign that identified the establishment as the Wild Boar Inn. "Perhaps it would be better to discuss matters of business somewhere other than in the street."

Mudge, who had been tracking the progress of an attractive lady mink, responded without taking his eyes from the passing tail. "Me friend an' me don't interrupt our day to shoot the shat with just anyone who accosts us in public." As the mink tail vanished, so too did the otter's interest. "You buyin'?" The stranger nodded again. Mudge's whiskers quivered appreciatively. "Then we're shootin'." He preceded the humans into the establishment, his short tail twitching expectantly from side to side.

Like most such Bellwoods establishments, the Wild Boar Inn was already crowded with drinkers and natterers, characters unsavory and tasteful, trolling wenches and amenable marks. The owner, a husky but amiable wild boar name of Focgren, paused in the careful measuring out of questionable libations long enough to grunt in the direction of an unoccupied booth near the back. Their order was taken by an obviously bored but nonetheless attractive vixen whose agility as she avoided Mudge's wandering fingers was admirable to behold. Spangles and beads jangled against the back of her dress and upraised, carefully coiffed tail. The booth's battered, thick wooden walls muted the convivial chaos that swirled around the conversing trio.

"You were saying something about assistance of an uncommon kind?" Jon-Tom sipped politely at his tankard while Mudge made a conscious effort to bury his snout in the one that had been set before him.

Having set his walking staff carefully aside, Wolfram indicated the duar that now rested next to the tall young human. "Your instrument is conspicuous, and not the sort to be carried by just any wandering minstrel. You are, perchance, a spellsinger?"

Jon-Tom's interest in the stranger rose appreciably. Recognizing a duar for what it was marked the older man as more sophisticated than originally supposed. There might be real business to be done here.

"While lacking in experience, I assure you I try every day to practice my art."

Wolfram nodded appreciatively. "Excellent! I am most of all in need simply of your musical talents, but a touch of wizardry is also required."

Suds dripping from his whiskers, a suddenly wary Mudge extracted his face from the tankard. His bright brown eyes flicked rapidly from friend to benefactor and back again. "Wizardry? Spellsingin'-type magic-making'?" He pushed the tankard aside. "Oh no, mate. Count me out! I've 'ad enough o' your so-called singin' o' spells to last me a lifetime!" Rising, he moved to depart.

While continuing his conversation with Wolfram, Jon-Tom kept the fingers of one hand wrapped around the otter's belt, thus preventing the frantic Mudge from escaping. Short legs struggled for purchase on the slippery stone floor.

Jon-Tom smiled reassuringly. "Don't mind Mudge. He's just anxious to get started."

"I'm anxious, alright, you bloody great stick-twit!" To no avail, the otter continued his furious struggle to free himself from his friend's grasp. "Let loose o' me pants!"

The three-way conversation was interrupted by a violent crash from the center of the floor. Peering out from the booth, their attention was drawn to a singularly unwholesome-looking human and his puma companion. Breathing hard, both were staring down at something on the floor. The human held the shattered remnants of a wooden mace, his snarling companion a club that had been broken in half. The upper, knobbed end of the mace hung from the handle by a splinter. As Jon-Tom tried to see what it was they were concentrating on, their expressions changed markedly.

An enormous dark mass was rising slowly from the floor. As it blotted out a wide section of inn, human and feline began to back away from it. Whirling abruptly, the man dropped his broken weapon and tried to run. A leather-wrapped wrist bigger around than his head reached out and enormous brown-furred fingers closed around his neck, lifting him off the floor. Rising, he clawed frantically at the grasping digits while his legs kicked uselessly at empty air. Waving the human over his head like a limp flag, the now erect leather-armored grizzly reached for the panicked puma. As he did so, a chair slammed into his back and shattered into kindling. When someone in the crowd took physical as well as verbal objection to this cowardly blow from behind, the inn's population descended (not entirely unwillingly) into instant and complete pandemonium.

Above it all the immense ursine could be seen clearly, still waving his now unconscious human assailant while bellowing above the increasingly thunderous fray, "*Stromagg stomp!*"

Mudge was already heading for the back exit, ducking flying utensils and other debris, some of it organic. Their host stayed close to him, anxious to be clear of the rapidly escalating skirmish. But Jon-Tom hung back. The otter bawled imploringly at his friend.

"Quickly, guv, quickly! The coppers'll be 'ere any minute! An' you know wot that'll mean."

Jon-Tom did, but still he lingered. "You two go on. I'll be right there." So saying, he plunged into the affray. Shaking his head in disbelief and venting a whistle of disgust, Mudge concentrated on chaperoning their erstwhile benefactor away from the chaos.

The tall human with sword and duar was largely ignored by the combatants, busily engaged as they were in removing one another's appendages and resolving old scores. Jon-Tom had to strike out only occasionally to remain above the fray as he worked his way towards its nucleus. When the enormous bear leaned in his direction, all massive chest and fur and long teeth, he found himself wondering if this was such a good idea after all. Despite his sudden apprehension, he managed to call out, "Come with me! The police are on their way."

Absently crushing to the floor with one massive fist an onrushing, sword-wielding wombat, the grizzly's heavy brows drew together as he considered the suggestion. "Why should I go with you? I don't know you."

There was a commotion near the entrance to the inn. Timswitty's deservedly feared finest were arriving. "Because I'm offering you a job—I think."

Whirling about, the sextet of uniformed skunks prepared to put an end to the fighting in a manner only they could manage, by means not even the strongest berserker could defy. Jon-Tom broke into a cold sweat. Still, the bear was reluctant.

"You help Stromagg?"

"My word on it." Instinctively, Jon-Tom found himself starting to edge toward the rear exit, wondering as he did so if there would be enough time to clear the room before the room needed clearing.

Fishing into the mob, the bear came up with the battered, bleeding body of the puma who had first attacked him. When smacking the sagging feline across its limp face failed to produce any reaction, Stromagg grunted heavily and tossed the cat into the roiling crowd.

"Hurry!" Jon-Tom pulled on the bear's forearm to urge it along. He might as well have been tugging on a sequoia. But the ursine moved.

They just did make it out before the police tactical squad let loose, so to speak. An unmusical chorus of mass retching pursued the escapees as they fled down a back alley.

As soon as they were clear of combative and olfactory intrusions, they slowed. Mudge guardedly eyed the mountainous newcomer in their midst. Stromagg endured the inspection thoughtfully. Or perhaps, Jon-Tom thought, "thoughtfully" was not the appropriate description. The bear's appearance hinted at a compassionate nature, but one that only infrequently strayed into the alien realm of higher cogitation.

"Wot's with the meat-mountain, mate?"

His breathing at last beginning to slow, Jon-Tom beamed and

put a reassuring hand on the grizzly's immense arm. "I've just taken on a little extra muscle."

"Wot for?" the otter snapped. "The job we ain't goin' to take?"

Ignoring his friend, Jon-Tom turned to the somewhat bedraggled Wolfram. "Now then, good sir. What exactly was it that you wished to employ my services for?"

Pulling his gaze away from the looming immensity of the bear, their benefactor gathered his wits. "I wish you to serenade a lady with whom I am deeply and hopelessly in love."

Jon-Tom and Mudge exchanged a glance. The graybeard's offer fell somewhat short of requiring them to Save the World, or some such life-threatening exercise. Mudge was too relieved to comment.

"That's all?" Jon-Tom wondered aloud.

Wolfram nodded slowly. "That's all. And for that I will pay you well. You see, I am a wise man, but a terrible singer."

Mudge jerked a furry thumb in Jon-Tom's direction. "Then this be a good fit, guv, as me mate 'ere is a good singer, but terrible stupid."

Ignoring the slur, Jon-Tom proved the otter wrong by asking, "If all that's needed is an amorous song, why not hire any troubadour? Why seek out a spellsinger like myself?"

Wolfram smiled approvingly. "A song to Larinda is all that is required. It is the reaching her that may require the application of some magic in concert with the music."

"Oi, I knew it," Mudge muttered under his breath.

"Calmness be upon you, my peripatetic friend." Wolfram tried to reassure the otter. "A simple spellsong should suffice. Nothing too elaborate. I would attempt it myself except that I, as previously stated, cannot carry a tune in a bucket."

"How simple a spellsong, guv'nor?" Mudge inquired warily.

"That is for the singer to decide. I will provide you with directions. I shall also pay your expenses, and half your fee in advance." Withdrawing a heavy purse from within the depths of his cloak, he proceeded to spill a tinkling pile of gold coins into Jon-Tom's cupped hands. Mudge's eyes widened, while Stromagg looked on appreciatively.

"'*Alf*, you say, guv?" The otter eyed the golden flood greedily.

Wolfram nodded as he slipped the now empty purse back into his cloak. "The other half when the object of my affection responds." Turning, he gestured with his staff. "Do you know the lands of the Agu Canyon, that lies between here and Hygria?"

Jon-Tom's expression wrinkled with thought. "I know the direction, though I've never been there."

"Nor I," Mudge added. " 'Eard 'tis a dry and homey place."

"There is an unclimbable cliff," Wolfram explained. "I will give you specific directions to it. On the far side lies Namur Castle, wherein dwells the beauteous Larinda. Serenade her on my behalf. Sing to her of my undying affection, then return to collect the rest of your well-earned due."

"'Scuse me 'ere a minim, guv'nor." The otter squinted skeptically at the graybeard. " 'Ow now are we supposed to get over an unclimbable cliff?"

Wolfram smiled from beneath the cowl of his blue and red cloak. "That, my energetic friend, is why I have sought out a spellsinger to do the singing. How you surmount the barrier is your problem. Or did you think I was paying you only for a love song?"

Jon-Tom was not discouraged "I'm a pretty decent climber. No ascent is 'unclimbable.' " He looked down at Mudge. "If necessary, I'll just sing us up the appropriate gear. Or perhaps a great bird to ferry us over."

Mudge winced. "You forget, guv, that I've seen 'ow all too much o' your spellsingin' as a way o' turnin' out."

"We'll cope." Jon-Tom stood a little straighter. "After all, I've had plenty of practice by now. I'm far more in command of my skills than I was when I first picked up this duar." He patted the instrument confidently, turned his gaze to the lingering, looming grizzly. "How about it, Stromagg? It's always useful to have someone like yourself along on a journey such as this? Are you with us?"

The bear's great brows furrowed. "Will there be beer?"

—||—

The granite cliffs and buttes that rose around them were streaked with gray and black, ivory and streaks of olivine green. Stromagg strode tirelessly forward on his hind legs, Jon-Tom riding on one shoulder and Mudge on the other. The twice-burdened bear seemed not to notice the weight at all. In any event, he did not complain. Not even when Mudge would rise to a standing position for a better view. Jon-Tom did not worry about his companion's awkward stance. For one thing, it would do no good: the otter held advice in the same regard as teetotaling. For another, otters have superb balance—and very low centers of gravity.

Overhead, vultures circled, gossiping like black-cloaked old women. They were as civilized as any bird that inhabited the

Warmlands, exceedingly polite, and fastidious in their table manners.

"There they are." Jon-Tom consulted the map their employer had sketched for them. There was no mistaking the twin buttes. From a distance, the spellsinger saw, the eroded massif known as Mouravi resembled a horned skull. "The cliff wall should lie just to the left of them."

Rising from the arroyo down which they had been hiking, they suddenly and unexpectedly encountered the truth of his observation in the form of a solid wall of rock. Slipping down from Stromagg's shoulder, Jon-Tom tilted his head back, back, until his neck began to ache. The cliff wall was at least five hundred feet high and as smooth as a marble slab. Swift inspection revealed that the featureless schist would make for a treacherous climb at best.

Examining the obstacle, Mudge let out a short, derisive whistle. "No problem, guv. I say we keep the half payment that old geezer gave us and hightail it up to Malderpot. Nice taverns in Malderpot. By the time the old geezer can track us down, we'll bloody well 'ave drunk away his gold."

"Now, Mudge." The spellsinger studied the seemingly impassable barrier. "That would hardly be honorable."

" 'Onorable, 'onorable." The otter scratched under his chin, his whiskers rising slightly. "From wot foreign tongue arises that strange word, wot I'm sure I never 'eard before and ain't quite familiar with?"

Stromagg frowned at the barrier and promptly sat down, dust rising from the fringes of his enormous brown behind. His leather armor hung loose against the vastness of his immense frame. "Stromagg not built for climbing."

"That's all right." Jon-Tom unlimbered his duar. "When Wolfram described this to us, I never expected to have to actually climb it. That's what he, and anyone else, would expect." Slipping the unique instrument across his front, he gently strummed the intersecting set of dual strings. A soft pulse of light appeared at the nexus. "We're not going over this barrier. We're going through it."

"Through it?" Mudge squinted at the solid rock, glanced meaningfully at Stromagg. "Through what, mate? Am I missin' something 'ere?"

"Why, through that tunnel." Jon-Tom pointed. "The one right there."

Once again, Mudge eyed the stone. Then he made the connection with the duar, the position of his friend's hovering hands, and his eyes widened slightly. "Now mate, are you sure this is a better idea than wastin' away old Wolfprick's money in lubricious Malderpot? You know wot 'appens when you open your mouth and somethin' kind o' like a song comes out."

"Just like I told Wolfram, Mudge. My skill has improved greatly with time and practice."

The otter grunted. "As opposed to the odds improvin'." He moved to stand close to, or rather behind, the bemused Stromagg as Jon-Tom approached the solid rock. The bear frowned down at the infinitely smaller otter.

"What happens now?"

Mudge put his hands over his ears. "If you've any sensitivity at all, large brother, you'll cover your bloomin' 'ears."

Stromagg hesitated, then raised his enormous paws. "There will be pain from the wizardry?"

"Not from the wizardry, guv." Mudge's expression tightened. "Trust me on this. You ain't 'eard old Jonnny-Tom sing. I 'ave."

His fingers strumming the duar, Jon-Tom launched into the song he had selected, a ditty of penetrating power from early Zeppelin. The grizzly's paws immediately clapped over his ears, bending them down forcefully against the top of his head.

Usually the eldritch mists that rose from the junction of the duar's intersecting sets of enchanted strings were pastel in hue: light blue, or lavender, bright pink or pale green. This time they were black and ominous. Mudge moved farther behind Stromagg, peering warily out from behind the grizzly's protective bulk. So peculiar, so enthralling was the coil of darkness that emerged from Jon-Tom's song that the otter could not take his eyes from it.

Detaching itself from the interdimensional wherever of the duar, the orb of ebon vapor drifted slowly toward the rock wall. It hesitated, and began to reverse direction. That movement prompted a redoubling of power chords by a suddenly anxious Jon-Tom. What might happen if the blackness fell back *into* the duar he couldn't imagine. The orb wavered, seeming to be considering something known only to eldritch orbs, and then resumed its drift toward the cliff face. Jon-Tom allowed himself to relax ever so slightly.

Upon making contact with the rock, the dark sphere spread itself across the perpendicular surface like a giant droplet of oil. When the last of it had seeped into the stone, Jon-Tom brought the vibrant song to a rousing conclusion that made both his furry companions wince.

Wiping sweat from his brow, the spellsinger pointed proudly. "There! I told you I could do it."

Emerging from Stromagg's shadow, Mudge warily approached the dark blot in the rock and peered—inward. " 'Tis a tunnel, all right." Pushing his feathered cap back on his forehead, he eyed his friend guardedly. "So I suppose all we 'ave to do now is stroll right on through the mountain?"

Jon-Tom nodded. "If everything has worked as it should, Namur Castle will lie on the other side." He drew himself up proudly. "And I'd say it's worked, wouldn't you?"

"Well now," Mudge muttered, argumentative to the last, "there's right enough a 'ole in this 'ere 'ill. But as to whether it leads to a castle or not remains to been seen, wot?"

"Only one way to find out." Striding confidently past his friend, Jon-Tom started in.

The spellsung tunnel was wide and high enough for Stromagg to enter without bending. Its floor was composed of smooth, clean sand. There was only one problem with it.

It was already occupied.

Drawing his short sword, a growling, whistling Mudge started to back up. Alongside him, Stromagg raised the huge mace that he carried slung across his broad back. "Oi, you've done it again, alright, mate. Now sing it closed!"

His expression falling, Jon-Tom strummed lightly on the duar as he backpedaled. "I only wanted the tunnel," he muttered to himself. "Just the tunnel."

The things that crawled and crept and slithered from the depths of the darkness had glowing red eyes and very sharp teeth. Multilegged puffballs with fangs, they resembled nothing in this world. Which made perfect sense, since Jon-Tom had sung them up from a different world entire. While Mudge and Stromagg hacked and sliced, Jon-Tom tried to think of an appropriate song to send the fuzzy horde back to the hell from which they had sprung.

Slashing wildly at something sporting tentacles and razor-lined suckers, Mudge spared a frantic glance for his friend. The tunnel continued to vomit forth more and more of the sinister, red-eyed assassins. "Sing 'em away, mate! Sing 'em gone. Sing the bloody tunnel *closed*!"

"Strange." Refusing to be distracted by the conflict, Jon-Tom was preoccupied with trying to remember lyrics appropriate to resolving their suddenly desperate situation. "I could try singing the same song backwards, I suppose." He did so, to no effect other than to further outrage Mudge's ears.

Using a kick to fend off something with long incisors and three eyes, he eventually began to sing once again. Mudge recognized the tune immediately. It was the same one his friend had sung moments earlier, to produce the tunnel.

"Are you mad, mate? We don't need twice as many of these 'orrors. We need less of 'em!" Ducking with astonishing speed, he cut the legs out from an assailant that had plenty of spares.

A second surging blackness emerged from the duar, drifted past the combatants, and struck the stone barrier. Once more a tunnel appeared. Fending off assailants, Jon-Tom raced toward it. "Come on! This is the right one, for sure. I was just a bit off on the rhythm the first time."

"A bit off? You've always been a bit off, mate!" Fighting a ferocious rearguard action, the otter and the grizzly followed the spellsinger into the new tunnel.

Unlike the first, this one was filled with a dim, indistinct light. Floor and walls were much smoother than those of their predecessor, devoid of sand, and harder. The tunnel looked to be composed of worked stone; an excellent sign, Jon-Tom decided. It was exactly the sort of access that might lead to a hidden underground entrance in something like a distant castle. Its dimensions were impressive.

Then they heard the roaring. Rising and coming toward them. "There!" Mudge pointed. A burning yellow eye was visible in the distance. As the roaring intensified, the fiery illumination grew brighter, washing over them.

"I think I liked the other critters better," an awed Mudge murmured.

Jon-Tom was looking around wildly. "Here, this way!" Turning to his right, he dashed up the stairs that lay in that direction. As they ascended, they could hear the monster approaching rapidly behind them. To everyone's great relief, it rushed past without turning, keeping to the main tunnel.

"The castle must be right above us." Shifting his duar around to his back, Jon-Tom slowed as new light appeared above them. Light, and a familiar, unthreatening noise. The sound of rain on pavement. "Probably the courtyard. Keep alert."

"Keep alert, 'e says." Gripping his sword tightly, Mudge strove to see through the brighter gloom above.

They emerged into a light rain that was falling, not on a castle courtyard, but on a narrow street. Storefronts, darkened and shuttered, were visible on the opposite side. There was no one in sight.

The otter's sensitive nose appraised their surroundings as his sharp eyes continued to scan the darkness. "No castle this, mate. Smells bleedin' nasty, it does." He looked up at his friend. "Where the blood 'ell are we?"

"I don't know." Thoroughly bemused, Jon-Tom walked out onto a sidewalk and turned a slow circle. "This should be Namur Castle, or its immediate vicinity." His eyes fell on a pair of rain-swept signs. Across the street, one hanging from an iron rod proclaimed the location of the Cork & Castle—pub. Light from within reached out into the street, as did muted sounds of polite revelry. The second sign hung above the entrance to the stairway from which they had emerged. It was a softly illuminated red and white circle with a single red bar running horizontally through it. The hairs on the back of his neck began to stiffen.

They had stumbled into an unsuspected path back into his own world.

—III—

Sounds of casual conversation reached the three stunned travelers. Retreating to the top of the gum-spotted, urine-stained stairway, he peered back down. Two young couples were mounting the steps from the underground, chatting and laughing about the casual inconsequentialities of a life he had long ago relinquished He looked around worriedly.

"We can't go back down this way. We've got to hide."

Stromagg looked baffled. "Why? More monsters come?"

"No, no. Somehow the song has broken through into my world. You and Mudge can't be seen here. Only humans talk and make sense here."

Unimpressed, Mudge let out a snort. "Who says 'umans make sense anywhere?" His nose twitched. "I *thought* this place stank."

"Hurry!" Espying an alley off the main street, Jon-Tom led his friends away from the subway entrance.

It was dark in the rain-washed passageway, but not so dark as to hide the overcoated sot standing with his bottle amid the daily deposit of debris expelled by the establishments that lined the more respectable street on the other side. Leaning up against the damp brick, he waved the nearly empty container at the new arrivals. Jon-Tom froze.

"Evenin' t'you, friends." The drunk extended the bottle. "Want a swig?"

Stromagg immediately started forward, forcing Jon-Tom to put out an arm to restrain the bear. "You two stay here!" he whispered urgently. Approaching the idling imbiber, he adopted a wide smile, hoping the man was too far gone to notice Jon-Tom's strange attire.

"Excuse me, sir. Can you tell us exactly where we are? We're kind of lost."

Squinting through the rain, the inebriated reveler frowned at him. His breath, Jon-Tom decided, was no worse than what he had experienced numerous times in the company of Mudge and his furry drinking buddies.

"What are you, tourists?" The drinker levered himself away from the wall. "Bloody ignorant tourists! You're in Knightsbridge, friend."

"Knightsbridge?" Jon-Tom thought hard. The name sounded sufficiently castle-like to jibe with his spellsong, but it didn't square with what he had just seen. "Where is that?"

" 'Where is that?' " the drunk echoed in disbelief. "London, man! Where did you think you were?" Squinting harder, he finally caught sight of the very large otter and far larger leather-armored grizzly standing silently behind his questioner. His bloodshot eyes went wide enough for the small veins to flare. "Oh, gawd." Letting the nearly empty bottle fall from his suddenly limp fingers, he whirled, stumbled and nearly fell, and vanished down the alley. They heard him banging and crashing through assorted trash receptacles and boxes for several minutes.

Picking up the bottle, Mudge sniffed the contents, made a disgusted face, shrugged, and promptly downed the remaining contents before Jon-Tom could stop him. Wiping his furry lips, he eyed his friend meaningfully.

"You spellsang us 'ere, mate. Now you bleedin' well better sing us a way back."

Jon-Tom looked helpless. "We could try the way we came. Maybe the creatures in the other tunnel have gone. I don't know what else to do." Discouraged and tentative, he started back toward the street. The rain was beginning to let up, turning to a heavy mist.

The exit back onto the street was blocked.

"A minute of your time, friend."

There were three of them. All younger than Jon-Tom, all more confident, two clearly high on something stronger than liquor. The speaker held a switchblade, open. The larger boy flashed a small handgun. The girl between them wielded a disdainful smirk.

Jon-Tom scrutinized them all and did not much like what he saw, or what he sensed. "We don't want any trouble. We're just on our way home."

The boy with the blade nodded contentedly. "American, is it? Good. I knew I heard American accents at the party. You'll have traveler's cheques. Americans always carry traveler's cheques." He extended the hand that was not holding the switchblade. "Hand 'em over. Also any cash. Also your watch, if you're wearing one. Your friends, too. Then you can go safely back to the stupid costume ball that your snooty friends wouldn't let us into."

Jon-Tom tensed. "I haven't got any traveler's checks on me. Or any cash, either. At least, not any you could use here."

"American dollars suit me just fine, friend." The kid gestured agitatedly with the open hand. "Hurry it up. We ain't got time for talk." His gaze flicked sideways. "Maybe you'd like me to cut the kid, here." He lunged toward Mudge.

Effortlessly, the otter bent the middle of his body out of the way. As the switchblade passed harmlessly to his left, he drew his short sword. Steel flashed in the dim light of the street.

Alarmed, the bigger boy raised his pistol. Emerging from the mist behind him, an enormous paw clamped over both weapon and hand. Stromagg squeezed. Bones popped. Startled, the big kid let out a subdued, girlish scream. Bared teeth dripping saliva, the grizzly put another paw around the punk's neck, lifted him bodily off the ground, and turned him. As he got his first glimpse of what had a hold of him, the street kid's eyes bugged out and gurgling sounds emerged from his throat. The bear drew the boy's face closer to his own. Low and dangerous, his voice was that of imminent death.

"You make trouble for Stromagg?" the grizzly growled.

"Urk . . . ulk . . ." Straining with both hands, legs flailing at empty air, the punk fought to disengage that huge paw from around his neck. Looking like white grapes, his eyes threatened to pop out of his head.

Holding his sword, Mudge easily danced around each swipe and cut of the switchblade that was thrust in his direction, not even bothering to riposte. Once, he ducked clear of a wild swing and in the same motion, bowed elegantly to the now incredulous and dazed girl, doffing his peaked cap in the process. Furious, the boy threw himself in the unstrikable otter's direction. Still bowing to the girl, Mudge brought the flat of his sword up between his young assailant's legs. All thoughts of combat suddenly forgotten, the kid went down onto the street and curled into a tight ball, moaning.

Still holding the bigger boy by his neck, Stromagg frowned and turned to Jon-Tom. "Uh, this one don't talk no more."

"Put him down." Jon-Tom approached the now apprehensive girl.

"Please, don't hurt me!" She gestured unevenly in the direction of the moaning coil of boy lying on the pavement. "It was all Marko's idea. He said we could make some easy money. He said American tourists never fight back."

Mudge eyed her with interest. "Wot's an American?"

"We're not going to hurt you," Jon-Tom assured her. "We just need some help getting home." He looked past her. "Your friend said something about a costume ball?"

"A-around the corner. In the hotel."

Thinking hard, Jon-Tom nodded at nothing in particular. "Might work. For a little while. I need some time to think. Thanks," he told her absently. He started off in the indicated direction. With a wink in the girl's direction that left her feeling distinctly non-plussed, Mudge trotted after his friend. Lowering the unconscious kid he still held gently to the wet pavement, Stromagg proceeded to follow.

The hotel was an older establishment and not particularly large. Motioning for his friends to remain behind, quiet and in shadow, Jon-Tom executed a quick survey until he found what he was looking for: a side entrance that would allow them entry without the necessity of passing through the main lobby. He was further relieved when he saw two couples emerge. One pair were clad in medieval garb, a third wore the guise of a large alien insect with a latex head, and the fourth was dressed in the silken body stocking and pale gossamer wings of a pixie. Having met real pixies, he almost paused to offer a critique of the latter costume, but settled for asking directions to the party. Returning to his companions and explaining the situation, he then boldly led them across the street.

Mudge remained wary. "'Ere now, mate. Are you sure this is goin' to work?"

As they approached the ancillary entrance, Jon-Tom replied with growing confidence. "I've heard about these convention balls, Mudge. For tonight, many of those attending are in full costume. They'll think you and Stromagg are fellow participants." He glanced back at the bear. "Try and make yourself look a little smaller, Stromagg." The grizzly obediently hunched his shoulders and lowered his head. "Also, there will probably be food."

The bear's interest picked up noticeably. "Food?"

No one challenged them as the entered the side lobby. After

asking directions of a pair of overweight warriors who would have
cut a laughable figure in Lynchbany Towne, they proceeded to a
large auditorium. It was packed with milling, chatting participants,
more than half of whom were in costume. A few glanced up at
the arrival of the newcomers, but no one appeared startled, or
otherwise alerted that they were anything other than fellow costumers. While Mudge and Stromagg surveyed the scene with
varying degrees of incredulity, Jon-Tom led them toward a line
of tables piled high with snack foods. Sniffing the air, the grizzly's
expression brightened perceptibly.

"Beer! Stromagg smell beer." Whereupon the bear, despite Jon-
Tom's entreaties, promptly angled off on a course of his own.

"Let the bleedin' oversized 'ulk 'ave a drink," Mudge advised his
suddenly concerned companion. " 'E deserves it, after the work 'e
did back at the first tunnel. I wish I could—oi there! Watch where
you're goin'!"

The girl who had bumped into him was dressed as a butterfly.
There wasn't much to her costume, and she was considerably more
svelte than the erstwhile warriors the travelers had encountered
in the hallway outside the auditorium. Mudge's anger dissipated
as rapidly as it had surged.

She gazed admiringly from him to Jon-Tom. "Hey, *love* your
costumes. Did you make them yourselves?"

Looking to terminate the conversation as quickly as possible,
Jon-Tom eyed the long table hungrily. Food was rapidly vanishing from the stained white covering cloths. "Uh, pretty much."

She eyed him interestedly, her wire-supported wings and other
things bobbing with her movements. "You're not writers, or art-
ists, because you don't have name tags on." She indicated the duar
resting against Jon-Tom's back. "That's a neat lute, or whatever.
It looks playable." She gestured in the direction of the busy stage
at the far end of the auditorium. "There's filksinging going on right
now. I'm getting this vibe that you're pretty good. I'm kind of
psychic, you see, and I have a feel for other people." Her smile
widened. "I bet you're a—computer programmer!"

"Not exac . . ." he tried to explain to her as she grabbed his hand
and fairly dragged him forward. Mudge watched with amusement
as his friend was towed helplessly in the direction of the stage.
Then he turned and headed for the food-laden tables.

Welcoming Jon-Tom, the flute player currently holding court
onstage cast his own admiring glance at the duar. "Cool strings.
You need a cord and an amp?"

Aware that others in the crowd had turned to face him, Jon-Tom played—but only for time. "Uh, no. Strictly acoustic."

The flute player stepped aside. "Right. Let's see what you can do." Conscious that Butterfly was still watching him intently, Jon-Tom decided that a quick, straightforward song would be the easiest, and safest, way to escape the unwelcome attention that was now being directed toward him. As his fingers began to slide across the strings of the duar, a familiar multihued mist began to congeal at the interdimensional nexus.

Someone in the forefront of the crowd pointed excitedly. "Hey, look—light show!" Responding with a lame grin, Jon-Tom tried to strum as simple and unaffecting a melody as possible. Gritting his teeth, he forced himself to remember the chords to a Barry Manilow tune. At least, he told himself, he would not have to worry about making any inadvertent magic.

Following his nose, Stromagg found himself approaching a bar near the far side of the auditorium. As he approached, someone thrust a tankard toward him.

"Here you go, big guy. Have one on me." The man dressed as Henry IX pressed a full tankard into the grizzly's paw. Accepting the offer, Stromagg took a suspicious sniff of the contents. His face lit up and he proceeded to drain the container in one long swallow. Looking on admiringly, the fan who would be king beckoned his friends to join the new arrival.

Scarfing finger food as fast as he could evaluate it with eyes and nostrils, Mudge was distracted from his gorging by the tapping of a furry forefinger on his shoulder. A ready if nervous retort on his lips, he turned—only to find himself struck dumb by the sight that confronted him.

The girl's otter costume was not only superbly rendered, it was, in word, compelling.

Twirling a whisker, he slowly put aside the piled-high plate of goodies he had commandeered from the table. "Well now. And wot might your name be, darlin'?"

Peering through the eye cut-outs in the papier-mâché head, the girl's gaze reflected a mix of admiration and disbelief. "And I thought I had had the best giant-otter costume in England!" Her eyes inspected every inch of him, analyzing thoroughly. "I've never seen such good sewing. I can't even see the stitches, or where you've hidden the zipper." Her eyes met his. "Costumers are good about sharing their secrets. Could you spare a couple of minutes to maybe give me some pointers?"

Mudge considered his platter. Food, girl. Food, girl. Cookies. . . .

—IV—

Onstage, Jon-Tom found himself, despite his reservations, slipping into the free-wheeling spirit of the occasion. Participants were dancing in front of him, twirling in costume, reveling in his music-making. So self-absorbed were they that they failed to see the small black ball of vapor that emerged from the center of the duar to flash offstage and vanish in the direction of the farthest doorway. Judging from its angle of departure, Jon-Tom guessed it to be heading fast in the direction of the underground stairway from which he and his companions had emerged earlier that same evening. Raising his voice excitedly while still strumming, Jon-Tom sought to alert his companions.

"Mudge, Stromagg! I think I've done it!" Ignoring the applause of the flute player, who took up the refrain, and the admiring stare of butterfly girl, he leaped off the stage and plunged into the crowd. There was no telling how long the revitalized, recharged tunnel would last. He and his friends had to make use of it before the thaumaturgic alteration was discovered by some wandering late-night pedestrians.

Stromagg wasn't hard to locate. The bear had by now gathered a small army of awed acolytes around him, who looked on in jaw-dropping astonishment as the grizzly continued to chugalug inhuman quantities of beer with no apparent ill effects.

Well, maybe a few.

Arriving breathlessly from the stage, Jon-Tom looked around uncertainly. "Stromagg, it's time to go. Where's Mudge?"

Weaving slightly, the more than modestly zonkered ursine frowned down at him and replied, in the tone of one only slightly interested, "Duhhh?"

"Oh great!" Latching on to the grizzly's arm, Jon-Tom struggled to drag him away from the crowd. Behind him, tankards and glasses and Styrofoam cups rose in admiring salute. "We've got to get out of here while we have the chance."

There was no sign of Mudge on the auditorium floor, nor out in the hallway, nor in an annex room. Confronting a participant made up as an exceedingly stocky, slime-dripping alien, Jon-Tom fought to keep Stromagg from falling down.

"This may sound funny, but have you seen a five-foot-tall otter come this way?"

"Nothing funny about it," the gray-green alien replied in an incongruously high-pitched voice. It jerked a thumb down the hall. "I just saw two of 'em."

"Two?" Jon-Tom's confusion was sincere. Then realization dawned, and he broke into a desperate sprint. "*Mudge!*"

He found his friend in the third room he tried: an empty office. Bursting in, he and Stromagg discovered Mudge and the otter other in a position that had nothing to do with passing along the finer points of advanced amateur costuming. Jon-Tom's outrage was palpable.

"Mudge!"

Rising from the couch, his friend looked back over his shoulder, not in the least at a loss.

" 'Ello, mate." He indicated the shape beneath him. "This 'ere is Althea. We been discussin' matters of the moment, you might say."

Stark naked except for otter mask and furry feet, the girl struggled to cover herself as best she could. Though surprised by the unexpected intrusion, she did not appear particularly distressed. Rather the contrary. Ignoring her, an angry Jon-Tom confronted his companion.

"What the hell do you think you're doing? Aren't matters complicated enough as it is?"

Hopping off the couch and into his short pants, the otter proceeded to defend himself. "Back off, mate. Me and Althea 'ere weren't 'aving no problems. It were all perfectly consentable, it were."

"That's right." Rising in all her admirable suppleness, she reached out with one hand to grab hold of Mudge's right ear. "And now that I've fulfilled my half of the bargain, it's time to see how your outfit is put together." She pulled hard.

Yelping, Mudge twisted around as his ear was yanked. "Owch! 'Ave a care there, darlin'."

Looking puzzled, the girl's gaze descended. Grabbing a fistful of fur in the otter's nether regions, she pulled again. Once more the otter let out a hurt bark. A look of confusion crossed her countenance, to be replaced by one of revelation, followed by one of shock. As this panoply of expression transformed her lovely face, Jon-Tom was half carrying Mudge, who was engaged in trying to buckle the belt of his shorts, toward the doorway where Stromagg kept tipsy watch.

"Omigod!" the girl suddenly screamed, one hand rising to her mouth, "*it's not a special effect!*"

Looking back as he was dragged out the door, an offended Mudge called back. "I resent that, luv!"

Hearing the girl's screams, a group of heavily armed attendees had begun to gather at the far end of the hallway. While any band of professionals from Lynchbany would have made short work of the lot, several of the costumed cluster did appear to be more than a little competent. And there was nothing slipshod or fragile about the assortment of swords and axes and lances they carried.

"This way!" With the increasingly outraged costumers following, Jon-Tom led his friends around the corner of the hallway that encircled the auditorium, searching for an exit that led back out onto the rain-washed side street.

"Here, you three." Up ahead, a neatly suited hotel security guard had materialized to block their path. "What's this I hear about you freaks causing trouble with—?" His slightly pompous accusation was cut off in mid-sentence as Stromagg stiff-armed him into the nearest wall, directly beside a painting of a skinny lord seated astride a decidedly astringent thoroughbred.

Bursting back out into the street, Jon-Tom led the way toward the underground station. It was darker than ever outside, but at least the rain had stopped falling. An oncoming car had to screech to a halt to avoid slamming into the fleeing trio.

Within the vehicle, a well-dressed middle-aged couple looked on as the tall, medievally clad spellsinger; a giant otter in feathered cap, vest, and short pants; and a rapidly sobering leatherarmored grizzly bear thundered past. They were followed soon after by an enraged mob of weapon-waving fans dressed as everything from a giant spider to a female Mr. Spock missing one ear. Peering through the windshield in the wake of this singular parade, the husband slowly shook his head from side to side before commenting knowingly to his equally mystified spouse. Pressing gently on the accelerator, he urged the car forward.

"I'm telling you, dear. There's no question about it. London gets worse every year."

Looking back over his shoulder, Mudge began to make insulting faces at their pursuers. He would have dropped his pants except that Jon-Tom threatened to brain him with the flat of his own sword. As usual, the otter reflected, the often dour spellsinger simply did not know how to have fun.

"There!" Jon-Tom pointed in the direction of the softly glowing split circle. A sphere of black mist was just visible plunging down the portal.

Racing past a brace of startled Underground travelers, he and Stromagg hurtled down the stairs in pursuit of the ebony globe. Mudge chose to slide gleefully down the central banister, looking back up the stairwell to flash obscene gestures in the direction of their pursuers. His scatological gesticulations transcended species.

Alongside the automatic gates that led to the boarding platform, a startled security officer looked up in the direction of the approaching commotion.

"See here, you lot need to slow down and . . ."

Accelerating to pass Jon-Tom, Stromagg shoved the officer aside. Grabbing one in each paw, he ripped two of the barriers out of the floor and flung them ceilingward. Mudge and Jon-Tom shielded their heads as thousands of Underground tokens from the crumpled barriers rained down on them.

Lying off to one side amid the rubble, cap and uniform askew, the unlucky guard looked up numbly. "Of course, if it's an emergency. . . ."

Slowing as they reached the Underground platform, a panting Jon-Tom looked back to see that pursuit had slowed as the angry fans stopped to gather up handfuls of tokens. Mudge was fairly dancing with fury.

"Puling 'umans! Shrew-pricked candy lobbers!" He had his short sword out and was stabbing repeatedly at empty air. "I'll skewer the bleedin' lot o' them!"

"You aren't going to skewer anyone." Climbing down off the platform onto the tunnel track, Jon-Tom started north, in the direction taken by the floating ball of black mist-magic. His companions followed. Unlimbering his duar as they plunged into the feebly illuminated tunnel, he began to play softly. The glow from the instrument served to show the way.

Sword rescabbarded, hands jammed in pockets, Mudge kicked angrily at the occasional rock or empty soda can underfoot. " 'Tis an unaccomodatin' world, is yours, mate. Unfriendly an' worse, no sense o' fellowship." Then he remembered the other otter, and a small smile played across his mouth.

As if recalling a fond and distant thought, Stromagg peered into the darkness ahead. "Beer?"

A light appeared, growing brighter as it came toward them. A light, and a roaring they had heard once before. Startled, Jon-Tom began to back-track. Literally.

"Oh shit."

Mudge made a face. "More incomprehensible spellsinger lyrics?"

"Run!" Turning, Jon-Tom broke into a desperate sprint. How far up the tunnel had they come? How far was it back to the passenger platform?

As the light of the oncoming train bore down on them, he fumbled with the duar and with memories of train-related songs. There was the theme from *Trainspotting*—no, that probably wouldn't work. He couldn't remember the words to "A Train A-Comin'." Heavy metal, punk, ska, even industrial had little use for trains.

He was still frantically seeking appropriate lyrics as the train bore down on them. The engineer saw the wide-eyed trio running in front of his engine and threw on the brakes. An ear-piercing *screeee!* echoed from the walls of the tunnel. Too little, too late.

Jon-Tom found himself stumbling, going down. As he fell, he saw something directly beneath him. It wasn't the empty plastic wrappers, or stubbed cigarettes, or torn, useless lotto tickets that drew his attention. It was a flat circle of softly seething black mist, lying neatly between but not touching the tracks or the center rail. He let himself fall, hoping his companions would see what was happening to him, hoping they would follow.

Of course, it might simply be a lingering patch of black fog, rising from the heat of the tracks.

He felt himself, thankfully, blissfully, continuing to fall long after he should have struck the ground.

Seeming to pass directly over his head, barely inches from his ear, the roar of the train faded. He hit the ground, rolled, and opened his eyes. They were still in his head, which was in turn still attached to his shoulders. These were good signs. Sitting up, he rubbed the back of his neck and winced. Reaching around behind him, he found that the precious duar was battered from the fall but still intact.

Nearby, Mudge cast a pain-wracked eye at his friend. "That's it, mate. I've bleedin' 'ad it, I 'ave. Give me me share o' old Wolfram's gold and I'll be quietly on me way." Behind him, a groaning Stromagg was just starting to regain consciousness.

Looking away from the angry otter, Jon-Tom found himself staring. "Don't you think you ought to have a look around, first?"

"Why? Wot the bloody 'ell should I . . ." The otter broke off, joined his friend in gawking silently.

Namur Castle rose from a narrow ridge of rock surrounded on all sides by sheer precipices. A wooden bridge crossed from the mountainside on which man and otter found themselves to a small intervening pinnacle, from where a second, slightly narrower bridge arched to meet a high wooden doorway. Towering granite spires rose on all sides, while a tree-lined flat-topped plateau dominated the distant horizon. Jon-Tom and his companions were enthralled. It was an impressive setting.

Starting across the first bridge, Mudge warily glanced over the single railing. Like a bright-blue ribbon dropped from a giant's hand, a small river wound and twisted its way through the deep canyon beneath. They reached the intervening pinnacle and crossed the second bridge, whereupon they found themselves confronting a massive, iron-bound door. Tilting back his head, Mudge rested hands on low hips and muttered aloud.

"Wot now, Mr. Spelltwit, sor? You goin' to sing us up a key, or wot?"

An irritated Jon-Tom contemplated the barrier. "Give me a minute, Mudge. I got us here, didn't I?"

The otter snorted softly. "Oi, that you did—though one might complain about the roundaboutness o' the route you chose. London!" He shook his head mournfully. "Give me Lynchbany any day."

While man and otter argued, the silent Stromagg approached the impediment, considered it a moment, and then balled both paws into fists the size of cannonballs. Raising them high over his head and rising on tiptoes (a sight in itself to behold), he brought both fists down and forward with all his considerable weight behind them. The center of the door promptly collapsed in a pile of shattered slats and splinters. Dust rose from the center of the destruction.

Approaching cautiously, Mudge peered through the newly made opening. "So much for a bloomin' key."

The interior of the foyer was dim, illuminated only by light shining through high windows. Nothing moved within, not even a piebald rat. Mudge's sensitive nose was working overtime, his long whiskers twitching.

"Sure you got the right foreboding castle 'ere, mate?"

Jon-Tom continued through the high vestibule, eyed the sweeping double stairway at the far end of the great room. "I sang for one and one only. This must be the right place."

Still, he found himself wondering and worrying, until their explorations eventually brought them to an expansive, exquisitely decorated bedchamber. Rainbow-hued light poured in through stained-glass windows, burnishing the furnishings with gold and turning the canopied, lace-netted bed at the far end to filigreed sunshine.

The woman who slept thereon might or might not be a princess, but she was certainly of ravishing beauty. She was sleeping peacefully on her back, her hands folded across her chest, a soft smile on her full lips. Slapping away Mudge's fingers, Jon-Tom considered the somnifacient figure thoughtfully.

"Something familiar about this. . . ."

—V—

"Not to mention somethin' irregular." Mudge contemplated the unconscious female with mixed emotions. "That Wolfsheep didn't say anythin' about 'is beloved bein' in a coma. 'Ow are you supposed to sing 'er a song o' love if she can't bleedin' 'ear you?"

The soft shush of fine leather on stone made the trio turn as one. Standing in the doorway was their erstwhile employer, but it was a Wolfram transformed. No longer the supplicating elder, he seemed to have grown taller in stature and broader of frame. His formerly simple cloth cloak glistened in the stained-glass light, and the vitreous globe atop his staff flickered with caged lightning. His entire being and bearing radiated barely restrained power.

"So you have done that which I could not." Stepping into the room, he ignored them to focus his attention on the figure lying supine in the bed. "Ignorant sots. Did you really think that I, Wolfram the Magnific, the All-Consuming, Master of the Warmlands, would consign the future of the Mistress of the Namur to your puerile attentions?"

As he replied, Jon-Tom slowly edged his duar around in front of him. "Somehow I knew you'd say something like that."

A belligerent Mudge stepped forward. "If you're so bloody all-whatever, guv'nor, then wot did you need us poor souls for?"

The sorcerer gazed down contemptuously. "Isn't it obvious? The bonds that conceal this place are such as I cannot penetrate. It needs the attention of a kind of magic different entirely from what I propound, powerful as that may be. It required someone such as an innocent spellsinger to blaze a path here and divert any dangers that might lie along the way. This so that I could follow safely in your wake—as I have done. Why should I take the risks?"

"Then," Jon-Tom said, indicating the figure reposing serenely in the bed, "this isn't your beloved?"

"Oh, but she is." Wolfram smiled thinly behind his narrow, pointed beard. "It is just that she does not know it yet. You see, whoever touches the princess in such a way as to rouse her from her sleep shall make of her a perfect match to the one who does the touching, and shall have her to wife, thus acquiring dominion over this portion of an important realm and its concurrent significant interdimensionality."

"Is that all?" Mudge was studying his fingernails. " 'Tis okay by me, guv."

"Oh no it isn't." Jon-Tom advanced to stand alongside the otter. "If an interdimensionality is involved here, it means that this piece of whiskery double-crossing scum might be able to make trouble in my world as well."

The otter shrugged. "Not me problem. Mayhap his meddlings might improve that revolting London place."

The sorcerer nodded knowingly. "I thought I would have no trouble with you three."

His fingers creeping across the strings of the duar, Jon-Tom mentally considered and discarded a dozen different songs. Which would be the most effective against a powerful, malign personality like Wolfram? Knowing little about the man, it was hard to conjure something specific. Then he recalled the sorcerer's words, and knew what he should do.

Whirling, he raced for the bed.

"*Hassone!*" Raising his staff, Wolfram thrust it in the spellsinger's direction. Gray vapor shot from the globe at its terminus to coalesce directly between the diving Jon-Tom and the bed. Slamming into the wall of solid gray rock, Jon-Tom stumbled once, staggered slightly, and then crumpled to the floor.

Gathering anxiously around their fallen comrade, Mudge and Stromagg exchanged a glance, then turned their rising ire on the serene figure of Wolfram. Raising their weapons, they rushed the sorcerer, each screaming his own battle cry.

"*Beeeer!*" The grizzly's below echoed off the walls and rattled the stained-glass windows.

"*No refunds!*" the otter howled.

"*Parimazzo!*" Wolfram countered, bringing his glowing staff around in a sweeping arc parallel to the floor.

Rising from the stone underfoot, all manner of fetid, armed horrors confronted the onrushing duo, swinging weapons made of the same stone as that from which they had arisen. Mildly amused, Wolfram leaned on his staff and solicitously observed the battle that ensued.

Behind the fracas, a groggy Jon-Tom slowly came around. Discerning what was taking place, he reached cautiously for his duar. Still lying on the floor, trying to avoid Wolfram's notice, he began to play, and started to sing.

"Once there was an—*urrrp!*"

The unexpected belch did more than put a crimp in the chosen spellsong. The visible result was a solid, softly glowing, jet-black musical note that hovered in the air a foot or so in front of the astonished Jon-Tom's face.

"Well, what do you know," he murmured to himself. "Music really *does* look like that."

Reaching up, he grabbed the note, rose, whirled it over his head, and flung it in Wolfram's direction. Seeing it coming, the sorcerer raised his staff to defend himself. The note passed right through the protective glow to smack the startled mage on the forehead and send him staggering backward.

Emboldened, avoiding the nearby swordplay, Jon-Tom strode determinedly toward the stunned sorcerer; playing, singing, and belching as never before.

"And ever the drink (*urp*) shall flow freely (*breep*) to the sea (*burk*). . . ."

Each belch produced a fresh glowing note, which he heaved one after another in the direction of the now quietly panicking Wolfram. Desperate, the wizard executed a small motion in the air with his staff.

"*Immunitago!*" A pair of large earmuffs appeared before him, drifted backward to settle themselves against his ears. Slowly, his confident smile returned. Staff upraised, he started toward Jon-Tom. Unable to hear the flung notes, they burst harmlessly in the air before reaching him.

Now it was a newly anxious Jon-Tom's turn to retreat. Changing tactics as he backpedaled, he also changed music. The roar of Rammstein thundered through the chaotic chamber. The duar glowed angrily, fiery with *bist* mist.

Shaken by the heavy chords, Wolfram halted and clutched at his stricken ears. Trying to keep the earmuffs from vibrating off his head, he flung a wild blast from his staff. Ducking, Jon-Tom watched as the flare of malevolent energy shot over his head.

To strike the grizzly, who was busy making gravel of his stony, stone-faced assailants.

"*Stromagg!*" a pained Jon-Tom yelled.

The force of the blast blew the bear backward into, and through, the stone wall that Wolfram had conjured earlier to encircle the sleeping princess. Rocks went flying as the bear landed, barely conscious, on the bed. Moaning, he rolled slightly to his right. His arm rose, arced, and fell loosely—to fall across the waist of the slumbering princess.

Aghast, a horrified Wolfram let out a shriek of despair. "*Nooo!*" Jon-Tom remembered the sorcerer's words.

"Whoever touches the princess in such a way as to rouse her from her sleep shall make of her a perfect match to the one who does the touching, and shall have her to wife."

A delicate haze enveloped the Princess Larinda. Her outline shimmered, shifted, and flowed. She was changing, metamorphosing, into . . .

When the mist finally cleared, not one but two grizzlies lay recumbent on the bed. One was clad in leather armor, the other in attire most elegant and comely. Rubbing at her eyes, the princess sat up, and turned slightly to gaze across at her savior. Blinking, holding one hand to his bleeding head, Stromagg looked up. Instantly, the pain of the sorcerer's perfidious blow was forgotten.

"Duhh—wow!"

"No, no, no!" Shrouded in tantrum sorceral, a despairing Wolfram was fairly jumping up and down, swinging his deadly staff indiscriminately.

Sitting up on the bed, which now creaked alarmingly beneath the unexpected dual weight, Stromagg took both of the princess's hands—or rather, paws—in his own and gazed deeply into dark-brown eyes that mirrored his.

"Duh, hiya."

Long lashes fluttered as she met his unflinching, if somewhat overwhelmed, gaze. "I always did like the strong, silent type."

"This shall not last! By my oath, I swear it!" Numinous cape swirling about him, Wolfram whirled and fled through the open doorway. "I shall find a way to renew the sleeping spell. Then it will most assuredly be I who awakens her the second time!"

Lightning flickering from his staff of theurgic power, he raced unimpeded down the stairway and back through the foyer. Outside the smashed main doorway, the bridge back to the rest of reality beckoned.

From a shadow there emerged a foot. A furry foot, sandal-clad. It interposed itself neatly between the sorcerer's feet.

Looking surprised, Wolfram went down and forward, his momentum carrying him right over the side of the bridge. As he fell, he looked back up at a rapidly shrinking fuzzy face, astonished that he could have been defeated by something so common, so ordinary. As he fell, he flailed madly for the staff he had dropped while stumbling. Though he never succeeded in recovering it, at least staff and owner hit the bottom of the canyon in concert.

Peering over the side of the bridge, Mudge let out a derisive whistle. "Bleedin' wizards never look where they're goin'."

By the time the otter rejoined his companions, Jon-Tom was facing a revitalized Stromagg and his new-found paramour. The two grizzlies held hands daintily.

"Sorry, guys," Stromagg was murmuring. "I think I'd kinda like to stay here."

Jon-Tom was grinning. "I can't imagine why."

A familiar hand tapped him on the arm. "You'd best lose that sappy grin now, guv', or they'll likely 'ang you for it back in Lynchbany. You look bloody thick."

"Be at peace, my good friends and saviors." Though rather deeper than was traditional, the voice of the restored princess was still sweet and feminine. "I have some small powers. I promise that upon your return home, you will receive a reward in the form of whatever golden coins you have most recently handled, and that these shall completely fill your place of dwelling. As Mistress of the Namur, this I vow."

"Well now, luv," declared a delighted Mudge. "That's more like it!"

It took some time, and not a small adventure or three, before they found themselves once more back in their beloved Bellwoods. Espying his riverbank home, a tired and dusty Mudge broke into a run.

"Time to cash in, mate! Remember the hairy princess's promise."

Following at a more leisurely pace, Jon-Tom was just in time to see his friend fling open his front door—only to be buried beneath an avalanche of gleaming golden disks. Hurrying forward, he dragged the otter clear of the mountain of metal.

"Rich, rich! At last! Finally!" The otter was beside himself with glee.

Or was, until he peered more closely at a handful of the disks. Doubt washed over his furry face. " 'Tis odd, mate, but I swear I ain't never before seen gold like this."

Gathering up a couple of the disks, Jon-Tom regarded them with a resigned expression. "That's because they're not gold, Mudge."

"Not gold?" Sputtering outrage, the otter sprang to his feet.

Which, given the shortness of his legs, was a simple enough maneuver. "But the princess bleedin' promised, she did. 'The last golden coin I 'andled,' she said. I remember! That were wot that slimy Wolfram character paid us with at the tavern back in Timswitty." His expression darkened. "You're shakin' your 'ead, mate. I don't like it when you shake your 'ead."

"She said '*golden* coin,' Mudge. Not 'gold coin.' " His open palm displayed the disks. "Remember when we were fleeing my world? These are London Underground tokens, Mudge." At the otter's open-mouthed look of horror, he added unhelpfully, "Look at it this way: you can ride free around greater London for the rest of eternity."

Sitting down hard on the useless hoard, the otter slowly removed his feathered cap from between his ears, let it dangle loosely from his fingers. "I don't suppose—I don't suppose you 'ave a worthy spellsong for rescuin' this sorry situation, do you, mate?"

Bringing the duar around, Jon-Tom shrugged. "No harm in trying."

But Pink Floyd's "Money" did not turn the tokens to real gold, nor did all the otter tears that spilled into the black river all the rest of that memorable day.

⪧ Child of Prophecy ⪦

A War of Light and Shadow Story

Janny Wurts

Meiglin all but wished for death on that clear winter morning, when the brothel's madam cupped her face between perfumed hands. Eyes shut, Meiglin endured as the woman assessed her fresh skin and, still considering, fingered the tangles the wind had wound in her lustrous seal-brown hair. The prick of the older woman's nails against her flesh was not another bad dream. Meiglin fought down tears and terror. Only a fool could have clung to belief that she might be allowed to stay innocent. Though her immature breasts had just started to bud, and the hips underneath her tattered skirt were as yet boyishly slim, one of last night's clients had winked at her as she had rushed in, cheeks flushed from an errand.

Today, the madam's shrewd eyes, cold blue, weighed up her assets as merchandise.

"Mistress, wait," Meiglin pleaded. "I'm surely too young."

"Not so young. A man has asked for you, dearie. Time we had Feylie cut you a gown." The powerful woman patted Meiglin's shoulder, not ungently, for all her hard heart. "Lavender, with black lace at the throat. That will bring out the unusual color of your eyes, and forgive the fact you have only promise filling the front of your bodice."

Meiglin jerked free, blazing with shame. Her future had been in plain sight, all along, her prospects no better than the other whores' daughters born comely enough for the house. Tomorrow,

145

she would have cream for her oatmeal, to fill out her coltish frame. She would no longer scrub dishes or wash soiled linen. By the time the new gown had been made to measure, her chapped hands would be soft, and her lips would be painted. She would be presented as the new, virgin jewel, and the clients would do more than wink.

"Come, now," chaffed the madam. "We don't feed any child who's not suited for the business. Nor any grown woman, either. Your mother's aging. She can't fill her bed as once she used to. Put a good face on this, Meiglin." Entwined ropes of pearls clicked over layered silk as the madam crossed the lush carpet. She slapped open her account book and started inscribing the writ for the dress maker. "These are hard times, with the wars and the mayor's exorbitant taxes. It's your earnings, now, girl, will pay for your shelter. Your mother's had her day. You'll now have to make your own way."

Left standing in chilled disarray, her unbound hair tumbled over the unlaced strings of her overdress, Meiglin trembled in shattered desperation. How had she ever dared hope for reprieve? The pilfered hoard of coins she had stashed away in secret could never have bought her escape. No man of decent family would wed a child of fourteen years, or employ one born and raised in a bawdyhouse. Meiglin swallowed back shock and anger. She drew a shaky breath, raised her chin and forced out a winsome smile. "I'll take the note to Feylie's and be measured?"

The madam's icy stare regarded her over the poised tip of the quill. "No, girl. You won't." She sighed in reproach. "Do you take me for an idiot?" A crisp snap of her fingers summoned Quincat.

The side door opened. A heavy tread entered. Meiglin bolted, too late. Quincat's massive hands caught her arms from behind. She had seen the way things went with a girl who fought her fate. Day after day, she would weep and rage behind a barred door, until she became too used and tired to dream, or care about running away.

"Best strip the clothes off that chit right now," the madam instructed her henchman. "There's defiance in her, make no mistake. She'd slip through the eye of a needle, she would, if you leave her the unguarded chance."

Meiglin did not weep. She refused to battle Quincat as he hauled her upstairs. To her worldly eye, the brute seemed to relish her sorry discomfort too much. She ignored the indignity, denied him the piquant satisfaction of a struggle as he did the madam's bidding and confiscated her clothing. Behind the locked door, wrapped up in a stale, musty sheet well used by last night's clients, Meiglin paced in helpless fury. Dread for the future made her sweat and shiver, until her throat felt hardened to glass, that might shatter with screams at a word.

When the soft step approached, and the key finally turned, it was not Quincat come to leer while Feylie's lisping seamstress prodded and mumbled over measurements. The hand at the latch was shaking and frail, fast followed by her mother's breathless whisper.

"Meiglin, hurry! No, girl, no questions! A bawd's life's not for you!" Her mother's touch was clammy with nerves as she bundled her terrified daughter over the threshold. "The door to the pantry's ajar for you, sweetling. There's no choice left. You have to run!"

"Like this?" Meiglin gasped. The sheet fluttered around her bare ankles. The draft cut with cruel chill as she pattered down the back stair. Outside in the alley, heavy snowfall would have rimed the mud into a slurry of glazed ice.

"You daren't stay!" Her mother paused, kicked off velvet slippers, then peeled the sheer, scarlet lace off her shift. "Here's the best I can do for you, child. Have you the courage? You'll need to go as you are."

Meiglin balked, aghast. "What about you? Mother, for this, the madam will—"

"Hush child! That can't matter." Through a rushed and desperate pause, thick with the overpowering musk of cheap scent, her mother hustled Meiglin into her own cast-off garments. The sequined fabric was woefully thin, and the ribbon-laced slippers, too large.

"I'll freeze inside an hour," Meiglin protested, afraid. This bid for escape was no less than stark madness. *Why, if a mother cared a straw for her daughter's secure future, had she thought to bear the child of a client?*

Her mother arrested her scathing questions; shook her head, to a rustle of curls dulled lusterless from too much henna. "No. Just listen, Meiglin! There are facts you must know, and no time to explain. You are no client's byblow! I was already bearing, do you hear? Married, and only a month from my time when the mayor's rebellion brought our family to ruin. My husband was an old-blood clansman. Egan s'Dieneval. He died at Earle, fighting the Mistwraith at the right hand of his king. I was left a widow, when the mob destroyed Tirans, driven out and hunted as a fugitive. I had no haven to give birth in safety. Not until the madam took me in. Oh, yes, she noticed what my accent could not hide. I had looks enough, then, to cozen her silence. She agreed to ask no questions, even helped to coach my speech. I sold myself in trade. But you were never to be any part of that bargain."

"Clanborn!" Meiglin shuddered, horrified, the last, secure bastion left in her life torn away at one stroke. "You're telling me *now*, you were clanborn?"

"Yes." Dimness hid her mother's face. Yet the unmasked force of her pride rang through, in crisp diction nothing like the downtrodden lisp she assumed to cajole madam's clients. "That is your true birthright, and your heritage, Meiglin."

"No inheritance at all," Meiglin whispered, shocked. She had never imagined herself to be on the wrong side of that round of bloodletting conflict. Clanborn were hated, even killed out of hand, since the uprising broke the ancient law of the High Kings. "And you say the madam knows? Dharkaron's mercy on us!"

Where the mayors ruled, their zealot factions bid to match the guilds' pledge to offer bounties. Packs of bloody reivers were now offered a rich purse to cut down the remnants of the clan bloodlines. That volatile fact explained all too well why the madam should force Meiglin to brothel service, so young. There would never be retirement, sewing gowns or washing linen, not for such as her mother.

Meiglin wrestled panic. "Now, more than ever, you're worth silver to them, dead."

"We both are." Her mother seized her hand, tugged her onward without mercy. "Can't you see? *That's why you have to run, child!*"

The madam had no scruples where her steely eye saw profit. She would peddle Meiglin's maiden assets for as long as eager clients paid to bed her for a premium. Once the novelty paled, the madam would sell out. Mother and child would inevitably be thrown to the swords of the mayor's headhunters.

"Get out of here and live!" Urgent fingers pressed Meiglin across the darkened pantry. "Go! Hurry, child! Egan s'Dieneval. Remember your lineage! Before everything else, that name matters."

Upstairs, Quincat's bellow showed the unlocked bedroom had been discovered.

"Go, Meiglin!" Weeping bitter tears, the doomed mother shoved her daughter through the doorway, into the cutting winter wind. "Leave Durn and never look back."

Meiglin fled.

She lost the slippers straightaway, their sodden cloth sucked off by the muddy slush clogging the street. Since the sheet made her conspicuous, and her narrow, bare prints left a track too easily followed, she snatched the first chance of refuge she found, beneath the loosened tarp of a trade wagon lumbering downhill toward the city gates. Huddled under flapping canvas, bound she knew not where, Meiglin wedged herself between a raw wool bale and a gunny sack of millet, probably hauled to feed the mule teams.

The cold seemed preferable to the butchery that waited if she was overtaken by a bountyman. Meiglin huddled in abject misery, silently cursing the lot that bound her to the mischance of her ancestry. She had no assets, no place to go. Her mother's people were scattered. Their proud history had been reduced to ashes in the turmoil that followed the Mistwraith's invasion, when shouting mobs had rampaged with fire and sword. They had cut down every old blood liegeman they could find, then turned in vengeful fury on their families. The clans' steadfast charge, to stand as liaison between humankind's needs and the world's ancient mysteries, had devolved into persecution and conflict. The hunted survivors hid deep in the wilds. Their armed scouts roved the land like secretive shadows, still defending the ground the old centaur guardians had forbidden to the ways of outsiders. A girl with no more to her name than a bed sheet would die of exposure, searching the hills, if she was not shot down by an arrow for trespass upon proscribed territory.

Despondent and alone, Meiglin suffered the insidious cold. Her blanched hands and aching feet slowly went numb. She slipped at length into somnolent grayness, overcome by a trance state of dreams that hurled her beyond the dimension of ordinary nightmare. The oddity had happened before; but never under the frightening, new knowledge that she sprang from a bloodline that *would* carry arcane gifts.

The visions came on, too fierce to deny, their brilliance stark and unsettling: of the scouring mists that had invaded through Southgate, and swallowed the fall of clean sunlight. As though past events revisited in review, she watched the rising that unseated the High Kings erupt in slaughter and flames. Then the Mistwraith's dank fog masked the horrors in white. Drifting like flotsam in the coils of the future, Meiglin looked down on a scene by a riverbank, where a gray-haired man wearing the crown colors of Shand lay in gasping extremity. A young man rode up, and leaped off his horse, crying aloud in his anguish. The man, who was mentor, died in his arms. Consumed by fierce grief, the boy reached to take the jeweled circlet from the brow of the corpse.

"Don't!" Meiglin cried.

Though her protest was made in the fabric of dream, the boy started and glanced up. For a stopped second, their eyes met and held, joined in the half world of mystery. He was young: as unmarked by life as newly forged steel, but beautiful in the purity of his unwritten potential.

"Don't." Meiglin whispered. Her beating heart seemed to freeze as she sensed the boy's determined fate. "You will meet your death."

He smiled, brash youth. "I must. What hope can survive if the last of the sunlight is lost to the Mistwraith's conquest?"

Time unfroze. His impetuous fingers closed over the circlet, and the dream narrowed in, vibrant as a shout that *should have* held power to rock the seat of the world.

Like a stone, Meiglin plummeted. Her awareness swooped toward the stream bank, as though the trapped cry of her mind and will could sever the spun strand of tragedy.

"Don't! You must not!"

Yet the choice had been made. Though Meiglin wept, the doomed prince faded beyond reach.

Fog closed, choking white. Tears of sorrow fell on a country swathed in lead. The boy would die, his brave sacrifice futile. The Mistwraith would seize its fell triumph. Meiglin cupped the drowned world between her two hands, her denial a silent shout wrenched from the dreaming core of her spirit.

Then the vision that gripped her snapped into light. She beheld the face of another old man, this one no king, but a creature mantled in power, with eyes that pierced time with a falcon's intensity, and perception that flayed her worth down to a word.

"S'Dieneval?"

He added a phrase in the Paravian tongue that Meiglin lacked learning to translate. But the mysteries answered. The shackling weight that constricted her chest burst and hurled her back into herself. . . .

Meiglin opened her eyes, choking on hot milk. The round face of a farm wife hovered above, set against a beamed wooden ceiling. Off to her left, a man finished a rambling dialogue in the lazy drawl of the southcoast.

" . . . don't know where along the route I picked her up," he ended, apologetic. "Found her huddled in the wagon under the tarps, shivering like a kit fox. If I'd left her, she'd have died of the cold, understand?"

"She's a pretty poppet," murmured the farm wife. Bowl and spoon clutched in her beefy hands, she paused for a moment to admire. "Such beautiful, sad eyes."

"Pretty enough to raise unwholesome trouble!" snapped a gruffer man, country bred, and likely the master of the croft. "And she's not sad enough to cry honest tears. Her sort know too well how to use winsome looks. It's her stock in trade to take advantage."

"She's only a child!" the woman said, shocked.

The crofter stayed adamant. "No child walks the streets clad in nothing but lace. Damn well, we can't harbor a sly, depraved creature. Not one with her habits. She'll have the boys fighting to try her shameless favors, and turn their minds for the worse."

The drover retreated, hands raised in consternation. "My caravan can't keep her, not with the outriders bored enough to dally, and randy as a pack of spring bulls. Turn the tart out on the road as you will, but for pity, at least see her off with a blanket."

Meiglin drew breath between chattering teeth. "I haven't, at least, there wasn't—" She colored, despite the chills that threatened to rattle her bones. "Not yet," she insisted lamely. "That's why I ran away."

"Well, she isn't any stranger to hard work!" snapped the wife. "Did you see? Her poor hands are chapped! T'would take a heart of stone to send a mouse out in this weather, with the wind blowing in another stormfront!"

"I can work," Meiglin whispered. "Sweep floors. Wash laundry. Even cook, a little. Send me on, if you must. Just, please, don't drag me back to Durn."

The farm wife's face softened. "How old are you, child?"

Meiglin told her.

In the blistering explosion of argument that followed, she was granted the chance for employment at a cousin's remote, wayside inn.

"It's honest work, child," the farm wife warned. "The tavern isn't fancy. It was built, with due permission, at the edge of the black desert, where it's hard to keep on decent help. The house draws from a well that's declared sacred ground. The tribefolk who tend the site won't tolerate wanton behavior. Not of any kind. The law of their goddess forbids the practice of whoring as unclean."

The crofter just bludgeoned into submission added his own brutal caution. "Those desertfolk aren't to be trifled with, girl. They can skewer a rat at eighty paces with their darts. Tawbas' inn was raised on the ruined foundation left by the last fool, who thought to let the drovers toss his wenches. We'll send you south with a cloak and decent clothes. But don't beg for pity from my kinsman should you stray. Get yourself caught in the hayloft with the grooms, Tawbas will be quick to turn you out. Then it's the waterfront brothels at Innish, for such as you, and belike an early grave at the fist of some drunken galleyman."

Grateful for the upright chance of reprieve, Meiglin took work for a servant's upkeep in the tavern amid the rolling, dark sands of Sanpashir. She swept floors, made beds, boiled linen and did a drudge's chores in the kitchen through the tempestuous years that Tawbas, in his forthright, southland drawl, took to calling the trouble times.

For the Mistwraith that smothered the lands to the west continued its inexorable invasion. The threat no longer seemed distant, or unreal, as inch by hard-fought inch, the northern kingdoms were lost. When the incursion rolled south and encroached on Melhalla, its creeping menace darkened even casual conversation. The looming possibility of a world lost to sunlight cast a pall of gloom over the future. The silk caravans moving from Atchaz to Innish brought news of the relentless defeats. In desperate increments, despite arcane help, the war-tattered remnants of Athera's defenders lost ground.

"The line's broken at Silvermarsh," a south bound merchant announced, wetting his parched throat with ale. "If we're going to grow lean when the harvest is stunted, I say the mayors did right to expunge the old law. A man can't have a pack of murdering clansmen gainsay his right to hunt game inside the free wilds. The farmers will have to plow up new fields. How else can they feed a family?"

"That's a slippery slope to tread," Tawbas said, arms folded over his polishing rag as he leaned on the edge of the bar. "Old law wasn't written for a Sorcerer's whimsy." Desertfolk insisted there was substance to the claim that the land's bounty increased with the unicorns. If their elders spoke truth, the charge given to the clans was not an arbitrary duty, born of high-handed arrogance. "A good deal worse than mist could blight our human fortune, if the ground the old law kept sacrosanct is given to the axe and the plow."

"Perhaps." The mule drover shrugged. "But a cousin of mine

herds sheep out in Vastmark. He's said no Paravians have migrated for years. Spring's come and gone, with no trace of a unicorn's track in the hills. Now, I've heard the uncanny creatures will vanish under the mist. Could be that's a fact, and the clanblood won't admit they've outlived their forefathers' purpose. I say the world's changed, and the mayors should be thanked. They'd do well to exterminate the whole stubborn breed, and open the land for prosperity."

Meiglin filled emptied tankards, quiet as a cat, while the fierce debate swirled around her. The greater trials of town politics were none of her affair. Sun still shone on the sands of Sanpashir. Her ancestry was not known to anyone. She lived each day as it came, unconcerned whether the scourge of the Mistwraith edged farther south, or the ancient magic waned from the countryside. Townborn, town raised, she had no incentive to pursue the arcane obligations of her ancestry. Nor was her parentage safe to disclose. Year after year, the new order waged its feud with ever more murderous ferocity.

Tawbas weathered the turmoil with his usual stoic tolerance, serving all travelers with an even hand, and asking no prying questions. More than once, Meiglin found herself pouring beer for clan survivors who still patrolled the borders of the wilds. They came by night, mantled in dusty, rough clothes, and bearing war-sharpened steel in concealment. They drew water from the well and bartered pelts for supplies in hurried, brisk spoken transactions. As silently they left, hampered in their charge to keep the proscribed lands free of violation.

Here, the blood price that hounded them was still a whispered threat. The tavern was bound under the desert tribes' law. Townsmen shunned the cruel sun and the desolate wastes. They also feared the dartmen, who were ever quick to anger, if a caravan strayed from the trade road.

Anonymously hidden as each season turned, Meiglin grew into striking beauty. Her skin tanned under Sanpashir's harsh sun, rich contrast to her violet eyes and her glossy, seal-brown hair. Wisely, she kept such attributes masked. She wore shapeless clothes and a linen head cloth when she served beer in the taproom. Her vivid smile hidden, she worked honestly and well, slapping off the smitten groping of the drovers, and refusing the tipsy blandishments of the merchants who tried to bedazzle her with their flashy rings. She tended the hens and cracked corn for the mule teams, grateful to stay safely in obscurity.

Yet as time passed, the fey talent born into her heritage refused to keep nondescript silence. Meiglin tossed, sleepless, through each windy spring, as if her blood knew when the centaur guardians escorted the dwindled herds of unicorns through the patterns of their seasonal migration. Her gifts stayed unschooled. No wise one lay at hand to guide the stirrings of her instinct. She had sighted dreams and visions, and not just during hallows, when the ancient rites were danced at the well to raise up the fire of the mysteries. Since she made no complaint, no one troubled to take notice when she arose, hollow-eyed in the morning. She drew water, dawn and dusk, from the mud-brick well, warned by a prickle of prescient gooseflesh when the secretive dartmen watched her out of the shadows.

Their surveillance was so light, they left only tracks, swiftly erased by the winds. Meiglin held no fear of their furtive presence. She had always been diligent, heeding the sanctions that granted Tawbas his right to maintain the tavern. She was never tempted to venture outside after midnight, when the tribefolk gathered to honor their goddess under the change of the moon. Content in her place, she masked her unease when the old women appeared, arrived without sound at her back.

Always, she bowed with her head turned, respectful. Their kind considered a stare rank impertinence. At first, Meiglin brashly offered them help, refilling their goatskin flasks. They smiled, veils lifted, their refusal soft spoken. *"Anshlien'ya,"* they called her, the archaic word for dawn. The nuance of their dialect was lost upon Meiglin. She smiled back and never realized the idiom meant hope.

Always, she presumed the phrase was a blessing, spoken in casual courtesy. A Sorcerer, perhaps, might have told her the truth, that Sanpashir's tribes revered silence. They never addressed anyone, unless their words were of vital importance.

The tavern kept Meiglin too busy for curiosity. As the only respite within two days' ride, the taproom served all comers. Sacred ground demanded that none be turned away. Meiglin poured beer and baked waybread for the travelers. She listened, entranced, to more than one conversation held in the lilted cadence of the old Paravian language. Where such speakers went, and on what obscure business, she was too prudent to ask. She knew nothing of the tongue used for centuries by her forebears, which was a clear blessing. The next hour, like as not, she could be serving a rowdy band of headhunters, seeking trophy scalps for their saddle cloths. Such men rode through increasingly often, as the mayors grew fat from their conquest.

Two trappers who boasted they had poached for game within the free wilds claimed the boldest of the killers had no mercy. "They'll ride down bearing women, even children." Armed parties now scoured deep into the hills to claim the reward for murdered clansmen.

"Greedy fools, every one of them," snapped a merchant dining at the next trestle. "One encounter with the old races, they're sure to go mad."

When the trappers scoffed, the fellow spoke of his grand-uncle. "He camped under a standing stone once, when the unicorns ran under moonlight. Turned him witless in a day. His wife had to spoon feed the wretch till he died, and change his breeches each time he pissed himself. You ask me, the world's mysteries are best left alone. Let the clanborn skulk as they will in the wilds. It's a miserable life their kind lead, anyway, with their witch blood bred to stand uncanny powers, and that curse on the seed of their children."

"I don't fear madness," the trapper declared. His burly companion shrugged also. "The sunchildren are gone out of Selkwood, as well as the centaurs who warded the forest. What cause is left for the clans to gainsay our right to hunt as we wish? We'll pay tax for their head price until they back down, and leave us the run of the country."

For as spring came round again, the rumors agreed. Under the Mistwraith's encroaching shadow, the ancient mysteries appeared to be fading. Paravian presence was increasingly scarce. Town bounties were taking their reiving toll, with the headhunters unafraid to ride out in force, and no centaur guardians to challenge their trespass.

For the first time, in Sanpashir, clan presence was suppressed. The scouts ceased treating with the inn for provisions. They seldom ventured into the open, even to draw from the well. One star-strewn nightfall, on a trip to haul water, Meiglin encountered a red-haired scout wearing a traditional clan braid. The dusk bolstered her courage. For the first time, curiosity overcame her better sense. She ventured to ask after the name that was all her mother had left her.

"He was a friend of my parents," she explained, stumbling over the lie as the scout turned a piercing glance upon her.

"Egan Teir's'Dieneval, *caithdein e'an*?" the clan woman inquired with raised eyebrows. She continued, still speaking in fluent Paravian.

Meiglin forced an awkward smile into a silence of hanging expectancy. "I never studied the ancient tongue," she confessed at self-conscious length.

"No?" The scout shrugged, not offended. "Townborn were you, yes? Or of an outbred clan descent, but too timid to try initiation?" Disinclined to linger for a tiresome explanation, the woman capped her brimming flask. "Then the name and the history of s'Dieneval are no proper business for your ears, I should think."

"Are there kinfolk?" Meiglin pressed.

The scout paused. Her hands hovered forbiddingly close to her weapons, and her weathered features turned grim. "None alive," she admitted, impatient. "If your parents weren't told, the last child of that lineage was slaughtered by the mob that savaged Tirans."

"I didn't know. I'm sorry." Meiglin bent to the task of filling her bucket yoke, then trudged the worn path to the tavern. No kin remained living. The knowledge reassured her. Surely no harm would come if the bloodline she carried was abandoned to nameless obscurity.

"Girl, you're mistaken."

Meiglin started in fierce surprise. An ancient desertman barred her way, his erect, scarecrow figure shrouded in layers of sun-faded robes. His eyes were obsidian, and his face, crinkled leather, and his approach had been eerily soundless. To further her upset, the yoke buckets swung at her jolted stop, and slopped water into the sand.

"Forgive," she murmured, appalled and afraid. The way of the tribes held such waste as a desecration. "Old one, I meant no wrong in your eyes."

"My eyes saw no wrong," the old man stated. The staccato emphasis of his native dialect came measured, and carefully dignified. "A wrong can be forgiven and righted. Yet the waste of a birth gift is not the same." His regard showed reproach. "Daughter," he chided, "Shroud a light in a blanket, it must start a fire. Your dreams will draw notice. Think carefully what you'll do when your talent fully awakens."

Meiglin edged back in denial. "My dreams are just nightmares."

"Ah. And are they, in fact?" The old man did not move aside. He bent down, scooped up the dollop of damp sand and cupped it between seamed brown fingers. "Water speaks truth, child. Here, perhaps, a thorn bush might sprout, that could not have grown but for carelessness. Yet for want of this moisture, somewhere else, another useful plant withers. A seed bears no harvest, and a child, perhaps, starves for the lack of its sustenance. That death in turn may become the one thing that brings on the ruin of a tribe. Worse than that, maybe, if the lost child's destiny was fated. The waste of that life might perhaps come to open the rift that unravels the world."

"Riddles." Meiglin sighed with cautious respect. "I don't understand a word of them."

"You will." The elder restored the damp earth with calm reverence. "Now, like spilled water, your bounty could fall anywhere. When what you are can no longer be masked, you will sprout the seed of its making. But then, heed me, daughter. The crop will be sown, and the choices you have will be few."

Meiglin returned to her duties, distressed. If her bloodline was fated, whom could she ask? Casual questions had become much too dangerous, with the least breath of gossip concerning the clans pursued by the mayors' informants.

Nor could she ponder the desertman's warning. Already the taproom was packed to the rafters with three caravans southbound from Atchaz. Merchants jammed the upstairs, two to a bed, with their dusty assemblage of muleteers and armed outriders grown boisterous with strong beer and boredom. The press and the noise forced the late courier bound for Innish to snatch supper in the inn's kitchen.

Meiglin overheard his ill news, while scouring the stacks of used crockery.

"Oh, you'll see business, come summer," the lean fellow told Tawbas, who had seized respite from the uproarious singing to sit smoking his squat pipe at the trestle. "More than you wish for, no doubt."

The innkeeper grunted. "Prosperity's no bad thing to wish for. But in summer? No civilized man boils his brains in Sanpashir. Not unless he's clanborn, and hunted, or a madman driven by devils."

"Devils indeed," the courier confided. Over the course of his hurried meal, he broke his shattering ill news. The defenders holding the Mistwraith in check had finally broken, at Spire. "Oh yes, there were deaths, a right tragic toll of them." He went on, though Tawbas' complaisant disposition was unlikely to mourn for the fallen. "Shand's liegemen foundered while fording the Ettin, which raged in the throes of spring flood. The High King was lost, and the next heir as well. The survivors are calling the new muster at Firstmark, and trying against hope to regroup. And of course, the Fellowship Sorcerers have summoned the next crown successor from Alland."

"That one better travel more guarded than bullion," Tawbas ventured across a strained pause. His cantankerous pipe had put itself out. Provoked by more than his usual irritation, he fussed over the steps to relight it. "The outpost at Ganish has turned for the mayors. Surely you knew? Best if you don't speak so freely of king's heirs. Desert law rules the road through these wastes, but fanatics still persecute clanblood. I can't risk my inn to vigilante justice. More than one man's had his business burned down for sympathy toward the wrong faction."

"That's why I can't stay," the courier confessed, and the discussion devolved into cut-throat haggling over the cost of a remount.

Meiglin scrubbed pots, chilled by dread thoughts. The sorrow seemed inevitable, that the sun shining over Sanpashir's bleak sands could be lost before summer solstice. If defenses at Firstmark could not be restored, the scourge that had swallowed the rest of the continent might strike through and drown all the world. The last patch of open sky would be gone. Even the southern reaches of Shand would become choked under fog that no Sorcerer's resource might lift.

That night, Meiglin dreamed. Blank billows of mist closed with strangling force, until she choked under a featureless shroud that muffled the landscape in white. Sunless, the greening earth languished. Crops failed, dusted with blight. Animals birthed stillborn offspring. On land and sea, the vigor of life waned away, until the weal of the world was left desolate.

"No!" Meiglin's cry raised a spurt of bright flame, a denouncement that sheared the dank quiet. When the cruel fog tightened its grip in response, she shouted again, and a third time sealed her denial. Horror for all of the land's spoiled grace drove her to desperate resistance. She would not give way, or let go of hope, though the whisper of fate insisted the end held no opening for salvation.

"Words carry power, child," a solemn voice answered, rolling thunder across the sere landscape. "Particularly words that are spoken three times, with heart and mind matched in conviction. Such fire as that creates binding magic."

"Who are you?" Meiglin snapped, too wounded to be cowed by the warning spun through her dream.

"I speak with the voice of the Fellowship Sorcerers, whose will shaped the line of your ancestry. S'Dieneval bears the power of prophecy. Beware how you wish, child. The mysteries are dwindled, not vanished from the world. They still tend the living heart of the earth. The last centaur guardian stands watch in Atainia. He will gather the thread of your steadfast desire. Through his hands, and the inherited ties to your bloodline, you could be claimed as the vessel to enact a far greater charge than you realize."

"I don't care!" The passion that moved Meiglin was already raised, and blazed beyond hope of quenching. "Three times spoken, or thrice three hundred, I won't endure a world plunged into darkness."

No more thunder rolled. The wise voice kept its counsel. Meiglin came softly awake in the garret that held her servant's pallet. No light burned but stars. Beyond the dusty panes of the casement, the night hung in suspended stillness. Meiglin drew in a shaken breath, thick with scent of parched sand, a heat brittle and dry as the scalded air over the coals of a forge fire. No breezes stirred. The earth seemed gripped in hush, the eerie hesitation in time that only occurred when the desert tribes' women held rites at the dark of the moon. Meiglin lay wakeful. Folded into that fabric of silence, she let its deep peace bring her ease. Unschooled as she was, she sensed nothing amiss. Nor did she know to look for the errant, sown seed to bear fruit as the moon swelled into full phase.

That day, when it came, began without fanfare. Meiglin fed the hens and raked out the stables. She kneaded the bread, then shouldered the unending task of washing and hanging out bed linens. Noon saw her gathering in the dry sheets, then serving tables in the close shade of the inn's shuttered taproom. Evening came on. The casements were latched back. A pall seemed to smear the northern horizon, perhaps the first harbinger of the dread mist. Tawbas lingered outside while the afterglow faded, afraid he had seen the last sunrise.

"Dust storm," said the outrider who jingled in after dark. "Just that and no more, though the sky you enjoy here abides on its last, borrowed time." The company at his heels was quite large, arrived as the inn usually closed for the night. The hour that had looked to be slow was made busy, with the trestles crowded to capacity. Meiglin poured beer, washed spoons and filled plates, too engrossed to care if the riders seemed closemouthed, with the odd man among them speaking low-voiced Paravian, or calling for food with the snap of clan accents.

"They're king's men," said Tawbas, too uneasy to smoke in the lull, when the taproom finally emptied. Under reddened light, as the cook banked the fires, he divulged perhaps more than was wise. "It's the crowned heir of Shand, riding to battle the Mistwraith, and not wanting to draw undue notice. He'll take water and provisions and leave before dawn, and not fare by way of the trade road."

"Ah, then they did come cross country?" said the cook, seated at last with her aching feet propped on the settle.

Tawbas nodded. "From the forest of Alland." Which explained why his inn had been visited unawares. No traffic moved between Atchaz and Innish, that the fast-riding couriers did not mark beforehand. "Meiglin," he added, "before you retire, please take the rind of leftover cheese and some bread and ale for the horse master's groom in the stable."

Meiglin fetched out the victuals. Willing to spare the exhausted cook, though too worn to retie her loose hair, she carried the tray through the open, back door, into the moon-washed yard.

The groom her errand charged her to find was not asleep in the hayloft. He had been at the well, stripped down for washing, when the rites of the tribes had displaced him. Lacking a towel, he had lingered outside for the winds to scour him dry. His soaked hair hung in an uncombed tangle. The soiled clothes he had intended to rinse still trailed from nonchalant fingers. He was gazing over the moon-flooded sands, too enthralled by the peace of the open sky to notice he had an observer. There, Meiglin beheld his naked form, bewitched herself by his beauty.

He was clanborn, to judge by the length of his hair, crimped in ripples from their custom of braiding. A creature just barely grown into his manhood, with his broadened shoulders sculpted with muscle, and his hips still boyishly slender. Meiglin froze between steps, the breath caught in her throat. Despite the shocked blush flaming her cheeks, she was unable to stop herself staring.

The inadvertent chink of a tankard betrayed her. The boy turned, all male, his features unveiled by the moonlight. Meiglin cried out with stunned recognition. Dreams had shown her that face, as well as the fate that must darken the course of the future.

"Don't go!" she blurted.

"You've seen me," he accused, as startled as she to discover himself under scrutiny. "You shouldn't. The Fellowship Sorcerers cast a glamour."

Meiglin's reply was unwontedly tart. "You're a bit hard to miss, are you not, in plain sight? And no groom as well, despite your claim to the contrary."

His eyebrows went up. "Then you know who I am?" He glanced, chagrinned, at the clothes in his fingers, too proud to retreat in embarrassment. "The glamour concealed me from everyone else. Are you warded, or just uncommonly fey?"

"I don't carry an amulet." Meiglin lingered, bereft of good sense, just as uselessly unable to recover the courtesy to turn away from the sight of him. His blue eyes held the same brash glint she recalled, touched silver under the moon.

"Don't go," she repeated. "I beg of you, don't. No good will come of your sacrifice."

His attentive gaze sharpened, as though, just that moment, he saw her for what she was. He strode forward. Breeches and shirt dropped from his heedless fingers, with only the tray's width between them. "If you're prophet enough to know who I am, then you'll see why I must go forward."

Meiglin shook her head. "I know nothing," she blurted, "except for your death, should you choose this road's bitter turning."

He regarded her, torn though by his anguish. "I can't go into exile through Westgate! Oh, the other kings' heirs went tamely enough. The Sorcerers were adamant that each royal bloodline should be secured in safety. Yet was I not born, except to stand guard for the soil under my feet? What life could I live, forsaking this ground, and fleeing the charge of my heritage? I am not going to run. This is my place! My crown oath of protection shall not be forsworn while the Mistwraith claims final triumph."

"Don't go," Meiglin begged, wide awake to the peril of words that were spoken thrice over. Yet the same stubborn hope that held him in denial kept her rooted until that fateful third time, he refused.

She dropped the tray. It fell with a crash of smashed crockery at her feet. Before she could bend, or exclaim in dismay, she found herself swept headlong into his arms.

"You'll cut yourself," he murmured in startled distress.

She opened her mouth, intending to chide. His concern was not worth foolish gallantry. Instead, she found herself meeting his kiss. Then his fingers captured the rich fall of her hair. He laid claim to her, there, while the moon shone down upon their twined forms and knotted a binding enchantment. He had silken, clean skin and a stag's rugged strength. The impetuous vitality behind his aware touch left Meiglin no breath for refusal. The spontaneous alchemy wrought by his embrace awoke her untapped, woman's passion.

He came to himself first, pulled back in dismay, and attempted a sensible apology. "Forgive me. You're beautiful. It's my bullish nature, charging ahead without manners. Never mind the broken plates. I'll pick up the mess. Go safely inside and forget me."

Meiglin looked into those moon-touched, clear eyes, possessed as though she was dreaming. Before he could loosen his grip, or stand off, she felt the cold wind from the future blow through, and scatter all prudence before it. "I won't go. Not inside. If the moon and the stars are as precious as that, let the Mistwraith not triumph, at least on this night." Whole hearted, she invited his eager heat. Her hands stroked his living, naked flesh, until she felt his response trample reason.

The warm sands of Sanpashir cradled their lovemaking through that night of wild abandon. They lay, oblivious to all but each other, while the desert tribes' women chanted completion, and danced the rites of full moon at the well.

By sunrise, he was gone, and with him, the name that Meiglin had neglected to ask of him. The throbbing, sweet ache of shared pleasure stayed with her, and a memory as rich as fine wine. That was all, so she thought; her gift nothing more than a comfort exchanged before his demise overtook him.

Except her monthly courses delayed, and then, never came. The queasy stomach that distressed her each morning soon raised the cook's ribald comment.

"Better cozen a wealthy merchant, my dear. A fat one who's older, and bedazzled enough to take you on as a mistress. Or else, sure's frost, the minute you're showing, Tawbas is bound to dismiss you. It's tribal law, did you not understand? The sacred ground of the spring cannot be defiled by lewd acts that offend their barbaric goddess."

Meiglin scrubbed pots, too wretched to argue. The child she carried could not be unmade. More than lust had arranged its conception. Nonetheless, the shame scalded. The uncanny power invoked through her dreams had dealt her an unkindly quandary. Now she faced the selfsame ruin that had undone her mother. The well-meant advice of the cook was no option. Meiglin could not bear the lie, to dizzy some gullible merchant with flirting kisses and flattery. The uglier prospect ran her blood cold, that she might be forced to seek haven at Innish, and earn living wage as a harlot. Though her agonized thoughts showed no better alternative, she refused to consider the herbal decoction the whores used to force an abortion. Bound by full knowledge of what she had done, she could not evade the harsh consequence. The child she harbored was a doomed father's legacy, sown under the shadow of prophecy.

Distraught with dread for her reckoning with Tawbas, Meiglin skulked like a ghost. She kept her head down, and finished the day's chores, one wearing week after the next.

When she went to the well, the desertfolk watched her. Their wise eyes surely read the fact she was bearing long before the first bulge strained her waistline. Once, a wizened matriarch grasped at her sleeve and gave warning in broken dialect.

"Dearie, the spirit you carry makes herself heard. She very well could draw the wrong sort of notice, with our world the more sorrowful for it."

Meiglin fled, her buckets abandoned. No voluminous apron or unbelted shift could shelter her for much longer. Once Tawbas noticed, she would be turned out, with no place to go, and no family name to grant her a stay of protection.

Yet before that momentous crisis could break, the unborn child herself attracted the eyes of an outside awareness. A party of three Koriani enchantresses ventured into Sanpashir, cloaked head to foot in their rich purple mantles, and the secrecy of their order. They traveled without escort, and ate in the common room, all to themselves in one corner. Meiglin felt their rapt gaze as she swept and fetched soup. Even through walls, she was made aware of their piercing, unnatural interest. Retreat to the stable failed to shake their spelled touch. These women with their uncanny arts had not visited the tavern by chance.

Meiglin shed tears in a mare's dusty mane, unable to shake looming dread. Power had found her. The gifts of her lineage were too brilliant to mask, and her straits left her desperately vulnerable.

Through the blinding heat of the late afternoon, the elder enchantress drew Tawbas aside and tried to buy Meiglin's service.

By then, Meiglin kneaded fresh dough in the kitchen. She heard the low-voiced exchange nonetheless, caught up in somnolent reverie.

"Your serving girl has fey blood, were you made aware when you took her in?" The senior with the red bands of rank on her sleeves went on to disclose the bald truth. "She dreams with the voice of a prophet."

Tawbas had not known. Nor was he at ease to find he had sheltered a clan foundling with errant talent.

The old woman conferred amid a rustle of silk robes. "We can pay, and quite well, for the privilege of taking the chit into Koriani fosterage."

Plainspoken Tawbas seemed lost for words, but not to the point of grasping the offer dishonestly. "She's not my kin, but only a hireling. In fairness, Meiglin should speak for herself."

Summoned forthwith, and granted the courtesy of a private room for the interview, Meiglin stood under the austere scrutiny of the sisterhood of enchantresses. The women measured her from under their hoods with the covetous interest of vultures.

They wasted no breath. "Your child will be born a mage-gifted girl. Come with us, take an initiate's oath with our order, and you can bear her with honor, in safety."

"And then?" Meiglin asked, uncertain and frightened. "What would become of us, after?"

The enchantresses stirred, as though touched by a breeze. The youngest of them offered answer. "Your daughter would be raised by the order, with all of her gifts given nurture. You are past the age to be trained to our arts, a sad loss, but not beyond salvage. Your life as a dedicate would be well spent in charitable service to humanity."

Meiglin met those unswerving, stony eyes, and found them darkened with secrets. "What aren't you telling me?"

"Initiates cannot be mothers," their senior admitted with arid impatience. "Our vows require us to renounce ties to family. Join us, and you and your child will never want. But your lives, by our custom, must be separate."

Ripped by formless doubt, as inflamed by headstrong will as she had been on the night she lay wanton under the moonlight, Meiglin straightened. "No. Keep your fee. I'll take my chances with Tawbas."

"He must turn you out," the crone warned, set back and sharply displeased. "Our scryers have already foreseen that future. It's a miserable, short life in the brothels of Innish, and no lot to inflict on a daughter who's sure to inherit the gifts of your bloodline."

"No," Meiglin stated, and then, "no," again, to seal her adamant rejection.

The Koriathain stood. Before they could move, or lock the closed door, Meiglin ducked past, her heart pounding. She would not turn back. The mere thought scared her white. She had experienced such jagged panic before: the same avarice had glittered in the eyes of the madam who had sold out her mother to bountymen.

"Girl!" snapped the cook, as Meiglin bolted through the kitchen. "Are you brainless? Would you spit in contempt at the only chance you'll ever have at salvation?"

"I'll not live in oath-bound confinement!" Meiglin plunged through the side door, clambered over the midden, and fled at reckless speed across the baked earth of the hen yard. She slammed the wicket gate, wrung breathless as the sun blazed down on her uncovered head, and her composure finally shattered.

She stumbled, blindly sobbing, and collided headfirst into the arms of a stranger.

"You've no wish to take vows as a Koriani witch? Truly, my colleagues thought you might not." The old man smelled of wild herbs and wood smoke, as though he had slept in his robes by a fire out in the open. His manner reflected astringent delight as he set her back on her feet. "If you like, we could make that the grounds for a friendly conversation."

Meiglin gasped. Released from a touch of such subtlety, she scarcely felt discomposed, she blotted her eyes, and regarded the being who addressed her with wry invitation.

"That depends on what you want." She raked tumbled hair from her face, unsettled enough to stay wary.

"Have I acted disreputable?" The old man looked chagrinned. "In strict fact, young mistress, your will binds mine. Any words we exchange depend on what you want, lastborn daughter of s'Dieneval."

Struck still, Meiglin stared. "Who are you?" she whispered. But the uncanny reach of his presence spoke for him. Without asking, she *knew*: this was no desert elder before her, although his brown, crinkled skin and salt hair lent him the same air of earth-chiseled dignity. His clothes were a tinker's, loomed from faded wool, and the lavender-gray mantle rolled on his back seemed to hold his scanty possessions. Nonetheless, he was no feckless wanderer. Meiglin's skin prickled before the awareness that those quiet, pale eyes looked straight through her.

Here stood living power, a force of pent stillness masked over in gentleness that could, if it moved, shift the world.

"You come from the Fellowship," Meiglin said in blanched shock. The Sorcerer raised amused eyebrows. "Did you expect less?" His eyes surveyed her, thoughtful, their tawny depths mild as sunlight struck through the shallows of a brook. "We are our own emissaries. As you wish, you may call me Ciladis."

Meiglin measured that statement, still taken aback by his unprepossessing appearance. Fellowship Sorcerers had made the first kings, were the power behind the compact that bound the clan forefathers into Paravian service. The blood heritage she had refused to acknowledge could not be evaded before such as he.

Meiglin stood dumbstruck, scarcely able to think.

Still gentle, he broke the silence for her. "Shall I give you the truth that the witches withheld? You will give birth to the child of a prophecy. In sorrow, I must tell you, the choice upholding that burden is great. Already, your unborn daughter is fatherless."

As though the firm ground had dissolved underfoot, Meiglin trembled, the pain a bright arrow struck through her. The name of the boy she had loved had not mattered. One night, he had touched her. Now, all her days, her sorrow must endure, a grief that would never be partnered. "He's lost so soon?"

The Sorcerer's hands caught and steadied her, then guided her unbalanced steps toward the shade. "Last night, he passed over. Your dream did not lie. Beside you, my Fellowship mourns for him."

Meiglin permitted herself to be set down on the stone wall that cut the stiff breeze off the desert. "The Mistwraith will triumph," she whispered, bereft.

The Sorcerer could not change that desolate fact. "Yet even defeat does not mean we are lost. The future could hold a last chance of reprieve, one spark upon which to build hope. The royal lineage of Shand is not ended. Because of your courage, a successor remains. She's the daughter you're carrying, Meiglin."

Hands closed over the swell of her womb, Meiglin found herself desperately shaking.

Ciladis' sure fingers laced over her own. "Here." His clasp affirmed what she had known all along, that this one precious life could become the lynchpin that hung the world's destiny.

"There's more," said the Sorcerer, as though his quizzical gaze tracked her thoughts. "Your child also bears the blood of s'Dieneval, a line that has served at the right hand of kings for more than a thousand years. That's a rather hair-raising legacy. In fact, she's twice endowed with precocious talent, a fix that could drive my six colleagues to fits, and bedevil her future descendents."

His irreverent humor sparked Meiglin to laughter. "You're warning me she'll be a trial to raise?"

Ciladis still chuckled. "Very. Does that knowledge please you? It should. I have come, because as the mother of royalty, you're entitled to ask for my help."

The words, foreordained, ripped through Meiglin like storm. "I would do anything, all that you ask, to deny the Mistwraith its conquest. Under such a binding, this child was conceived. I will name her Dari when she is born. Now tell me the fate that is best for her."

The Sorcerer smiled with forthright relief. "Dari s'Ahelas she must become, if you grant your consent to acknowledge her paternal birthright. Raise her in love, Meiglin. The Fellowship will provide you the means. If, when the time comes, you are still sincere, your daughter must be offered the path her wayward father rejected."

"Exile through Westgate?"

Ciladis nodded. "For safety's sake. If she chooses to go, if she shoulders the weight of her royal heritage, she must make her way in free will."

"She will go," Meiglin whispered. The tears burned her lids and spilled over again, for a love she had held for one moment, and lost. "Had her father done the same, I would never have lain with him, and he would still be alive."

The Sorcerer raised a fingertip to her brow, testing, that light touch all he needed be reassured of her steadfast commitment. "Meiglin," he stated. "Your courage is blessed. Did you know, your true heart may yet forge the path that will hold the light for the future?"

⋘ The Afterlife of St. Vidicon ⋙ of Cathode

A Warlock Story

Christopher Stasheff

With thanks to Morris McGee,
honorary Father-General, and to Laurie Patten,
honorary Mother Superior of the Order of Cassettes.

(INTRODUCTION)

The abbot waited in the convent's audience chamber, fascinated by the beauty drawn from its flat planes and minimal furniture by the glow of waxed golden paneling, the vivid color of the spray of flowers in a ceramic vase of elegant simplicity, and the two pictures adorning the walls, lighted by the windows opposite— an old woman next to a young on the wall facing the bench on which he sat, and on the wall at his left, the cowled face of a man in middle age, his brooding expression softened by the twinkle in his eye. If he was the man the abbot suspected, the artist had caught his character perfectly, leaving an elegant legacy to her successors. The whole room spoke of the care and devotion of the women of the Order, and of their dedication to their vocation.

The door opened to admit a woman of his own age, no longer slender, but with a kind though firm look to her eyes. The abbot rose in deference.

"Sit, please, my lord," the nun said with a slight frown. "Surely the abbot of the Order of St. Vidicon should not stand to a mere nun."

"Any gentleman should stand when a lady enters a room." But the abbot sat as she bade. "Certainly the abbot should show respect for the Mother Superior of the Order of Cassettes."

"I am only Sister Paterna Testa, a simple nun like all my sisters," the woman said primly. "As you know, my lord, we are not officially sanctioned nor formally an Order, so our leaders have never claimed such a title."

"If it comes to titles, I am not a lord," the abbot said with a smile of amusement. "I am a peasant, the son of peasants."

"Then you do not use the title when you speak with dukes and earls?" Sister Paterna Testa was skeptical.

"I will admit to that much of worldly vanity," the abbot said without the slightest sign of contrition. "I cannot risk their contempt when I berate them for their treatment of their peasants, after all."

"I have heard that you do just that," Sister Paterna Testa said, "when most of your predecessors rarely emerged from their monastery, and then only by royal summons."

"Or in outrage at the actions of the monarch." The abbot nodded. "It has seemed to me that if I remonstrate with the lords, or even Their Majesties, while their sins are still minor, I may be able to prevent the growth of conditions great enough that I am forced to speak in indignation."

"And so it has occurred, from what rumor tells me." Sister Paterna Testa nodded. "So are you come to remonstrate with me, and demand that my Order be brought within your jurisdiction?"

"Heaven forfend!" The abbot raised his palms as though to ward off a horror. "But it does seem to me that the only two Orders in the land should be in communication, and that your Order should be officially recognized as being in every way the equal of mine."

"That is quite generous," Sister Paterna Testa said slowly, "but we have managed well for centuries without such recognition—indeed, without your knowledge. How did you learn of us?"

"Word of your aiding the High Warlock and the High Witch might have been kept to yourselves," the abbot said with a smile, "but not news of the battle you fought to aid him. Minstrels have spread the tale throughout the length and the breadth of the land, so it finally reached even my ears."

"Minstrels! I like not the sound of that." Sister Paterna Testa turned away, frowning. "The Queen shall no doubt summon us now to be sure we count ourselves her vassals."

"She is more likely to summon you to heal those sunk in melancholy or beset by delusions," the abbot said, "but no matter her motive, it would strengthen your position to be officially constituted, and recognized by the Pope."

"I had heard that His Holiness had finally found Gramarye." Sister Paterna Testa turned her frown back to the abbot.

"He has, but felt it sufficient to leave us to the ministrations of the Father-General of our Order," the abbot said.

"Then we stand on quicksand," Sister Paterna Testa said, "for we have no abbess or mother-general."

"Quite so," said the abbot, "since there is no Order of Cassettes anywhere but in this convent, whereas the Order of St. Vidicon has chapter houses on every Terran-colonized planet."

"We have as firm a claim to his founding as have you!"

"I do not doubt it," said the abbot, "and you thereby have as good a claim to exist as in independent Order, subject only to the Holy Father."

Sister Paterna Testa knit her brows, searching his eyes for duplicity and finding none. Slowly, then, she said, "How could we prove such a claim, though? The Vatican will scarcely accept our unsupported word."

"This picture will support your claim by itself." The abbot nodded at the painting of the monk. "If it matches photographs in the archives of our Order, few can gainsay you. It is painted from life, is it not?"

"From memory, at least." Sister Paterna Testa turned to the portrait. "It was drawn by the young woman who became our second leader, some years after the visitation of the monk who saved her, and our founder. He would not say his name, though."

"Yet he told you tales of St. Vidicon that we know not," the abbot said, "or so the minstrels have even sung—that you have knowledge of the Saint that we have not."

"So that is why you have come!" Sister Paterna Testa turned back to him, amused. "You mean to trade your support for our knowledge, is that it?"

"Our support will be freely given if you will have it." It was the abbot's turn to be prim.

"And you expect our knowledge to be freely given also?" Sister Paterna Testa asked with a trace of irony. "Well, it shall be so, for we believe that knowledge should be free to all who wish to learn it."

"I have seen your school for the peasant children, and it is elegant proof of that claim," the abbot said. "If you wish to share, I shall not refuse."

"Be skeptical," Sister Paterna Testa warned him. "This may be only tales of imagination, that some gifted nun made up to while away a winter's evening for her sisters—and if it is, I am sure it has gained episodes from other tellers as the winters have rolled."

"Or it could indeed be words left to you by that monk." The abbot nodded at the portrait. "I promise I shall not be credulous, sister, for who could know the events that befell the Saint *after* his death?"

"Only one inspired by St. Vidicon himself," Sister Paterna Testa sighed, "or one who delighted in imagining what befell the Foe of Perversity in the afterlife. You remember how St. Vidicon died?"

"Who does not?" the abbot asked. "Though it is hard for any of us to believe that a world so full of people as Old Earth could be so blinded by prejudice and ignorance as to seek to obliterate the Roman Catholic Church."

"Impossible though it seems, our traditions speak of it."

The abbot nodded. "We have histories of Terra that testify to it, ones brought by our ancestors when they came to this world—and not Church histories only, but also those by lay scholars, non-Catholics, agnostics, and even an atheist."

"Do you really?" Sister Paterna Testa looked up with interest. "Do they also tell that only a speech by our Holy Father the Pope was able to save the Church?

"They do indeed, for apparently he was an extremely charismatic speaker."

"But how could the whole world hear him?'

"You must promise me not to speak of this to any outside our Orders," the abbot admonished, "and swear your nuns to silence, too, for we do not wish the people of Gramarye to be contaminated by too much knowledge of advanced technology."

"Even so was the wish of our ancestors, though I sometimes question their wisdom," Sister Paterna Testa said. "Well, as you ask, I shall promise. How was it done?"

"By a magical instrument called 'television,' by which the picture of the Holy Father was projected into every living room on the planet," the abbot said, "or at least those who chose to see it—and since the issue was hotly debated, more than half the planet watched. Certainly all the Catholics did, and the fallen-away Catholics, of whom there were many, many more."

"And St. Vidicon was responsible for maintaining this magic spell?"

"This electronic miracle, let us say," the abbot answered. "It was he who was the engineer who oversaw the operation of the transmitter—but the instrument was old and faulty, and kept burning out resistors and failing."

"So he took the place of that resistor," Sister Paterna Testa said in awe.

"He did indeed, and the Pope's speech was heard through to the end," the abbot said. "Fallen-away Catholics came flooding back into the churches, and the world's governments saw that they could not rule against so very many of their citizens—so the Church was saved."

"But Father Vidicon was dead," Sister Paterna Testa whispered.

The abbot nodded. "The electrical fire that had burned out the resistors, also burned out his life. He was declared a saint within the year, for none could doubt that he was a martyr for the Faith."

"None could," Sister Paterna Testa agreed, "though by the time the Pope declared his knowledge, many miracles had already saved those who called upon the Saint for aid."

The abbot nodded. "Any who worked with magical equipment, even as Father Vidicon had."

"Of course." Sister Paterna Testa smiled. "By the time they called upon him, St. Vidicon had already bested the worst of the spirits that plague humankind with the urge to fail, and thereby turn their own devices against them."

"What spirits were those?" The abbot leaned forward, the intensity of his hunger for learning finally unveiled. "How did Father Vidicon defeat them?"

Sister Paterna Testa laughed softly, then began the tale.

(ENDING)

"So our Order was founded by one who served as the channel for Creation?" the abbot asked, his eyes alight with the glory of the tale.

"So the tales say." Sister Paterna Testa's eye twinkled. "But would it not be a victory for Finagle if we were to believe such a tale as might be made up by a nun with a wild imagination?"

"Or by a priest like our own Father Ricci, his was not above a prank or two." The abbot grinned, sharing her amusement. "Well, Sister, when I write down this account, I shall caution all who read it to take it as pure imagination—an amusing tale only, but one that illustrates Father Vidicon's essential nature."

"Which is?"

"Devout, but with a sense of humor—and a huge enjoyment of irony, and a delight in solving paradoxes." The abbot throttled back his amusement and nodded. "Have no fear, Sister—this tale may not be true, but it is an inspiration."

"Indeed—for any member of your order must be an engineer before he can become a monk, is that not so?"

"It is."

"Then how shall we claim descent from St. Vidicon?" Sister Paterna Testa demanded. "We are not engineers, after all, but teachers and healers."

"Healers of the human mind," the abbot pointed out, "and I cannot help but think, Sister Paterna Testa, that so complex an entity as the brain must easily be liable to as much confusion and paradox as any computer."

Now Sister Paterna Testa smiled with her full warmth, face radiant as she leaned forward and rested her hand on his. "Trust me, Father Abbot—it surpasses them all."

When that the blessed Father Vidicon did seize upon a high-voltage line and did cleave unto it, aye, even unto death, so that the words of our blessed Holy Father the Pope might reach out through the satellites to all the television transmitters of the world, for the saving of our most Holy and Catholic Church—aye, when that he did thus die for the Faith and did pass into one enduring instant of blinding pain, he was upheld and sustained by the knowledge that, dying a martyr, he would pass straightway to Heaven and be numbered among the Blest.

How great was his dismay, then, to find himself, as the pain dimmed and awareness returned, falling through darkness, amidst a cold that did sear his soul. Distantly did he espy certain suns, and knew thereby that he did pass through the Void, and that his eternal fall was not truly so, but was only the absence of gravity. Indeed, he knew the place for an absence of all, and fear bit his soul—for thus, he knew must Hell be: a place of lacking, of absence of being.

Then, in his terror, did he cry out in anger, "My God! For Thee did I give my life! Wherefore hast thou doomed me?" Yet no sooner were the words said than he did repent, and cursed himself for a faithless fool, thus to doubt even now in death, that the Christ would uphold him.

And straightway on the heels of that thought, came the shock of insight—for he saw that, if he did die to cheat the Imp of the Perverse, defeating Finagle himself by his very perversity, he must needs expect reversal of expectation—which is to say that, if he died expecting the vistas of Heaven, he would most certainly discover the hollowness of Hell.

Then courage returned, and resolution; for he did come to see that the struggle was not ended, but only begun anew—that if he did desire Heaven, he would have to win to it. Then did he wonder if even the saints, they who dwelt in God, could count their toils ended—or if they chose eternally to struggle 'gainst greater forces.

Then did his Mission become clear to him, and the blessed knew wherefore he had come to this Void. The enemy 'gainst whom he had striven throughout his life, endured still—and now would Father Vidicon confront him, and look upon his face.

With the thought, his fall slowed, and he saw the mouth of a tunnel ope in the darkness before him, and it did glow within, a sullen red. Closer it did come, and wider, stretching and yawning to swallow him; yet Father Vidicon quailed not, nor tried to draw back. Nay, bravely he stood, stalwart in nothingness; yea, even eagerly did he strain forward, to set foot upon infirm, fungoid flesh and stride into Hellmouth.

As he strode, the sullen glow did brighten, gaining heat until he feared it would sear his flesh, then remembered that he had none. Brighter and hotter it flowed, until he turned thorough a bend in its tube, and found himself staring upon the Imp of the Perverse.

Gross it was, and palpable, swollen with falsehood and twisted with paradoxes. Syllogisms sprouted from its sides, reaching toward Father Vidicon with complexes of bitterness, and it stood but did not stand, on existential extensions.

"Turn back!" roared the Imp, in awesome sardonicism. "Regress, retrograde! For none can progress that do come within!"

"Avaunt thee!" cried Father Vidicon. "For I know thee of old, bloody Imp! 'Tis thou who dost drive every suicide, thou who dost strengthen the one arm of the Bandit who doth rob the gambler compulsive, thou who dost bring down freezing snow upon the recumbent form of the will-leached narcotic! Nay, I know thee of old, and know that he who retreats from thee, must needs pursue thee! Get THEE behind ME—for I shall surpass thee!"

"Wilt thou, then?" cried the Imp. "Then look to thy defense—for I shall undo thee!"

Then a great calm came upon the Blessed One, and he slowly stood straight, smiling gently and saying, "Nay, I shall not—for I know now that to become defensive is to bend the sword so that it strikes against thyself. Nay, I shall not defend, but offend!" And so saying, he leaped upon the Imp, striking out with his fist.

But the Imp raised up a shield, a plane of white metal, flat as a fact and bare as statistics, and polished to so high a gloss that it might not have existed. "See!" cried the Imp, full of glee. "See the monster thine offense hath wrought!"

And staring within, Father Vidicon did behold a face twisted with hatred, tortured with self-doubt, bare-faced as a lie and bound by the Roman collar of law.

Yet the Blessed One did not recoil. Nay, he did not so much as hesitate to question himself or his cause; only, with a voice filled with agony, did he cry, "Oh my Lord! Now preserve me! Give me, I beg of Thee, some weapon against the wiles and malice of the Imp's Shield of Distortion!"

He held up his hands in supplication—and Lo! In his left, a blade did appear, gleaming with purity, its edge glittering with exquisite monofilament sharpness—and in the Blessed One's palm, its handle nestled, hollow to the blade folded.

The imp sneered in laughter and cried, "See how they master doth requite thee! In exchange for thy life, he doth grant thee naught but a slip of a blade, which could not pierce so much as a misapprehension!"

"Not so," cried Father Vidicon, "for this Razor is Occam's!"

So saying, he slashed out at the shield. The Imp screamed and cowered away—but the Blessed One pursued, slicing at the Shield of Distortion and crying, "Nay, thou canst not prevail! For I could have wasted eternity wondering where the fault lay in me, that could so twist my face and form into Evil! Yet the truth of it is shown by this Razor as it doth cleave this Shield!"

So saying, he swung the blade, and it cleaved the Shield in twain, revealing hidden contours, convexities and concavities of temporizing and equivocating. The Imp screamed in terror and the Blessed One cried,

" 'Tis not my image that is hideous, but thy shield that is warped!"

Dropping its shield, the Imp spun away, whirling beyond Father Vidicon, to flee toward the Outer Dark.

Filled with righteous rage, the Blessed One turned to follow it—but he brought himself up short at a thought; for 'twas almost as though a voice spoke within him, saying, *Nay! Thou must not seek to destroy, for thus thou wouldst become thyself an enemy of Being. Contain only, and control; for the supporting of Life will lead Good to triumph; but the pursuit of Destruction in itself doth defeat good!*

The Blessed One bowed his head in chagrin—and there, even there in the throat of hell, did he kneel and join his hands in penitence. "Pardon, my Master, that in my weakness, I would have forgotten the commandment of thine example." And he held up the Razor on his open palm, praying, "Take again the instrument wrought for Thee by Thy faithful servant William—for I need it not, now. For thou, oh God, art my strength and my shield; with Thee, I need naught."

Light winked along the length of the blade, and it was gone.

Father Vidicon stood up then, naked of weapons and solitary in his feelings; yet his heart was light and his resolution was strengthened. "Whither Thou wilt lead me, my Lord," he murmured, "I will go; and with what adversaries thou shalt confront me, I shall contend."

So saying, he strode forth down the throat of Hell; but the song that rose to his lips was a psalm.

St. Vidicon strode bravely onward though the throat of Hell. Having routed the Imp of the Perverse, he did not seek escape, but strode ahead in answer to the Call he felt, the new vocation the Lord had given him.

But as he went, the crimson of the walls about him darkened down toward ruby, then darkened further still, toward purple. Protuberances began to rise up from the floor, each taller than the last, excrescences that did stand upon slender stalks as high as his waist. Then did their tips begin to broaden and to swell, until he saw that, every few paces, he did pass a glowing ball that stood by his hip. And he did see a strip upon the ceiling that did widen, with decorations that did glow upon it, curliques and arabesques. It sprouted chandeliers, and square they were, or rectangular; and they did hang down from chains at each corner. Yet neither were they chains, but cables, or aye, rods. "These are like to tables," Father Vidicon did muse, "tables inverted." Then he noticed that a bulge, extruding from the ceiling, did broaden out, then sprouted up upon a side. The good Father Vidicon frowned and bethought him, " 'Tis like unto a chair." And it was, in truth.

Thus did the Saint realize that he did pace upon the ceiling of a hallway, with a strip of carpet Oriental, and with chairs and tables hanging up above his head. And lo! He did pass by a mirror set into the wall, that did glow with the maroon of the wall across from it; and as he did step past, he saw himself inverted, with chest and hip vanishing upward. He squeezed his eyes shut and shook his head, to rid himself of the sight; and when he did ope his eyes he did see that the walls now did flow past him toward his front; indeed, the mirror did slide past a second time, from back to fore. With every step he took, the walls went farther past, and dizziness did claim him. Then did thrills of danger course throughout his nerves, for he saw that he had come upon a region of inversion, where all was upside down, and progress turned to regress; where every step forward took him two steps backward, and all was opposite to how it should have been. "I near the Demon," he bethought himself, and knew that he came nigh the spirit of illogic.

Yet the Saint perceived that he could not approach that spirit, unless it chanced that he might discover some way to progress. He stopped; the motion of the wall stopped with him, as it should; and Father Vidicon did grin with delight, then took one step backward. In truth, the wall did then move from front to back. He laughed with joy, and set off, walking backward. The mirror slid past him again, going from the front then toward the back, as was fit and proper. So thus, retreating ever, Father Vidicon went onward toward the Spirit of Contrariness.

And lo! The Spirit did come nigh, though he moved not; for he stood, arms akimbo, feet apart, smiling at Father Vidicon as he watched the good Saint come; and the Spirit's eyes were shielded behind two curving planes of darkness. From head to foot he was clothed in khaki, aye even to his shirt, where it did show between lapels, and his necktie was of brown. Clean-shaven he was, and long-faced, smiling with delight full cynical, and crowned with a cap high-peaked, with a polished visor, and insigniae did gleam upon his shoulder boards.

Then Father Vidicon did halt some paces distant, filled with wariness, and quoth he, "I know thee, Spirit—for thou art Murphy!"

But, "Nay," quoth the Spirit, "for any trace of any person who dwells in thy real world hath been swallowed up in the mythic figure that hath grown of its own accord and become myself. I am not Murphy, therefore, but someone else by that same name."

Father Vidicon's face did darken then. "Deceive me not. Thou it is who hath enunciated that fell principle by which all human projects come to doom."

"The doom's within the doer," the Spirit answered. "How may I exorcise it? Nay, 'tis they who bring it out, not I."

"Thou speakest false, fell foe!" Father Vidicon did cry. "Well dost thou know the wish to fail is buried deep in most and, left to lie, would sleep quiescent. 'Tis thou dost invest each mortal, thou who dost nurture and encourage that doom-laden wish!

But the Spirit's smile remained, untouched. "If I do, what boots it? Wouldst thou truly blame me for encouragement?"

"For nurture of foul folly, aye! As thou wouldst know, if thou didst not look upon the world through thy fell filters of Inversion!" Thereupon did Father Vidicon leap forth to seize those darkened lenses of the Spirit, to rip away the shadow's shades, crying, "Look not through your glasses, darkly!"

They came away within his hand, yet not only those dark lenses, but all the face, peeling off the Spirit's head like shriveled husk, exposing there within, a mass of hair.

Father Vidicon gazed on the coiffure, stunned.

Slowly, then, the Spirit turned, hair sliding aside to show another face. Hooded eyes now gazed upon the Saint, darkened indeed, but not in frames; for his eyes were naught but frosted glass, and his twisting mouth a grinning grimace.

Father Vidicon did swallow thickly, and looked down into his hands, where he beheld the back side of the empty face. "Truth," he cried, "I should have thought! Thou hast backward worn thy wear!"

But the Spirit chortled then, "Not so! Behold my buskins!"

Then Father Vidicon looked down and found the Spirit spoke in sooth. The back sides of his shoes were there, and his toes did point away upon the other side. "Alas!" the good Saint cried, "What boots it?" Then up he raised his gaze and did declare, "Thy head's on backwards!"

"In sooth." The Spirit grinned. "Wouldst thou expect aught else?"

"Nay, surely!" Father Vidicon now clamped his haw and folded all his features in a frown. "I should have known! Thou art the jaundiced Janus."

"Two-faced in truth," the Spirit did agree.

"That thou art not! Truth there cannot be in him who's two-faced. Thy hinder face was false!"

"What else?" The Spirit shrugged. "Yet canst thou be sure of the falsehood of that face? Mayhap another countenance doth lie beneath my hair, and I have truly eyes behind, as well as those before."

"Nay, that sight must be seen," the Saint then said, and looking up to Heaven he did pray: "Good Father, now forgive that in my false pride and folly I did think myself so fit for fighting such fell foes. I pray Thee now Thine aid to give, and send me here a weapon to withstand this Worker of our Woe!"

But the Spirit chuckled. "What idle plea is this? What instrument could the Patron place in thy palm, that could reverse the perverse?"

A spark of light did gleam within the good priest's hand, glaring and glowing into glass, and Father Vidicon help up a mirror.

His foe laughed outright. "What! Wilt thou then fight the Spirit of Defeat with so small a service?"

"Aye," quoth Father Vidicon, "if it shows truly."

"Nay—for it is '*darkly*,' though a glass. Dost thou not recall?"

But Father Vidicon held up the mirror to reflect the Spirit's face into his eyes.

"Nay, I have another," then it cried. Its arm slipped backward into its inner pocket, and did whisk out another glass, a foot or more in width, and opposed it to the plate the good Saint held, reflecting back reflections into the Reverend's regard.

"It will not serve!" the good priest cried; and even as he spoke, his mirror grew to half against the size of the Spirit's, throwing back into the Spirit's eyes the sight of its own face with a glass beside it, within which was his face within a glass, and within it a smaller image of his face beside a glass, within which was his face beside a smaller glass, and so on until the reflection was too small to see. The Spirit shrieked and yanked his own glass aside away; but his image held within the priest's reflector.

" 'Tis too late to take away!" the good priest cried. "Dost thou not see thou hast begun a feedback uncontrolled?

And so it was.

"It cannot serve!" the Spirit wailed. "*No* feedback can sustain without a power input!"

"I have the Input of the greatest Power that dost exist," the Saint explained with quiet calm. "All power in the Universe doth flow from this one Source!"

The mirror grew still brighter, within each other's view—brighter then and brighter, white-hot, flaring, burning up the image of the imp, and as his image burned, did he. For, "In truth," quoth Father Vidicon, "he was naught *but* image."

So, with wailing howl, the Spirit frayed and dwindled, shimmering, burned to tatters, and was gone.

"So, at bottom, he was, at most, a hologram," Father Vidicon mused, "and what was formed by mirrors, can by them be undone."

He laid the glass that had swallowed the Spirit most carefully on its face and, folding his hands, cast his gaze upward. "Good Lord, I give Thee thanks that Thou hast preserved Thine unworthy servant a second time, from such destruction! I pray Thee only that Thou wilt vouchsafe to me the strength of soul and humility that I will need to confront whatever adversary Thou wilt oppose to me."

The mirror winked, and glimmered, and was gone.

Father Vidicon gazed upon the place where it had been, and sighed. "I thank Thee, Lord, that Thou hast heard me. Preserve me, thus, I pray, 'gainst all other hazards that my hover."

So saying, then, he sighed himself with the Cross, and stood, and strode on further down toward Hell.

Long did St. Vidicon stride onward down that darkly ruddy throat, 'til he began to tire—then heard a roar behind him, rising in pitch and loudness as though it approached. Looking back, he saw an airplane approaching, the propeller at its nose a blur. He stared, amazed that so large an object could navigate so small a space, then realized that it was a model. Further, he realized that it swooped directly at him, as shrewdly as though it had been aimed. "Duck and cover!" he cried, and threw himself to the floor, arms clasped over his head. The aircraft snored on past him, whereupon he did look up to remark upon it, but heard the pitch of its propeller drop and slow as the craft did lower, then touch its wheels to the palpitating deck and taxi to a halt, its propeller slowing until it stopped.

Father Vidicon stared in wonder, then frowned; it seemed to much a coincidence, too opportune, that a conveyance should present itself when he was wearied. Still, a machine was a challenge he could not ignore; the thrill of operating a strange device persisted even after life; so he did quicken his steps until he stood beside a fuselage not much longer than himself, with an open cockpit into which he might squeeze himself—and so he did.

Instantly the propeller kicked into motion, in seconds blurring to a scintillating disk, and the aircraft lurched ahead, bouncing and jogging till it roared aloft and shot onward down that darkling throat. St. Vidicon, no stranger to ill chance, searched for a seat belt, but there was none, and shivered with the omission. The plane's arrival might be mere chance, the lack of a seat belt might be only coincidence, but he braced himself for a third unpleasant occurrence.

Sure enough, the engine coughed, then sputtered, then died; he stared in horror at a propeller that slowed to a halt. Galvanized by ill fortune, he seized the wheel, set his feet to the rudder pedals, and glanced at his gauges. No, there was fuel enough, so he dealt with malfunction.

Enough! The plane did tilt downwards, rushing toward that obscene and jellied floor. Father Vidicon did haul back upon the wheel, and the nose tilted upward again. Relying on what little he'd read, he held his wing flaps down, keeping the airplane's nose upward as the craft settled. It struck that fleshly floor with as much impact as though it had hit upon asphalt; it bounced, then struck again, bounced again, and so, by a series of bounces, slowed until at last it came to rest.

Father Vidicon clambered down from that falsely welcoming cockpit, telling himself sternly that never again would he operate a machine that he had not inspected—for once may have been accident and twice coincidence, but this third time was definitely enemy action.

But which enemy?

There was as yet insufficient data for a meaningful conclusion. Staggering for his first few steps, then stabilizing to stride, he made his way onward down that darkling throat, lit only by the luminescence of certain globular growths upon the walls.

An object loomed before him, at first dim and indistinct in the limited light, then becoming clear—and Father Vidicon stared upon a scaled-down Sherman tank, a treaded fortress scarcely higher than his shoulder, that sat in the middle of the tunnel as though waiting for him, though in friendly fashion, for its cannon pointed ahead.

The Blessed One reminded himself that he had but minutes before promised himself never to drive a mechanism unverified, so he examined the treads most carefully, then opened the engine compartment and scrutinized the diesel. Satisfied that nothing was defective—ready but wary—he set foot upon a tread, climbed up, and descended through the hatch.

The slit above the controls showed him that dim-lit tunnel. He sat before it, grasped the levers to either side, and pushed them forward quite carefully. The tank cranked, then coughed, then clanked into motion. Warily, though, Father Vidicon held its speed to crawling, not much faster than he could walk. His gain was that he could travel sitting down, but in truth 'twas the thrill of adventure in operation a device hitherto unknown.

So he went grinding down that tunnel, allowing a little more speed, then a little more, until he was traveling at a pace quite decent— 'til a sudden crash did sound upon his right and the tank did slew about. At once Father Vidicon did throttle down and the tank slowed dutifully—but slewed as it slowed, and Father Vidicon realized that he swinging about and about in a circle.

He pulled back on the levers, killed the engine, then clambered out of the hatch, setting foot down onto the right tread—and found nothing there beneath his step. He froze, then levered himself up and about to climb down the left-hand tread instead, then walked around the machine and saw that the right-hand tread was gone indeed. Looking back down the tunnel, he saw it lying like a length of limber lumber on the ground. Frowning then, he came close and sat upon his heels to study the end, and saw where the connection had broken, crystallized metal fractured, as indeed it might have if this Sherman tank had really sat in wait through six decades. "'Nature always sides with the hidden flaw,'" he mused, then stiffened, remembering that he quoted a corollary of Murphy's Law. Yet he had defeated Murphy—so which of his henchmen had engineered this mishap?

Or was it a henchman? It might well have been a monstrosity quite equal, for Murphy's Law was itself a corollary of Finagle's General Statement, and many were the minions of Finagle.

Suspending judgment, the Blessed One rose to stand and turned his face ahead. Onward he strode down the tunnel.

Then came he to a bank of recorders whose reels spun two-inch tape. He frowned, remembering such things from his youth, but finding no television cameras or control chains nearby—but his eye did light upon an antique electric typewriter without a platen. "A computer terminal!" he cried in delight, and went to sit by the console and log on.

Behind him reels did hum, and he froze, reminding himself that he dealt with a device unknown. Casually, then, he typed in a program he knew well—but when he directed the computer to run, the reels spun only for a minute before the printer chattered. Looking over to it, he saw the words, "Error on Line 764"—but the type-ball flew on until it had drawn a picture in marks of punctuation. Peering closer, Father Vidicon beheld the image of a beetle. "It doth generate bugs!" quoth he, then realized that he was in a realm in which any device would have a hidden flaw.

Rising from that place, he resolved most sternly that he would ignore any other device he found, and onward marched.

Full ten minutes did he stride before a doorway blocked his path, and a lighted panel lit above it in the yellow-lettered word REHEARSAL. The Blessed One's pulse did quicken, resolution forgotten, for in life he had been a video engineer, and he quite clearly did approach a television studio much like the one in which he first had learned to operate camera, in the days of his youth.

He wondered if he should enter, but saw no reason not to, if the souls within were only in rehearsal. He hauled open the sand-filled door, discovering a small chamber six feet square with a similar door set opposite him and another in its side, as a proper sound lock should have. He closed the door behind him carefully, so that sound might not be admitted, then opened the door to the side and stepped into the control room.

It lay in gloom, with three tiers of seats rising, all facing bank upon bank of monitors—the first tier of seats for the engineers, the second for the switcher, director, and assistant director, and the third for observers. Each position sat in its own pool of light from tiny spotlights hung above.

None were peopled. He stood alone.

Looking out through the control room window, he saw the studio likewise unpeopled, but the huge old monochrome cameras aimed at easels, each with a stack of pictures. Even as he watched, the tally light on Camera One went out as its mate atop Camera Two came on, and on Camera One's easel, one picture fell to the floor, revealing another behind it.

Father Vidicon frowned; it was clearly an automatic studio, and even more clearly a temptation. Still, he saw no harm in it, and since the studio blocked the tunnel, it had to be navigated—so he sat down before the switched, smiling fondly as he saw only a preview bank, two mixing banks, and a downstream key cluster; the memories that it evoked were dear.

But he could not wallow long in nostalgia, for a voice called from the intercom, "Air in five . . . four . . . three . . ."

Quickly, the saint split the faders and went to black.

" . . . two . . . one . . . You're on!" the voice cried.

Father Vidicon faded in Camera One, seeing a vision of St. Mark's Plaza appear on the program monitor as a mellow voice began to narrate a travelogue. Father Vidicon glanced at Camera

Two's monitor, saw a close-up of the gilded lion, and readied a finger over the button "Two" on the air bank. As the voice began to speak of the lion, he punched the button, and the close-up of the lion appeared on program. Grinning then, he began to fall into the old rhythm of a program, taking from one detail to another, then seeing a photograph of a gondola on a canal and dissolving to it.

Just as the picture became clear though, the picture fluxed, shrinking, then expanding, then shrinking to die. Instantly did Father Vidicon dissolve back to Camera One—and it too bloomed and died.

"Telecine!" he roared, that his voice might be heard through the director's headset (since he wore none). "Trouble slide!"

And Lo! The telecine screen lit with a picture of an engineer enwrapped in layers of videotape as he spooled frantically through an antique videotape recorder, attempting to clear a jam. It was a still picture only, so Father Vidicon leaned back with a sigh, then rose on rather wobbly legs. "I should have known," he muttered, "should have remembered." Then he walked, though rather unsteadily, back into the sound lock, then on into the studio. Around the cameras he went and drew aside the heavy velvet drape that hid the back wall—and sure enough, it had hidden also the double door to the scenery storage room. He hauled open portal, stepped in among the ranked flats, threaded his way through piled sofas and stacked chairs, and found the entry door beyond. He opened it, stepped through, and found himself back in the dim light of the maroon tunnel. He set off again, mouth in a grim line, for, said he unto himself, "Now, then, we know which minion of Finagle's we shall face"—for surely there could be no doubt who sided with the hidden flaw, who made machinery fail in crucial moments, who was attracted to devices more strongly as they became more complicated, and it was not Nature.

And Lo! The monster did approach—or, more precisely, the Saint did approach the monster, who smiled as he saw the Blessed One approach, glanced down to make a check mark on his clipboard, then looked up again to grin—or his lips did; Father Vidicon could not see his eyes, since they were shadowed by a visor of green, and his face that of a gnome, not a man. He wore a shirt that was striped and held by sleeve-garters, its collar tightened by a necktie, though over it he was clothed in coveralls (but they were pin-striped), and he left hand bore socket wrenches in place of fingers. Clean-shaven he was, and round-faced, smiling with delight full cynical, the whiles his right hand did play upon a keyboard.

Then Father Vidicon did halt some paces distant, filled with wariness, and declared, "I know thee, Spirit—for thou art the Gremlin!"

"I do not make policy," the creature replied, "I only execute it."

"Seek not to deceive!" Father Vidicon rebuked. "Thou art the one who dost seek to find the hidden flaw and doom all human projects."

" 'Tis in the nature of humans to bring it out," the Gremlin retorted. "I only execute what they themselves have overlooked."

"Wouldst thou have me believe 'tis Nature who doth side with the hidden flaw, though well we know that Nature makes not machines?"

"Nature sides with me," the Gremlin returned. "Canst thou blame me for the nurture of the natural?"

" 'Tis not Nature thou dost serve, but Entropy!"

"What else?" the spirit jibed. "Humans seek to build, when 'tis the way of Nature to fall apart."

"Only in its season," Father Vidicon admonished, "when the time of growth is behind."

"Not so," the Gremlin answered, "if the flaw's inherent in the newborn creature. Thus only when it doth come to maturity doth its undoing become manifest."

"And what of those whose flaws emerge before they're grown?"

The Gremlin shrugged. "Then they never come to the age at which they can build, and only looking backward can they see a life worth living."

"Thou dost lie, thou rogue," Father Vidicon said sternly, "for that cannot be behind which is before!"

"Oh, so? Hast thou, then, heard never of the Mule?" The Gremlin's hand did beat upon the keyboard, and letters of a glowing green did glimmer in the gloaming 'fore his face: "BOOT MULE." Father Vidicon did step back with a presentiment of foreboding; then the words did vanish, and beside the Gremlin stood a stocky quadruped, with longish ears laid back, teeth parting in a bray.

"I should have thought," the priest did breathe. "This is the beast most susceptible to thee, for 'tis also the most contrary; when we most wish it to work, it will not."

"All who will not work are with me," the Gremlin answered, "as are those who, in the name of standing firm, give way to stubbornness." He reached out to stroke the beast, and chanted,

"The mule, we find,
Hath two legs behind,
And two we find before.
We stand behind before we find
What the two behind be for."

And the Saint did find the mule's tail confronting him, and the hooves kicked up and lashed out at his head. But St. Vidicon did bow, and the feet flashed by above. "Affront me not," quoth he, "for I do know this beast hath fallibility."

"Then make use of it," the Gremlin counseled, "for he doth set himself again."

'Twas true, the mule did once again draw up his hooves to kick. Father Vidicon did therefore run around the beast up toward his head.

But, "What's before, and what's behind?" the Gremlin cried. "Behold, I give the beast his head, and he doth lose it! For if we know what that behind be for, then assuredly, what's behind's before!"

Father Vidicon did straighten up before the mule's head—and found it was a tail, with hooves beneath that did lash out.

"Surely in his stubbornness," the Gremlin said, "the mule has lost his head!"

The good priest did shout as he did leap aside, quickly, but not quite quickly enough, and a hoof did crack upon his shoulder, and pain shot through his whole side. He cried out, but his cry was lost in the Gremlin's laughter, which did echo all about.

"Thou canst not escape," the spirit cried with gloating glee, "for if thou dost run around the beast, thou wilt but find what thou hast lost!"

Hooves slashed out again, and the priest did throw himself upon the ground. The mule's feet whistled through the air above him, then drew back to stand, and began to hobble toward him.

"Come, come!" the Gremlin cried. "Thine heart was ever in thy work! Wouldst thou now lie about and trouble others? Wouldst thou be underfoot?"

But the priest had scrambled to his feet, a-running, and heard the thunderous echo of galloping hooves behind. At a thought, however, he turned back. "Two backward sets both running must go against each other; they thereby must stand in place!"

Assuredly, the poor beast did; for each pair of legs, in leaping forward, did naught but counter the other's thrust.

"Let it not trouble thee," the Gremlin counseled, "for I've held him close thus far—yet now I'll give the beast his head!"

Father Vidicon knew then that he had but a moment to draw upon the strength of Him to Whom he was in all ways dedicated; and holding up his hands to Heaven, he did pray, "Good Father, now forgive! That in my pride I did think myself equipped to defeat the Finder of Flaws. Lend me, I pray Thee, some tool that will find and hinder all bugs that this creature doth engender!"

Of a sudden, his hands weighed heavy. Looking there, he found a halter.

A bray recalled him to his conflict, and he saw the mule's tail grow dim, then harden again to show forequarters topped by a head that did reach out, teeth sharp to bite, as the mule leaped forward.

Father Vidicon shouted and spun aside, flailing at the mule with the halter—and sure enough it caught. The mule swerved and reared, braying protest, but Father Vidicon did hold fast to reins and turn the mule toward its master, then leaping to its back. Still under the Gremlin's mandate to attack, it galloped ahead, teeth reaching for its master.

"How now!" the creature screeched, drumming at its keyboard. "How canst thou turn my own artifact against me?"

The mule disappeared, leaving the saint to plummet toward the floor, the halter still in his hand—but he landed lightly.

"Thou didst expect that fall!" the Gremlin accused. "How couldst thou have known?'

"Why, by preparing 'gainst every eventuality," the Saint replied, "then expecting some other malfunction that I could not name, because I had not thought of it."

"Thou dost not mean thou didst expect the unexpected!"

"Surely, for I have always expected thee, since first I learned to program Cobol." The Saint advanced, holding out the halter. "Know that with my Master's power, these straps can harness any who their energy expend." Then he advanced, the halter outheld.

"Thou dost speak of those who embody Entropy," the Gremlin protested, and did back away.

" 'Tis even so," the Saint replied, "for to live is to expend energy, but to grow is to gain structure."

"You are not fool enough to think to reverse entropy!" the Gremlin cried, still backing.

"Only for some little while," the Saint replied, "but each little while added to another can constitute a lifetime entire."

"Yet in the end your race shall die! In mere billions of years, your sun shall explode, and all will end in fire! Thus all is futile, all is done in vain, all's absurd!"

"Yet while life endures, it contradicts absurdity—if it has structure." Father Vidicon relaxed the halter, then swung it at the Gremlin to ensnare.

The Gremlin wailed and winked out as though he'd never been.

Father Vidicon stared at the place where he had been and bethought him somberly, "He is not truly gone, but will recur wheresoever people try to build—for against such as him we struggle to find meaning." Then he looked down at the halter, contemplating it a moment before he held it high in offering. "O Father, I thank Thee for giving Thine overweening servant the means to banish this Foe of Humankind, no matter how briefly. I return unto Thee the Halter Thou hast lent me to rein in our impulses of self defeat, for the use of which I thank Thee deeply."

For half a minute, then, the halter began to glow, then scintillated as it vanished.

The Blessed One stood alone, reflecting that once again he was unarmed; but he recalled the words of the psalm and murmured them aloud: " 'For Thou, O God, art my wisdom and my strength.' Nay, I shall never lack for defense within this realm, so long as Thou art with me."

So saying, he strode forth once more, further downward in that tunnel, wondering what other foe the Lord might send him to confront.

As Father Vidicon strode onward down the throat of Hell, he was resolved to confront whatsoever the Good Lord did oppose to him. Even as he went, the maroon of the walls did darken to purple and farther, till he did pace a corridor of indigo. Then the light itself began to dwindle and to darken, until he groped within a lightless place. Terror did well up within him, turning all his joints to water and sapping strength from every limb, yet he did resolve upon the onward march, rebuked his heart most sternly, and held the fear within its place. He did reach out to brace himself against the wall—yet it was damp and soft and yielding, and did seem to move beneath his palm. He did pull his hand away right quickly and did shudder, and was nigh to losing heart then; yet he did haul his courage up from the depths to which it had plummeted, and did force his right foot forward, and his left foot then to follow; and thus he onward moved within that Hellish tunnel.

Then as he went, the floor beneath him did soften, till he did walk upon a yielding surface; and he stumbled and did fall, and caught himself upon his hands. He did cry aloud, and backward thrust himself with a broken prayer for strength, for that floor had felt as moist and yielding as tissue living. "In truth," he muttered, "I walk indeed within the throat of Hell."

He plucked himself up and pushed himself onward, bowed against the weight of his fear, yet going.

Sudden light did glare, and did sear his eyes, so that he did clench them shut, then did slowly ope, allowing them to accustom themselves to such brightness, whereupon the glare was gone, and Father Vidicon did see a grinning death's head that did glow there—yet not if its own light, for it was of a pale and sickly green that did shine too brightly for the light to be within. Yet naught else could Father Vidicon see there about him. He did frown, and held his hand before his face; yet he could see it not. "In sooth," he breathed, "what light is this, that is itself a darkness—what light is this, that doth not thus illuminate? How can light cast darkness?"

The answer came at once within his mind, and he did pull his Roman collar from out its place and did hold it out before him, to behold it as a strip of glaring bluish-white. "It doth fluoresce!" he cried in triumph, and he knew thereby that light did truly fill the hall, but was of a color that human eyes see not. Yet his collar, in consequence of the detergent held within it, did transform that color, and did reflect it as a one that human eyes see as glowing.

Father Vidicon replaced his collar then within his shirt with hands that trembled only slightly, and he murmured, "I have, then, come within the land of the Spirit of Paradox." His heart did quail within him, for he knew that the perversities he'd faced ere now were naught indeed when set against the reversals and inverted convolutions of the Spirit that he soon would face. Yet he bowed his head in prayer and felt his heart did lighten. With a silent thought of thanks, he lifted up his head and set forth again down that gigantic throat. The death's head passed upon his left, and on his right he did behold a skeleton frozen at odd angles, as though it were running and was small, or as though the person were now distant. And onward he did pace, past skulls and crossed bones on his left, and on his right, skeletons in postures that might have been provocative, had they worn flesh—and as they must have been to the Spirit of Paradox. Father Vidicon did pray that he would not behold a being fully-fleshed, for he felt sure that it would lie as one who's dead.

The passage then did curve downward toward his left, past bones and left-hand helices inverted widdershins. A galaxy did reel upon his left; yet the spiral arms were on the rim, and darkness dwelt within its heart, a disc of emptiness. Stars did coalesce upon his right to form a globe elongate, and it did seem as though the universe entire did move backward, and invert.

The throat he paced did upward curve, still bending leftward, and he did hear above him footsteps, that did approach in front, then did recede behind. He frowned up at them, yet still did march ahead, past glowing signs of death in birth, on and on through hallways that did ever curve unto his left. Yet it did begin to once again curve downward also, down and down, a mile or more, till at least, he did behold, upon his left —

A grinning death's head.

Father Vidicon stopped and stood stock still. A chill enveloped him, beginning at the hollow of his back and spreading upward to embrace his scalp, for he was certain that this death's head was the first he had beheld within this sightless tunnel. Then did he bethink him of the footsteps he had heard above his head, and knew with certainty (though he knew not how he knew) that those had been his own footsteps going past this place. They'd seemed inverted for, at the time, he had walked upon the outside of the throat he was now within; yea, now he walked within it once again. "In truth," he whispered, "I do wander a Klein flask."

And so it was—a tube that did curve back upon itself, then curved within itself once again, so that he passed from inside to outside, then back to inside, all unawares. Aye, forever might he wander this dark hall and never win to any goal except his own point of origin. He might well press onward ageing more and more, till at last he wold stumble through this hall, a weak, enfeebled, ancient spirit. Yet, "Nay," he cried, "for here's the place of paradox— and as time goes forward, I shall grow younger!" And hard upon the heels of that realization came another: that he might wander where he would yet never find that Spirit within whose throat he wandered—the Spirit that did invest this place.

Or did the place invest the Spirit? "Aye!" he cried in triumph. "'Tis not Hell's mouth that I did enter, but Finagle's!" and his throat was like unto a Klein flask. Therefore, Father Vidicon did set forth again, with heart renewed and fear held in abeyance, to pace onward and onward, downward to his left, then upward left gain, until the wall did fall away beneath his hand and the floor did curve away beneath him. Then he cried in triumph, "I have come without! Nay, Spirit, look upon me—for I have come from out to stand upon thy skin! Nay, behold me!"

A door thundered up scant feet away, nearly knocking him backward with the wind of its passage. He did fall back, plunging downward and crying out in fear, flailing about him, near to panic—and his hand caught upon a spoke which did grow from that surface there below. More such spikes caught him, pressing most painfully against him, for their points were sharp; yet he heeded not the pain, but did gaze upward, and did behold a great and glowing baleful eye that did fill all his field of vision.

"Indeed, I see thee now," a great voice rumbled. "May there be praise in censure! I had begun to think I would never have thee out from my system!"

"Nor wilt thou," Father Vidicon did cry in triumph, "for the outside of thy system is the inside! Indeed, thine inside is thine outside, and thine outside's inside! They are all one, conjoined in endlessness!"

"Do not carol victory yet," the huge voice rumbled, "for thou dost address Finagle, author of all that doth twist back upon itself. I am the fearsome spirit that doth invest all paradox, and doth make two aspects of any entity separate and opposed as thesis and antithesis, in Hegelian duality."

"Ah, is it Hegel's, then?" Father Vidicon did cry; but,

"Nay," Finagle rumbled, "for Hegel thus was mine."

"Thou dost afright me not," Father Vidicon did cry. "I know thee well at last! Thou art the bridge from Tomorrow to Yesterday, for Positive to Negative, from nucleus's strong force thus to weak! Thou art the bridge that doth conjoin all those that do appear opposed!"

"Thou hast said it." Finagle's voice did echo all about him. "And I am thus the Beginning and the End of all. Bow down and adore me, for I am He whom thou dost call thy Lord!"

"Thou art not!" the Saint did cry, and righteous wrath arose within him. "Nay, thou art a part of Him, as are we all—yet but a part! Thou must needs therefore be within His limit and control."

"Art thou so certain, then?" The great eye did narrow in anger. "For an I were the Beginning and the Ending joined, how could I lie?"

"Why, for that," Father Vidicon replied, "thou art the Spirit of all Paradox, and canst speak true words in such a way that they express mistruth! Thus thou dost lie by speaking sooth!'"

"Thou hast too much of comprehension for my liking," Finagle then did rumble. "Ward thee, priest! For I must annihilate thy soul!"

Light seared, and did shock the darkness, turning all to fire, lancing the good Saint's orbs sightless with light. He did clap his palms over them, and closed them tightly—yet the light remained. Recalling then that he was within the Paradox of Lands, he did ope his eyes to slits, and the little light admitted did darken dazzle, till the Saint could once again distinguish form and detail.

He beheld a gigantic, fiery bird that did drift up from ashes, its wings widespread and cupped for hovering, beak reaching out to slash at him. Then terror struck the priest's stout heart, and he grasped the spikes that held him kneeling on Finagle's flesh and, throwing back his head, did cry, "Oh Father! Hear me now, or I must perish! Behold thy servant, kneeling here in helplessness, beset by that dread raptor called the Phoenix, in whom resides vast power, for in its end doth it begin! Give me now, I pray thee, some shield, some weapon here for my defense, or I must perish quite! Even the last shreds of my soul must be transformed and subsumed into pure, unmodulated energy devoid of structure, and that fearsome predator doth smite me!'

He held up hands in supplication—and light did glare within his palm, pulling back and pulling in, imploding, gathering together, coalescing—and the Saint did hold an Egg of Light!

Then did the Spirit's vasty laugh fill all the Universe, bellowing in triumphant joy, "Nay, foolish priest! For all thy pleas to thy Creator, nothing more than this hath he to give thee! An egg— and thou wouldst oppose it 'gainst the bird full-flown! Now yield thee up, for thou must perish!"

But, "Not so," the Saint did cry, "for I know thee well, and know that when thou most doth laugh, thou art most in dread—and when thou dost most gloat on victory, thou art most in terror of defeat. Thou must needs be, for to thy Phoenix grown out of an ending, I do bring a beginning that must needs bear its death!'

Then he did rise, that he might face the greatest peril of his existence upright and courageous; and he held the Egg out in his two hands cupped, as though it were an offering.

The Phoenix screamed, and fiery wings beat downward to surround him. The beak of flame seared toward him, like unto a laser; and he bore himself bravely, but felt his spirit quail within

him. Fire did surround him on every side, closer then and closer—
and the Spirit of pure energy did envelop him and did sink in
upon him . . .

And inward passed him. The heat of that passing did sear his
face, and he closed his eyes against it. Cool breath then touched
his cheek and, opening his eyes, he saw the bird, shrunken now
unto a hand's breadth, shrinking still, diminishing and growing
smaller. Its despairing cry did pierce his ears and heart; for as it
shrank, it sank. The Egg absorbed all flame and every erg of energy,
until the phoenix's head did shrink at last within the shell. There
it sat, glowing within Father Vidicon's cupped palms, brighter and
more pure than e'er it had been.

The priest breathed a sigh and cried, "All praise be to Thee, my
Lord, who hath saved me from the mountain of the Light of
Death."

Then the dazzle faded from his eyes, and again he saw that huge
orb, still glinting balefully upon him. "How now, then, priest,"
Finagle's voice did rumble. "Thou hast defeated my most puissant
servant. What shalt thou, therefore, do with me?" His voice did
sneer. "Shalt thou now annihilate me? Nay, do so—for then thy
race shall be free of this urge to self-defeat that doth invest them!"

Fathomless tranquility enveloped the priest. "Nay," quoth he, "for
I cannot make thee cease to exist, nor can any—for thou art part
of God, as are we all, and thou art spirit—the Spirit of fell Paradox.
Nay, tempt me not to *hubris*, arrogance—for I do know that, did
I eliminate thee, thou wouldst turn even that about, and make of
it Creation. Thus wouldst thou blaspheme—for none can create,
save God. Thou wouldst not die, but wouldst simply change thy
form—and 'tis better to have thee as thou art, so that we know
thine appearance. Go thy ways—thou art a necessary part of
existence."

"So, then." And the huge voice ran with disappointment quite
profound—nay, almost with despair. "Thus thou wilt let me live."

But Father Vidicon knew that when the spirit of Paradox did
seem desperate, it was in truth triumphant. "Be not so proud," he
did admonish it, "for thou art even now within the hand of God,
and 'tis that which he hath proven though me—that even thou
canst be comprehended, and accepted within a person's harmony
of being. Thus thine urge to self-defeat can be transformed to
growth. Thou wilt ever be with Adam's breed, fell Spirit, and with
Eve's—but never again need any man or woman fear thee. For they
will know thou art as much a part of the world about them as

the rain and wind, and as much of the world within them as the urge to charity."

"So thou dost say," the spirit rumbled, "yet doth that not make a mockery of thy victory? Dost thou not see that I have triumphed finally? What shalt thou do, with that Phoenix thou hast at long last slain by bringing within the scope of Birth? Wilt thou then destroy it, and with it, all beginnings?"

The priest then shook his head. "Nay; for 'tis not mine to do with any wise. I must surrender it unto its Source." Then he cried, "Oh, Father! I give thee now thine Egg of Rebirth, with all the thanks and praise that I do own—thanks that thou hast preserved me, but more—that thou hast deemed me worthy to become Thine instrument for this restarting!" He thrust the Egg up high, an offering there within his hands, and it rose above his palms and arced upward, and farther upward and farther, and Father Vidicon did cry out, "See! This is the Egg of All, the Cosmic Egg, the Monobloc!"

Then at its zenith did the Egg explode, filling all that emptiness with light, searing all the Void with its seeding of Energy and Matter, fulfilling all with the Cosmic Dust and with it, the structure of Time and Space, thus bringing Order out from Chaos.

And Father Vidicon did rise within it, like to a flaring candle, for flame surrounded him transcendent and unburning; and thus did he ascend through Space and Time, unto the Mind of God.

⇠ The Elf House ⇢

An Isles Story

David Drake

Cashel didn't need to carry his quarterstaff in the corridors of the Vicar's palace—what'd been the Count of Haft's place till Prince Garric arrived the week before—but he was more comfortable holding the smooth, familiar hickory than he'd be otherwise. He didn't dislike big buildings, but he disliked being in them; and this palace had a nasty feel all its own.

Besides, the staff had been a friend in places where Cashel had no other friends. He wouldn't feel right about leaving it alone in the huge suite assigned to him while he went off to dinner with Garric in the roof garden. If the servants, officials, and the amazing number of other people crowding the palace stared at him, well, a man as big as Cashel or-Kenset was used to being stared at whether he carried a quarterstaff or not.

For a wonder there wasn't anybody around at the moment. Cashel sauntered down the hall looking at the cherub mural painted just above shoulder level. In the dim light through the transoms of the rooms to either side, there was something new to catch every time he passed.

Cashel started to grin at the little fellow with his wings spread as he struggled to lead a goat who didn't want to go. The sound of a girl crying jerked his head around.

He'd been holding the quarterstaff straight up and down in one hand. Now, without him thinking about it his left hand slipped into position a span below the right and he slanted the staff before him. "Ma'am?" he said, ready to deal with whatever was making a woman cry.

The girl wore servant's clothing: a cap and a simple gray tunic set off by a sash of bleached wool. She knelt a little way down a corridor which joined the main one from the right. Cashel didn't remember there being anything but a blank wall there, but he guessed he'd always missed it because he'd been intent on the mural opposite.

She gave another vain push at the inward-opening door in front of her, then looked up at Cashel with eyes glittering with tears. "Oh, sir!" she said. "I dropped the key and it slipped under the door. The steward will beat me if I don't get it back!"

"I don't guess he will," Cashel said. The notion that somebody'd beat a little slip of a girl surprised him into speaking in a growl. He didn't know her, but he didn't think men ought to hit any girls. He was *real* sure no man was going to try that twice in front of Cashel or-Kenset.

He cleared his throat and went on in a normal voice, "But anyhow, let's see if I can't get your key."

The door stood a finger's breadth ajar. Cashel pressed with the fingertips of his right hand without budging it further. It was stuck, that was all; rusty hinges, he figured, since the panel didn't bind to the lintel or transom. Through the crack at the edge he could see a glint of gold in what was otherwise darkness; the key was there, all right. It must've bounced wrong off the stone floor.

Cashel leaned his quarterstaff against the wall beside him and placed his hands one above the other on the latch side of the panel. The girl looked up at him intently. She seemed older, all of a sudden, and there was no sign of her frightened despair of a moment ago. He made sure his feet were set, then put his weight against the wood.

More people lived in the palace than did in all Barca's Hamlet where Cashel'd grown up. Even though there wasn't any traffic in the main corridor, sounds constantly echoed through the hallways and made the floor quiver. All that stopped; Cashel pressed against the panel in dead silence. Maybe it was the effort, because the door still didn't want to give—

And then it did, though with creaking unwillingness. It opened another finger's breadth, twice that....

The girl stuck her arm in, calling something that Cashel could barely hear through the roar of blood in his ears. "I can't quite...," she said, so he kept pushing and the door gave some more, enough that she squeezed her torso into the room beyond.

Cashel shoved harder yet. He could feel the wood fighting him like the staff of a bent bow, ready to snap back if he let up the pressure.

"I've got it!" the girl said, only her legs from the knees down out in the hallway where Cashel could see them. "I've—"

And then she shrieked "Milord, I'm falling!" shrilly. Her legs slid out of sight, following the rest of her. She was wearing sandals with straps of green-dyed cut-work.

Cashel didn't understand what was happening, but as the girl slipped inward he slammed his shoulder hard against the panel instead of just shoving with his hands. He hadn't done that before because he didn't want to smash the door, but now he didn't care.

The door didn't break, neither the thick fir panel nor the squealing hinges that fought him all the way, and he swung it open at right angles. The room within was small and dingy. There was no furniture, and part of the rotten wainscoting had fallen onto the floor.

The girl had the key in one hand and reached toward Cashel with the other. She looked like she was sliding backward, but she was already farther away than the far wall of the room.

Cashel grabbed the staff with his left hand and stretched it out to the girl. She couldn't reach it and screamed again. Her voice was growing fainter; he could see her body shrink as the distance increased.

"Duzi!" Cashel bellowed. He strode into the room, holding the quarterstaff out in both hands. The girl grabbed it, but Cashel's feet slipped like he was standing on an icy hillside.

The door slammed behind him. The only light was a dim, yellow-brown glow that silhouetted the girl's body and he and she plunged down an unseen slope.

Cashel felt himself spinning as he dropped, but his body wasn't touching anything. The girl held the other end of his staff; he couldn't see her expression, but she didn't bawl in fear or make any sound at all that he noticed.

They skidded onto a gritty hillside and stopped. Cashel looked over his shoulder. All there was there was gray sky and a rising slope. There wasn't any sign of the room where they'd come from. He looked all around and didn't see anything he liked better.

The bare hills ranged in color from yellow-white to the red of rusty iron. For the most part the rock had weathered into gravel, but there were outcrops where the stone must've been harder. The general landscape wasn't pretty, but the outcrops were worse. Whenever Cashel looked hard at one, he started to see a large, angry face.

He got up, brushing crumbled rock from the back of his tunic. He hadn't come down hard, for all that they'd seemed to be rushing headlong through emptiness. He glanced at the girl, already on her feet. She smiled and said, "My name is Mona, Lord Cashel. Do you know where we are?"

"Just Cashel, please, mistress," he said with a grimace. "I'm not Lord anything."

He cleared his throat, looking around again. The landscape wasn't any more appealing on a careful survey than it'd been when he first landed in it. "And I don't know anything about this place, except I wish we were someplace else."

"It's where the house elf lives," Mona said. She was looking at the landscape also, turning her head slowly. "Used to live, I mean. There can't be anything alive here except the dwelling itself."

She held her arms across her bosom; her expression was coldly disapproving. From Mona's features she was younger than Cashel's nineteen years, but her eyes were a lot older than that.

Cashel followed the line of her gaze up a series of streaked, ragged slopes. On top of a butte was what at first he'd taken for white stone weathered into a spire. When he squinted and let it sink in angle by angle, he realized he was seeing a man-made tower with battlements on top. A slant of windows curved around the shaft the way they'd do to light a circular staircase.

"You mean that castle?" Cashel said, nodding toward the structure instead of pointing. "That there's people living there?"

"There's no people here and no elves either," the girl said as she stared toward the tower. "Only us. And I don't mean the building, Cashel. This whole world was the dwelling for the house elf."

Cashel cleared his throat. He took out the pad of raw wool he carried in his belt wallet and wiped the smooth hickory surface of his quarterstaff as he thought.

"Mona," he said while keeping his eyes fixed on his task. "The only house elves I've heard of are the little fellows who live under the hearth and, well, make things go right. The Luck of the House, some people call them."

He cleared his throat again. "Not that I've ever seen one. Or known anybody who did."

"How could anybody live under a hearth?" Mona asked, with a pretty smile that took the sting out of words that could've been cutting if said the wrong way. "But they *could* live between the cracks of the real world, in a place that grew for them. A place like this was."

She looked around, no longer smiling. "When the elf died," she said, "the dwelling should've fallen apart like a web when the spider dies. This dwelling took a life of its own instead. A sort of life."

The sky was getting darker. It was solidly overcast, as heavy and oppressive as a block of gray stone. Cashel could feel a storm in the air. Duzi, the little god of shepherds, knew how many times he'd been caught by the weather while he was minding sheep; but he didn't have sheep to worry about this time, so he could go somewhere else.

"Ah, Mona?" he said. "I think we'd best get under cover while we can. Unless you've got a better idea, let's head for the castle up there."

"Yes," she said. "We'll do that. Though the storm will catch us anyway."

They had about a half mile to go. The route was uphill on average, but Cashel could see there were several ridges and gullies between them and the castle. Experience had taught him that the terrain was always worse than it seemed at a distance, but he didn't foresee anything they couldn't cross even if he had to carry the girl part of the way.

He looked at Mona again. She wasn't the frail little girl that she'd seemed when he first saw her in the palace corridor. She stepped with determination across the rough terrain, avoiding head-sized chunks of rock but seemingly unperturbed by the coarse gravel. Maybe the soles of her sandals were sturdier than they seemed. Cashel himself was wearing thick boots. He didn't like the feel of footgear, especially in warm weather, but the stone floors of the palace and cobblestone streets of the city beyond were too much for the calluses he'd developed going barefoot on the mud and meadows where he grew up.

Lightning flashed somewhere above the clouds, giving them texture if not shape for an instant. Cashel held his staff crosswise, ready to brace himself with an iron butt-cap if the gravel slid or a rock turned under his foot. You couldn't trust your footing here. . . .

"I'm surprised there's nothing growing here," Cashel said. The girl was a couple steps in front of him, choosing each step and keeping in perfect balance. "This isn't good soil—" his boot toe gouged into the slope "—but with rain, there ought to be something."

"Nothing can live here," Mona said bitterly. She reached down and brushed at the loose grit. "Look."

The underlying rock was mostly dark brown and cream, with streaks of maroon and other colors. Cashel frowned as he let his eyes grapple with the pattern.

"It's a tree trunk," he said at last. "It's a stone statue of a tree trunk."

"It *was* a tree trunk," the girl said. "The house has turned it to stone to reabsorb it. Lesser vegetation is—"

She swept her left hand in a short arc, palm down.

"—already gone. Stone and dust. The house has only a half-life; it hates the real thing."

She smiled wryly at Cashel. "Forgive me if I get carried away," she said. "There's nothing evil about what's happening here, any more than there is with cancer or a wolf tree. But it's a perversion and can't be allowed."

Cashel nodded. "We'd best be getting on," he said, nodding toward the tower ahead of them. The hill was particularly steep right here; he could only see the crowning battlements from where he stood. "Though you were right about us not beating the storm."

They resumed, climbing steeply now. The girl dabbed a hand down frequently while Cashel used the butt of his staff to steady him where he didn't trust the grip of his feet.

He knew what a wolf tree was. If a forest grew wild, there'd always be a few trees, oaks more often than not, that through a combination of luck in soil and the weather spread over ground that could've supported a dozen ordinary trees. Their limbs shaded out lesser growth, and their trunks grew gnarled and rotted at the heart, useless for anything but firewood.

Forests didn't grow wild, of course: wood was too valuable a resource for that. If a tree started taking more than its share, the woodlot's owner hired a husky young man like Cashel to cut it down.

A steep-sided gully barred their way, not broad but deeper than twice Cashel's height. He figured he could get over it, but the girl'd have to climb down and then—

Mona jumped over the gully from a standing start, looking like nothing so much as a squirrel hopping the gap between trees. She glanced over her shoulder. "I'll wait for you here, Master Cashel," she said with a trace of laughter in her tone.

Cashel grunted. He checked the ground, then backed two steps and came on again in a rush. He butted his quarterstaff firmly at the edge of the gully and used the great strength of his shoulders to loft him over. He landed beside her, flexing his knees to take his weight.

"You're graceful despite your size," the girl said as she resumed her way toward the tower.

"Who are you, Mistress Mona?" Cashel asked. "*What* are you?"

"I'm a servant," she said. "We're all servants of one kind or another, aren't we? You used to serve sheep, for example."

"I didn't serve sheep," Cashel said, shocked at the thought. "I—"

He broke off. A shepherd did a lot of things, but when you boiled them all down they amounted to making sure his sheep were safe and comfortable. Put like that it sure enough sounded like being a servant.

"Well, maybe that's so," he admitted, saying the words instead of just holding his tongue and pretending he hadn't been wrong to begin with.

The rain hit, violent slashes from straight ahead. Each gust drove at Cashel's face like he was standing in the sluice of the mill back home in Barca's Hamlet. He didn't see how Mona could stand against it but she did, lowering her head and striding on.

The lightning was nearly constant, dancing in the clouds as the air shuddered with thunder. Run-off gouged fresh rivulets which gushed down the slopes as streams of thin mud.

The gully they'd crossed must be a raging freshet now. It'd be a bad time to lose your footing and slide into a torrent.

The storm stopped as abruptly as it'd begun. It paused, at any rate; the rain no longer fell, but the sky stayed the same dark matte. Mona had a little peaked cap as part of her livery. It'd blown away, and her simple tunic stuck to her torso, sopping wet and three shades darker than its original light gray. Cashel figured he looked like a drowned rat himself.

He grinned and slicked the water off his staff between his thumbs and forefingers, sliding first his right hand to the ferrule and then cleaning the other half with his left. A drowned ox, maybe. On his worst day, nobody was going to confuse Cashel or-Kenset with a rat.

They'd reached the base of the great outcrop on which the tower stood. The cliff was pretty steep, but there was a path slanting up to the left. It looked badly worn . . . well, no. It looked more like the rock had been melted somehow. Anyway, they'd be able to get up it even if the rain started again.

"Wait!" the girl said, staring intently at the cliff to the side of the pathway. Her index finger traced a bump in the rock. It was about the size of a ripe cantaloupe and had a pearly luster instead of the dull, chalky surface holding it.

Now that Mona'd pointed out the first one, Cashel saw that there were more balls, as many as he could count on the fingers of one hand, in the rock beside it. They looked as much like frog's eggs as anything Cashel could think of, though much bigger, of course.

"The seeds of new dwellings," the girl said softly. She took her hand away from the stone. "Each seed should grow into a home for a young elf who'd make the people of a house in the waking world a little happier. This place is absorbing them too."

She turned her head toward Cashel. "I was wrong, I think," she said. Her voice didn't sound angry, but it rang as hard as a sword edge. "What's happening here *is* evil."

"Let's go on," said Cashel, but Mona had started up the path before he got the words out.

The wind rose again before they'd climbed halfway. It whirled around the outcrop, buffeting Cashel head-on no matter which direction he was facing as he walked along the curving path. Rain began to fall, a few drops at a time but big ones that stung like hard-thrown pebbles.

Mona's tunic was sleeveless and only knee-length. Even so Cashel was afraid that it'd give the storm's violence enough purchase to snatch her from the path and throw her onto the broken landscape below. Her balance remained perfect and her steps stayed steady despite the gusts.

The top of the outcrop was as flat as a table. The tower stood in the center with no more margin than Cashel could span by stretching his arms out to either side. He wondered if the spire itself was artificial, a pedestal built at the same time the tower was; though if what Mona said was true, this whole world had been made—or grown, which he supposed was the same thing.

The entrance was partway around the tower from where the path reached the top. Mona started for it with Cashel right behind. Now that they were close, Cashel saw that the windows in the tower were blocked up—filled with stone rather than just shuttered. What he'd seen were the outlines where the sashes used to be.

The rain resumed in torrents, now mixed with hail the size of quails' eggs. Cashel threw his left arm up to shield his eyes. He'd have bruises when this was over, that was for sure. Balls of ice shattered against the stone, cracking like a fire of pine boughs. Sharp bits bounced from the ground, pricking Cashel's ankles and lower legs.

The tower's doorway was recessed. Mona bent toward it, doing something with the panel. Cashel hunched behind her, trying to shelter her from the hailstones that slipped past the overhang.

The rattling hail drowned the thunder, but its deeper notes still vibrated through Cashel's boots. Lightning was a constant rippling presence overhead. The tower's walls were alabaster; Cashel ran his fingertips over them, trying to find joints between the courses. If there were any, they were too fine for his touch or eyesight, either one, to identify them.

"Mona, maybe I can break it down," Cashel said, speaking louder with each word of the short sentence. The hail made more noise than he appreciated until he tried to talk over it.

A crust flaked off the wall when Cashel rubbed it. Though the tower stood in open air, the stone was rotting like a statue buried in the acid soil of a forest.

"I've got it!" said the girl, and as she spoke the tower opened; she stepped inside.

Cashel was close on her heels, bumping the door as he entered. It was made of the same white stone as the rest of the building, pivoting on pins carved from one block with the panel. As soon as Cashel was past, it banged shut with a ringing sound more like a xylophone than that of stone on stone.

The storm's noise ended abruptly when the door closed. They were in an anteroom.

"There's light!" Cashel said in surprise, and there was: a soft, shadowless glow from the stone itself. The room was unfurnished, but on the walls were carved patterns as rich and fanciful as the engravings on a nobleman's gold dinner service.

Only a few patches remained to show what the original decoration had looked like, though. The scaly rot disfiguring the tower's exterior had claimed most of the inner surfaces too.

Mona stepped through the inner doorway. Cashel followed, keeping his elbows close to his sides. The passage was so narrow that if he'd tried to swagger through arms-akimbo, he'd have bumped the jambs.

A slender woman stood in the center of the hall, her right hand out in greeting. "Oh!" Cashel said, straightening in surprise. The tower was so silent that he'd convinced himself it was empty.

"Her name was Giglia," Mona said, walking toward the other woman. "She was the luck of the palace ever since the Count of Haft built it. There was never a house elf who could match what Giglia did with glass. She made the palace windows gleam like a thousand rainbows every sunrise."

Cashel touched his tongue to his lower lip. His staff was slant-ways before him, not so much a threat as a barrier between him and the silent Giglia. "Why doesn't she move?" he asked.

"Because she's dead, Cashel," Mona said. "She grew old and died; as things should do. Without death there can be no renewal."

She reached toward the dead woman; their faces were as like as those of twins. When her fingers touched the other's cheek, Giglia disintegrated into dust motes. Her right arm fell to the floor intact, then erupted as a geyser of fine dust swirling in the air.

There was a dry, sweetish smell. Cashel threw his arm over his nose to breathe through the waterlogged sleeve of his tunic, though he didn't suppose it mattered. "Mona?" he said. "How can we get out of here? Back to the palace, I mean? Or somewhere!"

Instead of answering, the girl walked toward the door on the other side of the central room. Her feet stirred Giglia's remains into umber whorls. Grimacing, Cashel followed.

The room beyond was darker than the others. Against the far wall was a throne inexpertly hacked out of stone; on it sat a statue as brutal and primitive as the throne itself. It was male, but it had tusks and a crude ape's face. In its right hand was a stone club the length of Cashel's arm.

"Is this a chapel?" Cashel said. "Is that the god they worship here?"

The tower shuddered. Cashel heard the sharp *crack/crack/crack* of stone breaking. The statue trembled side to side on its throne.

Cashel turned; the outer door had slammed behind them, but maybe he could smash it open again. "Earthquake!" he cried. "We've got to get out!"

"It's not an earthquake," Mona said impassively; she didn't move. "And we can't get out while this remains. The dwelling must have a master to exist, so it's created a master in its own image."

The statue stood up. It looked even bigger standing than it'd seemed while seated; Cashel didn't think he could reach to the top of its head flat-footed. Not that he was likely to need to do that.

It started forward, raising its club. "Mona, get out of the way!" Cashel said in a growl.

He lifted the quarterstaff before him and began backing toward the door to the central room. The light was better there, and there was more space besides. He and his staff covered a lot of territory when the fight started.

Rock groaned against itself. The statue's face shifted as its mouth moved. "I will destroy you ... ," the stone said in a rumble almost too low for human ears.

Cashel knew where the doorway was behind him. He feinted at the statue's head, then stepped back quickly and surely. He kept his staff vertical to clear the narrow opening. Mona was somewhere nearby, a presence without form because all Cashel's attention was on the statue. He hoped the girl'd stay clear, but he couldn't worry about that right now.

The statue clumped through the doorway after him, barely clearing the jambs. It looked even uglier than it had in the relative shadow of the farther room. "You cannot escape me ... ," it grated in a voice of emotionless menace.

Cashel spun his staff in a short sun-wise arc, crashing his left ferrule into the lumpish fist which gripped the stone club. There was a crack and flash of blue wizardlight; the creature growled like an approaching avalanche.

Cashel wasn't looking for escape. He'd come to fight.

The statue rushed him, swinging the stone club in an overhead blow. Cashel rammed his staff forward like a spear. The blunt butt-cap slammed into the thing's throat with another blue flash.

The creature's head jerked back. The mighty arc of its club touched nothing but air till it smashed inself on the floor, cratering the alabaster. The grip flew out of the stone hand.

Cashel backed, gasping in deep breaths. He'd struck swiftly and as hard as he could, and the quivers of wizardlight meant he was using more than the strength of his great muscles. He was uncomfortable about that other business—he was a shepherd, not a wizard—but when he was facing a creature like this he was glad of any help he could get.

The thing held its hands up in front of its face. Its fingers were thin scorings in stone mitts; only the thumbs were separate. Its blunt features were those of a bestial doll a child had molded from clay.

The creature's mouth opened. It screamed like millstones rubbing.

"Watch—" Mona cried, but Cashel didn't need to be told what to do in a fight. The creature leaped toward him like a missile from a huge catapult. Cashel stepped back and sideways, thrusting his quarterstaff low. He slipped the thick hickory pole between the stone ankles; it flexed but held. The creature plunged headfirst into the wall with a crash that rocked the tower.

The alabaster fractured in scalloped flakes, leaving a crater at the point of impact. The creature dropped flat on the floor. It braced its stone arms beneath it, starting to rise.

Cashel, holding the staff like a battering ram, struck the back of its head, bouncing it into the wall again. Light as blue as the heart of a sapphire flared at the double *crack!* of iron on stone and stone on stone.

Cashel stepped back, bending slightly and sucking air through his open mouth. The creature's arms moved feebly, like an infant trying to swim. The ferrule Cashel had just struck with glowed orange, cooling to dull red. He switched ends, then brought the staff back with both arms.

The creature got its hands under it and lifted its head slightly. Cashel lunged forward, driving the staff down with the whole weight of his body. The butt hammered the creature at the same point as before. The statue's head exploded in a flash and thunderclap. The massive body began to crumble the way a sand castle dissolves in the surf.

Cashel felt himself wavering. He planted the quarterstaff against the floor and used it to brace him as he let himself kneel. His breath was a rasping thunder, and his blood hammered in his ears.

The only part of the creature still remaining was the outstretched right arm. When it suddenly collapsed to a spill of sand, Cashel caught a brief reminder of the dry, sweet odor in which Giglia had vanished. Then nothing remained but air harsh with the faint brimstone reek of nearby lightning.

Cashel stayed like that for—well, for a time. He figured he could move if he had to, but since he didn't he was just going to rest till he felt like doing something else.

Though he'd kept his eyes open, he didn't have much awareness of his surroundings. There wasn't a lot to see, after all; just the trail of coarse grit that'd been a statue there on the floor in front of him. It looked like what he'd seen on the hills he'd climbed to reach the tower. . . .

"Are you ready to go home, Cashel?" Mona said.

Cashel's world clicked back into hard focus again. He turned his head and smiled at the girl, feeling a little embarrassed. How long had she been standing there, waiting for him to come to himself?

"I'm all right," he said, wondering how true that was. He stood, lifting himself partly by the strength of his arms on the quarterstaff. He swayed a little, but no worse than you always did when you'd been bent over and got up suddenly.

He grinned wider and said, "I'm fine," meaning it this time. "But how do we get back home, Mona?"

As Cashel spoke, he took a closer look at the walls. His eyes narrowed. "Mona?" he said. "Things don't look right. The stone looks *thin*. It wasn't like that before."

"This world is decaying," the girl said, "and not before time. We have to get you out of here, though. Come."

She stepped through the doorway to the room where the statue had waited; the gold key was out in her hand again. Cashel followed, as he'd been doing ever since he met the girl—except when there was the fighting.

He grinned again. That was all right. Mona was better at leading than Cashel ever wanted to be, and she'd kept out of the way when *he* went to work.

Mona looked back at him. "I'm sorry I had to trick you," she said. "Your help was very important."

Cashel shrugged. "You didn't have to trick me, Mona," he said. "You could just have asked. But that's all right."

The throne had fallen into a pile of sand and pebbles like the thing that'd sat on it. On the wall behind was another door. Mona stuck the key into the door—there hadn't been a keyhole that Cashel could see, but he was sure about what she'd just done—and pulled the panel open.

"Go on through, Cashel," she said, smiling like the sun rising. "Thank you. We all thank you."

Cashel hesitated. "You're coming too, aren't you, Mona?" he said. Light and color without shape swirled in the door opening.

Her smile became pensive. She raised the key in the hand that didn't hold the door open. "I have to free the seeds we found," she said. "Otherwise they'll rot instead of growing as they should."

"But what happens to you?" Cashel said.

"Go on back to your own world, Cashel," Mona said, her voice hard without harshness. "There must be renewal."

Cashel cleared his throat. He didn't have anything to say, though, so he nodded and walked toward the opening. As his leading foot entered the blur of color, Mona said, "Your house will always be a happy one, dear friend."

For a moment Cashel stepped through nothingness so silent that he heard his heart beating; then his bootheel clacked on stone. He was standing in the familiar hallway down which he'd been going to dinner.

"Oh!" cried a servant, dropping the pair of silver ewers he'd been carrying to refill from the well in the courtyard at the end of the passage. They rang on the floor, sounding sweet or hollow by turns as they rolled.

Cashel squatted, holding his staff upright in one hand as he caught the nearer pitcher. It might have a few new dings in it, but he didn't guess the servant would get in real trouble.

"Oh, your lordship, I'm so sorry!" the fellow babbled. He took the ewer from Cashel's hand but he was trembling so bad he looked like he might drop it again. "I didn't see you!"

Cashel glanced at the door he'd come out of . . . and found there wasn't one, just a blank wall between the entrances to a pair of large suites. He stood up. "Sorry," he said apologetically. "I didn't mean to startle you."

Cashel headed on in the direction he'd been going when he'd first heard the girl—well, first heard Mona—crying. He'd never really liked this palace. It was a dingy place, badly run down before Garric arrived and replaced the Count of Haft with a vicar.

Nothing Cashel could see was different about it now, but the corridor seemed a little cheerier than it used to be. He smiled. He'd have started whistling if he could carry a tune.

❧ Gifts ❧

A World of Paksenarrion Story

Elizabeth Moon

In the fullness of spring, with flowers everywhere and the scent of them filling the nose, Dall Drop-hand, Gory the Tall's third son, quarrelled with his father and brothers, and went off to find adventure.

"You'll regret it," his father said.

"You'll come crawling back as soon as your belly gripes," said his oldest brother.

"You'll find out nobody wants a fool whose only talent is dropping things," said his second-oldest brother.

His younger brothers and two of his sisters merely jeered. But the last sister cried, and hugged him, and begged him to stay. The others watched, still laughing, and he turned away.

"Wait," she said. "I'll give you a parting gift."

"The only parting gift he needs is a kick in the pants," said his father. But he stood aside to let the girl scamper to her bed and pull out her treasure, a bit of wood carved in the likeness of a knife. She had found it lying loose among the leaves while nutting the year before. She ran back to her brother, and put it in his hand.

"Take this," she said. "You may need it."

It was only wood, and not very sharp, but hers was the only kind voice that day. "Are you sure, Julya?" he asked.

"I am," she said, standing straight as young children do, upright

211

as a pine, and she flung her arms around him and kissed him. Then she stood back, and he was bound to go, a gawky lad of no particular beauty or skill, out into the world all alone, at the very season when food was shortest, for no one can live on flowers.

He walked off down the path that led to the ford, and stopped to drink deeply of that fast, cold water. He would have taken some in a waterskin, but he had no waterskin. Still it was spring, with water running fast in every brook and rill, and he was sure he would find water at need. Food was another matter. He had no bow, no line for setting snares. In all this wealth of flowers, no fruit had set but wild plums, and they were green and hard as pebbles still. His eye fell on a ruffle of green leaves trembling in the moving water. They looked very much like the greens his mother grew in the back garden. He picked off a piece, and tasted it. Yes. The very same. He picked a handful, and stuffed them into his shirt and set off away from the stream, on a path that narrowed here to a foot's width from little travel.

By midafternoon, he had passed through the woods near the stream and come out into open country, fields grown up into tall grass and flowers that reached his waist. He had lost the path in that tall growth, and found it again by stumbling over its groove; now he walked slowly, letting his feet feel their way and hoping no snake lurked below, where he could not see through the lacework of white and yellow. In the distance, the land rose in billows to blue hills, but he could not tell how far off they were.

At sunfall, he was still in the fields, wading slowly through the flowers. He trampled out a circle his own length, with the groove of the footpath running across it, and sat down. The footpath made a little tunnel, forward and back, under the tall growth. If he'd been a small animal, he could have used it as a private road and traveled hidden. The thought amused him; he wondered what it would be like to be so small, to see the meadow as a forest. For him, the footpath would make a comfortable hole for his hip, when he lay down to sleep.

The leaves he'd gathered were a limp, unappetizing mess when he pulled them from his shirt, but he ate them anyway and tried not to think of his family at their supper. He lay down then, and sat up quickly as his sister's gift poked him in the side. He pulled it out and rubbed his finger along the rib of wood. There was still enough light to see that it gleamed a little, where his sister had rubbed it with fat, but not enough to see the design that his finger felt, something carved, not deeply, into it. He kissed the thing, blessing the sister who had given it—useless though it was, it had been her treasure—and lay down to sleep with it in his hand.

He woke in darkness, uneasy, at first not knowing where he was. His shirt had rucked up, baring his back to the chill spring breezes; he yanked it down one-handed but could not go back to sleep. Around him, over him, the grass and flower-stalks rustled in the breeze. So did something else; he sat up, eyes wide. Was that more than star-shadow, that dark movement on the trail? Meadow mice, probably, or the slightly larger field rats. A stoat? A fox?

Laughter ringed him in so suddenly that he felt a shock like cold water. They were all around him, tattered shadows in the starlight, holding weapons that already pricked his back, his sides. Weapons that glinted slightly in that faint light. Laughter stilled to uneasy silence.

"Mortal man, you trespass." That voice was high, higher than his youngest sister's, but very clear.

"I'm not a man," he said. His voice broke on the absurdity of that; he had told his father he was man enough, when his father called him boy once too often.

"Not a man?" the voice asked, mocking. Laughter rimmed the circle again, and again died. "And what, pray, art thou if not man? Art too tall for rockfolk, too uncomely for elvenkind, and having speech canst not be a mere beast, despite the smell . . ." More laughter.

He found his voice again. "I'm a boy." Most of the elder folk were kinder to children than adults; he would claim that protection if he could. Surely if his father considered him a mere boy, so also would beings far older than his father.

"I think not," the voice said. "I think thou art man grown, at least in some things . . ." The voice insinuated what things, and he felt himself going hot. "And since we found thee asleep athwart our high road, man-grown as thou art, I say again: mortal man, you trespass. And for your trespass, mortal man, you shall be punished."

The shift of tone, from common to formal and back again, jerked at his mind, confused him. He fell back on childhood's excuse. "I didn't know . . ."

"Did not know what? That this was our highway, or that it was forbidden to such as you?"

"Either—both. I was only trying to get away from home . . ." That sounded lame as a three-legged cow in the night, with sharp points pricking him.

"You drew a circle across our highway," the voice said. "You drew a circle and then lay athwart, your loins on the path, and you thought nothing of it? No loss to the world then, such an oaf as you."

"But a circle is holy," he said. "A circle protects . . ."

Hisses all around him, as sharp as sleet on stubble; his belly went cold.

"A circle with a line across it negates the protection of the circle," the voice said. "And when that line is our highway—you have made a grave error, mortal man, and you will indeed be punished. Away from home, you wanted to go? Away from home you shall go indeed, never to return . . ."

His fists clenched, in his fear, and in the heart hand his sister's gift bit into the insides of his fingers. But what use a little wooden knife-shape against the creatures here, whose sharp weapons were surely harder and sharper than wood?

He had to try. He shifted the knife forward in his hand, and the blade caught the starlight and flashed silver.

"Ahhhh . . . so you would fight?"

"I . . . just want to go," he said. He felt one of the weapons behind prick through his shirt, and jerked forward, away from that pain. The shadows in front retreated, as if that knife were a real weapon. He waved it experimentally, and they flinched away.

"Do you know what you bear?" the voice asked.

"It's a knife," he said.

"Thou art a fool, mortal man," the voice said. "Stay away from our highways; thy luck may change." The pricks at his side and back vanished; a huddle of dark shapes ran together, vanishing into the tunnel beneath the grass.

Dall stood up, his heart pounding. He could see nothing across the field but a blurred line where he had come from, his body pushing the grass and flowers aside, but nothing ahead. Yet now he knew the footpath was perilous, he could not go back to it. He did not know what those beings were. He never wanted to see them again.

From the line of his passage the day before, he struck out at an angle, pushing his way through the waist-high growth. As anyone who has ever tried it, he found walking in the dark more difficult than he expected. Where the surface of the flowers seemed level, the land below dipped and rose beneath his feet, here a hummock like a miniature hill just high enough to catch his toe, and there a hollow deep enough to jar his teeth when he staggered into it. He pushed on, careless of the noise he made and any hazards he might wake, until—witless with fatigue—he caught his foot on yet another hummock and measured his length in the tall growth, falling hard enough to knock the breath from his lungs. And there he slept, overcome by all that had happened, until the sun rose and an early bee buzzed past his ear.

In the morning, he could scarcely understand his panic of the night. He stood, stretched, and looked around him. His backward path was clear, a trampled line that twisted and turned like that of a fleeing rabbit. He thought he had gone straight, but by day he could see that he had not come half so far from the . . . the highway . . . as he hoped.

Remembering that, he looked again at his sister's gift. Clearly wood, carved to the likeness of a knife, and polished. In the low slanting light, he could see the incised design he'd felt before. He ran his forefinger over it, but nothing happened, and the lines themselves meant nothing to him. Whatever it was, it had driven away those . . . whatever they were.

He was hungry, but he often woke hungry at home, and nothing to eat until chores were done. He was thirsty, but he would come to water soon; all he had to do was go on. He looked around at the wide, green, flower-spangled world, and saw nothing he knew. He told himself he was happy about that. No father and brothers to bully him; no sisters to scold and laugh.

As morning wore on, hunger and thirst vied for his attention. Thirst won; by afternoon, he could think of nothing but water . . . and no water could he see, or sign of it. No friendly line of trees beside a brook or river . . . all around the grass lifted and flattened in the wind, billowing . . . the hills as distant as ever, flat and shimmery against the pale sky. He went on, into the lowering sun, hoping to get to the hills . . . surely he would find trees and water there.

Instead, he trod on something that yielded beneath his foot, and sharp pain stabbed his leg. With a gasp and cry, he threw himself away from whatever it was, and caught a glimpse of a long, sinuous body, checkered brown and yellow, as he landed hard on his side. He scrambled to his feet, but whatever it had been did not follow him. His leg burned and throbbed; the pain ran up and down his leg like scalding water. Groaning, he sat down again, and pulled up his trews. Two tiny dark holes a thumbwidth apart, and a rapidly purpling bruise around them. He felt sick and shaky. It must have been a serpent, but the little grass and water snakes near home had been smaller. They never bit anyone—of course he'd never stepped on one . . .

Suddenly his mouth was full of sour mucus; he spat, and blinked away tears. Poison. It was some kind of poison. His mother's mother, before she died, had said something about poison from evil creatures. Cut it out, she'd said, or cut it off. The wooden knife could not be sharp or strong enough, but it was all he had.

He touched the point of it to one of the fang-marks, but he could not make himself push it in . . . the pain was already beyond bearing, and how could he cause more. Thick yellow ooze came from the wound, running down over his leg like honey. He stared, blinked, and realized he felt better. The flow of liquid stopped. He moved the knife point to the other fang-mark, holding his breath . . . and again, the thick yellow oozed out, ran down his leg. His belly steadied back to the simple ache of hunger; his mouth was dry again. As he watched, the fang-mark closed over, leaving a dry pale dimple. The other one still gaped; he moved the knife tip back to it, and it too closed over.

Grass rustled; he jerked up, stared. Unwinking eyes stared at him from a narrow head on a long, coiled body. Another serpent, this one much larger. A pink forked tongue flickered out; he flinched, scooting backward, and held the knife forward. The serpent's head lowered.

Slowly, trembling, he clambered to his feet. He wanted to back away but what if there was another one . . . ? Holding the knife toward the serpent, he dared a quick glance behind him.

At his back stood someone he had never seen, someone who had appeared . . . he almost forgot the serpent, in that astonishment, but the serpent moved, and that caught his eye. Slowly, without appearing to move at all, it lowered its coils until it lay flat to the ground, and then, too fast to follow, whipped about and vanished into the grass.

"You're very lucky," the person said.

Dall could say nothing. He shook his head a little in his confusion. How could a full-grown man, dressed in fine leathers and a shirt with a lace collar, and boots to the thigh, have walked up on him without making a noise?

"I surprised you," the person said. "As you surprised the serpent's child."

"I don't know you," Dall said. He could think of nothing else to say.

"Nor I you," the stranger said. "But it needs no names to befriend someone, does it?"

"I—I'm Dall," Dall said. He almost added *Gory the Tall's third son*, but didn't because he had left home and could no longer claim his father's name.

"And I am Verthan," the stranger said. "You're a long way from a village, Dall. Gone hunting a lost sheep?"

"No . . . I left home," Dall said.

"You travel light," the stranger—Verthan—said. "Most men setting out would take at least a waterskin."

"Didn't have one," Dall muttered.

"Then you're thirsty, surely," Verthan said. "Have a drink of mine." He unhooked from his belt a skin dyed scarlet, bound in brown.

Dall reached for it, his mouth suddenly dryer than ever, but then pulled his hand back. He had nothing to trade, nothing at all, and the deepest rule he knew was hearth-sharing. He shook his head and shrugged.

"Nothing to share? You must have left in a hurry." Verthan shook his head. "You've set yourself a hard road, lad. But you'll not go much farther without water—water you must have."

Dall felt the words as if they were a hot summer wind in the hayfield; he felt dryness reach down his throat to his very marrow.

"I'll tell you what," Verthan said. "Why not trade your knife? Come evening, if you'll travel with me, we'll come to a place where you can gather early fruits, and we can trade it back to you. How's that?" He held out the water skin. Dall could see the damp surface of it; he could almost smell the water inside it; he could certainly hear it as the man shook it.

His hand jerked, as if someone had caught it from behind, and he felt the edges of the knife against the insides of his clenched fingers. The memory of the snake venom oozing out, and the sickness leaving . . . the memory of Julya's face, as she handed him the knife . . . He shook his head, mute because his mouth was too dry to speak.

Verthan's expression sharpened into anger, then relaxed again into humor. "You are not as stupid as you look," he said. Then, as wind blows a column of smoke, he blew away, and where he had stood a rustle in the grass moved off downslope.

Dall's knees loosened and he slumped down into the grass, frightened as he was of the grass and all that lived in it. He sat huddled a long time, hardly even aware of his thirst and hunger, while fear fled ice-cold up and down his veins.

Some while later, when fear had worn itself out, he became aware of something wet touching his hand. Too tired now to jump away, he looked. The wooden knife in his heart hand, blunt as it was, had poked a little way through the grass stems into the soil beneath. The wet soil, he now saw, for the base of the grass stems around it glistened with water, and his hand and the knife.

At once his thirst returned, fierce as fire, and he scrabbled at the place, digging with the knife. He could see it, he could smell it . . . when he had opened a space the size of his cupped palm, he pushed his face into it and a sucked in a half-mouthful of water flavored with shreds of dry grass and dirt. He spat out the mud, and swallowed the scant water. The tiny pool refilled; he drank again, this time with less mud in his mouth. Again. Again. And again. Each a scant mouthful, but each restoring a little of his strength.

When he had drunk until he could hold no more, he sat up and looked again at his sister's gift. Through his mind ran the events since he'd left home—the attack of the little people, the snakes, the phantom of the air, his thirst. Each time the thing had saved him, and he did not understand how. It looked like something an idle boy might whittle from any handy stick of wood. He himself had no skill at carving, but he had seen such things: little wooden animals and people and swords. As far as he knew— which seemed less far than the day before—none of those were magical. And so . . . his mind moved slowly, carefully, along the unaccustomed paths of logic . . . this must not be what it looked like. It must be something else. But what?

By now the sun hung low over the hills. He looked around. He had no idea where to go, or how to avoid the dangers he now knew inhabited these apparently harmless meadows. Only the gift that had saved him . . . could it help him find his way?

He bent again to the tiny pool of water, and then stood, holding the knife as always in his heart hand. How could he tell it his need? His hand twitched, without his intention. The thought came into his mind that he had not needed to tell the knife what his need was before. He held out his hand, palm up, and opened it. The knife squirmed on his hand—he almost dropped it in a moment of panic—and the tip pointed the way he least expected, downslope and back the way he had come. Toward that perilous footpath. Even—if he thought about it—toward home.

He did not want to go that way. Surely, with the knife's help, he could go on the way he wanted, into the hills . . . he might find more dangers, but the knife would protect him. It might even feed him.

His hand fell with the sudden weight of the knife, and lost its grip; the knife disappeared into the tall grass.

Dall cried out, wordless surprise and fear, and threw himself into the grass, feeling among the springy stems for something stiff, unyielding, wooden. Nothing. He tried to unthink the thought he'd had, promising the thing that he would follow its guidance always, in everything, if it would only come back.

Always? The question hung in the air, unspoken by mortal voice, but ringing in Dall's ears like the blow of a hammer.

"I'm sorry," he muttered aloud. "Julya gave it to me, and she loved me . . ."

A gust of wind flattened the grass over his head; pollen stung his eyes. He turned to blink and clear them, and there it lay, on top of the grass he had flattened while sitting on it. He reached out gingerly, wondering if it would let him touch it, and picked it up.

No heavier than at first. No less plain wood than at first. It lay motionless in his hand and when he stood he was facing the way the blade had pointed.

"All right then," he said. "Show me."

With water enough in his belly, the worst of the day's heat past, and the sun and high ground behind him, he made quick progress down and across the slope. Now his feet found good purchase wherever he trod, now the wind at his back cooled him without burning his face.

In the last of the light, he came to a stream fringed with trees. Was it the same stream he had crossed at the ford near his home? He could not tell, in the gloom. The knife had led him between the fringing trees to a flat rock beside the water, and there he drank his fill again, and there he found ready to hand the green leaves he knew could be eaten safely. He fell asleep on the rock, warded on three sides by clean running water, and woke before dawn, cold and stiff but otherwise unharmed, the knife still in his hand.

He expected the knife to lead him back home, to return it to his sister Julya, but instead it led him upstream, and insisted (for its guidance strengthened as the day went on) that he stay within the trees beside the stream, and on this hither side. Because of the trees, he could not see the land around, but he knew it rose by the ache in his legs from climbing, always climbing, ever more steeply as the water's note changed from the quiet gurgle lower down to the high, rapid laugh as it fell over taller and taller rocks.

Near the stream he found a few early berries, gleaming red, and ate them, along with more of the greens. He pried loose a few clingshells from rocks and sucked out the sweet meat inside; he managed to tickle one fish in the noon silence, when the knife had made it clear (how he was still not sure) that he should rest by the stream awhile. Always he had water to drink, so by nightfall he was well content to sleep again, this time in a hollow between oak roots.

Midmorning the next day, following the stream ever higher, he came out of the woods into a wide bare land of low grass, with here and there tussocks of reeds and an occasional gnarled shrub. Now he could see over the land—see how the trees traced out the stream below in its twists and turns and joinings with others . . . see little columns of smoke far in the distance that might have come from farmhouse chimneys . . . see the great green sea of grass breaking on the hills' knees, washing up this high as grass that would not cover the top of his foot.

Upslope, where the stream leaped in silver torrents from rock to rock, the land heaped up in mounds as far as he could see, all the way to the pale sky. Off to his right a great rocky wall, blue-shadowed and white-topped, had risen as if from nowhere . . . far higher than the hills he'd seen from home.

You wanted adventure. Again that voiceless voice, those words with no breath, hung in the air. *Now will you follow? Or shall I take you home?*

Against the memory of home—sweeter now than it had been when he left—came the memory of that first night and day of terror, and then the pleasanter but still strenous days of travel since. What finally determined him to keep going was the memory of Julya. She would be glad to see him come home, but she alone had believed he might do something . . . become something. For her he would keep going until he could bring her . . . something worth the gift she had given him.

"I'll go on," Dall said.

Silence. He scrubbed one leg with the other foot, and waited. The knife lay quiescent in his hand. That had not, he realized, been the question. It had been *follow or go home*, not *go on or go home*.

"I'll follow," he said.

The knife twitched, and Dall headed on up the steepening slope, following the knife and the cold rush of water.

Finally, legs trembling with fatigue, he staggered up yet another slope to find that the water gushed from a cleft in the rocks beside the thread of trail. Above him the slope broke into vertical slabs of rock, bare and forbidding in the evening shadows beneath a darkening sky. Dall looked back, where the land beyond sloped down again, down and down into a purple gloom that hid every place he had ever been. Did the knife expect him to climb those rocks? He was sure he could not. He looked around for someplace to sleep, finally creeping between two massive boulders each bigger than his family's hut, but an insistent breeze chilled him wherever he tried to curl up, and he could not really sleep.

He was awake, and just this side of shivering in the chill, when he heard the cry. He was on his feet, peering wide-eyed into the darkness, when he felt the knife twitch in his hand. "But it's dark," he said. "I can't see where I'm going." He thought perhaps the knife would glow, giving light for him to see. Instead, it pricked his fingers, a sharp sting.

Another cry, and hoarse shouts. Shaking with fear, Dall started that way, only to run into one of the rocks. He scrabbled back; his foot landed on loose rubble, and he fell, rocks rolling about him and down below, loud and louder. He slid with them, flung out his arms and tried to stop himself. He had scrambled up over a ledge . . . and now his legs waved in the cold air, his belly lay against a sharp irregular edge, his bruised, skinned fingers dug in.

He pulled himself up a little, panting with fear, and felt around with his use-hand for a better purchase. Then his foot bumped the rock below, and he remembered where the foothold had been. He let himself slide backward, into the air and darkness, and another rock fell from the ledge, bounced loudly below, and hit something that clanged louder than his mother's soup-kettle.

This time he heard, though he did not understand the words, the angry voice below. He pressed himself against the cold rock, shivering. But his heart hand cramped, and he had to move, and again rocks fell from under his feet, and he lost his grip on the rock, falling his own length in a rattle of small stones to land on something that heaved and swore, this time in words he'd heard before. Hard hands clamped on his bare ankle, on his arm, angry voices swore revenge and stank of bad ale and too much onion . . . and without thought his heart hand swept forward, and the hand on his ankle released it with a hiss of pain, and with another swipe the grip on his arm disappeared.

"Back!" he heard someone say, panting. "It's not worth it—" And there was a scramble and rattle and clang and clatter of rocks on stone, and metal on rocks, and shod feet on rocks and someone falling and someone cursing—more than one someone—all drawing away into the night and leaving him crouched breathless and shaking.

He drew a long breath and let it out in a sigh that was almost a sob. Like an echo of his own, another sigh followed, then a groan. He froze, staring into darkness, seeing nothing . . . he could hear breathing. Harsh, irregular, with a little grunt at each exhalation. Off to his left a little, the way the knife pulled at him now. He took a cautious step, his left foot landing on a sharp pebble—a quick step then, and his foot came down on something soft, yielding.

The scream that followed knocked him to the ground like a blow, his fear came so strongly. Once there he fell asleep all at once, heedless of his scrapes and bruises and the danger.

In the first cold light of dawn, the man's face might have been carved of the stone he lay on, flesh tight to the bone with care and pain. Dall stared at the face. Longer of jaw than his father's, it still had something of the same look in the deep lines beside the mouth, the deep-cut furrows of the brow.

Color seeped into the world with the light. That dark stain, almost black at first, was blood—bright red where it was new, the color of dirty rust where it had dried. The man's shirt had once been white, and edged with lace; now it was filthy, soaked with blood, spattered with it even where it was not soaked. His trews were cut differently than any Dall had seen, fitted closer to his legs, and he had boots—real leather boots—on his feet. They were caked with dried mud, worn at the instep, with scuffed marks on the side of the heels. The dangling ends of thongs at his waist showed where something had been cut away. Dall could smell the blood, and the sour stench of ale as well.

The man groaned. Dall shuddered. He knew nothing of healing arts, and surely the man was dying. Dead men—men dead of violence, and not eased into the next world by someone who knew the right words to say—could not rest. Their angry spirits rose from their bodies and sought unwary travelers whose souls eased their hunger and left the travelers their helpless slaves forever. Such tales Dall's grandda had told by the winter fireside; Dall knew he was in danger more than mortal, for he knew none of the right words to smooth a dying man's path.

He tried to push himself up, but he was too stiff to stand up and his ankle—he could just see, now, that it was swollen as big as a cabbage and he could feel it throbbing—would not bear his weight even as he tried to get away on hands and knees.

The man shifted in his blood-soaked clothes, groaned again, and opened his eyes. Dall stared. Bloodshot green eyes stared back.

"Holy Falk," the man said. His voice was breathy but firm, not the voice of a dying man. He sounded more annoyed than anything else. He glanced down at himself and grimaced. "What happened, boy?"

Dall gulped, swallowed, and spoke aloud for the first time in days. "I don't know . . . sir."

"Ah . . . my head . . ." The man lay back, closed his eyes a moment, and then looked at Dall again. "Bring water, there's a good lad, and some bread . . ."

The incongruity made Dall giggle with relief. The man scowled.

"There's no bread," Dall said. His stomach growled loudly at that. "And I don't have a waterskin."

"Am I not in the sotyard . . . ?" The man pushed himself up on one elbow, and his brows raised. "No, I suppose I'm not. What place is this, boy?"

"I don't know, sir." This time the *sir* had come easily.

"Are you lost too, then?"

"I—aren't you dying, then?"

The man laughed, a laugh that caught on a groan. "No, boy. Not that easily. Why did you think—?" He looked down at himself, and muttered "Blood . . . always blood . . ." then squeezed his eyes shut and shook his head. When he next looked up, his face was different somehow. "Look here, boy, I hear a stream. You could at least fetch some water from there . . . I have a waterskin . . ." He patted his sides, then shook his head. "Or I suppose I don't. It must've been thieves, I imagine. Were there thieves, boy?"

"I didn't see them," Dall said. Odds on this man was a thief himself. "I heard yells in the dark. Then I fell . . ."

Now the man's eyes looked at him as if really seeing him. "By the gods, you did fall—you look almost as bad as I feel. You saved my life," the man said. "It was a brave thing, to come down on unknown dangers in the dark, and take on two armed men, a boy like you."

Dall felt his ears going hot. "I . . . didn't mean to," he said.

"Didn't mean to?"

"No . . . I fell off the cliff."

"Still, your fall saved me, I don't doubt. Ohhhh . . ." Another groan, and the man had pushed himself up to sitting, and grabbed for his head as if it would fall off and roll away. "I don't know why I drink that poison they call ale . . ."

"For the comfort of forgetting," Dall said, quoting his father.

A harsh laugh answered him. "Aye, that's the truth, though you're over-young to have anything worth forgetting, I'd say. You—" The man stopped suddenly and stared at the ground by Dall's hand. "Where did you get that?" he asked.

Dall had forgotten the knife, but there it lay, glinting a little in first rays of the sun. He reached and put his hand over it. "My sister gave it to me," he said. "It's only wood . . ."

"I see that," the man said. He shook his head, and then grunted with pain. Dall knew that sound; his father had been drunk every quarter-day as long as he could remember. The man pushed himself to hands and knees, and crawled to the tiny stream, where he drank, and splashed water on himself, and then, standing, stripped off his bloody clothes. There was plenty of light now, and Dall could see the bruises and cuts on skin like polished ivory, marked as it was with old scars on his sides.

While the man's back was turned, Dall pushed himself up a little, wincing at the pain—he hurt everywhere—and picked up the wooden knife. If it could mend a serpent bite, what about a swollen ankle? And for that matter the bloody scrape some rock had made along his arm? He laid the knife to his arm, but nothing happened. Nor when he touched it to his ankle.

The man turned around while Dall still had the knife on his ankle. "What are you doing?" he asked sharply.

"Nothing," Dall said, pulling his hand back quickly. "Just seeing how bad it hurt if I touched it."

"Hmmm." The man cocked his head. "You know, boy—what is your name, anyway?"

"Dall Drop—Dall, son of Gory," Dall said.

"Dall Drop? That's one I haven't heard."

"My father calls me 'Drop-hand'," Dall said, ducking his head.

"Drop-*body*, if last night was any example," the man said, chuckling. Dall felt himself going hot. "Nay, boy—it's not so bad. Your dropping in no doubt scared those thieves away. Maybe it was all accident, but you did good by it. Let's see about your wounds . . ."

"They're not wounds," Dall said. "Just cuts and things."

"Well, cuts or whatever, they could use some healing," the man said. He looked around. "And none of the right herbs here. We'll have to get you down to a wood, and you can't walk on that ankle."

" 'M sorry," Dall muttered.

"Nonsense," the man said. "Just let me get the blood off this—" He took his wadded shirt back to the creek. Dall gaped. Was he going to pollute the pure water with his blood? But the man sat down, pulled off one of his boots, and scooped up a bootful of water, then stuffed his shirt into the boot and shook it vigorously. The water came out pink; he dumped the wet shirt on the ground, emptied the bloody water into a clump of grass, and did it again. That was bad enough, but at least he wasn't dipping the shirt itself in the water.

After several changes of water, he came back to Dall with the sopping mess of his shirt, wrung it out, and reached for Dall's foot. "This'll hurt, boy, but it'll help, too."

It did hurt; every movement of the foot hurt, and the wet shirt was icy. The man wrapped it around his ankle, and used the sleeves to tie it tightly. Dall could feel his bloodbeat throbbing against the tight wrapping.

"Now, boy, give me your hand."

Dall had reached out his hand before he thought; the man took it and heaved him up in one movement.

"You'll have to walk; I'm still too drunk to carry you safely on this ground," the man said. "I can help, though. Let me guide you."

"Sir," Dall said. His foot hurt less than he expected as he hobbled slowly, leaning on the man's shoulder. The other aches also subsided with movement, though his cuts and scrapes stung miserably.

It was a slow, painful traverse of the slope, down and across, even when they came to the thread of a path the man said he'd followed the night before. "Sheep are not men," the man said, when they came to the first drop in the path. He slid down first, and Dall followed. The man caught him before his bad ankle hit the path. That was almost all the man said, other than the occasional "Mind this" and "That rock tips."

The sun was high overhead when the path widened abruptly at the head of a grassy valley, where several sheep trails came together. Ahead, smoke rose from a huddle of low buildings. Dall could smell cooked food for the first time in days; his stomach growled again and he felt suddenly faint. He sagged; the man muttered something but took more of his weight. "Come on, boy— you've done well so far," he said.

Dall blinked and gulped, and managed to stand more on his own feet. The man helped him down the wider track to an open space where someone had placed a couple of rough benches around a firepit. No one was visible outside the buildings, but from the smell someone was busy inside them. The man lowered Dall to one of them, then bent to unwrap his ankle. "I need a shirt, boy, if I'm to talk someone into giving us food. And down here I should be able to find the right leaves for your injuries."

Dall's ankle had turned unlovely shades of green and purple; now his foot was swollen as well. The man shrugged into the wet, dirty shirt, and headed for one of the huts as if he knew it. Dall glanced around, and caught sight of someone peeking around a house-wall at him. A child, younger, smaller. He looked away, then looked back quickly. A boy, wearing a ragged shirt much like his own over short trews . . . barefoot as he was. The boy offered a shy smile; Dall smiled back. The boy came nearer; he could have been Dall's younger brother if he'd had one.

"What happened to you?" the boy asked. "Did he beat you?"

"No," Dall said. "I fell on the mountain."

"You need to wrap that," the boy said, pointing to his ankle. "Are you hungry?"

"I have nothing to share," Dall said.

"You're hurt. It's Lady's grace," the boy said. "Don't you have that where you come from?"

"Yes . . . I just . . ."

"I'll get something," the boy said, and was gone like a minnow in the stream, in an instant.

He was back in a moment, with a hunk of bread in his hand. "Here, traveler; may the Lady's grace nourish us both."

"In grace given, in grace eaten, blessed be the Lady." Dall broke the bread, giving a piece back to the boy, and looked around for the man. He had disappeared; an empty doorway suggested where he'd gone. Dall took a bite of bread and the younger boy did also.

The bread tasted better than anything he'd ever eaten, so much better that he forgot the pain in his foot, and his other pains. He could've eaten the whole piece, but he set aside a careful half for the man, in case no one shared with him.

But the man was coming back now, carrying a jug and another loaf. "I see you've made friends," he said.

"I saved you a bit," Dall said. "It's Lady's grace."

The man raised his eyebrows. "I suppose we could all use grace."

He ate the piece Dall had set aside, then broke the loaf he carried. "Here—you could eat more, I daresay. And here's water."

Dall wanted to ask if this too had been given as Lady's grace, but he didn't. The man sat a few minutes, eating, and taking sips of the water. Then he stood. "I'd best be going to work," he said. "There's a wall to mend." He nodded at the far end of the village, where one wall of a sheepfold bulged out, missing stones at the top. Dall started to push himself up and the man shook his head. "Not you, boy. You're still hurt. Just rest there, and one of the women will be out to tend you shortly. She's boiling water for boneset tea for you."

That night Dall lay on straw, his injured ankle wrapped in old rags. Sleeping under a roof again after so many nights in the open made him as wakeful as his first nights on the trail. He could hear the breathing of others in the cottage, and smell them all too. He wanted to crawl outside into the clean night air scented with growing things, but that would be rude. Finally he fell asleep, and the next morning ate his porridge with pleasure. Cooked food was worth the discomforts of the night, he decided.

He and the man stayed in the village for six hands of days; the man worked at whatever chores anyone put him to, without comment or complaint. As Dall became able to hobble around more easily, he too worked. It was strange to do the familiar work he had grown up with, but for strangers. When he dropped something—less often than before—he waited for the familiar jibes, but none came. Not even when he dropped a jug of new milk and broke the jug.

"Never mind," said the woman for whom he'd been carrying that jug and two others. "It's my fault for giving you more than you could carry, and the handle on that one's been tricky for years." She was a cheerful dark-haired woman with wide hips and a wider smile; all her children were like her, and the boy who had first given him bread was her youngest.

One evening after supper, Dall had an itch down his back, and scratched at it with the point of the wooden knife. The man watched him, and then asked, "Where did you get that knife?"

"I told you—my sister gave it to me." Dall sighed with relief as the tip found the perfect itchy spot to scratch.

"And where did she get it?"

"She found it in the woods last fall; we were all out nutting together, and she was feeling among the leaves in between the roots, and there it was."

"By itself?"

"I don't know. I didn't see her find it. Why, what could have been with it?"

The man sat down, heavily. "Dall, I carved that knife myself, two winters gone. I had thrown away my sword—oh, aye, I had a sword once, and mail that shone like silver, and a fine prancing horse, too. I had a dagger yet, and while I was snowed in, that first winter of my freedom, I whittled away on the kindling sticks. Most I burnt, but a few I kept, for the pleasure of remembering my boy's skill. Then spring came, and when I set out again I tossed them in the stream one summer's day to watch them float away."

"So the knife is yours," Dall said.

"I threw it away," the man said. "Like my sword. And unlike my sword it has come back, in a hand that valued it more." He cleared his throat. "I just wondered . . . if any of the others were found. Some flowers—mostly rose designs, over and over—and one fairly good horse."

"I don't know," Dall said. "But if the knife is yours . . ." He held it out.

The man shook his head. "No, lad. I threw it away; it's yours now."

"But it's special," Dall said. "It saved me—" He rattled on quickly, sensing the man's unwillingness to hear, about the little people in the grass, and the serpent's bite, and the strange being that appeared from nowhere and vanished back into nowhere, and the water . . .

The man stared at him, open-mouthed. "That knife?"

"This knife," Dall said. He held it out again. "Your knife. You made it; the magic must be from you."

"'To ward from secret treachery, from violence and from guile, from deadly thirst and hunger, from evil creatures vile . . .'" The man's voice trailed off. "It can't be . . ." His fingers stretched toward it, then his fist clenched. "It can't be. It's gone; what's loosed cannot be caught again."

"That's silly," Dall said. He felt silly too, holding out the knife. "When we let the calf out of the pen, we just catch it and bring it back."

"Magic is not a cow, boy!" The man's voice was hoarse now; Dall hardly dared look at his face for the anger he expected to see, but instead there were tears running down the furrows beside his mouth. "I forswore it . . ."

And will the wind not blow? And will not the spring return? The man's head jerked up; he must have heard it too.

Dall took a small step forward, and laid the knife in the man's hand, folding the man's fingers around it. As he stepped back, he saw the change, as if the sun had come out from behind a cloud. Light washed over the man, and behind it the man's filthy old shirt shone whiter than any cloth Dall had seen. His scuffed, worn boots gleamed black; his mud-streaked trews were spotless. On his tired, discouraged face, a new expression came: hope, and love, and light. What had seemed gray hair, once clean, now gleamed a healthy brown.

And the knife, the simple wooden knife, stretched and changed, until the man held a sword out of old tales. Dall had never seen a sword at all, let alone such a sword as that.

Vows are not so easily broken, or duties laid aside. Dall had no idea what that was about, but the man did; his quick head-shake and shrug changed to an expression of mingled awe and sorrow. He fell to his knees, holding the sword carefully, hilt upright. Dall backed away; a stone nudged the back of his legs and he sat down on it. He watched the man's lips move silently, until the man looked straight at him out of those strange green eyes, eyes still bright with tears.

"Well, boy, you have done quite a work here."

"I didn't mean to," Dall said.

"I'm glad you did," the man said. He stood, and held out his hand. "Come, let me call you friend. My name's Felis, and I was once a paladin of Falk. It seems Falk wants me back, even after—even now." He looked at the sword, the corners of his mouth quirking up in what was not quite a smile. "I think I'd better find this wood where your sister found the knife I carved, and see if any of the other bits washed up there. Something tells me the road back to Falk may prove . . . interesting."

Dall took the proferred hand and stood.

"What about me?" he asked.

"I hope you will travel with me," the man said. "You saved my life and you brought me back my knife . . . my life, actually, as a servant of Falk. And surely you want the sister who found it to know that it saved you."

"Go *home*?" Dall's voice almost squeaked. He could imagine his father's sarcasm, his brother's blows.

"It seems we both must," Felis said. "We both ran away; the knife called us both. But neither of us will stay with your father, I'm sure. What—do you think a boy who has saved a paladin remains a drop-hand forever?"

〜   〜   〜

In the days of high summer, when the trees stood sentinel over their shade at noon, still and watchful, and spring's racing waters had quieted to clear pools and murmuring riffles, Dall no longer Drop-hand returned to his home, walking across the hayfield with a tall man whose incongruous clothes bore no sweat-stains, even in that heat. Gory the Tall recognized Dall the moment he came out of the trees, but the man with the spotless white shirt and the sword he did not recognize. Dall's brothers stood as if struck by lightning, watching their brother come, moving with the grace of one who does not stumble even on rough paths.

That evening, in the long soft twilight, Felis told of Dall's courage, of the magic in the knife he'd carved, of his oaths and his need to return.

"Then—I suppose this is yours too," said the youngest girl, Julya. She fished out of her bodice a little flat circle of wood carved with rose petals and held it out to him. Dall could hear the tears in her voice.

Felis shook his head. "Nay, lass. When I carved the flowers, I thought of my own sisters, far away. If it has magic, let it comfort you." He touched it with his finger. Then the air was filled with the perfume of roses, a scent that faded only slowly. The girl's face glowed with joy; she sniffed it again and tucked it back into her clothes.

"And he really saved you?" Dall's oldest brother asked.

"I slipped and fell," Dall said.

"At exactly the right moment," Felis said, a wave of his hand shutting off the gibes Dall's brothers had ready. "I hope he'll come with me, help me find the rest of the carvings I must find before I go back to my order."

"But—" Gory the Tall peered through the gloom at his son and at Felis. "If he's not the boy he was ..."

"Then it's time for him to leave," Felis said. He turned to Dall. "If you want to, that is."

He was home without blows and jeers; he had triumphed. If he stayed, he would have that to fall back on. Stories to tell, scars to show. If he left, this time it would be for such adventures as paladins find—he knew far more about real adventures now than he had ... and he was no longer angry and hurt, with every reason to go and none to stay.

An evening breeze stirred the dust, waking all the familiar smells of home. At his back, Julya pressed close; he could just smell the rose-scent of the carving in her bodice. But beyond that, he could smell the creek, the trees, the indefinable scent of lands beyond that he had only begun to know.

"I will go with you," he said to Felis. And then, to his family, "And someday I will come home again, with gifts for you all."

❧ The Amorous Broom ❧

A John Justin Mallory story

Mike Resnick

John Justin Mallory, his feet up on his desk, his battered fedora worn at an angle, was studying the *Racing Form*.

"You know," he announced, "I think I just may take a run out to the track this afternoon."

"Oh my God!" breathed Winnifred Carruthers, his pudgy, pink-faced, gray-haired partner. "That poor creature is entered again, isn't he?"

"How did you guess?" asked Mallory.

"It's the only time you ever go to the track—when Flyaway's running."

" 'Running' is an overstatement," said the not-quite-human creature perched atop the refrigerator in the next room. "Flyaway plods."

"When I want advice from the office cat," said Mallory irritably, "rest assured I'll ask for it."

"That's what Flyaway does," continued Felina from atop the refrigerator. "He rests assured."

"If you ever leave here," said Mallory, "don't apply for a job as a comedian."

"Why should I leave here?" purred Felina. "It's warm and dry and you feed me."

"How many races has Flyaway lost in a row now, John Justin?" asked Winnifred.

"Fifty-three."

"Doesn't that suggest something to you?" she persisted.

"That it's past time for him to win."

"You are the finest detective in this Manhattan," continued Winnifred. "How can you be so stupid?"

"O ye of little faith," said Mallory.

"You've solved a lot of tricky cases, and put yourself in harm's way at least half a dozen times. Did you do it solely so you could keep losing your money on Flyaway?"

"When I go out on a case, my function is to detect," replied Mallory. "When I go to the track, my function is to bet. Why do you have such a problem with that? Mallory & Carruthers is paying its bills. This is discretionary income."

"I don't have a problem with betting," shot back Winnifred. "But betting involves an element of chance. Putting your money on Flyaway doesn't."

"You're going to look mighty silly when he finally wins one," said Mallory.

"Well said!" cried a voice. "You tell 'em, John Justin Mallory!"

Mallory was on his feet in an instant. "Who said that?" he demanded.

Felina leaped catlike to the floor and bounded into the office. She grinned, extended a shining claw at the end of her forefinger, and pointed it toward a broom that was leaning against a wall in the far corner.

"Come on," said Mallory. "Brooms don't talk."

"I most certainly do," said the broom.

Mallory stared at the broom for a moment, then looked at Winnifred. "Yours?" he asked.

"I never saw it before," she said.

"Then what's it doing here?"

"Why not ask it?" suggested Winnifred.

"I've never spoken to a broom before. How does one address it?"

"You may call me Hecate," said the broom.

"Isn't that a witch's name?" asked Winnifred.

"She was my first owner."

"All right, Hecate," said Mallory. "Who and what are you, and more to the point, what are you doing in my office?"

"I want to be near you, John Justin Mallory," said Hecate.

"Why?"

"The Grundy hates you. Isn't that enough?"

"Okay, he's behind this, right?"

"No, he doesn't know I'm here," said the broom.

"It's pretty hard to keep a secret from the most powerful demon on the East Coast," said Mallory. He paused. "Where does the Grundy *think* you are?"

"Hanging on his wall with his other magical trophies."

"Why aren't you there?"

"He's mean and cruel and unfeeling," complained the broom. "He put me there a year ago and hasn't let me down since. I made up my mind to escape months ago, but I didn't know where to find sanctuary until he started complaining about you. Mallory did this, and Mallory did that, and Mallory thwarted him again— so I knew that you were the one person who could protect me from the Grundy." Hecate paused. "He was wrong about you. You're beautiful, John Justin Mallory."

Mallory turned to Winnifred. "Call a cab."

"What are you going to do?" asked Hecate apprehensively.

"I'm going to return you to your owner before he rips my office apart looking for you."

"But you can't! He'll just hang me on that wall again!"

"We all have problems," said Mallory, walking across the room toward the broom. "Yours will have to be resolved without my help."

He picked up the broom and began carrying it to the front door.

It squealed.

"Oh, my! What strong, manly hands you have, John Justin Mallory!"

"Where the hell's your voice coming from?" asked Mallory.

"Why?"

"I want to shut you up. I thought I'd put some tape over your mouth."

"I'll never tell!"

Mallory opened the door, then looked back over his shoulder. "Tell them I'll pay double if the cabbie doesn't ask any questions."

"Right," said Winnifred.

It took Mallory twenty minutes to drive to the Grundy's Gothic Baptist castle at the north end of Central Park. He handed the broom to one of the Grundy's trolls, then walked back across the drawbridge, climbed into the cab, and had it drive him home.

When he entered the office the broom was propped against his desk, waiting for him.

"I forgive you, John Justin Mallory," it said.

"How the hell did you get back ahead of me?"

"I'm a magic broom. I can fly. My original mistress and I used to fly everywhere. She loved the loop-the-loop, before my arthritis made it too difficult."

"Forget all that," said Mallory. "You don't seem to understand the situation here. You belong to my mortal enemy, a being who can bring freezing weather to the whole damned city just by blowing on it. He touches things and they die. If he finds you here, he's going to think—"

"Think what?" interrupted a familiar voice.

"*Oh, shit!*" muttered Mallory, turning to face his newest visitor. "Doesn't anyone ever knock or even use a door anymore?"

The creature facing Mallory was tall, a few inches over six feet, with two prominent horns protruding from his hairless head. His eyes were a burning yellow, his nose sharp and aquiline, his teeth white and gleaming, his skin a bright red. His shirt and pants were crushed velvet, his cloak satin, his collar and cuffs made of the fur of some white polar animal. He wore gleaming black gloves and boots, and he had two mystic rubies suspended from his neck on a golden chain. When he exhaled, small clouds of vapor emanated from his mouth and nostrils.

"Why should I knock?" replied the Grundy. "Did you knock when you stole my broom from me?"

"I didn't steal it," said Mallory. "Hell, I just drove across the city to return it."

"Yet here it is," said the Grundy, pointing to Hecate.

"Take it," said Mallory. "I didn't ask for it and I don't want it. It's yours."

"How can you say that after all we've been to each other?" demanded the broom.

"We haven't been a thing to each other, and we're never going to see each other again!" snapped Mallory. He picked the broom up and thrust it into the Grundy's hands. "Take it and get the hell out of here."

"You still have no fear of me, have you?" asked the Grundy curiously.

"Let's say I have a healthy respect for what you can do," answered Mallory.

"But no fear."

"Not today. I didn't steal the damned thing, and you must know it. It's not *my* fault that your broom has a crush on me." He paused thoughtfully. "Maybe you should introduce it to a nice, masculine mop."

"No!" cried the broom. "It's *you* that I want!"

Mallory and the Grundy exchanged looks, and for the first time since arriving in this Manhattan from his own, the detective actually felt a surge of sympathy for the demon. What could one, even a demon, do in the face of such earnest if misdirected passion?

"Mallory!" screamed the broom, as the Grundy secured his grip on it. "Aren't you going to say anything?"

"We'll always have Paris," answered Mallory.

And then the Grundy and the broom blinked out of sight, all trace of them gone in the smallest fraction of a second.

"Well," said Mallory, "what did you think of that?"

"I felt sorry for it," said Winnifred.

"We've got Felina. One freeloader is enough."

"But to spend the rest of its life hanging on a wall..."

"It's a *broom*, for God's sake!" said Mallory irritably. "It doesn't *have* a life."

"It feels and it thinks," insisted Winnifred stubbornly.

"It feels foolishly and it thinks irrationally," replied Mallory.

"So says the man who's about to bet on Flyaway again."

"Maybe I'll just go to the Emerald Isle Pub and hang one on," muttered Mallory. "I've got to get away from this place."

"I'll go with you," said a voice.

"Shit! You're back *again*?" growled Mallory, looking around the room until he finally spotted the broom leaning against the fireplace. "Didn't the Grundy just take you away about two minutes ago?"

"He adjusts time for his own convenience," said the broom. "I've been back at the castle for almost three days of subjective time. I had to wait until the room was empty of trolls, goblins, and leprechauns before I made my escape."

"You know that I'm just going to send you back," said Mallory wearily.

"No!" cried the broom. "You can't send me back to a life of humiliation and degradation. Everyone looks at me as if I'm... I'm some kind of *object*."

"I don't know how to tell you this gently," said Mallory, "but you *are* an object."

"No! I'm a living entity, with hopes and dreams and fears and sexual needs!"

"I don't think I want to hear about this," said Mallory.

"You *can't* send me back! I beg of you, Mallory—I live only for you! Let me come out and catch criminals with you!"

"I'm not a cop. I don't go out and walk a beat and catch criminals. I'm a detective. I wait until someone hires me."

"You need management. Advertising. Let me write your phone book ads." It lowered its voice to a whisper. "And lose the fat broad. I'm all you'll ever need."

"Well, I like *that!*" snorted Winnifred.

"Have you any other requests?" asked Mallory sardonically.

"Make sure the cat thing doesn't sharpen her claws on me."

"That's all?"

"That's all—except that I'm dying to see you work. When do you expect to be tailing a villain up a dark alley?"

"Not for at least five or ten minutes," said Mallory sardonically.

"Then I'll just stay right here and admire you," said the broom. "You're beautiful, John Justin Mallory. Exquisite. Perfection personified."

"Thank you," said Mallory in bored tones.

"I'll bet you'd be hell in a heart-shaped waterbed with a mirror on the ceiling."

"Goddammit!" snapped Mallory. "I've been in this Manhattan for almost two years now, and every time I think I'm starting to really understand it, someone says something like that!"

"*I* understand it," offered Felina. "It's filled with people who were put here to scratch me and feed me." She sidled over to Mallory. "Ask it if it drinks milk."

"You want to share your milk with it?" asked Mallory, surprised.

"If it says it does, I'll scratch it until it's nothing but a pile of wood shavings."

"I heard that!" said the broom sternly. "What kind of monsters do you keep in your office, Mallory?"

The detective sighed. "The kind that won't go away."

"In answer to the cat thing's question, I don't drink milk."

"Just out of curiosity, what *do* you eat and drink?" asked Mallory, still wondering where its mouth was.

"It's been so long since I've eaten, I can't remember," said the broom. "Not all of us lead a life of privilege. Some of us undergo endless privation while the object of our affection continues to ignore us."

"I've been the object of your affection for about ten minutes, tops," said Mallory.

"Not so. I've loved you from afar for years."

"Years?" demanded Mallory.

"Well, weeks, anyway," said the broom. "Why must you insist

on precision, John Justin Mallory? Why don't you just sweep me up in your arms and tell me you return my love?"

"You want a list of reasons?"

"My God, you know how to hurt a person!" moaned the broom. "This is so humiliating—especially in front of the fat broad and the cat thing."

"I'm sure they both appreciate your sensitivity."

"How could they? They're still here!"

"They belong here. You don't."

"How can you say that to me?" demanded the broom. "Who else loves you so completely and unselfishly? Who else hears heavenly music at the sound of your voice? This is the passion of the eons! How can you be so blind to it?"

"I have cataracts," said Mallory dryly.

"I pour my heart out in front of these two unwanted hangers-on, and you make puny little jokes. Do you enjoy causing me such pain?"

"I hadn't really thought about it," admitted Mallory. "But now that you mention it, somehow I don't feel guilty at all."

The broom screamed in agony. "Cut me to the quick! Spit on my love! See if I care!"

"This has gone on long enough," said Mallory. He picked up his phone and dialed the letters G, R, U, N, D and Y in succession. An instant later the Grundy materialized in front of the detective's desk.

"Will you please take your emotionally unstable broom back?" said Mallory.

The Grundy stared at the broom for a long moment, then turned back to the detective. "This broom is proving to be more trouble than it's worth. I hereby give it to you."

"I don't want it."

The broom moaned.

"What you want doesn't interest me," said the Grundy. "The broom is yours."

"You're all heart, Grundy," said Mallory.

"Save your sarcasm, Mallory," said the Grundy. "You will need it for comfort when I am slowly and painfully disemboweling you."

"Were you planning on doing that sometime soon?"

"Soon, late, what is the difference? Death always wins in the end."

"I don't know why you're so anxious to kill me," said Mallory. "I'm the only person you know who's never lied to you."

"Why do you think you're still alive?" said the demon, and vanished.

"Everyone comes and goes so fast here," said Mallory sarcastically. "Somehow, I don't think we're in Kansas anymore, Toto."

"My name is Hecate, not Toto," said the broom. "And now we can be together forever and ever. Isn't it wonderful?"

Mallory looked across the room at Winnifred. "You know, I could really grow to hate that goddamned demon."

"What do you plan to do about . . . well, you know?"

"The broom?" he said. "Well, it's here and it's ours. We may as well put it to work."

"I don't do dishes or windows," said the broom.

"You're magic. You have powers. I was thinking of taking you on a case and seeing what you can do."

"You and me? Together? Stalking super-villains to their lairs? Breaking up international espionage gangs?"

"We've got a lady goblin who thinks her husband is cheating on her," said Mallory. "I've got to follow him until I find out if she's right or wrong."

"How mundane!"

"They give you medals for tracking down super-villains," explained Mallory. "They give you money for tracking down straying husbands. We're running a business."

"It makes no difference," said the broom after a moment's consideration. "As long as I can be with you . . . uh . . . can I call you darling?"

"I'd rather you didn't."

"Okay, sweetie," said the broom. "Let's go tracking unfaithful goblins."

Monday night—the first case:
They had followed the goblin to the corner of Lust and Despair. Then it took a sharp turn down Lust Street.

"We've got the goods on him!" cried the broom excitedly. "He's going to patronize a brothel!"

The goblin turned at the sound of the broom's voice, peered into the darkness until it saw Mallory, and then took off like a bat out of hell.

"Thanks a heap," muttered Mallory.

Wednesday night—the second case:
They stood in the shadows near the Kringleman Arms Hotel,

watching one ersatz Santa Claus after another enter the place with a pot of money in hand.

"So how do you know which ones are legitimate and which are keeping the money themselves?" asked the broom in its normal speaking voice.

Three Santas instantly emerged from the lobby and began firing Saturday Night Specials into the shadows. Mallory could almost feel the bullets whistle by as he raced around the corner and dove for safety behind a pair of trash cans.

"Whatever would I do without you?" said Mallory, checking to make sure he still possessed the requisite number of arms and legs.

Saturday night—the third case:
An old man, his hair white and thinning, sparse whiskers on his chin, his eyes hidden by a pair of sunglasses, walked down Broadway, beggar's cup in one hand, an ancient cane in the other.

Behind the shades, Mallory was concentrating his gaze on Creepy Conrad's Bizarre of the Exotic, where he was certain that Conrad was showing his client prints of some very revealing, if inartistic, photos prior to blackmailing him.

A woman stopped to toss a few coins into Mallory's cup. She inadvertently brushed against him as she walked by, and to keep in character he pretended to momentarily lose his balance. The woman instantly stopped and helped him regain his equilibrium.

"Take your hands off the man I love!" roared the broom.

Creepy Conrad looked out at the distraction, stared long and hard at Mallory, grinned as he finally recognized him, and quickly substituted some photos of Tassle-Twirling Tessie Twinkle, the lizard girl who shed her skin four times a night at the Rialto Burlesque, for the blackmail shots.

"Well?" asked Winnifred, looking up from her paperwork as Mallory shuffled into the office.

"If I take that damned broom on two or three more cases, we'll be looking for a new line of work."

"Where is Hecate now?"

"Down at the corner, getting some coffee and a donut."

"Why didn't she just—?"

"She doesn't want me to know where her mouth is," interrupted Mallory. "Right now I'm more interested in locating her jugular."

"So what are we going to do?"

"I've been giving it some thought," said Mallory. "After all, we're detectives. Our job isn't necessarily catching crooks or preventing crimes, it's solving problems . . . so I think it's time we solved our own."

"How?"

"I've got an idea, but I can't do it myself. That damned broom'll never let me out of its sight long enough." He pulled a roll of bills out of his pocket and stared mournfully at it. "This was what I was going to bet on Flyaway the night Hecate showed up."

"What do you want me to do, John Justin?"

He tossed the roll to her. "Buy a gallon of glue, and a few bottles of glitter, and then go over to Morgan the Gorgon's hardware store and . . ."

"What's going on here?" demanded Hecate.

"Business as usual," said Mallory. "Why?"

"There's nothing usual about this!" said the broom.

"Oh, you mean *these*?" said Mallory, gesturing to twenty brand-new brooms lined up on the wall, each totally covered with gold and silver glitter.

"Yes, I mean these!" snapped the broom. "They weren't here before! What's going on, Mallory?"

"You were so helpful the last few nights that I decided we could use even more brooms," said Mallory. "And as long as I'm going to be spending all my time with them, why not surround myself with beauty?"

"But . . . but—" sputtered Hecate.

Mallory picked up a broom at random. "Isn't this one gorgeous?" he said, stroking it lovingly. "I'll never be bored on a stakeout again."

"You ingrate!" screamed Hecate. "You heathen! You ungrateful swine! How dare you forsake me for another broom!"

"Another twenty brooms," Mallory corrected it pleasantly.

"And I would have married you!" said the broom. It began weeping copiously. "I'm going back to where I was appreciated. Maybe the Grundy didn't spend much time with me, but I was well-cared for and people stopped by to admire me every day and . . ." Its voice tailed off.

"You can stay here," said Mallory. "I promise to take you out of the broom closet at least twice a year, for exceptionally easy cases. And think of all the fun you can have hanging around with all these truly beautiful brooms. Who knows? Some of their elegance might rub off."

"My mother was right!" cried the broom. "Never trust a man!"

And then, with one final heart-wrenching sob, it vanished as quickly and completely as the Grundy ever had.

"Well, you got rid of it, John Justin," said Winnifred.

"I feel like shit," said Mallory grimly. "Still, it had to be done."

"Don't feel bad," said Felina. "I certainly won't feel bad when I desert you under duress."

"Thanks," said Mallory ironically. "*I* take enormous comfort in that."

Felina smiled happily. "I knew you would."

"Remind me to check on the broom in a few months and make sure it's doing okay," said Mallory.

"I will, John Justin," said Winnifred.

"Good." He pulled out a tissue, blew his nose, and tossed it into the waste basket next to his desk. "When did you buy that?"

"Buy what, John Justin?"

"The waste basket with the fancy trim," he said. "I don't remember seeing it before."

"I didn't buy any waste basket," said Winnifred.

The waste basket approached Mallory and rubbed gently against his leg.

"I think I'm in love with you," it said.

❧ Web of Deception ❧

A Bahzell story

David Weber

It was raining again.

It seemed to do an awful lot of that on the Sothōii Wind Plain, Kaeritha thought. Especially in the spring.

She leaned moodily against the deep-cut frame of a tower window and stared out across Hill Guard Castle's battlements at the raindrops' falling silver spears. The sky was the color of wet charcoal, swirled by gusty wind and lumpy with the weight of rain not yet fallen, and the temperature was decidedly on the cool side. Not that it wasn't immensely warmer than the bone-freezing winter she had just endured.

Thunder rumbled somewhere above the cloud ceiling, and she grimaced as a harder gust of wind drove a spray of rain in through the open window. She didn't step back, though. Instead, she inhaled deeply, drawing the wet, living scent of the rain deep into her lungs. There was a fine, stimulating feel to it, despite the chill—one that seemed to tingle in her blood—and her grimace faded into something suspiciously like a grin as she admitted the truth to herself.

It wasn't the rain that irritated her so. Not really. As a matter of fact, Kaeritha rather liked rain. She might have preferred a little less of it than the West Riding had received over the past several weeks, but the truth was that this rain was simply part and parcel of the real cause of her frustration. She should have been on

245

her way at least two weeks ago, and instead she'd allowed the rain to help delay her travel plans.

Not that there hadn't been enough other reasons for that same delay. She could come up with a lengthy list of those, all of them entirely valid, without really trying. Unfortunately, "reasons" were beginning to turn into something entirely too much like "excuses" for her taste. Which meant that, rain or no rain, it was time she was on her way. Besides—

Her thoughts broke off as a tall, red-haired young woman rounded the passageway corner with a hurried stride that was just short of a trot. The newcomer, who came to an abrupt halt as she caught sight of Kaeritha, was both very young and very tall, even for a Sothōii noblewoman. At fourteen, she was already over six feet—taller than Kaeritha herself, who was considered a tall woman, by Axeman standards—and she was also beginning to show the curves of what promised to be an extraordinarily attractive womanhood.

Her expression was a curious blend of pleasure, half-guilt, and semi-rebellion . . . and her attire of the moment was better suited to a stable hand than an aristocratic young lady, Kaeritha thought wryly. She wore a worn pair of leather trousers (which, Kaeritha noted, were becoming more than a bit too tight in certain inappropriate places) under a faded smock which had been darned in half a dozen spots. It also showed several damp patches, and there were splashes of mud on the girl's riding boots and the thoroughly soaked poncho hanging over her left arm.

"Excuse me, Dame Kaeritha," she said quickly. "I didn't mean to intrude on you. I was just taking a shortcut."

"It's not an intrusion," Kaeritha assured her. "And even if it were, unless I'm mistaken, this is your family's home, Lady Leeana. I imagine it's appropriate for you to wander about in it from time to time if it takes your fancy."

She smiled, and Leeana grinned back at her.

"Well, yes, I guess," the girl said. "On the other hand, if I'm going to be honest about it, the real reason I'm taking a shortcut this time is to stay out of Father's sight."

"Oh?" Kaeritha said. "And just how have you managed to infuriate your father so badly that you find it necessary to avoid his wrath?"

"I haven't infuriated him at all . . . yet. But I'd like to get back to my quarters and changed out of these clothes while that's still true." Kaeritha cocked her head, her expression questioning, and the girl shrugged. "I love Father, Dame Kaeritha, but he gets, well, *fussy* if I sneak out to go riding without half a dozen armsmen clattering around behind me." She made a face. "And he and Mother are both beginning to insist that I ought to dress 'as befits my station.' " This time she rolled jade-green eyes with a martyred sigh, and Kaeritha was hard put not to chuckle.

"However annoying it may be," she said instead, with commendable seriousness, "they probably have a point, you know." Leeana looked at her skeptically, and Kaeritha shrugged. "You *are* the only child of one of the four most powerful nobles of the entire kingdom," she pointed out gently, "and men like your father always have enemies. You'd make a powerful weapon against him in the wrong hands, Leeana."

"I suppose you're right," Leeana conceded after a moment. "I'm safe enough here in Balthar, though. Even Father is willing to admit that, when he isn't being stuffy just to make a point! And," she added in a darker tone, "it's not as if I'm not a weapon against him anyway."

"I don't think that's exactly fair," Kaeritha said with a quick frown. "And I'm certain that's not how *he* thinks of it."

"No?" Leeana gazed at her for several seconds, then gave her head a little toss that twitched her long, thick braid of damp golden-red hair. "Maybe he doesn't, but that doesn't really change anything, Dame Kaeritha. You know as well as I do how many people want him to produce a *real* heir. The entire King's Council certainly goes on at him enough about it whenever he attends!"

"Not the entire Council, I'm sure," Kaeritha objected, her eyes widening slightly as she sensed the true depth of bitterness Leeana's normally cheerful demeanor concealed.

"Oh, no," Leeana agreed. "But the only ones who don't are the ones who have sons they think are just the right age to marry off to the heir to Balthar and the West Riding. Or think they're still young enough for the job themselves." She grimaced in disgust. "All the rest of them, though, use it as an excuse to go on at him, like a pack of mongrels snarling at a leashed wolfhound, because they know I make a safe excuse to gnaw away at his power base."

"Is it really that bad?" Kaeritha asked, and Leeana looked surprised by the question. "I may be a champion of Tomanak, Leeana," Kaeritha said wryly, "but I'm also an Axewoman, not a Sothōii. Tomanāk!" She laughed. "As far as that goes, I'm only even an Axewoman by adoption. I was born a peasant in Moretz! So I may be intellectually familiar with the sorts of machinations that go on amongst great nobles, but I don't have that much firsthand experience with them."

Leeana appeared to have a little difficulty with the idea that a belted knight—and a champion of Tomanāk, into the bargain—could be that ignorant of things which were so much a part of her own life. And she also seemed surprised that Kaeritha seemed genuinely interested in *her* opinion.

"Well," she said slowly, in the voice of one manifestly attempting to be as fair-minded as possible, "it probably does seem even worse to me than it actually is, but it's bad enough. You do know how Sothōii inheritance laws work, don't you?"

"That much I have down," Kaeritha assured her.

"Then you know that while I can't legally inherit Father's titles and lands myself, they'll pass through me to my own children. Assuming he doesn't produce a son after all, of course."

Kaeritha nodded, and Leeana shrugged.

"Since our enlightened customs and traditions won't permit a woman to inherit in her own right, whatever fortunate man wins my hand in matrimony will become my 'regent.' He'll govern Balthar and hold the wardenship of the West Riding 'in my name,' until our firstborn son inherits them. And, of course, in the most unfortunate case that I might produce only daughters, he'd continue to hold the wardenship until one of *them* produced a son." The irony in her soprano voice was withering, especially coming from one so young, Kaeritha thought.

"Because of that," Leeana continued, "two-thirds of the Council want Father to go ahead and set Mother aside to produce a good, strong, *male* heir. Some of them say that it's because of his duty to the bloodline, and others argue that a matrimonial regency always creates the possibility of a succession crisis. Some of them may even be sincere, but most of them know perfectly well he won't do it. *They* see it all as a club to beat him with, something he has to use up political-capital fighting off, like a constant drain on his position. The last thing he needs, especially now, is to give his enemies any more weapons to use against him! But the ones who are sincere may be even worse, because the real reason they want him to produce a male heir is that none of them like to think about the possibility that such a plum might fall into the hands of one of their rivals. And the third of the Council who don't want him to set Mother aside probably hope that they're the ones who will *catch* the plum."

Kaeritha nodded slowly, gazing into the younger woman's dark-green eyes. Tellian Bowmaster's marriage eighteen years before to Hanatha Whitesaddle had not only united the Bowmasters of Balthar with the Whitesaddles of Windpeak; it had also been a love match, not just a political alliance between two powerful families. That had been obvious to anyone who'd ever laid eyes on them.

And if it hadn't been, the fact that Tellian had furiously rejected any suggestion that he set Hanatha aside after the riding accident which had left the baroness with one crippled leg and cost her her fertility would have made it so. But that decision on his part did carry a heavy price for their only child.

"And how does the plum feel about being caught?" Kaeritha asked softly.

"The plum?" Leeana gazed back into Kaeritha's midnight-blue eyes for several silent seconds, and her voice was even softer than Kaeritha's when she finally replied. "The plum would sell her soul to be anywhere else in the world," she said.

The two of them looked at each other, then Leeana shook herself, bobbed a quick half-bow, and turned abruptly away. She walked down the passage with quick, hard strides, her spine pike staff-straight, and Kaeritha watched her go. She wondered if Leeana had actually intended to reveal the true depths of her feelings. And if the girl had ever revealed them that frankly to anyone else.

She frowned in troubled thought, then shook herself and turned back to the window as fresh thunder grumbled overhead. Her heart went out to the girl—and to her parents, for that matter—but that wasn't what had brought her to the Wind Plain, and it was past time that she got on with what *had* brought her here. She gazed out the window a few moments longer, inhaled one more deep breath of rain from her relatively dry perch, and then turned away and walked briskly towards the tower's spiral stair.

Bahzell Bahnakson of the Horse Stealer Hradani looked up an instant before the library door opened. The red-haired human sitting across the gaming table from him looked up in turn, and then shook his head as the door swung wide and Kaeritha Seldansdaughter stepped through it.

"I wish you two would stop doing that," Baron Tellian complained in the tenor voice which always seemed a bit odd coming from a man who stood six and a half inches over six feet in height.

"And just what is it the two of us are after doing?" Bahzell inquired genially in the deep, subterranean bass which sounded not a bit odd rumbling up out of the deep chest of a hradani who stood over *seven* and a half feet in his stockings.

"You know perfectly well what," Tellian replied, setting the black pawn he had just picked up back down on the chessboard. "*That.*" He waved at Kaeritha, still standing in the doorway and smiling at him. "You could at least *pretend* that you have to wait until the other one knocks, like normal people!"

"With all due respect, Milord," the third individual seated in the library—also a hradani, although he was actually a few inches shorter than the human—said, never looking up from the book in his lap, "I don't believe anyone's ever been foolish enough to suggest that there was anything 'normal' about either of them."

"But they could at least try, Lord Brandark," Tellian objected. "Damn it, it's uncanny . . . and it worries my men. Phrobus! It worries *me*, sometimes!"

"I apologize, Milord," Kaeritha said with a small smile. "It's not really anything we do, you know. It just . . . happens."

"Aye," Bahzell agreed, and the smile he gave the baron was much broader than hers had been. "And come to that, I've not heard yet that champions of Tomanāk weren't supposed to be after being 'uncanny.' "

"That's because they are," Brandark said in a slightly more serious tone, looking up from his book at last and cocking the foxlike ears he shared with his fellow hradani. "Uncanny, that is. And the truth is, Milord," he went on as Tellian turned his head to look at him, "that it's so unusual to have two champions as houseguests at the same time that very few people have ever had the opportunity to watch them being uncanny together."

Tellian considered that for a few seconds, then nodded.

"You have a point," he conceded. "But then, everything about the current situation is on the unusual side, isn't it?"

"It is that." Heartfelt agreement rumbled in Bahzell's deep voice as he leaned back in his chair—specially built by Tellian's master woodworker to Bahzell's size and weight—and gazed across the neat ranks of chessmen at the human host who was technically his own paroled prisoner. "And I hope you won't be taking this wrongly, Baron, but it's in my mind that there's more than a few of your folk who'd sooner see my head on a pike over your gate than see my backside sitting in this chair."

"Of course there are," Tellian agreed. "Just as quite a few of your father's subjects would prefer to see *my* head on a pike, if our positions were reversed. Surely you didn't expect anything different when less than two hundred hradani took several thousand Sothōii warriors 'prisoner,' did you?"

"Of course not," Bahzell said. "Not that that's after making it any more pleasant—or keeping my shoulder blades from itching whenever daggers are about—now that it's here."

"On the other hand," Kaeritha observed mildly, "nobody ever said being a champion of Tomanāk would be an endless pleasure jaunt, either. Or, at least, no one ever said so to *me*, anyway."

"Nor to me," Bahzell admitted, and his foxlike ears twitched in wry amusement as he recalled the conversation in which the God of War had recruited one Bahzell Bahnakson as the first hradani champion of any God of Light in the past twelve millennia. "Pleasure jaunt" was one phrase which had never passed Tomanāk's lips.

"I can well believe that." Tellian shook his head. "It's bad enough being a simple baron without having a god looking over my shoulder all the time!"

"That's as may be," Bahzell said, "but I'm thinking it wasn't all that 'simple' for you, either, when we ran up against each other in The Gullet."

"Oh, I don't know about that." Tellian leaned back in his chair and smiled. "If nothing else, at least I assured that I'll go down in history. After all, how many men have ever managed to surrender to a force they outnumbered twenty or thirty times over?"

All four of them chuckled, but there was an undertone of seriousness to the laughter. The unauthorized invasion of hradani lands which Mathian Redhelm, one-time Lord Warden of Glanharrow, had led down the narrow passage known as The Gullet, could all too easily have ended in catastrophe for all concerned. But Tellian's solution to avoiding that catastrophe, after overtaking Redhelm, had struck many of his fellow Sothōii as . . . a less than ideal one. His "surrender" of the entire invasion force to Bahzell and the first hradani chapter of the Order of Tomanāk was also the only thing which had prevented the massacre of that same chapter and, almost certainly, of the undefended citizens of the city of Hurgrum. Yet it had put Tellian—and Bahzell—in positions which were more than a bit awkward.

Officially, Tellian and the entire force he had surrendered remained Bahzell's paroled prisoners. Everyone considered that no more than a ludicrous fiction, but there was little anyone could do about it so long as Bahzell and Tellian presented a united front and insisted upon maintaining it. Which, given the millennium or so of mutual hatred between Sothōii and Horse Stealer, was also the only way to maintain the fragile peace between their two peoples. Both Bahzell and the baron were determined to keep up the pretense for as long as it took to give that peace some stability, but all too many on both sides—human and hradani alike— would have loved to see them fail. And at the moment, Tellian was under far more fire from his Sothōii peers than anything Bahzell had to put up with from the hradani.

"I have a feeling that you'll go down in history for more than just that, Milord," Kaeritha said after a moment. "But I'm afraid that it's past time I was off on one of those 'pleasure jaunts' Bahzell and I were never promised."

"Ah?" Bahzell cocked his head. "And has himself been talking to you again, Kerry?"

"Not directly." She shook her head. "On the other hand, He doesn't speak directly to me as often as He seems to speak to you."

"Perhaps," Brandark murmured in the tone of one in whose mouth butter would adamantly refuse to melt, "that's because it doesn't require something quite that, um . . . *direct* to get through to you."

"I wouldn't know about that," Kaeritha said primly, and her blue eyes twinkled as Bahzell made a rude gesture at his friend. "But," she went on, "He does have His own ways of getting messages through to me. And the one I'm getting now is that I've been sitting around your house too long, Milord."

"My house has been honored by your presence, Dame Kaeritha," Tellian said, and this time his voice was completely serious. "I would be most pleased for you to remain here however long you like. And while I know a champion's duties take precedence over all other considerations, could you not wait at least until the rain stops?"

"*Does* the rain ever stop on the Wind Plain, Milord?" Kaeritha asked wryly.

"Not in the spring," Bahzell replied before Tellian could. "It may be after pausing a bit, here and there, though."

"Bahzell is right, I'm afraid," Tellian confirmed. "Winter weather is worse, of course. They say Chemalka uses the Wind Plain to test her foul weather before she sends it elsewhere, and I believe it. But spring is usually our rainiest season. Although, to be fair, this spring has been rainier than most, even for us."

"Which I'm sure will be doing wonderful things for the grass and crops, assuming as how it doesn't wash all of them away before ever they sprout. But that won't be leaving you any dryer right this very moment, Kerry," Bahzell observed.

"I've been wet before." Kaeritha shrugged. "I haven't melted or shrunk yet, and I probably won't this time, either."

"I see you're serious about leaving," Tellian said, and she nodded. "Well, I'm not foolish enough to try to tell a champion of Tomanāk her business, Milady. But if He insists on sending you out in such weather, is there at least anything I can do to assist you on your way?"

"It might help if you could tell me where I'm going," Kaeritha said ruefully.

"I beg your pardon?" Tellian looked at her as if he half suspected her of pulling his leg.

"One of the more frustrating consequences of the fact that He doesn't talk to me as directly as He does to Bahzell here," Kaeritha told him, "is that my directions are often a bit less precise."

"Well, Bahzell does require as much clarity—not to say simplicity—as possible," Brandark put in with a wicked grin.

"Just you be keeping it up, little man," Bahzell told him. "I'm sure it's an impressive splash you'll be making when someone kicks your hairy arse halfway across the moat."

"This castle doesn't *have* a moat," Brandark pointed out.

"It will as soon as I've finished digging one for the occasion," Bahzell shot back.

"As I was saying," Kaeritha continued in the tone of a governess ignoring her charges' obstreperousness, "I haven't really received any specific instructions about exactly what I'm supposed to be doing here."

"I should think that helping to destroy an entire temple of Sharnā and to establish a brand-new chapter of your order amongst Bahzell's people—not to mention playing some small part in preventing that idiot Redhelm from committing all of us to a disastrous war—constitutes a worthwhile effort already," Tellian observed.

"I'd like to think so," Kaeritha agreed with a small smile. "On the other hand, I was already headed this direction before Bahzell ever came along. Not that I knew exactly why then, either, of course. But one thing I do know, Milord, is that He doesn't normally leave His champions sitting around idle. Swords don't accomplish much hanging on an armory wall. So it's time I was about figuring out whatever it is He has in mind for me next."

"You've no clue at all?" Bahzell asked.

"You know Him better than that," Kaeritha replied. "He may not have actually discussed it with me, but I know that whatever it is, it lies east of here."

"With all due respect, Dame Kaeritha," Tellian pointed out, "three-quarters of the Wind Plain 'lies east of here.' Would it be possible for you to narrow that down just a bit more?"

"Not a great deal, I'm afraid, Milord." She shrugged. "About all I can say is that I'm probably within a few days' travel—certainly not more than a week's or so—of where I'm supposed to be."

"While it would never do to criticize a god," Tellian said, "it occurs to me that if I attempted to plan a campaign with as little information as He appears to have provided you, I'd fall flat on my arse."

"Champions do require a certain . . . agility," Kaeritha agreed. "On the other hand, Milord, that's usually because He's careful to avoid leading us around by the hand." Tellian quirked an eyebrow at her, and she shrugged again. "We need to be able to stand on our own two feet," she pointed out, "and if we started to rely on Him for explicit instructions on everything we're supposed to be doing, how long would it be before we couldn't accomplish anything *without* those instructions? He expects us to be bright enough to figure out our duty without His constant prompting."

"And himself is after having his own version of a sense of humor, as well," Bahzell put in.

"And that." Kaeritha nodded.

"I'll take your word for that," Tellian said. "You two are the first of His champions I've ever personally met, after all. Although, to be honest, I have to admit that I harbor a few dark suspicions about how typical the pair of you are." Bahzell and Kaeritha both grinned at him, and he shook his head. "Be that as it may," he continued, "I'm afraid that I can't really think of anything to the east of here—within no more than a few days' travel, at least— that would seem to require a champion's services. If I did know of anything that serious, I assure you that I'd already have been trying to do something about it!"

"I'm sure you would, Milord. But that's frequently the way it is, especially when the local authorities are competent."

"I'm not sure I'd consider someone who could let that idiot Redhelm come so close to succeeding 'competent,' " Tellian said a bit sourly.

"I doubt that anyone could have stopped him from making the attempt," Kaeritha objected. "You could scarcely have stripped him of his authority before he actually abused it, after all. And once you discovered that he had, you acted promptly enough."

"Barely," Tellian said.

"But promptly enough, all the same," Bahzell said. "And, if you'll pardon my saying so, I'm thinking that betwixt us it was effective enough, as well."

"It certainly was," Kaeritha agreed. "But my point, Milord, is that champions frequently end up dealing with problems which have succeeded in hiding themselves from the local authorities' attention. Often with a little help from someone like Sharnā or one of his relatives."

"You think whatever it is you're here to deal with is that serious?" Tellian sat up straight in his chair, his sudden frown intense. "That there could be another of the Dark Gods at work here on the Wind Plain?"

"I didn't say that, Milord. On the other hand, and without wanting to sound paranoid, Bahzell and I *are* champions of one of the Gods of Light. Tomanāk doesn't have that many of us, either, so we tend not to get wasted on easy tasks." She grimaced so wryly that Tellian chuckled. "Of course, a great deal of what we do in the world requires us to deal with purely mortal problems, but we do see rather more of the Dark Gods and their handiwork than most people do. And the Dark Gods are quite accomplished at concealing their presence and influence."

"Like Sharnā in Navahk," Brandark agreed grimly.

"Well, yes, but—" Tellian began, then stopped. His three guests looked at him expressionlessly, and he had the grace to blush.

"Forgive me," he said. "I *was* about to say that that was among hradani, not Sothōii. But I suppose that sort of 'It couldn't possibly happen to *us*' thinking is what does let it happen, isn't it?"

"It's certainly a part of it," Kaeritha said. "But infections are always hard to see before they rise to the surface, and one of a champion's functions is to bring things to a head and clean the wound before it gets so bad that the only alternative is amputation."

"A charming analogy." Tellian grimaced, but it was obvious he was thinking hard. He leaned back in his chair, the fingers of his right hand drumming on the armrest, while he pondered.

"I still can't think of anything that *seems* serious enough to require a champion," he said finally. "But as you and Bahzell—and Brandark—have all just pointed out, that doesn't necessarily mean as much as I'd like to think it does, so I've been trying to come up with anything that may have seemed less important to me than it actually is. If you can delay your departure for perhaps another day or two, Kaeritha, I'll spend some time going over the reports from my local lords and bailiffs to see if there is something I missed the first time around. Right off the top of my head, though, the only ongoing local problem I'm aware of is the situation at Kalatha."

"Kalatha?" Kaeritha repeated.

"It's a town a bit more than a week's ride east of here," Tellian told her. "I realize you said you were within a 'few days' of whatever your destination is, but you could probably make the trip in five days if you pushed hard on a good horse, so I suppose it might qualify."

"Why is it a problem?" she asked.

"Why *isn't* it a problem?" he responded with a harsh chuckle. She looked puzzled, and he shrugged. "Kalatha isn't just any town, Milady. It holds a special Crown charter, guaranteeing its independence from the local lords, and some of them resent that. Not just because it exempts the Kalathans from their taxes, either." He smiled crookedly. "The reason it holds a free-city charter in the first place is because Lord Kellos Swordsmith, one of my maternal great-great-grandfathers, deeded it to the war maids—with the Crown's strong 'approval'—over two centuries ago."

Kaeritha's eyes narrowed, and he nodded.

"The war maids aren't so very popular," he said with what all of his listeners recognized as massive understatement. "I suppose we Sothōii are too traditional for it to be any other way. But for the most part, they're at least respected as the sort of enemies you wouldn't want to make. However much they may be *disliked*, very few people, even among the most convinced traditionalists, are foolish enough to go out of their way to pick quarrels with them."

"And that isn't the case at the moment with Kalatha?" Kaeritha asked.

"That depends on whose version you accept," Tellian replied. "According to the local lords, the Kalathans have been encroaching upon territory not covered by the town charter, and they've been 'confrontational' and 'hostile' to efforts to resolve the competing claims peaceably. But according to the war maids, the local lords—and especially Trisu of Lorham, the most powerful of them—have been systematically encroaching upon the rights guaranteed to them by their charter for years now. It's been going on for some time, but there's always something like this. Especially where war maids are concerned. And it's worse in Kalatha's case—inevitably, I suppose. Kalatha isn't the largest war maid free-town or -city, but it *is* the oldest, thanks to my highly principled ancestor. I like to think that he didn't realize just how much of a pain in the arse he was going to be dumping on all of his descendants. Although, if he didn't, he must have been stupider than I'd prefer to think."

Kaeritha had started to ask another question, but she paused almost visibly at the baron's tone. It would have been too much to call it bitter or biting, but there was a definite edge of sourness to it. So instead of what she'd been about to ask, she nodded.

"I agree it doesn't sound like an earthshaking problem," she said. "On the other hand, I have to start somewhere, and this sounds like it might very well be the place. Especially since each of Tomanāk's champions has his—or her—particular . . . specialties, call them."

Tellian furrowed his brow in apparent puzzlement, and Kaeritha chuckled.

"Any of us are expected to be able to handle any duty any of His champions might encounter, Milord, but we each have our own personality traits and skills. That tends to mean we're more comfortable, or effective, at least, serving different aspects of Him. Bahzell here is obviously most at home serving Him as God of War, although he's done *fairly* well serving Him as God of Justice, as well. For someone who's most at home breaking things, anyway."

She grinned at Bahzell, who looked back affably, with an expression which boded ill for the next time they met on the training field.

"My own reasons for joining His service, though," she went on, returning her attention to Tellian, "had more to do with a burning thirst for justice." She paused and frowned, eyes darkening briefly with old and painful memories, then shook herself. "That's always been the aspect of Him I'm most comfortable—or happiest, anyway—serving, and my talents and abilities seem best suited to it. So if there's a legal dispute between this Kalatha and the neighboring nobility, it certainly seems like a logical place for me to start looking. Can I get a map to show me how to find it?"

"Oh, I can do better than that, Milady," Tellian assured her. "Kalatha may hold a Crown charter, but Trisu and his neighbors are my vassals. If you can wait until the end of the week to depart, I'll make some additional inquiries and provide as much background information as I can. And of course I'll send along letters of introduction and instructions for them to cooperate fully with you during your visit."

"Thank you, Milord," Kaeritha said formally. "That would be very good of you."

"That was delicious, Tala—as always," Kaeritha said with a deeply satisfied sigh. She laid her spoon neatly in the empty bowl of bread pudding and patted her flat stomach as she leaned back in her chair, smiling at the sturdy, middle-aged hradani woman who'd been sent along by Prince Bahnak of Hurgrum as his son's house-keeper.

"I'm glad you enjoyed it, Milady," Tala said in a pronounced Navahkan accent. "It's always a pleasure to cook for someone who knows good food when she tastes it."

"Or devours it—in copious quantities," Brandark observed, eyeing the empty platters on the table he shared with Kaeritha and Bahzell.

"I didn't seem to notice you shirking your share of the devouring, Milord," Tala replied dryly.

"No, but there's more of me to maintain," Brandark replied with a grin, and Kaeritha grinned back at him. At six feet two inches, Brandark was of less than average height for even a Bloody Sword hradani, far less one of the towering Horse Stealers like Bahzell. But that still left him a good three inches taller than Kaeritha, and he was far more massively built. Indeed, his shoulders were almost as broad as Bahzell's.

"Aye," Bahzell agreed. "For a sawed-off runt of a hradani who's after sitting on his arse with a pen and a bit of parchment all day, you've a bit of meat on your bones, I suppose."

"I'll remember that the next time you need some obscure Sothōii text translated," Brandark assured him.

"Speaking of obscure Sothōii texts," Kaeritha said as a smiling Tala withdrew, "I wonder if you've come across a copy of the war maids' charter in your forays through Tellian's library, Brandark?"

"I haven't been looking for one," the Bloody Sword replied. "I've done a little research on the entire question of war maids since you and Tellian discussed them this morning, but I've really only scratched the surface so far. I assume there's probably a copy of the charter and its amending documents somewhere, though. Would you like me to take a look for them?"

"I don't know." Kaeritha grimaced. "It's just that I've realized that I'm really pretty appallingly ignorant where any detailed knowledge about the war maids is concerned. Tellian's suggestion that whatever I'm supposed to be dealing with concerns them and their prerogatives may well be right, but my training in Sothōii jurisprudence is a bit shakier than my training in Axeman law. If I am supposed to be investigating the war maids' claims, it would probably be a pretty good idea to know what their prerogatives are in the first place."

"I'm not so sure that laying hands on a copy of their original charter would be enough to be telling you that," Bahzell put in. He leaned back in a chair which creaked alarmingly under his weight.

"Why not?" Kaeritha asked.

"The war maids aren't so very popular with most Sothōii," Bahzell said in the tone of one speaking with deliberate understatement. "Not to be putting too fine point on it, there's those amongst the Sothōii who'd sooner see an invading hradani army in their lands than one of the war maids' free-towns."

"They're that unpopular?" Kaeritha looked surprised, and Bahzell shrugged.

"An invading army is likely to be burning their roofs over their heads, Kerry. But roofs can be rebuilt, when all's said. Rebuilding a way of life, now—that's after being just a mite harder."

"And that's exactly how your typical conservative Sothōii would see having a batch of war maids move in next door," Brandark agreed.

Kaeritha nodded in acknowledgment, yet there was still a baffled edge to her expression. As she'd told Leeana, she'd been born a peasant in Moretz, which was at least as feudal a society as that of the Sothōii, but she'd fled that land when she'd been even younger than Leeana was now. And she'd also been educated in the Empire of the Axe, where women enjoyed far broader choices and possibilities then were generally available to Sothōii women.

"Kerry," Bahzell said, "I'm thinking you've too much of the Axewoman in you. You, if any, ought to have realized by now how hard any Sothōii is after finding it to wrap his mind round the very notion of a woman as a warrior."

Kaeritha nodded again, more emphatically, and Bahzell chuckled. If he found his position in Balthar difficult as a hradani, Kaeritha had found hers only marginally less so. Tellian's men had taken their cue from their liege lord and extended to her the same deference and respect any champion of Tomanāk might have expected, but it was only too obvious that they found the entire concept of a female knight—not to mention a knight who was also a champion of the war god *him*self—profoundly unnatural.

"Well, for all that our folk've spent the best part of a thousand years massacring one another," Bahzell continued, "there's much to be said for the Sothōii. But one thing no one is ever likely to be suggesting is that they've an over abundance of innovation in their natures, especially where matters of tradition and custom are concerned. Don't let Tellian be fooling you. For a Sothōii, he's about as radical as you're ever likely to meet, and well educated about foreign lands, to boot. But your typical Sothōii is stiffer-necked then even a hradani, and the real conservatives are still after thinking the wheel is a dangerous, newfangled, harebrained novelty that will never really be catching on."

Kaeritha chuckled, and Brandark grinned.

"I won't say there isn't an element of the pot and kettle in that pithy description," the Bloody Sword said after a moment. "But there's a lot of accuracy in it, too. And the very existence of the war maids is an affront to those conservatives' view of the way their entire society—or the rest of the world, for that matter—is supposed to work. In fact, the war maids undoubtedly wouldn't exist at all if the Crown hadn't specifically guaranteed their legal rights. Unfortunately—and I suspect this is what Bahzell was getting at—calling that royal guarantee 'a charter' is more of a convenient shorthand then an accurate description."

Kaeritha cocked an eyebrow, and he shrugged.

"It's actually more of a bundle of separate charters and decrees dealing with specific instances than some sort of neat, unified legal document, Kerry. According to what I've learned so far, the original proclamation legitimizing the war maids' existence was unfortunately vague on several key points. Over the next century or so, additional proclamations intended to clarify some of the obscurity and even the occasional judge's opinion were bundled together, and the whole mishmash is what they fondly call their 'charter.' I haven't actually looked at it, you understand, but I'm familiar enough with the same sort of thing among the hradani. When something just sort of naturally grows up the way the war maids' 'charter' has, there's usually a substantial degree of variation between the terms of its constituent documents. And that means there's an enormous scope for ambiguities and misunderstandings . . . especially when the people whose rights those decrees are supposed to stipulate aren't very popular with their neighbors."

"You have a positive gift for understatement," Kaeritha sighed, and shook her head. "Just what rights *do* the war maids have? In general terms, I mean, if there's that much variation from grant to grant."

"Basically," Brandark replied, "they have the right to determine how they want to live their own lives, free of traditional Sothōii familial and social obligations."

The Bloody Sword scholar tipped back in his chair, folded his arms, and frowned thoughtfully.

"Although they're uniformly referred to as 'war maids,' most of them aren't, really." Kaeritha raised an eyebrow, and he shrugged. "The Kingdom of the Sothōii is a lot more feudal than the Empire of the Axe. Virtually every legal right up here on the Wind Plain is associated in one way or another with the holding of land and the reciprocal obligation of service to the Crown, and the war maids are no exception. As part of the core charter which originally recognized their existence, their free-towns are obligated to provide military forces to the Crown. In my more cynical moments, I think that obligation was included as a deliberate measure intended to effectively nullify the charter, since it's hard for me to conceive of any Sothōii king who could honestly believe that a batch of women could provide an effective military force."

"If that *was* after being the case, then the king in question was in for a nasty surprise," Bahzell put in, and Brandark chuckled.

"Oh, he was that!" he agreed. "And in my *less* cynical moments, I'm inclined to think King Gartha included the obligation only because he had to. Given how much of the current crop of Sothōii nobles is hostile to the very notion of war maids, the opposition to authorizing their existence in the first place must have been enormous. Which means his Council probably could have mustered the support to block the initial charter without that provision. For that matter, the opponents to the measure would have been the ones most inclined to believe that requiring military service out of a bunch of frail, timid women would be an effective, underhanded way of negating Gartha's intentions without coming out in open opposition.

"At any rate, only about a quarter of all 'war maids' are actually warriors. Their own laws and traditions require all of them to have at least rudimentary training in self-defense, but most of them follow other professions. Some of them are farmers or, like most Sothōii, horse breeders. But more of them are shopkeepers, blacksmiths, physicians, glassmakers, even lawyers—the sorts of tradesmen and craftsmen who populate most free-towns or -cities up here. And the purpose of their charter is to ensure that they have the same legal rights and protections, despite the fact that they're women, that men in the same professions would enjoy."

"Are they *all* women?"

"Well," Brandark said dryly, "the real war *maids* are. But if what you're actually asking is whether or not war maid society is composed solely of women, the answer is no. The fact that a woman chooses to live her own life doesn't necessarily mean she hates all men. Of course, many of them become war maids because they *aren't* very fond of men, and quite a few of them end up partnering with other women. *Not* a practice likely to endear them to Sothōii men who think the entire notion of women making decisions for themselves is unnatural. But it would be a serious mistake to assume that any woman who chooses to become—or, for that matter, is born—a war maid isn't going to fall in love with a man and choose to spend her life with him on her own terms. Or at least to dally with one from time to time. And war maid mothers do tend to produce male children, just like any other women. Of course, those two facts lead to some of the thornier 'ambiguities' I mentioned earlier."

"Why?" Kaeritha leaned forward, elbows on the table, her expression intent, while she cradled her wineglass in her hands, and Bahzell hid a smile. He'd seen exactly that same hunting-hawk expression when she encountered a new combat technique.

"There's always been some question as to whether or not the war maids' charter automatically extends to their male children," Brandark explained. "Or, for that matter, to their *female* children, in the eyes of some of the true reactionaries. When a woman chooses to become a war maid, her familial and inheritance obligations to her family are legally severed. Even your true sticks-in-the-mud have been forced to admit that. But a fair number of nobles continue to assert that the legal severance applies only to *her*—that whatever line of inheritance or obligation would have passed through her to her children is unimpaired. For the most part, the courts haven't agreed with them, but enough of them have to mean that it's still something of a gray area. I suppose it's probably fairly fortunate that most 'first-generation' war maids come from commoner stock, or at most from the minor nobility—the squirearchy, you might call them. Or maybe it isn't. If the higher nobility had been forced to come to grips with the question, the Crown courts would have been forced to make a definitive ruling on the question years ago.

"At any rate, the exact question of the legal status of war maids' children is still up in the air, at least to some extent. And so is the question of their marriages. Their more diehard opponents argue that since their precious charter severs all familial obligations, it precludes the creation of new obligations, which means that no war maid marriage has any legal validity in their eyes. And there really is some question, I understand, in this instance. I doubt very much that Gartha had any intention of precluding the possibility of war maid marriages, but Baron Tellian's senior magistrate tells me that some of the controlling language is less precise than it ought to be. According to him, everyone knows it's a matter of technicalities and reading the letter of the law, not its spirit, but apparently the problems do exist. And, to be perfectly honest, from what he said—and a couple of things he *didn't* say—I think the war maids have done their own bit to keep the waters muddied."

"Why would they do that?" Kaeritha asked. "Unless . . . Oh. The children."

"Exactly. If war maid marriages have no legal standing, then every child of a war maid is technically illegitimate."

"Which would take them out of the line of inheritance, unless there were no legitimate heirs at all," Kaeritha said with a nod of understanding, but her expression was troubled.

"I can follow the logic," she continued after a moment, "but it seems awfully shortsighted of them. Or maybe like the triumph of expedience. It may prevent their children from being yanked away from them and drawn into a system they wanted out of, but it also prevents them from extending the legal protections of their own families to those same children."

"Yes, it does," Brandark agreed. "On the other hand, their own courts and judges don't see it that way, and for the most part, the charters which create their free-towns extend the jurisdiction of their judges to all of the citizens of those towns. The problem comes with legal cases which cross the boundaries between the war maids' jurisdiction and those of more traditional Sothōii nobles."

"Tomanāk," Kaeritha sighed. "What a mess!"

"Well, it isn't after being just the tidiest situation in the world," Bahzell said. "Still and all, it's one the Sothōii have been working at for two or three centuries now. There's those as have some mighty sharp axes to grind, but for the most part, they've learned how to be getting on with one another."

" 'For the most part' still leaves a lot of room for potential trouble, though," Kaeritha pointed out. "And somehow, I don't think

He would be sending me off to deal with a crop of Sothōii who were 'getting on with one another.' Do you?"

"Well, as to that," Bahzell replied with a crooked smile, "no."

It was still raining when Kaeritha left Hill Guard—of course.

At least it wasn't a torrential downpour, she told herself encouragingly as she started down the steep approach road to Baron Tellian's ancestral keep. The Wind Plain was actually a huge, high plateau which, for the most part, was one vast, flat ocean of grass. There weren't very many hills on it, so, over the centuries, those which did exist had exhibited a distinct tendency to attract towns and fortifications. Hill Guard had come into existence in exactly that fashion the better part of eight hundred years ago when Halyu Bowmaster, the first Lord Warden of Balthar, had looked about for a suitable spot for the capital of his new holding. Now the city of Balthar sprawled out for several miles from the castle which brooded down over it from above.

The Sothōii weren't great city builders. For the most part, their people continued to follow the pastoral lifestyle of their ancestors. While the Wind Plain remained the heart of their realm, they had also acquired extensive holdings to the east, below the towering plateau. Those lower regions enjoyed a far milder climate, and a substantial portion of the huge Sothōii horse and cattle herds were wintered in those more salubrious surroundings. But the huge stud farms where the magnificent Sothōii warhorses were bred and trained remained where tradition insisted they must—atop the Wind Plain. And for whatever reason, the Sothōii coursers flatly refused to live anywhere else.

Horses—and coursers—required a lot of space, and the Sothōii population by and large was scattered sparsely about the Wind Plain, watching over its vast herds. That produced a lot of villages and small towns, but not very many cities. Which, conversely, meant that what cities there were tended to be quite large.

They were also well maintained, and Kaeritha moved briskly along the wide, straight avenue on the new mount Tellian had insisted upon giving her. She'd argued about accepting it, but not, she was guiltily aware, very hard. Any Sothōii warhorse was worth a prince's ransom, and the mare Tellian had bestowed upon Kaeritha was a princess among her own kind. Smaller and lighter than the heavier cavalry horses of other lands, the winter-hardy Sothōii warhorse was perfectly suited to the swift, deadly archery-dominated tactics of the people who had bred it. Indeed, only the

coursers themselves excelled its combination of speed and endur-
ance.

And unlike Kaeritha, the warhorses seemed perfectly content with
the Wind Plain's soggy spring weather.

She chuckled damply at the thought and reached down to pat
the mare's shoulder. The horse flicked her ears in acknowledgment
of the caress, and Kaeritha smiled. The mare's dark chestnut
coloring, even darker at the moment thanks to the rain, probably
accounted for her name, but Kaeritha still felt that naming such
an affectionate creature "Dark War Cloud Rising" was just a bit
much. She'd promptly shortened it to "Cloudy," which had earned
her a rather pained look from Tellian. His stable master, on the
other hand, had only grinned, and from the readiness with which
Cloudy answered to her new name, Kaeritha suspected that the
stable hands had employed a similar diminutive before she ever
came along.

A packhorse trotted along at Cloudy's heels. Even he, although
far more plebeian than the aristocratic warhorse, was a magnificent creature. He would have been happily accepted as a superior
light cavalry mount anywhere but among the Sothōii, and Kaeritha
knew she had never been better mounted in her entire life. Which,
she reflected, was saying something, given the care the Order of
Tomanāk took when it came to equipping their god's champions.

Despite Balthar's size, there was very little traffic as she
approached the city's East Gate. The weather undoubtably had
a little something to do with that, she thought, looking past the
open gate to the rain blowing across the road beyond and rippling the endless spring grass of the Wind Plain. Sothōii roads were
not, by and large, up to Axeman standards. Few highways outside
the Empire itself were, of course, but the Sothōii's efforts came
up shorter than most, and Kaeritha felt an undeniable sinking
sensation as she contemplated the one before her. It was straight
enough—not surprisingly, given the flat, unobstructed terrain of
the Wind Plain—but that was about all she could say for the broad
line of mud stretching out before her.

The officer commanding the gate guard saluted her respectfully
as she passed, and she nodded back with equal courtesy. Yet even
as she did, she wondered how the officer might have greeted her
if not for the gold and green badge of the Order of Tomanāk
Tellian's seamstresses had embroidered across the front of her
poncho.

Then she was through the gate, and the gentle pressure of a heel sent Cloudy trotting down the last bit of slope towards the waiting road.

Steam rose gently from the stew pot. More steam rose from the far from occasional drops of rain which found their way through the open side of the lean-to Kaeritha had erected to protect her cooking fire. Centuries of Sothōii had planted trees along the lines of their roads, mainly to provide windbreaks, but also for the purpose to which Kaeritha had put this dense patch of trees. Although it was still spring, the branches above her were densely clothed in fresh, green leaves, which offered at least some protection to her campsite. And, of course, there was firewood in plenty, even if it was a bit on the damp side.

The blanket-covered packhorse was picketed beside the brawling, rain-fed stream at the foot of the slight rise on which she had encamped. Cloudy wasn't picketed at all—the idea that she might require picketing would have been a mortal insult to any Sothōii warhorse—but she'd ambled over and parked herself on the up-wind side of the fire. Kaeritha wasn't sure whether that was a helpful attempt to shield the fire from the rainy wind or an effort to get close enough to soak up what warmth the crackling flames could provide. Not that she was about to object in either case.

She stirred the stew again, then lifted the spoon and sampled it. She sighed. It was hot, and she knew it was going to be filling, but one thing she had never been able to do was cook. She was going to miss Brandark's deft hand at the cook fire, and the mere thought of Tala's cooking was enough to bring a glum tear to the eye when she contemplated her own efforts.

She grimaced and sat back on her heels under the cover of her open-fronted tent. She'd positioned the tent and her fire with the careful eye of hard-won experience. The lean-to she'd constructed, and a rising swell of ground, served as reflectors to bounce the fire's warmth back into her tent, and only a little of the smoke eddied in along with it. Given the general soddeness of the Wind Plain, she was as comfortable—and as close to dry—as she was likely to get.

Which wasn't saying a great deal.

She got up and began moving additional firewood under the crude lean-to, where it would be at least mostly out of the rain and the cook fire could begin drying it out. She was just about finished when Cloudy suddenly raised her head. The mare's ears came up, pointed forward, and she turned to face back towards the road.

Kaeritha reached up under her poncho and unbuttoned the straps across the quillons of her matched short swords, then turned casually in the same direction.

Cloudy's hearing was considerably more acute than Kaeritha's. Kaeritha knew that, yet how even the mare could have heard anything through the steady drip and patter of rain surpassed her understanding. For a moment, she thought that perhaps Cloudy *hadn't* heard anything, but then she saw the rider emerging ghost-like from the rainy, misty evening gloom and knew the mare hadn't been imagining things after all.

Kaeritha stood silently, watching the newcomer and waiting. The Kingdom of the Sothōii was, by and large, peaceful and law-abiding . . . these days, at least. It hadn't always been so, though, and there were still occasional brigands or outlaws, despite the ruthless justice nobles like Tellian dealt out to any they caught up with. Such predators would be likely to think of a lone traveler as easy prey, especially if they knew that traveler was a woman . . . and *didn't* know she was one of Tomanāk's champions. As far as Kaeritha could tell, there was only one rider out there, but there might be more, and she maintained a prudent watchfulness as the other slowly approached her fire.

The possibility that the stranger might be a brigand declined as Kaeritha got a better look at his mount. That horse was almost as good as Cloudy, and no prudent horse thief would dare to keep such a readily recognizable and remarked animal for himself. Which didn't bring her any closer to being able to guess what the newcomer was doing out here in the rain with night coming on.

"Hello, the fire!" a soprano voice called, and Kaeritha closed her eyes as she heard it.

"Why me?" she asked. "Why is it always *me?*"

The cloudy night vouchsafed no reply, and she sighed and opened her eyes again.

"Hello, yourself, Leeana," she called back. "I suppose you might as well come on in and make yourself comfortable."

The Lady Leeana Glorana Syliveste Bowmaster, heir conveyant of Balthar, the West Riding, and at least a dozen other major and minor fiefs, had mud on her face. Her red-gold braid was a thick, sodden serpent, hanging limp down her back, and every line of her body showed her weariness as she sat cross-legged across the fire from Kaeritha and mopped up the last bit of stew in her bowl with a crust of bread. She popped it into her mouth, chewed, and swallowed contentedly.

"You must have been hungry," Kaeritha observed. Leeana looked at her questioningly, and she shrugged. "I've eaten my own cooking too often to cherish any illusions about my culinary talent, Leeana."

"I thought it was quite good, actually, Dame Kaeritha," Leeana said politely, and Kaeritha snorted.

"Flattering the cook isn't going to do you any good, girl," she replied. "Given the fact that you look more like a half-starved, half-drowned, mud-spattered rat then the heir of one of the kingdom's most powerful nobles, I was willing to let you wrap yourself around something hot before I began the interrogation. You've done that now."

Leeana winced at Kaeritha's pointed tone. But she didn't try to evade it. She put her spoon into the empty bowl and set it neatly aside, then faced Kaeritha squarely.

"I'm running away," she said.

"That much I'd already guessed," the knight told her dryly. "So why don't we just get on to the two whys?"

"The two whys?" Leeana repeated with a puzzled expression.

"Why number one: why you ran away. Why number two: why you don't expect me to march you straight home again."

"Oh." Leeana had the grace to blush slightly, and her green eyes dropped to the fire crackling between them. She gazed at the flames for several seconds, then looked back up at Kaeritha.

"I didn't just suddenly decide overnight to run away," she said. "There were lots of reasons. You know most of them, really."

"I suppose I do." Kaeritha studied the girl's face, and it was hard to prevent the sympathy she felt from softening her own uncompromising expression. "But I also know how worried and upset your parents must be right now. I'm sure you do, too." Leeana flinched ever so slightly, and Kaeritha nodded. "So why did you do this to them?" she finished coldly, and Leeana's eyes fell to the fire once more.

"I love my parents," the girl replied after a long, painful pause, her soft voice low enough that Kaeritha had some difficulty hearing her over the sound of the rain. "And you're right—they are going to be worried about me. I know that. It's just—"

She paused again, then drew a deep breath and raised her eyes to Kaeritha's once more.

"Father received a formal offer for my hand the night after you left Hill Guard," she said.

It was Kaeritha's turn to sit back on her heels. She'd been afraid it might be something like that, but that didn't make having it confirmed any better. She thought of several things she might have said, and discarded each of them just as promptly as she recalled her earlier conversation with Leeana.

"Who was it from?" she asked instead after a moment.

"Rulth Blackhill," Leeana said in a flat voice. Kaeritha obviously looked blank, because the girl grimaced and continued. "He's Lord Warden of Transhar . . . and he'll be fifty years old this fall."

"*Fifty?*" Despite herself, Kaeritha couldn't quite keep the surprise out of her voice, and she frowned when Leeana nodded glumly. "Why in the world would a man that age believe even for a moment that your father might consider accepting an offer of marriage on your behalf from him?"

"Why shouldn't he?" Leeana asked simply, and Kaeritha stared at her.

"Because he's three times your age, that's why!"

"He's also incredibly wealthy, a favorite of the King's chief minister, a member of the King's Council in his own right, and related by both blood and marriage to Baron Cassan," Leeana replied.

"But you said he's almost fifty!"

"What difference does that make?" Leeana asked. "He's a recent widower with four children, two of them boys, by his first wife, and the youngest is less than a year old. So it's obvious he can still sire children—preferably sons."

She said it so reasonably that Kaeritha had to bite her own tongue hard. For just a moment, she was furious with Leeana because she *did* sound so reasonable. But then she made herself step back a full pace from her own anger. Leeana's tone was that of someone who knew that the world in which she had been raised would find what she was saying reasonable, not that of someone who *agreed* with it.

"Do you really think," the knight asked quietly after another brief pause, "that your father would let someone that age have you?"

"I don't think he'd do it willingly," Leeana said in a very low voice. "In fact, I think he'd probably refuse to do it at all. But I can't be certain. And even if he did refuse, it would only make things worse."

She stared into Kaeritha's eyes, her own pleading for something. Sympathy, Kaeritha thought, but that was only a part of it. Possibly even the smallest part. No. What Leeana wanted wasn't sympathy—it was understanding.

"What do you mean, 'worse'?" she asked.

"Rulth Blackhill is a greedy, powerful man," Leeana replied. "He's ambitious, and he's very closely allied with his cousin and brother-in-law, Baron Cassan. And Baron Cassan and Father . . . don't get along. They don't like each other, they don't agree on most matters of policy, and Baron Cassan is the leader of the faction at Court most opposed to anything resembling 'appeasement' of the hradani. In fact, it was Cassan who almost convinced the King to deny Father's petition to strip Mathian Redhelm of his wardenship, and Blackhill supported him. The two of them—and the ones who think like them—would love to see Father's heir married off to one of Cassan's allies."

Her young face was taut with distaste and anger, and Kaeritha nodded slowly. Of course, unless this Rulth Blackhill was unlike any other man she'd ever met, the thought of bedding someone as lovely as Leeana would probably figure in his thinking as well, the knight thought sardonically. But this might not be the best time in the world to be bringing that up.

"I'd think that Cassan would realize that all of that would make your father even less likely to accept Blackhill's offer," she said instead.

"He probably does," Leeana agreed. "In fact, he's probably counting on it."

"Now you have me really confused," Kaeritha admitted.

"Cassan hates Father. He also wants to discredit Father with the King and his Council in any way he can. And however I might feel about marrying someone Blackhill's age, it's a perfectly appropriate match by most standards. Given the fact that everyone knows Balthar and the entire West Riding is going to face a succession crisis when Father dies—unless he's prepared to set Mother aside and marry someone else who can give him sons—there would be enormous pressure from several members of the Council for him to accept it. They'd argue that Balthar is too important for the succession to be left up in the air when such an appropriate marriage to a nobleman of mature years who's already demonstrated his own abilities—and potency—stands ready to resolve it. So if Father *does* refuse the offer, it may cost him dearly in terms of political support. Especially when he's already upset so many people by his 'surrender' to Prince Bahzell."

Kaeritha shook her head.

"That's too complicated and devious for my poor peasant-born brain to wrap itself around," she said. Leeana looked at her, and she snorted. "Oh, I don't say I disbelieve you, girl. And intellectually, I suppose I can even understand the twisty sort of thinking that would go into something like that. I just can't understand it on any sort of *personal* level."

"I wish *I* didn't," Leeana told her. "Or that I didn't have to, at least."

"I can believe that," Kaeritha said. She put some more wood on the fire, listening to the hiss as the flames began exploring its damp surface. Then she looked back up at Leeana.

"So someone you don't like and certainly don't want to marry has asked your father for your hand, and you're afraid that if he refuses the offer it will make serious problems for him. That's why you ran away?"

"Yes." There was something about that one-word reply that made Kaeritha cock an eyebrow. It wasn't a lie—that much she was certain of. Yet somehow she was certain it wasn't the *entire* truth, either. She thought about pushing harder, then changed her mind.

"And how does running away solve any of those problems?" she asked instead.

"I'd have thought that was obvious, Dame Kaeritha," Leeana said in a surprised tone.

"Humor me," Kaeritha said dryly. "Oh, I think I can figure out your basic strategy. I don't flatter myself that you followed me just to place yourself under my protection, champion of Tomanāk or not. So I suspect that what you're really doing is heading for Kalatha with some scatterbrained, romantic notion of becoming a war maid in order to avoid your unwelcome suitor. Is that about right?"

"Yes, it is," Leeana said just a touch defensively.

"And have you really considered all you'll be giving up?" Kaeritha countered. "I've been a peasant, *Lady* Leeana. I doubt very much that your lot would be quite that hard among the war maids, but it would be very, very different from anything you've ever experienced before. And there won't be any going back. Your birth and family won't protect you any longer—in fact, for all intents and purposes, you'll be dead as far as your family is concerned."

"I know," Leeana said very, very softly, staring into the fire once more. "I know." She raised her eyes to Kaeritha again. "I *know*," she repeated for a third time, jade eyes brimming with tears. "But I also know Mother and Father will always love me, whether I'm still legally their daughter or not. Nothing will ever change that. And if I go to the war maids, I take the decision out of Father's hands. No one can possibly blame him for refusing to allow Blackhill to marry me if I'm no longer his daughter. And," she managed a crooked smile, "the disgrace of what I'm doing should put me so far beyond the pale that not even someone as ambitious as Rulth Blackhill would consider offering me honorable marriage."

"But you're not yet fifteen years old," Kaeritha said. She shook her head sadly. "That's too young to make this sort of decision, girl. I haven't known your father as long as you have, but I know he'd agree about that. You may be doing this for him, but do you really think he'd *want* you to?"

"I'm fairly certain he wouldn't," Leeana admitted with a sort of forlorn pride. "He'll *understand* it, but that isn't the same as wanting me to do it. In fact, I'm pretty sure he and his armsmen aren't too far behind me by now. If he catches up, he'll figure that he doesn't have any choice but to take me home again, whether I want to go or not. Because he loves me, and because, like you, he's going to argue that I'm too young to make this decision.

"But I'm *not* too young according to the war maids' charter. I have the legal right to make that decision myself if I can reach one of their free-towns before Father catches up, and once it's made, he can't make me go home again, no matter how much he loves me or I love him. And if he can't make me go home, Blackhill and Cassan can't use me against him anymore, ever."

A tear broke free at last, spilling down her cheek, and Kaeritha drew a deep breath. Then she let it out again.

"Then I suppose we'd better turn in," she said. "I'm sure we can both use the sleep . . . and we'll have to make an early start if we're going to see to it that he doesn't catch up with us."

At least the rain had stopped when they broke camp in the morning. That was something, Kaeritha told herself as she swung lightly up into Cloudy's saddle and settled the butt of the quarterstaff she carried instead of a more traditional lance into the holder on her right stirrup. In fact—she sucked in a deep, lung-filling draft of clear, cool morning air—it was quite a bit.

She'd watched Leeana as unobtrusively as possible as they went about preparing to take the road once more. The girl had been almost painfully ready to undertake any task, although it was obvious that she'd never been faced with many of those tasks before in her life.

Like any Sothōii noble, male or female, she'd been thrown into a saddle about the same time she learned to stand up unassisted, and her horsemanship skills were beyond reproach. Her gelding, who rejoiced in a name even more highfaluting than "Dark War Cloud Rising," answered perfectly amiably to "Boots," and Kaeritha wondered if *any* Sothōii warhorse actually had to put up with its formal given name. However that might be, Boots (a bay brown who took his name from his black legs and the white stockings on his forelegs) was immaculately groomed, and his tack and saddle furniture were spotless, despite the wet and mud. Unfortunately, his rider was considerably less adept at others of the homey little chores involved in wilderness travel. At least she was willing, though, as Kaeritha had noted, and she took direction amazingly well for one of her exalted birth. All in all, Kaeritha was inclined to believe there was some sound mettle in the girl.

And there had better be, the champion thought more grimly as she watched Leeana swing nimbly up into Boots' saddle. Kaeritha found herself unable to do anything but respect Leeana's motives, but the plain fact was that the girl couldn't possibly have any realistic notion of how drastically her life was about to change. It was entirely possible that, assuming she survived the shock, she would find her new life more satisfying and fulfilling. Kaeritha hoped she would, but the gulf which yawned between the daughter of one of the four most powerful feudal magnates in the entire kingdom and one more anonymous war maid, despised by virtually everyone in the only world she had ever known, was far deeper than a fall from the Wind Plain's mighty ramparts might have been. Surviving that plunge would be a shattering experience—one fit to destroy any normal sheltered flower of noble femininity—however assiduously Leeana had tried to prepare herself for it ahead of time.

Of course, Kaeritha had never had all that much use for sheltered flowers of noble femininity. Was that the real reason she'd agreed to help the girl flee from the situation fate had trapped her into? A part of her wanted to think it was. And another part wanted to think that she was doing this because it was the duty of any champion of Tomanāk to rescue the helpless from persecution. Given Leeana's scathing description of Rulth Blackhill it was impossible for Kaeritha to think of a marriage between him and the girl as anything but the rankest form of persecution, after all, and Tomanāk, as the God of Justice, disapproved of persecution. Besides, Leeana was right; she *did* have a legal right to make this decision if she could reach Kalatha.

Both of those reasons were real enough, she thought. But she also knew that at the heart of things was another, still deeper reason. The memory of a thirteen-year-old orphan who had found herself trapped into another, even grimmer life . . . until she refused to accept that sentence.

For a moment, Dame Kaeritha's sapphire-blue eyes were darker and deeper—and colder—than the waters of Belhadan Bay. Then the mood passed, and she shook herself like a dog, shaking off the water of memory, and gazed out through the cool, misty morning. The sun hovered just above the horizon directly in front of them in a molten ball of gold, with the morning mists rising to enfold it like steam from a forge, and the last of the previous day's clouds were high-piled ramparts in the south, their peaks touched with the same golden glow, as the brisk northerly wind continued to sweep them away. The road was just as muddy as it had been, but the day was going to be truly glorious, and she felt an eagerness stirring within her. The eagerness to be off and doing once again.

"Are you ready, Lady Leeana?" she asked.

"Yes," Leeana replied, urging Boots up beside Cloudy. Then she chuckled. Kaeritha cocked her head at the younger woman, and Leeana grinned. "I was just thinking that somehow it sounds more natural when you call me 'girl' than when you call me 'Lady Leeana,'" she explained in answer to Kaeritha's unspoken question.

"Does it?" Kaeritha snorted. "Maybe it's the peasant girl in me coming back to the surface. On the other hand, it might not be such a bad thing if you started getting used to a certain absence of honorifics."

She touched Cloudy very gently with a heel, and the mare started obediently forward. Leeana murmured something softly to Boots, and the gelding moved up at Cloudy's shoulder and fell into step with the mare, as if the two horses were harnessed together.

"I know," the girl said after several silent minutes. "That I should started getting used to it, I mean. Actually, I don't think I'll miss that anywhere near as much as I'll miss having someone else to draw my bath and brush my hair." She held up a dirty hand and grimaced. "I've already discovered that there's quite a gap between reality and bard's tales. Or, at least, the bards seem to leave out some of the more unpleasant little details involved in 'adventures.' And the difference between properly chaperoned hunting trips, with appropriate armsmen and servants along to look after my needs, and traveling light by myself has become rather painfully clear to me."

"A few nights camping out by yourself in the rain will generally start to make that evident," Kaeritha agreed. "And I notice you didn't bring along a tent."

"No," Leeana said with another, more heartfelt grimace. "I had enough trouble getting a few days' worth of trail rations smuggled into the stable and stowed away in Boots' saddle bags without trying to bring along proper travel gear." She shivered. "That first night was *really* unpleasant," she admitted. "I never did get a fire started."

"Hard to do without dry wood," Kaeritha observed, carefully hiding the deep pang of sympathy she felt as she pictured Leeana— a pampered young noblewoman, however much she may have wanted and striven to be something else—all alone in a cold, rainy night without a tent or as much as a fire. It must have been the most wretched night of the girl's entire existence.

"Yes, I found that out." Leeana's grin was remarkably free of self-pity, and she actually chuckled. "By the next morning, I'd figured out what I'd done wrong, so I spent about an hour finding myself a nice, dead log and hacking half a saddlebag or so of dry heartwood out of it with my dagger." She held up her right palm, examining the fresh blisters which crossed it with a rueful chuckle. "At least the exercise got me warmed up! And the next night, I had something dry to start the fire with. Heaven!"

She rolled her eyes so drolly Kaeritha had no choice but to laugh. Then she shook her head severely, returned her attention to the road, and asked Cloudy for a trot. The mare obliged, with the smooth gait which was steadily becoming addictive, and they moved off in a brisk, steady splatter of mud.

Yes, Kaeritha thought, treasuring green eyes that could laugh at their owner's own wet, cold, undoubtedly frightened misery. *Yes, there is some sound mettle in this one, thank Tomanāk.*

"Father isn't far behind now."

Kaeritha looked up from the breakfast fire. Leeana was standing beside the road, her raised arm hooked up across Boots' withers while she stared back the way they'd come the day before. Her expression was tense, and she stood very still, only the fingers of her right hand moving as they caressed the gelding's soft, warm coat.

"What makes you so certain?" Kaeritha asked, for there had been no question at all in the sober pronouncement.

"I could say it's because I know he had to have missed me by the second morning and that it's easy to guess he's been pushing hard after me ever since," the girl said. "But the truth is, I just *know*." She turned and looked at Kaeritha. "I always know where he and Mother are," she said simply.

Kaeritha chewed on that for a few moments, while she busied herself turning strips of bacon in her blackened camp skillet. Then she whipped the bacon out of the popping grease and spread it over their last slabs of slightly stale bread. She dumped the grease into the flames and watched the fire sputter eagerly, then looked back up at Leeana.

The girl's face was drawn, and Boots and Cloudy were both beginning to show the effects of the stiff pace they had set. Of course, Leeana and Boots had covered the same distance in twenty-four hours less than she and Cloudy had, but she'd been pushing hard herself ever since the girl caught up with her. The baron and his wind brother Hathan were both wind riders. However furious and worried he might be, Tellian was too levelheaded to risk riding in pursuit with only Hathan—the Lord Warden of the West Riding would be too juicy a target for the ill-intentioned to pass up—but he and his wind brother would be setting a crushing pace for the rest of his armsmen, and Kaeritha knew it.

"What do you mean, you know where they are?" she asked after a moment.

"I just do." Leeana gave Boots one more caress, then stepped closer to Kaeritha and the fire and accepted her share of the bread and bacon. She took an appreciative bite of the humble repast and shrugged.

"I'm sorry. I'm not trying to be mysterious about it—I just don't know a good way to explain it. Mother says the sight has always run in her family, all the way back to the Fall." She shrugged again. "I don't really know about that. It's not as if there have been dozens of magi in our family, or anything like that. But I always know where they are, or if they're unhappy . . . or hurt." She shivered, her face suddenly drawn and old beyond its years. "Just like I knew when Moonshine went down and rolled across Mother."

She stared at something only she could see for several seconds, then shook herself. She looked down at the bread and bacon in her hand, as if seeing them for the first time, and gave Kaeritha a smile that was somehow shy, almost embarrassed, as she raised the food and bit into it again.

"Do they always 'know' where *you* are?" Kaeritha asked after moment.

"No." Leeana shook her head. Then she paused. "Well, actually, I don't know for certain about Mother. I know that when I was a very little girl, she always seemed to know just when I was about to get into mischief, but I always just put that down to 'mommy magic.' I do know *Father* doesn't have any trace of whatever it is, though. If he did, I'd have gotten into trouble so many times in the last few years that I doubt I'd be able to sit in a saddle at all! I'd never have gotten away with running away in the first place, either. And I can tell from how unhappy and worried he feels right now that he doesn't realize they're no more than a few hours behind us."

Her eyes darkened with the last sentence, and her voice was low. The thought of her father's unhappiness and worry clearly distressed her.

"It's not too late to change your mind, Leeana," Kaeritha said quietly. The girl looked at her quickly, and the knight shrugged. "If he's that close, all we have to do is sit here for a few hours. Or we can go on. From the map and directions your father's steward gave me, Kalatha can't be more than another two or three hours down the road. But the decision is yours."

"Not anymore," Leeana half-whispered. Her nostrils flared, and then she shook her head firmly. "It's a decision I've already made, Dame Kaeritha. I can't—won't—change it now. Besides," she managed a crooked smile, "he may be unhappy and worried, but those aren't the only things he's feeling. He knows where I'm going, and why."

"He does? You're certain of that?"

"Oh, I wasn't foolish enough to leave any tear-spotted notes that might come to light sooner than I wanted," Leeana said dryly. "In fact, I left right after breakfast, and I sent both of my personal maids off to visit their parents the night before. I didn't tell either of them the other one had the evening off, either, so no one was likely to miss me until sometime after breakfast the next day. Father *is* a wind rider, you know. If I hadn't managed to buy at least a full day's head start, he'd have forgotten about waiting for his personal bodyguard and he and Hathan would have come after me alone. And in that case, he'd have been certain to catch up with me, even on Boots.

"Since he didn't, I have to assume I did manage to keep anyone from realizing I'd left long enough to get the start I needed. But Father isn't an idiot, and he knows I'm not one, either. He must have figured out where I was going the instant someone finally realized I was missing, and he's been coming after me ever since. But, you know, there's a part of him that doesn't want to catch me."

She finished the last bite of her bread and bacon, then stood, looking across at Kaeritha, and this time her smile was gentle, almost tender.

"Like you, he's afraid I'm making a terrible mistake, and he's determined to keep me from doing it, if he can. But he knows why I'm doing it, too. And that's why a part of him doesn't want to catch me. Actually *wants* me to beat him to Kalatha, because he knows as well as I do that the war maids are the only way I'll avoid eventually being forced to become a pedigreed broodmare dropping foals for Blackhill . . . or someone. Mother was never that for him, and he knows *I'll* never be that for anyone. He taught me to feel that way—to value myself that much—himself, and he knows that, too."

"Which won't prevent him from stopping you if he can," Kaeritha said.

"No." Leeana shook her head. "Silly, isn't it? Here we both are—me, running away from him; him, chasing after me to bring me back, whether I want to come or not—and all of it because of how much we love each other."

A tear glittered for an instant, but she wiped it briskly away and turned to busy herself tightening the girth on Boots' saddle.

"Yes," Kaeritha said softly, emptying the teapot over the fire's embers and beginning to cover the ashes with dirt. "Yes, Leeana. Very silly indeed."

"You have to be out of your bloody mind!"

The gray-haired woman on the other side of the desk stared at Kaeritha and Leeana in disbelief. The bronze key of her office hung on a chain about her neck, and her brown eyes were hard, almost angry.

"I assure you, Mayor Yalith, that I am *not* out of my mind," Leeana replied sharply. She and Kaeritha were tired, mud-spattered, and worn to the bone from long days in the saddle, but she was obviously fighting hard to hang on to her temper. Equally obviously, her life as the daughter of the Baron of Balthar had not exactly suited her to dealing with attitudes like Yalith's.

"Madwomen seldom *think* they're out of their minds," the mayor shot back. "And whatever you may think, and however much you may believe that the war maids are a way out of some social inconvenience, there are aspects of this situation which could only lead to disaster."

"With all due respect, Mayor," Kaeritha put in, intervening for the first time, "this girl is not talking about 'some social *inconvenience.*' She is talking, unless I was very much mistaken when I read King Gartha's original proclamation granting the war maids the right to exist, about the exact thing you and your people are supposed to guarantee to *any* woman."

"Don't you go quoting the charter to *me*, thank you, *Dame* Kaeritha!" Yalith shot back. "You may be a champion of Tomanāk, but Tomanāk's never done anything for the war maids that *I* ever heard about! And the war maids are scarcely a convenient bolthole for some pampered noblewoman—the daughter of a baron, no less!—to use just to avoid an engagement when her family hasn't even accepted it yet!"

Kaeritha started to speak again, quickly, despite her awareness that her own anger would only guarantee that Yalith would refuse to listen to anything she said. But before she could open her mouth, Leeana laid a hand on her forearm and faced the mayor of Kalatha squarely.

"Yes," she said quietly, holding Yalith's brown eyes with her own jade stare. "I am avoiding an engagement my family hasn't accepted. I'm not aware, though, that the war maids are in the habit of asking a woman why she seeks to join them—aside from making certain that she isn't simply a criminal trying to avoid punishment. Was I mistaken?"

It was Yalith's turn to bite off a hot return unspoken. She glared at Leeana for several tense seconds, then shook her head curtly.

"No," she admitted. "We aren't 'in the habit' of asking questions like that. Or, rather, we *do* ask them, but the answers don't—or shouldn't—affect whether or not we grant someone membership. But I trust that you're willing to admit that this is not a usual situation. First, I'm quite certain you're the highest-ranking young woman who's ever sought to become a war maid, and the gods only know where *that* might end. Second, the most common reason women who later regret asking to become one of us sought us out in the first place is to escape an arranged marriage. We always make a special effort to be positive women like that are certain in their own minds of what they want. And, third, this is the worst possible time, from Kalatha's perspective, for us to be antagonizing someone like Baron Tellian!"

"I'll want to speak to you about that later, Mayor Yalith," Kaeritha put in, snapping the mayor's eyes back to her. "For now, though, I don't think you need to fear antagonizing Tellian. I don't expect him to be happy about this, and I don't know what his *official* position is likely to be. But I do know he isn't going to blame you for doing precisely what your charter requires you to do just because the applicant in question is his daughter."

"Oh no?" Yalith snorted in obvious disbelief. "All right, then. Let's say you're right, Dame Kaeritha—about her father, anyway. But what about Baron Cassan and this Blackhill? If they're hunting this young woman—" she jabbed a finger at Leeana "—as greedily as the two of you are suggesting, how do you think they're going to react if the war maids help her slip through their filthy little fingers? You think, perhaps, they'll send us a sizable cash donation?"

"I expect they'll be as pissed off as hell," Kaeritha said candidly, and despite Yalith's own obvious anger and anxiety, her earthy choice of words lit a very slight twinkle in the mayor's eyes. "On the other hand," the knight continued, "how much harm can it really do you? From what Leeana's told me, Blackhill and Cassan are probably already about as hostile to you war maids as they could possibly get."

"I'm afraid Dame Kaeritha is right about that, Mayor Yalith," Leeana said wryly. Yalith looked back at her with another, harsher snort, and the young woman shrugged. "I'm not trying to say they won't be angry about it, or that they won't do you an ill turn if they can, if I manage to drive a stake through their plans by becoming a war maid. They certainly will. But in the long term, they're already hostile to everything the war maids stand for."

"Which is a *marvelous* reason to antagonize them further, I'm sure," Yalith replied. Her sarcasm was withering, yet it seemed to Kaeritha that her resistance was weakening.

"Mayor Yalith," Leeana said quietly, "the war maids antagonize every noble like Blackhill or Cassan every single day, simply by existing. I know I'm a 'special case.' And I understand why you feel concerned and anxious at the thought of all the complications I represent. But Dame Kaeritha is right, and you know it. *Every* war maid is a 'special case.' That was exactly why the first war maids came together in the first place—to give all those special cases someplace to go for the first time in our history. So if you deny my application because of my birth, then what does that say about how ready the war maids truly are to offer sanctuary to *any* woman who wants only to live her own life, make her own decisions? Lillinara knows no distinctions among the maidens and women who seek Her protection. Should an organization which claims Her as its patron do what She will not?"

She locked eyes once again with the mayor. There was no anger in her gaze this time, no desperation or supplication—only challenge. A challenge that demanded to know whether or not Yalith was prepared to live up to the ideals to which the mayor had dedicated her life.

Silence hovered in the office, flawed only by the crackle of coal burning on the hearth. Kaeritha sensed the tension humming between Yalith and Leeana, but it was a tension she stood outside of. She was a spectator, not a participant. That was a role to which a champion of the war god was ill-accustomed, yet she also knew that this was ultimately not a battle anyone could fight for Leeana. It was one she must win on her own.

And then, finally, Yalith drew a deep breath and, for the first time since Leeana and Kaeritha had been ushered into her office, she sat down behind her desk.

"You're right," she sighed. "The Mother knows I wish you weren't," she went on more wryly, "because this is going to create Shīgū's own nightmare, but you're right. If I turn you away, then I turn away every woman fleeing an intolerable 'marriage' she has no legal right to refuse. So I suppose we have no choice, do we, Milady?"

There was a certain caustic bite in the honorific, yet it was obvious that the woman had made up her mind. And there was also an oddly pointed formality in her use of the address, Kaeritha realized—one which warned Leeana that if her application was accepted, no one would ever extend it to her again.

"No, Mayor," Leeana said softly, her voice accepting the warning. "We don't. Not any of us."

"Baron Tellian is here. He demands to speak to you and his daughter."

Yalith of Kalatha gave the messenger a resigned look, then glanced at Kaeritha with a trace of a "look what you've gotten me into" expression. To her credit, it was only a trace, and she returned her attention to the middle-aged woman standing in her office doorway.

"Was that your choice of verbs, or his, Sharral?"

"Mine," Sharral admitted in a slightly chagrined tone. "He's been courteous enough, I suppose. Under the circumstances. But he's also quite . . . emphatic about it."

"Not surprising, I'm afraid." Yalith pinched the bridge of her nose and grimaced wryly. "You did say he was close behind you, Dame Kaeritha," she observed. "Still, I would have appreciated at least a little more time—perhaps even as much as a whole hour— to prepare myself for this particular conversation."

"So would I," Kaeritha admitted. "In fact, a certain cowardly part of me wonders whether or not this office has a back door."

"If you think I'm going to let you sneak out of here, Milady, you're sadly mistaken," Kalatha's mayor replied tartly, and Kaeritha chuckled.

It wasn't an entirely cheerful sound, because she truly wasn't looking forward to what she expected to be a painful confrontation. On the other hand, once Yalith had made her decision and the initial tension between them had eased a bit, she'd found herself liking the mayor much more than she had originally believed she ever might. Yet there was still an undeniable edge there, rather like the arched spines of two strange cats, sidling towards one another and still unsure whether or not they should sheath their claws after all. She wasn't certain where it came from, and she didn't much care for it, whatever its source. But there should be plenty of time to smooth any ruffled fur, she reminded herself. Assuming she and Yalith both survived their interview with Tellian.

"I suppose you'd better show him in, then, Sharral," Yalith sighed after moment.

"Yes, Mayor," Sharral acknowledged, and withdrew, closing the door behind her.

It opened again, less than two minutes later, and Baron Tellian strode through it. It would have been too much to call his expression and body language "bristling," but that was the word which sprang immediately to Kaeritha's mind. He was liberally bespattered with mud, and—like Kaeritha's own—his bedraggled appearance showed just how hard and long he'd ridden to reach Yalith's office. And in his effort to overcome her own two-day lead on him. Even his courser must have found the pace wearying, and she suspected that most of his armsmen—those not mounted on coursers—must have brought along at least two horses each to ride in relays.

"Baron," Yalith said, rising behind her desk to greet him. Her voice was respectful and even a bit sympathetic, but it was also firm. It acknowledged both his rank and his rightful anxiety as a parent, but it also reminded him that this was *her* office ... and that the war maids had seen many anxious parents over the centuries.

"Mayor Yalith," Tellian said. His eyes moved past her for a moment to Kaeritha, but he didn't greet the knight, and Kaeritha wondered just how bad a sign that might be.

"I imagine you know why I'm here," he continued, returning his gaze to the mayor. "I'd like to see my daughter. Immediately."

His tenor voice was flat and crisp—almost, but not quite, harsh—and his eyes were hard.

"I'm afraid that's not possible, Baron," Yalith replied. Tellian's brow furrowed thunderously, and he started to reply sharply. But Yalith continued before he could.

"The rules and customs of the war maids are unfortunately clear on this point, Milord," she said in a voice which Kaeritha considered was remarkably calm. "Leeana has petitioned for the status of war maid. Because she's only fourteen, she will be required to undergo a six-month probationary period before we will accept her final, binding oath. During that time, members of her family may communicate with her by letter or third-party messenger, but not in person. I should point out to you that she was not aware upon her arrival that she would be required to serve her probationary time, or that she would not be permitted to speak to you during it. When I informed her of those facts, she asked Dame Kaeritha to speak to you for her."

Tellian's jaw had clenched as the mayor spoke. If there had been any question about whether or not he was angry before, there was none now, and his right hand tightened ominously about the hilt of his dagger. But furious father or no, he was also a powerful noble who had learned from hard experience to control both his expression and his tongue. And so he swallowed the fast, furious retort which hovered just behind his teeth and made himself inhale deeply before he spoke once more.

"My daughter," he said then, still looking directly at Yalith, as if Kaeritha were not even present, "is young and, as I know only too well, stubborn. She is also, however, intelligent, whatever I may think of this current escapade of hers. She knows how badly her actions have hurt her mother and me. I cannot believe that she would not wish to speak to me at this time. I don't say she would look forward to it, or be happy about it, but she is neither so heartless nor so unaware of how much we love her that she would refuse to see me."

"I didn't say she had refused, Milord. In fact, she was extremely distressed when she discovered it would be impossible for her to do so. Unfortunately, our laws permit me no latitude. Not out of arrogance or cruelty, but to protect applicants from being browbeaten or manipulated into changing their minds against their free choice. But I will say, if you will permit me to, that I have seldom seen an applicant who more strongly desired to speak to her parents. Usually, by the time a young woman seeks the war maids, the last thing she wants is contact with the family she's fled. Leeana doesn't feel at all that way, and if it were her decision, she would be here this moment. But it isn't. Nor is it mine, I'm afraid."

Tellian's knuckles whitened on his dagger, and his nostrils flared. He closed his eyes for a moment, then opened them again.

"I see." His tone was very, very cold, but for a man who had just been told his beloved daughter would not even be permitted to speak to him, it was remarkably controlled, Kaeritha thought. Then his eyes swiveled to her, and she recognized the raging fury and desperate love—and loss—blazing within them.

"In that case," he continued in that same, icy voice, "I suppose I should hear whatever message my daughter has been permitted to leave me."

Yalith winced slightly before the pain in his voice, but she didn't flinch, and Kaeritha wondered how many interviews like this one she had experienced over the years.

"I think you should, Milord," the mayor agreed quietly. "Would you prefer for me to leave, so that you may speak to Dame Kaeritha frankly in order to confirm what I've said, and that Leeana came to us willingly and of her own accord?"

"I would appreciate privacy when I speak to Dame Kaeritha," Tellian said. "But not," he continued, "because I doubt for a moment that this was entirely Leeana's idea. Whatever some others might accuse the war maids of, I am fully aware that she came to *you* and that you did nothing to 'seduce' her into doing so. I won't pretend I'm not angry—*very* angry—or that I do not deeply resent your refusal to allow me to so much as speak to her. But I know my daughter too well to believe anyone else could have convinced or compelled her to come here against her will."

"Thank you for that, Milord." Yalith inclined her head in a small bow of acknowledgment. "I'm a mother myself, and I've spoken with Leeana. I know why she came to us, and that it wasn't because she didn't love you and her mother or doubted for a moment that you love her. In many ways, that has made this one of the saddest applications ever to pass through my office. I'm grateful that despite the anger and grief I know you must feel, you understand this was *her* decision. And now, I'll leave you and Dame Kaeritha. If you wish to speak to me again afterward, I will, of course, be at your service."

She bowed again, more deeply, and left Tellian and Kaeritha alone in her office.

For several seconds, the baron stood wordlessly, his hand alternately tightening and loosening its grip on his dagger while he glared at Kaeritha.

"Some would call this poor repayment of my hospitality, Dame Kaeritha," he said at length, his voice harsh.

"No doubt some would, Milord," she replied, keeping her own voice level and as nonconfrontational as possible. "If it seems that way to you, I deeply regret it."

"I'm sure you do." Each word was carefully, precisely spoken, as if bitten clean-edged from a sheet of bronze. Then he closed his eyes and gave his head a little shake.

"I could wish," he said then, his voice much softer, its angry edges blurred by grief, "that you'd returned her to me. That when my daughter—my only child, Kaeritha—came to you in the dark, on the side of a lonely road, running away from the only home she's ever known and from Hanatha's and my love, you might have recognized the madness of what she was doing and stopped her." He opened his eyes and looked into her face, his own eyes wrung with pain and bright with unshed tears. "Don't tell me you couldn't have stopped her from casting away her life— throwing away everything and everyone she's ever known. Not if you'd really tried."

"I could have," she told him unflinchingly, refusing to look away from his pain and grief. "For all her determination and courage, I could have stopped her, Milord. And I almost did."

"Then *why*, Kaeritha?" he implored, no longer a baron, no longer the Lord Warden of the West Riding, but only an anguished father. "Why *didn't* you? This will break Hanatha's heart, as it has already broken mine."

"Because it was her decision," Kaeritha said gently. "I'm not a Sothōii, Tellian. I don't pretend to understand your people, or all of your ways and customs. But when your daughter rode up to my fire out of the rain and the night, all by herself, she wasn't running away from your heart, or your love, or from Hanatha's love. She was running *to* them."

The unshed tears broke free, running down Tellian's fatigue-lined, unshaven cheeks, and her own eyes stung.

"That's her message to you," Kaeritha continued quietly. "That she can never tell you how sorry she is for the pain she knows her actions will cause you and her mother. But that she also knows this was only the first offer for her hand. There would have been more, if this one was refused, Tellian, and you know it. Just as you know that who she is and what she offers means almost all those offers would have been made for all the wrong reasons. But you also know you couldn't refuse them all—not without paying a disastrous political price. She may be only fourteen years old, but she sees that, and she understands it. So she made the only decision she thinks she *can* make. Not just for her, but for everyone she loves."

"But how could she *leave* us this way?" Tellian demanded, his voice raw with anguish. "The law will take us from her as surely as it takes her from us, Kaeritha! Everyone she's ever known, everything she ever had, will be taken from her. How could you let her pay that price, *whatever* she wanted?"

"Because of who she is," Kaeritha said quietly. "Not 'what'—not because she's the daughter of a baron—but because of *who* she is . . . and who you raised her to be. You made her too strong if you wanted someone who would meekly submit to a life sentence as no more than a high-born broodmare to someone like this Blackhill. And you made her too loving to allow someone like him or Baron Cassan to use her as a weapon against you. Between you, you and Hanatha raised a young woman strong enough and loving enough to give up all of the rank and all of the privileges of her birth, to suffer the pain of 'running away' from you and the even worse pain of knowing how much grief her decision would cause you. Not because she was foolish, or petulant, or spoiled—and certainly not because she was stupid. She did it because of how *much* she loves you both."

The father's tears spilled freely now, and she stepped closer, reaching out to rest her hands on his shoulders.

"What else could I do in the face of that much love, Tellian?" she asked very softly.

"Nothing," he whispered, and he bowed his head and his own right hand left the dagger hilt and rose to cover the hand on his left shoulder.

He stood that way for long, endless moments. Then he inhaled deeply, squeezed her hand lightly, raised his head, and brushed the tears from his eyes.

"I wish, from the bottom of my heart, that she hadn't done this thing," he said, his voice less ragged but still soft. "I would never have consented to her marriage to anyone she didn't choose to marry, whatever the *political* cost. But I suppose she knew that, didn't she?"

"Yes, I think she did," Kaeritha agreed with a slight, sad smile.

"Yet as badly as I wish she hadn't done it, I know why she did. And you're right—whatever else it may have been, it wasn't the decision of a weakling or a coward. And so, despite all the grief and the heartache this will cause me and Hanatha—and Leeana— I'm proud of her."

He shook his head, as if he couldn't quite believe his own words. But then he stopped shaking it, and nodded slowly instead.

"I *am* proud of her," he said.

"And you should be," Kaeritha replied simply.

They gazed at one another for a few more seconds of silence, and then he nodded again, crisply this time, with an air of finality . . . and acceptance.

"Tell her . . ." He paused, as if searching for exactly the right words. Then he shrugged, as if he'd suddenly realized the search wasn't really difficult at all. "Tell her that we love her. Tell her we understand why she's done this. That if she changes her mind during this 'probationary period' we will welcome her home and rejoice. But also tell her it is *her* decision, and that we will accept it—and continue to love her—whatever it may be in the end."

"I will," she promised, inclining her head in a half-bow.

"Thank you," he said, and then surprised her with a wry but genuine chuckle. One of her eyebrows arched, and he snorted.

"The *last* thing I expected for the last three days that I'd be doing when I finally caught up with you was *thanking* you, Dame Kaeritha. Champion of Tomanāk or not, I had something a bit more drastic in mind!"

"If I'd been in your position, Milord," she told him with a crooked smile, "*I'd* have been thinking of something having to do with headsmen and chopping blocks."

"I won't say the thought didn't cross my mind," he conceded, "although I'd probably have had a little difficulty explaining it to Bahzell and Brandark. On the other hand, I'm pretty sure that anything I was contemplating doing to you pales compared to what my *armsmen* think I ought to do. All of them are deeply devoted to Leeana, and some of them will never believe she ever would have thought of something like this without encouragement from someone. I suspect the someone they're going to blame for it will be you. And some of my other retainers—and vassals—are going to see her decision as a disgrace and an insult to my house. When they do, they're going to be looking for someone to blame for *that*, too."

"I anticipated something like that," Kaeritha said dryly.

"I'm sure you did, but the truth is that this isn't going to do your reputation any good with *most* Sothōii," he warned.

"Champions of Tomanāk frequently find themselves a bit unpopular, Milord," she said. "On the other hand, as Bahzell has said a time or two, 'a champion is one as does what needs doing.'" She shrugged. "This needed doing."

"Perhaps it did," he acknowledged. "But I hope one of the consequences won't be to undermine whatever it is you're here to do for Scale Balancer."

"As far as that goes, Milord," she said thoughtfully, "it's occurred to me that helping Leeana get here in the first place may have been a part of what I'm supposed to do. I'm not sure why it should have been, but it *feels* right, and I've learned it's best to trust my feelings in cases like this."

Tellian didn't look as if he found the thought that any god, much less the War God, should want one of his champions to help his only child run away to the war maids particularly encouraging. If so, she didn't blame him a bit . . . and at least he was courteous enough not to put his feelings into words.

"At any rate," she continued, "I will be most happy to deliver your message—*all* of your message—to Leeana."

"Thank you," he repeated, and the corners of his eyes crinkled with an edge of genuine humor as he looked around Yalith's office. "And now, I suppose, we ought to invite the mayor back into her own office. It would be only courteous to reassure her that we haven't been carving one another up in here, after all!"

At least Chemalka seemed to have decided to take her rainstorms somewhere else.

Kaeritha grinned at the thought as she stood on the porch of the Kalathan guesthouse with a mug of steaming tea and gazed out into a misty early morning. Tellian and his armsmen had refused the war maids' hospitality and departed late the previous afternoon. Kaeritha felt certain that the baron hadn't declined Yalith's offer out of anger or pique, but it had probably been as well that he had. Whatever he might feel, the attitudes—and anger—of several of his retainers would have been certain to provoke friction and might well have spilled over into an unfortunate incident.

Her grin vanished into a grimace, and she shook her head with an air of resignation before she took another sip of tea. Tellian's warning that many of his followers were going to blame Kaeritha for Leeana's decision and actions had proved only too well founded. All of them had been too disciplined to say or do anything overt about their feelings in the face of their liege lord's public acceptance of the situation, but Kaeritha hadn't needed to be a mage to recognize the intense hostility in some of the glances which came her way. She hoped their anger with her wasn't going to spill over onto Bahzell and Brandark when they got back to Balthar. If it did, though, Bahzell would simply have to deal with it. Which, she thought wryly, he would undoubtedly accomplish in his own inimitable fashion.

She drank more tea, watching the sun climb above the muddy fields which surrounded Kalatha. It was going to be a warmer day, she decided, and the sun would soon burn off the mists. She'd noticed the training field and an extensive weapons salle behind the town armory when she passed it on the day of her arrival, and she wondered if Yalith's guard captain would object to her borrowing it for an hour or so. She'd missed her regular morning workouts while she and Leeana pressed ahead as rapidly as possible on their journey. Besides, from all she'd heard, her own two-handed fighting technique was much less uncommon among war maids. If she could talk some of them into sparring with her, she might be able to pick up a new trick or two.

She finished the tea and turned to step back into the guesthouse to set the mug on the table beside her other breakfast dishes. Then she looked into the small mirror—an unexpected and expensive luxury—above the fireplace. Welcome as the guesthouse bed had been, the communal bathhouse had been even more welcome. She actually looked human again, she decided, although it was still humid enough that it had taken her long, midnight-black hair hours to dry. Most of her clothes were *still* drying somewhere in the town laundry, but she'd had one decent, clean change still in her saddlebags. There were a few wrinkles and creases here and there, but taken all in all, she was presentable, she decided.

Which was probably a good thing. It might even do her some good in her upcoming interview with Yalith.

Then again, she thought ruefully, *it might not*.

∽   ∽   ∽

"Thank you for agreeing to see me so early, Mayor," Kaeritha said as Sharral showed her into Yalith's office and she settled into the proffered chair.

"There's no need to thank me," Yalith replied briskly. "Despite any possible . . . lack of enthusiasm on my part when you handed me a hot potato like Leeana, any champion deserves whatever hospitality we can provide, Dame Kaeritha. Although," she admitted, "I am a bit perplexed by exactly what a champion of Tomanāk is doing here in Kalatha. However exalted Leeana's birth may have been, I don't believe we've ever had a war maid candidate delivered to us by *any* champion. And if that was going to happen, I would have expected one of the Mother's Servants."

"Actually," Kaeritha said, "I was already headed for Kalatha when Leeana overtook me on the road."

"Were you, indeed?" Yalith's tone was that of a woman expressing polite interest, not surprise. Although, Kaeritha thought, there was also an edge of wariness to it.

"Yes," she said. Her left elbow rested on the arm of her chair, and she raised her hand, palm open. "I don't know how familiar you are with champions and the way we get our instructions, Mayor Yalith."

Her own tone made the statement a tactful question, and Yalith smiled.

"I've never dealt directly with a champion, if that's what you mean," she said. "I once met a senior Servant of the Mother, but I was much younger then, and certainly not a mayor. No one was interested at the time in explaining how she got her instructions from Lillinara. Even if anyone had been, my impression is that She has Her own way of getting Her desires and intentions across, so I assume the same would be true of Tomanāk or any of the other gods."

"It certainly is," Kaeritha agreed wryly. "For that matter, He seems to tailor His methods to his individual champions. In my own case, however, I tend to receive, well, *feelings*, I suppose, that I ought to be moving in a particular direction or thinking about a particular problem. As I get closer to whatever it is He needs me to be dealing with, I generally recognize the specifics as I come across them."

"That would seem to require a great deal of faith," Yalith observed. Then she wrinkled her nose with a snort of amusement at her own words. "I suppose a champion *does* need rather more 'faith' than the most people do, doesn't she?"

"It does seem to come with the job," Kaeritha agreed. "In this instance, though, those feelings He sends me already had me headed in this direction. As nearly as I can pin things down at this point, Kalatha was where He wanted me."

"And not just to escort Leeana to us, I suppose."

"No. I had some discussion with Baron Tellian before I left Balthar, Mayor. Frankly, the reports from his stewards and magistrates which he shared with me lead me to believe that relations between your town and its neighbors are ... not as good as they might be."

"My, what a tactful way to describe it." Yalith's irony was dry enough to burn off the morning's mist without benefit of sunlight. She regarded Kaeritha without saying anything more for several more seconds, then leaned back in her chair and folded her arms across her chest.

"As a matter of fact, Dame Kaeritha, our 'neighbors' are probably almost as angry with us as we are with them. Although, of course, my town council and I believe we're in the right and *they* aren't. I hope you'll forgive me for saying this, however, but I fail to see why our disagreements and squabbles should be of any particular interest to Tomanāk. Surely He has better things to spend His champions' time on than refereeing fights which have been going on for decades. Besides, with all due respect, I should think that matters concerning the war maids are properly the affair of Lillinara, not the War God."

"First," Kaeritha said calmly, "Tomanāk is the God of Justice, as well as the God of War, and from Tellian's reports, there seems to be some question of exactly what 'justice' means in this case. Second, those same reports also seem to suggest that there's something more to this than the same sort of quarrels which usually go on between war maid communities and their neighbors."

Yalith seemed less than pleased by the reminder that Tomanāk was God of Justice—or perhaps by the implication that in that capacity he might have a legitimate interest in a matter which she clearly considered belonged to Lillinara. But if that was the case, she chose not to make a point of it. Yet, at least.

"I suppose there may be a bit more to it this time," she conceded with a slightly grudging air. "Trisu of Lorham has never been particularly fond of war maids in general. His father wasn't, either, but at least the old man realized we aren't going away and that he had to learn to live with our presence. Trisu only inherited his title three years ago, and he's still young ... and impatient. I sometimes think he actually believes he can make himself sufficiently unpleasant to convince us to all just—" she wiggled the fingers of one hand in midair "—move away and leave him in peace."

She grimaced, then drew a deep breath and shook her head.

"On the other hand, I doubt even Trisu could really be stupid enough to think that's going to happen. Which means he's making such an ass out of himself for some other reason. My own theory is that it's simple frustration and immaturity. I've been hoping he'll simply outgrow it."

"With all due respect, Mayor Yalith," Kaeritha kept her voice as level and uninflected as possible, "from his own reports—and complaints—to Baron Tellian, he seems to feel he has legitimate cause for his unhappiness with Kalatha." She raised one hand in a pacifying gesture as Yalith's eyes narrowed. "I'm not saying you're wrong about his underlying hostility, because from the tone of his letters, you're certainly not. I'm only saying that he clearly believes he has legitimate grievances over and above the fact that he simply doesn't like you very much."

"I'm aware of that," Yalith said a bit frostily. "I've heard about water rights and pasturage complaints from him until, quite frankly, I'm sick of it. Kalatha's charter clearly gives us control of the river, since it passes through our territory. What we do with it is up to us, not to him. And if he wants us to make a greater share of *our* water available to him, then he's going to have to make some concessions to us, in return."

Kaeritha nodded—in understanding, not agreement, although she wasn't certain Yalith recognized the distinction. Given the quantity of water which had fallen out of the sky over the past several weeks, the thought that Kalatha and the most powerful of the local nobles were at dagger-drawing over the issue of water rights might have struck some as silly. Kaeritha, however, had been born and spent her earliest years in a peasant farming community. That meant she was only too well aware of how desperately important such issues could become when soggy spring gave way to the hot, dry months of summer. On the other hand, it was entirely possible—even probable, she suspected—that the quarrel over water was only an outward manifestation of other, more deeply seated enmities.

"From his arguments to Tellian's magistrates," she said after moment, "it seems fairly evident Trisu doesn't agree that your control of the river is as straightforward and unambiguous as you believe it is. Obviously, he's going to put forward what he believes are his strongest arguments in that respect, since he's trying to convince the courts to rule in his favor. I'm not saying he's correct or that his arguments are valid—only that he appears to *believe* they are."

Yalith snorted derisively, but she didn't say anything, and Kaeritha continued.

"To be honest, at the moment I'm more interested in those return 'concessions' to which you just referred. Trisu has complained to Tellian that the war maids have been hostile and confrontational towards his efforts to work out a peaceable compromise solution to his disputes with you. As far as I'm aware, he hasn't gone into any specifics about just how you've been hostile and confrontational. Do you suppose that would have anything to do with the concessions you want from him?"

"Hostile and confrontational, is it?" Yalith glowered. "I'll 'hostile and confrontational' *him*! We've been as reasonable as we *can* be with such a pigheaded, greedy, stubborn, opinionated young idiot!"

Despite herself, Kaeritha found it difficult not to smile. Yalith's evident anger made it a bit easier, since it was obvious her resentment of Trisu burned much deeper and hotter than she wanted to admit to Kaeritha . . . or possibly even to herself. At the same time, the knight could see how even a man considerably more reasonable than she suspected Trisu was could feel that the war maids were just a trifle hostile towards him.

"I'm sure you have," she said after a second or two, when she was confident she could control her own voice. "What I need to know before I move on to Lorham is exactly what concessions you've been seeking."

"Nothing that earthshaking," Yalith responded. "Or they shouldn't be, anyway. We want a right-of-way across one of his pastures to a stud farm which was donated to us six or seven years ago. We want a formal agreement on how the river's water will be divided and distributed in dry seasons. We want a guarantee that our farm products—and farmers—will receive equal treatment in local markets from his factors and inspectors. And we want him to finally and formally accept the provisions of our charter and Lord Kellos' land grant—*all* of their provisions."

"I see." Kaeritha sat back and considered what Yalith had just said. The first three points did, indeed, sound as if they were less than "earthshaking." She was only too well aware of how simply and reasonably someone could describe her own viewpoint on an issue which was bitterly contested, yet she was inclined to think it must be the fourth point which lay at the heart of the war maids' current confrontation with the Lord of Lorham.

"What specific provisions are in dispute?" she asked after a moment.

"Several." Yalith grimaced. "King Gartha's charter defines specific obligations to local lords from which war maids are to be exempted, and, to be fair, Trisu and his father and grandfather have generally accepted that. They've been less interested in enforcing the provisions which require those same local lords to grant war maid crafters and farmers equal protection and treatment in their markets.

"That's bad enough, but it's also been going on literally for generations, and we'd managed to live with it. But another serious dispute has arisen in the last few years concerning the water rights I spoke of and the integrity of the surrounding land which Lord Kellos originally granted to us. Lord Kellos' grant defined specific boundaries and landmarks, obviously, but Trisu's family— and, for that matter, some of the other local lords, although not to the same degree—have been encroaching upon those boundaries for years. In fact, Trisu's father built a grist mill on what is clearly our land, and Trisu has refused to acknowledge that Lord Darhal was in the wrong when he did. In fact, Trisu insists that *he* owns that land and always has, despite the fact that the original grant puts the boundary almost half a mile *beyond* the mill. That's just one instance of the way in which our boundaries are being routinely violated.

"Another point is that the grant clearly specifies that we're exempt from tolls on the use of roadways crossing Lorham. Lord Kellos and Trisu's great-great-grandfather did some horsetrading back and forth over the exact boundaries of our holdings, and Lord Rathman gave us the exemption in return for a couple of offsetting concessions from Lord Kellos. But Lord Trisu's father began charging us the tolls about thirty years ago.

"Admittedly, this isn't a point we've made an issue out of before, since the tolls Lord Darhal levied weren't all that high. More to the point, they were clearly intended for the maintenance of the roads in question, and we *were* using them to transport our goods and produce. But Trisu began raising the tolls immediately after he became Lord of Lorham. He's obviously trying to use them to raise additional revenues, over and above the cost of maintaining the roads themselves. We may have been willing to pay a toll we weren't legally obligated to pay so long as the funds were being used to repair and maintain roadways that benefitted us, as well as Lorham. But we are not prepared to subsidize other parts of his treasury while he's violating our boundaries and attempting to deny us our legitimate water rights.

"There are several other, minor points—most of them procedural, really. Some of them, to be completely honest, probably aren't worth fighting over. But they're part and parcel of our overall quarrel with him, and we're not prepared to concede any of them without getting something in return. But there is one additional, major problem."

The mayor paused, and Kaeritha quirked an eyebrow.

"As I said, our charter clearly and unambiguously provides that our craftspeople, farmers, traders, and anyone else who may be a citizen of Kalatha or any of the free-towns which were founded later are guaranteed the same rights as any other citizens of the Kingdom, regardless of whether they're men or women. Trisu doesn't seem to think that that applies in Lorham."

"In what way?" Kaeritha asked, leaning forward and frowning intently.

"Our merchants and some of our farmers have been harassed in local markets, and Trisu's magistrates have done nothing about it," Yalith replied. She waved a hand in a back-and-forth gesture. "That, in itself, isn't all that important. There's always going to be some bigoted farmer or townsman who's going to give women doing 'man's work' a hard time, and war maids can't afford to be too thin-skinned when it comes along. But it's symptomatic of a more serious problem."

"What sort of problem?"

"There have been . . . incidents concerning the temple of Lillinara at Quaysar," Yalith said. It was obvious she was picking her words carefully, and also that she was trying hard to restrain a volcanic surge of anger. She paused, and Kaeritha waited for the mayor to be certain she had control of her temper before she continued.

"As a follower of Tomanāk, not Lillinara, you may not be aware that the temple in Quaysar has special significance to the Mother," she said, after a few moments. "It's not an especially large temple, but it's a very old one. Quaysar itself is a tiny town. In fact, the town proper has pretty much disappeared over the last fifty or sixty years. What's left of it has been effectively absorbed by the temple itself. But the Quaysar Temple has always been especially important to the war maids—just as Kalatha itself has been, despite our small size—because it was at Quaysar that our original charter from King Gartha was first officially and formally proclaimed. You might say Quaysar is the 'mother chapter' of all war maids everywhere and that Kalatha is the 'mother free-town' to match it. Quaysar is also located in Lorham, unfortunately. As a matter of fact, one of the reasons Lord Kellos originally granted Kalatha to the war maids and why the Crown recognized it as a free-town was our proximity to Quaysar."

"I wasn't aware of that," Kaeritha murmured. "Tellian told me Kalatha was your oldest free-town, but I didn't know about Quaysar or its importance to you."

"There's no reason why you should have," Yalith pointed out. "Obviously, we would have preferred to have been able to include Quaysar under our charter. Unfortunately, the lords of Lorham have always been much less sympathetic to us than Lord Kellos was. It didn't seem to matter much, though, given the respect and autonomy enjoyed by any temple. Whether Trisu or his ancestors approved of war maids or not, surely no sane person was going to harass or insult the temple of *any* god . . . or goddess. Or so we thought."

"You mean he *has* done that?" Kaeritha demanded sharply.

"I mean," Yalith said grimly, "that he's repeatedly demonstrated his disrespect—I would even say contempt—for the temple at Quaysar. He's insulted the Voice of Quaysar in personal conversation. He's made it clear to her that he is not impressed by the fact that she speaks for the Mother. For that matter, he's all but openly stated that he doesn't believe she *does* speak for the Mother at all."

Kaeritha was shocked. Different rulers always evidenced different degrees of reverence and respect, and some people seemed to believe that if they worshiped one god—or goddess—all of the others were irrelevant. But what sort of idiot openly showed the sort of disdain and contempt Yalith was describing? Regardless of what he himself believed or disbelieved, such an attitude was guaranteed to offend and infuriate his subjects.

"That's all bad enough," Yalith continued in a flat, bitter voice, "but it isn't all. Two of the Voice's handmaidens were sent from Quaysar to Kalatha with a message from the Voice to me. They never arrived."

This time, Kaeritha was far more than merely shocked.

"Mayor Yalith, are you suggesting—?"

"I'm not prepared to suggest that Trisu personally had anything to do with their disappearance," Yalith interrupted before Kaeritha could complete the question. "If I had any proof—or even strongly suggestive evidence—of that, I can assure you that I would already have charged him with it before Baron Tellian, as his liege, or demanded that the case be investigated by the Crown Prosecutor. But I do believe that whoever was responsible—who must have shared Trisu's attitude towards war maids generally to have done something so insane—probably took his cue from Trisu. And I am not at all satisfied with Trisu's so-called 'investigation' of the incident. He claims he can find no evidence *at all* to suggest what happened to the Voice's handmaidens. Indeed, he's gone so far as to suggest that they never disappeared at all. That the entire story is a fabrication."

Kaeritha frowned. There had been no mention of this incident in any of Trisu's correspondence with Tellian or his magistrates. In the wake of what Yalith had just told her, that omission took on ominous overtones.

"The Voice hasn't been able to determine what happened to her handmaidens?" she asked after a moment.

"Apparently not," Yalith said heavily. She sighed. "All the Voice can discover is that both of them are dead. How they died, and exactly where, she cannot say."

A chill ran down Kaeritha's spine. The murder of the consecrated Servants of any temple, and especially that of two acolytes sworn to the personal service of a Voice of Lillinara, was an incredibly serious matter. The fact that Trisu wasn't tearing Lorham apart stone by stone to find the guilty parties was frightening.

And perhaps it's also the reason Tomanāk needed one of His champions involved, she thought grimly.

"How long ago did this happen?" she asked crisply.

"Not very long," Yalith replied. She glanced at the calendar hanging on the wall. "A bit less than six weeks ago, actually."

Kaeritha's mood eased just a bit. If the murders had happened that recently, then it was at least possible that Trisu hadn't mentioned it to Tellian because he was still investigating it himself. After all, if it had happened in Lorham, it was *Trisu's* responsibility to solve the crime, not Tellian's. If he was unable to do so, he had the right—and, some would argue, the responsibility—to call upon his liege for assistance, but he might simply feel he hadn't yet exhausted all of his own resources.

Sure. He might *feel that*, she told herself.

And the fact that it had happened that recently undoubtedly

explained why nothing had been said to Tellian by Yalith or the Voice at Quaysar. Kalatha held a Crown charter. That meant that, unlike Trisu, Yalith was *not* one of Tellian's vassals, and as such, she had no responsibility to report anything to him. Nor, for that matter, was Tellian legally obligated to take any action on anything she *did* report to him, although he undoubtably would have acted in a matter this serious which involved or might involve one of his vassals. As for the Voice, Trisu was the appropriate person for her to turn to for an investigation and justice. If he failed to provide them, only then was she entitled to appeal to *his* liege.

"Perhaps now you can see why I was surprised to see a champion of Tomanāk rather than one of the Mother's Servants," Yalith said quietly.

"To be honest, so am I, a little," Kaeritha admitted, although she privately thought that the Servants of Lillinara were a little too intent on avenging victims rather than administering justice. All the same, she *was* surprised Lillinara hadn't dispatched one or more of them to deal with the situation. The Silver Lady was famed for the devastating retribution she was prepared to visit upon those who victimized her followers.

"Perhaps," she went on slowly, thinking aloud, "if Trisu is as hostile towards you as you're saying—hostile enough to extend his feelings towards the war maids into public disrespect for Lillinara—She and Tomanāk felt it might be better for Him to send one of His blades. The fact that I'm a woman may make me a bit more acceptable to you war maids and to the Voice, while the fact that I serve Tomanāk rather than Lillinara may make me acceptable to Trisu *despite* the fact that I'm a woman."

"I hope *something* does, Dame Kaeritha," Yalith said soberly. "Because if something doesn't bring about a marked improvement in what's happening here in Kalatha and Lorham sometime soon, it's going to spill over."

Kaeritha looked at her, and she grimaced.

"Kalatha's status as our oldest free-town means all war maids tend to keep up with events here, Milady, and I just explained why Quaysar is important to all of us. If Trisu and those who think like him are able to get away with running roughshod over us *here*, then they may be inspired to try the same thing anywhere else. That would be bad enough, but to be perfectly honest, I'm actually more concerned about how the *war maids* will react. Let's be honest. Most of us aren't all that fond of men in positions of authority, anyway. If Trisu proves our distrust is well founded, it's going to cause our own attitudes to harden. I can assure you that at least some of the war maids are just as bitter and just as prejudiced against the Trisus of the world as Trisu could ever be against us, and some of those women are likely to begin acting upon their bitterness if they feel we've been denied justice in this case. And if that happens, then everything we've accomplished over the past two hundred and fifty years is in jeopardy."

Kaeritha nodded, blue eyes dark as she contemplated the spiraling cycle of distrust, hostility, and potential violence Yalith was describing.

"Well, in that case, Mayor," she said quietly, "we'll just have to see to it that that doesn't happen, won't we?"

Thalar Keep, the ancestral seat of the Pickaxes of Lorham, was a considerably more modest fortress then Hill Guard Castle. Then again, the town of Thalar (calling it a "city" would have been a gross exaggeration) was far, far smaller than Balthar. Still, the castle, with its two curtain walls and massive, square central keep, was of respectable antiquity. Indeed, it looked to Kaeritha's experienced eye as if the outer walls were at least a couple of centuries younger than the original keep.

There was nothing remotely like finesse about the castle's architecture or construction. It was uncompromisingly angular, laid out with an obvious eye for fields of fire for the archers expected to man its battlements in time of emergency. Whoever had designed it, though—assuming anything like an actual "design" process had been part of its construction—had clearly been less concerned about what an enemy with capable siege engineers might have done to it. It was dominated by a higher ridge to the east, beyond accurate bow range but well within reach for the sort of ballistae someone like the Empire of the Axe might have deployed. Nor was the castle moated. It was built on what appeared to be an artificial mound, too, rather than bedrock, which would have been highly vulnerable to mining operations.

Of course, she mused as Cloudy carried her up the very slight slope towards Thalar, the people who'd built that castle had probably had their fellow Sothōii, or possibly Horse Stealers, in mind. Neither the cavalry-oriented Sothōii nor the relatively unsophisticated hradani would have been in much of a position to take advantage of the weaknesses evident to Kaeritha.

Despite its small size, compared to Balthar, Thalar appeared to be relatively prosperous. There were few houses over two stories in height, but all of the dwellings Kaeritha could see appeared to be well maintained and clean. Despite the incessant spring rains, the local farmers had managed to get their fields plowed, and the first blush of green crops showed vividly against the furrows' rich, black topsoil. And, of course, there were the endless paddocks, training rings, and stables of Trisu's home stud farm.

There were laborers in the fields, and most of them paused to look up and study Kaeritha as Cloudy trotted past. Like Thalar itself, they seemed to be sturdy and well fed, if not wealthy, and almost despite herself, Kaeritha was forced to concede that first appearances suggested that Trisu, whatever his other failings, took excellent care of his people and his holding.

The road up to Thalar Keep was at least marginally better maintained than the muddy track Kaeritha had followed across the Wind Plain. She was grateful for that, and so was Cloudy. The mare picked up her pace as she recognized journey's end. No doubt she was looking forward to a warm stall and a bucketful of oats and bran.

Kaeritha chuckled at the thought, then drew rein as she approached the castle's outer gatehouse and a bugle blared. Her eyebrows rose as she recognized the bugle call. It was a formal challenge, a demand to stand and be recognized, and it was unusual, to say the least, for a single rider to be greeted by it. On the other hand, she could see at least six archers on the wall. Under the circumstances, she decided, compliance was probably in order.

She and Cloudy stopped just beyond the gatehouse's shadow, and she looked up as a man in the crested helmet of an officer appeared on the battlement above her.

"Who are you? And what brings you to Thalar Keep?" the officer shouted down in a nasal bass voice. It was unfortunate that his natural voice made him sound querulous and ill-tempered, Kaeritha thought.

"I am Dame Kaeritha Seldansdaughter," she called back in her clear, carrying soprano, carefully not smiling as his helmeted head twitched in obvious surprise at hearing a woman's voice. "Champion of Tomanāk," she continued, fighting not to chortle as she pictured the effect *that* was likely to have upon him. "Here to see Lord Trisu of Lorham on the War God's business," she finished genially, and sat back in the saddle to await results.

There was a long moment of motionless consternation atop the battlements. Then the officer who had challenged her seemed to give his entire body a shake and whipped around to gabble orders at one of the archers. The archer in question didn't even wait to nod in acknowledgment before he went speeding off. Then the officer turned back to Kaeritha.

"Ah, you *did* say a champion of Tomanāk, didn't you?" he inquired rather tentatively.

"Yes, I did," Kaeritha replied. "And I'm still waiting to be admitted," she added pointedly.

"Well, yes—" the flustered officer began. Then he stopped. Clearly, he had no idea how to proceed when faced with the preposterous, self-evidently impossible challenge of a woman who claimed to be not only a knight, but a champion of Tomanāk, as well! Kaeritha understood perfectly, but she rather hoped the average intelligence level of Trisu's officers and retainers was higher than this fellow seemed to imply.

"I'm getting a crick in my neck shouting up at you," she said mildly, and even from where she sat in Cloudy's saddle she could see the fiery blush which colored the unfortunate man's face.

He turned away from her once more, shouting to someone inside the gatehouse.

"Open the gate!" he snapped, and hinges groaned as someone began obediently heaving one of the massive gate leaves open.

Kaeritha waited patiently, hands folded in plain sight on the pommel of her saddle, until the gate was fully open. Then she nodded her thanks to the still flustered officer and clucked gently to Cloudy. The mare tossed her head, as if she were as amused as her mistress by the obvious consternation they'd caused, then trotted forward with dainty, ladylike grace.

The unfortunate officer from the battlements was waiting for her in the courtyard beyond the gatehouse by the time she emerged from the gate tunnel. Seen at closer range, he was rather more prepossessing than Kaeritha's first impression had suggested. Not that that was particularly difficult, she thought dryly.

His coloring was unusually dark for a Sothōii, and he stared up at her, his brown eyes clinging to the embroidered sword and mace of Tomanāk, glittering in gold bullion on the front of Kaeritha's poncho. From his expression, he would have found a fire-breathing dragon considerably less unnatural, but he was at least trying to handle the situation as if it were a normal one.

"Ah, please forgive my seeming discourtesy, Dame . . . Kaeritha," he said. There was a slight questioning note in his pronunciation of her name, Kaeritha noticed, and nodded pleasantly, acknowledging his apology even as she confirmed that he had it right. "I'm afraid," the officer continued with a surprisingly genuine smile, "that we're not accustomed to seeing champions of Tomanāk here in Lorham."

"There aren't that many of us," Kaeritha agreed, amiably consenting to pretend that that had been the true reason for his confusion.

"I've sent word of your arrival to Lord Trisu," he continued. "I'm sure he'll want to come down to the gate to greet you properly and in person."

Or to kick me back out of the gate if he decides I'm not a champion after all, Kaeritha added silently. *On the other hand, one must be polite, I suppose.*

"Thank you, Captain—?"

"Forgive me," the officer said hastily. "I seem to be forgetting all of my manners today! I am called Sir Altharn."

"Thank you, Sir Altharn," Kaeritha said. "I appreciate the prompt and efficient manner in which you've discharged your duties."

The words were courteously formal, but Sir Altharn obviously noticed the gently teasing edge to her voice. For a moment he started to color up again, but then, to her pleased surprise, he shook his head and smiled at her, instead.

"I suppose I had that coming," he told her. "But truly, Dame Kaeritha, I'm seldom quite so inept as I've managed to appear this morning."

"I believe that," Kaeritha said, and somewhat to her own surprise, it was true.

"Thank you. That's kinder then I deserve," Sir Altharn said. "I hope I'll have the opportunity to demonstrate the fact that I don't always manage to put my own boot in my mouth. Or, at least, that I usually remember to take my spurs off first!"

He laughed at himself, so naturally that Kaeritha laughed with him. There might be some worthwhile depths to this fellow after all, she reflected.

"I'm sure you'll have the chance," she told him. "In fact, I—"

She broke off in mid-sentence as four more men, one of them the messenger Altharn had dispatched, arrived from the direction of the central keep. The one in the lead had to be Trisu, she thought. His stride was too imperious, his bearing too confident—indeed, arrogant—for him to be anyone else. He was fair-haired, gray-eyed, and darkly tanned. He was also very young, no more than twenty-four or twenty-five, she judged. And as seemed to be the case with every male Sothōii nobleman Kaeritha had so far met, he stood comfortably over six feet in height. That would have been more than enough to make him impressive, but if his height was typical of the Sothōii, his breadth was not. Most of them tended—like Sir Altharn or Baron Tellian—towards a lean and rangy look, but Trisu Pickaxe's shoulders were almost as broad in proportion to his height as Brandark's. He must, she reflected, have weighed close to three hundred pounds, and none of it was fat.

He was unarmored, but he'd taken time to belt on a jewel-hilted saber in a gold-chased black scabbard, and two of the men behind him—obviously armsmen—wore the standard steel breast-plates and leather armor of Sothōii horse archers.

"So!" Trisu rocked to a halt and tucked his hands inside his sword belt as he glowered up at Kaeritha. She looked back down at him calmly from Cloudy's saddle, her very silence an unspo-ken rebuke of his brusqueness. He seemed remarkably impervi-ous to it, however, for his only response was to bare his teeth in a tight, humorless smile.

"So you claim to be a champion of Tomanāk, do you?" he continued before the silence could stretch out too far.

"I do not '*claim*' anything, Milord," Kaeritha returned in a deliberately courteous but pointed tone. She smiled thinly. "It would take a braver woman than me to attempt to pass herself off falsely as one of His champions. Somehow, I don't think He'd like that very much, do you?"

Something flashed in Trisu's gray eyes—a sparkle of anger, perhaps, although she supposed it was remotely possible it might have been humor. But whatever it had been, it went almost as fast as it had come, and he snorted.

"Bravery might be one word for it," he said. "Foolishness—or perhaps even stupidity—might be others, though, don't you think?"

"They might," she acknowledged. "In the meantime, however, Milord, I have to wonder if keeping a traveler standing in the courtyard is the usual courtesy of Lorham."

"Under normal circumstances, no," he said coolly. "On the other hand, I trust you will concede that women claiming to be knights and champions of the gods aren't exactly normal travelers."

"On the Wind Plain, perhaps," Kaeritha replied with matching coolness, and, for the first time, he flushed. But he wasn't prepared to surrender the point quite yet.

"That's as may be, Milady," he told her, "but at the moment, you're *on* the Wind Plain, and here what you claim to be is not simply unusual, but unheard of. Under the circumstances, I hope you'll not find me unduly discourteous if I request some proof that you are indeed who and what you say you are." He smiled again. "Surely, the Order of Tomanāk would prefer that people be cautious about excepting anyone's unsubstantiated claim to be one of His champions."

"I see." Kaeritha regarded him thoughtfully for a long moment. It would have been handy, she reflected, if Tomanāk had seen fit to give to gift her with a sword like Bahzell's, which came when he called it. It was certainly an impressive way to demonstrate his champion's credentials when necessary. Unfortunately, her own blades, while possessed of certain unusual attributes of their own, stayed obstinately in their sheaths unless she drew them herself, no matter how much she might whistle or snap her fingers for them.

"I've come from Balthar," she said, after a moment, "where Baron Tellian was kind enough to offer me hospitality and to gift me with this lovely lady." She leaned forward to stroke Cloudy's neck, and smiled behind her expressionless face as the first, faint uncertainty flickered in those gray eyes. "He also," she continued blandly, "sent with me written letters of introduction and, I believe, instructions to cooperate with me in my mission." Those eyes were definitely less cheerful than they had been, she noted with satisfaction. "And if you should happen to have anyone here in the keep who is injured or ill, I suppose I could demonstrate my ability to heal them. Or—" she looked straight into Trisu's eyes "—if you insist, I suppose I might simply settle for demonstrating my skill at arms upon your chosen champion, instead. In that case, however, I hope you won't be requiring his services anytime soon."

Trisu's face tightened, its lines momentarily harder and bleaker than its owner's years. The people who had described him as "conservative" had been guilty of considerable understatement, Kaeritha thought. But there appeared to be a brain behind that hard face. However angry he might be, his was not an *unthinking* reactionism, and he made his expression relax.

"If you bear the letters you've described," he said after a moment, with what Kaeritha had to concede was commendable dignity under the circumstances, "that will be more than sufficient proof for me, Milady."

"I thank you for your courtesy, Milord," she said, bending her head in a slight bow. "At the same time—and I fear I owe you an apology, because I did make the offer at least partly out of pique—if there are any sick or injured, it would be my pleasure as well as my duty to offer them healing."

"That was courteously said, Milady," Trisu replied, still more than a bit stiffly but with the first genuine warmth she'd seen from him. "Please, Dame Kaeritha—alight from your horse. My house is yours, and it would seem I have a certain unfortunate first impression to overcome."

Kaeritha's initial impression of Sir Altharn had been misleading. Her first impression of Lord Trisu, unfortunately, and despite his promise to overcome it, had not.

It wasn't that there was anything wrong with Trisu's brain; it was simply that he chose not to use it where certain opinions and preconceptions were concerned. Kaeritha could see only too well why Yalith and the war maids found it so difficult to work with him. However determined one might be to be diplomatic and reasonable, it must be hard to remember one's intention when all one wanted to do was strangle the stiff-necked, obstinate, bigoted, prejudiced, quintessential young Sothōii reactionary on the other side of the conference table.

His obvious native intelligence never challenged his opinions and prejudices because it was enlisted in their support, instead. That might not prevent him from being an excellent administrator, as was obvious from the condition of his lands and the people living on them. But it was a serious handicap when he was forced to deal with people or events he couldn't hammer into submission to his own biases.

On the other hand, perhaps it's time someone jerked him up short, she thought as she settled into her place at his right hand at the high table in Thalar Keep's great hall.

"I fear Thalar's hospitality must appear somewhat modest compared to that of Balthar." Trisu's words were courteous enough, as was their tone, but there was a challenging glint in his eyes. Or perhaps there wasn't. It was always possible, Kaeritha reminded herself, that her own prejudices were unfairly ascribing false attitudes and motives to him.

"Balthar is considerably larger than Thalar, Milord," she replied, after a moment. "But it's been my experience that simple size has less to do with hospitality and the gracious treatment of guests than the graciousness of the host. Certainly no attention to my own comfort has been omitted here in Thalar."

She hid an inner grimace at the stiltedness of her own turn of phrase. Trisu seemed to have that effect on her. But what she'd said had been only the truth, at least in physical terms. The fact that Trisu's retainers and servants took their lead from their lord's own attitudes probably explained why there had been a certain lack of genuine welcome behind their courteous attentiveness, but good manners forbade her from mentioning that.

"I'm pleased to hear it," Trisu said, looking out across the crowded tables below them as serving women began bringing in the food. Then he returned his attention fully to Kaeritha.

"I've read Baron Tellian's letters, Dame Kaeritha," he said. "And I will, of course, comply with his wishes and instructions." His smile was thin, and his gray eyes glittered. "Lorham stands ready to assist you in any way we may."

"I appreciate that," she replied, forbearing to observe that it was marvelous that it appeared to have taken him no more than the better part of seven hours to work his way through all two of the letters Tellian had sent along.

"Yes. But that's for tomorrow. For tonight, allow my cooks to demonstrate their skill for you." A serving maid deposited a stuffed, roasted fowl before him, and he reached for a carving knife. "Would you prefer light meat, or dark, Milady?" he inquired.

Trisu's office was on the third floor of his family's somewhat antiquated keep. Once she saw it, however, Kaeritha's initial surprise that he hadn't moved to more spacious and comfortable quarters elsewhere faded as quickly as it had come. It was part and parcel of the man's entire character. One look at the office itself, with its spartan, whitewashed walls decorated without softening with shields and weapons, made it abundantly clear that no other place else could possibly have been as comfortable to Trisu, however much more spacious it might have been.

The armsman who had ushered her into Trisu's presence, withdrew at his lord's gesture, and the office door closed quietly behind him. Sunlight spilled in through the narrow, diamond-pane windows behind Trisu's desk, and for all its trophy-girt walls, the square, high-ceilinged room did have a certain airy warmth.

"Good morning, Dame Kaeritha. I trust you slept well? That your chambers were comfortable?"

"Yes, thank you, Milord. I did, and they were." She smiled. "And thank you for seeing me so promptly this morning."

"You are, of course, welcome, although no thanks are necessary. Duty to my liege lord—and to the War God, as well—requires no less." He leaned back in his high-backed chair and folded his hands atop one another on the desk before him. "At the same time," he continued, "I fear Baron Tellian's instructions, while clear, were less than complete. In what way may I assist you?"

"The Baron *was* less than specific," Kaeritha conceded. "Unfortunately, when he wrote those letters, before I set out, neither he nor I were certain what I would discover or what sorts of problems I might find myself dealing with."

He raised an eyebrow, and she shrugged.

"Champions of Tomanāk often find themselves in that sort of situation, Milord. We get used to dealing with challenges on the fly, as it were. Baron Tellian knew that would be the case here."

"I see." Trisu pursed his lips as he considered that. Then it was his turn to shrug. "I see," he repeated. "But may I assume that since you've sought me out and presented the Baron's letters, you now know what problem you face?"

"I believe I've discovered the nature of the problem, at least, Milord." Kaeritha hoped her tone sounded more courteous than cautious, but she was aware that his obvious prejudices had awakened a matching antipathy in her and she was watching her tongue carefully. "It involves your ongoing . . . dispute with Kalatha."

"*Which* dispute, Milady?" Trisu inquired with a thin smile. His response was just a bit quicker than Kaeritha had expected, and her eyes narrowed. "Several matters stand in contention between the war maids and me," he continued. The words "war maids" came out sourly, but Kaeritha would have expected that. What she didn't care for was something else in his tone—something which seemed to suggest he anticipated less than complete impartiality out of her.

"If you'll forgive my saying so, Milord," she said after a moment, "all of your disputes with Kalatha—" she carefully refrained from using the apparently incendiary "war maids" herself "—are the same at the heart."

"I beg to differ, Dame Kaeritha," Trisu replied, his jaw jutting. "I am well aware that *Mayor* Yalith chooses to ascribe all of the differences between us to my own deep-seated prejudices. That, however, is not the case."

Kaeritha's expression must have revealed her own skepticism, because he gave a short, barking laugh.

"Don't mistake me, Milady Champion," he said. "I *don't* like war maids. I think their very existence is an affront to the way the gods intended us to live, and the notion that women—*most* women at any rate—" he amended as Kaeritha's eyes flashed, although his tone remained unapologetic "—can be the equal of men as warriors is ridiculous. Obviously, as you yourself demonstrate, there are some exceptions, but as a general rule the idea is ludicrous."

Kaeritha made herself sit firmly on her temper. It wasn't easy. But at least the young man sitting across the desk from her had the courage—or arrogance—to say exactly what he thought. And, she admitted after a moment, the honesty to bring his own feelings openly to the table rather than attempt to deny them or dress them up in fine linen. In fact, and although she found herself hesitant to rush to assign virtues to him, that honesty seemed to be an integral part of his personality.

Which undoubtedly makes him even more difficult to live with, she thought wryly. *But it also makes me wonder how he can be maintaining his position so strongly now when he must know inside that he's in the wrong. Is it that his prejudices against war maids are strong enough to overcome that innate honesty of his?*

"I don't much care for 'general rules,' Milord," she said when she was certain she could keep her own tone level. "I've found that, for most people, 'general rules' are all too often little more than an excuse for ignoring realities they don't care to face."

She held his eye across the desktop, and neither gaze flinched.

"I'm not surprised you should feel that way," he said. "And I imagine that if our positions were reversed, I might feel much as you do. But they aren't reversed, and I don't." The words weren't—quite—as challenging as they might have been, Kaeritha noted. "Because I don't, I chose to say so openly. Not simply because I believe I'm right—although, obviously, I do—but so that there should be no misunderstanding on your part or mine."

"It's always best to avoid misunderstandings," she agreed in a dust-dry voice.

"I've always thought so," he said with a nod. "And having said that, I repeat that my . . . difficulties with Kalatha have very little to do with my opinion of war maids in general. The fact of the matter is that Kalatha is clearly in violation of its own charter and my boundaries and that Mayor Yalith and her town council refuse to admit it."

Kaeritha sat back in her chair, surprised despite herself by his blunt assertion. He'd taken the same position in his correspondence with Tellian's magistrates, but Kaeritha had read the relevant portions of Kalatha's original charter and Lord Kellos' grant in Yalith's office before riding to Thalar. The mayor and Kalatha's archivist,

Lanitha, had pointed out the specific language governing the points in dispute, and Kaeritha had been grateful for the guidance. Her own command of the written Sothōii language was far inferior to Brandark's, and the archaic usages and cramped, faded penmanship of the long-dead scribe who'd written out Gartha and Kellos' original proclamations hadn't helped. But she'd been able to puzzle her way through the phraseology eventually, and it was obvious that Yalith's interpretation was far more accurate than Trisu's assertions.

"With all due respect, Milord," she said now, "I've read King Gartha's original proclamation and the terms of Lord Kellos' grant to the war maids. While I realize many of the subsequent points in dispute between you and Kalatha have arisen out of later customary usages and practices, I think the original language is quite clear. On the matter of water rights, high road tolls, and the location of your father's grist mill on land which belongs to Kalatha, it would appear to me that the war maids are correct."

"No, they aren't," Trisu said flatly. "As any fair reading of the documents in question amply demonstrates."

"Are you suggesting that a Champion of Tomanāk would *not* read evidentiary documents fairly?" Kaeritha was aware that her own voice was both colder and harder than it had been, but she couldn't help it. Not in the face of his bald denial of the documents she'd read with her own eyes.

"I'm suggesting that the documents clearly say the opposite of what Mayor Yalith claims they say," Trisu replied, refusing to back down. Which, Kaeritha, admitted to herself, required a certain moral courage on his part. Whatever his reservations about women warriors might be, he'd had ample proof the day before, when she healed three of his sick and injured retainers, that she most certainly was a champion of Tomanāk. And only a man absolutely certain of his own ground—or a fool—would so flatly challenge a direct, personal servant of the God of Justice.

"Milord," she said after a pause, "while I would normally hesitate to contradict you, in this instance I fear you are incorrect." His mouth tightened and his eyes narrowed, but he said nothing, and she continued. "Once I reached Kalatha and realized where the dispute lay, I took particular care to examine the originals of the relevant documents. Admittedly, my command of your language is less than perfect, but as a champion of Tomanāk, I've been well trained in jurisprudence. It took me quite some time to feel confident I'd read the documents correctly, but I must tell you that, in my opinion, Mayor Yalith is correct . . . and you aren't."

A silence hovered between them. It was very quiet in the sun-filled, whitewashed room, but Kaeritha sensed the fury blazing incandescently within her host. Yet for all his prejudices, he was a disciplined man, and he kept that fiery temper securely leashed. For the most part.

"Milady Champion," he said at length, and despite his control, there was a bite in the way he pronounced "champion" which Kaeritha didn't care for at all, "I make all due allowance for the fact that our language is not your native tongue. As you yourself have just pointed out. However, I, too, have copies of the original charter and grant in my library. They were made at the same time, by the same scribe, as the documents you examined at Kalatha. I am quite prepared, if you so desire, to allow you to examine them, as well. I am also prepared to allow you to discuss—freely, and in private—my interpretation of them with my senior magistrate. Who is also my librarian and, I might point out, served my father before me, and whose interpretation is identical to my own. As I say, any *fair* reading not prejudiced by . . . differences of opinion as to proper ways of life, let us say, must come to the same conclusion."

Kaeritha's jaw clenched, and she was forced to throw a leash on to her own temper at the pointed emphasis of his final sentence. Yet even through her own anger, she felt a fresh sense of puzzlement. As she'd told him, she was at least as thoroughly trained in matters of law as most royal and imperial judges in the King Emperor's service. To be sure, she was more familiar with Axeman law than that of other countries, but the Code of Kormak was the basic foundation of *all* Norfressan law, not just the Empire's. And there was no way in the world that anyone could possibly stretch and strain the language of the documents in question to support Trisu's bald contention. Yet she'd already come to the conclusion that he was an intelligent man, despite his prejudices. He must know the language *wouldn't* support his position . . . so why was he offering—indeed, almost demanding—that she examine them?

She made herself sit very still and draw a deep, tension-cleansing breath. Trisu's anger was resonating with her own, threatening to undermine the impartiality any champion of Tomanāk must maintain when called upon to consider matters of justice. She knew that, and so she knew she must proceed carefully and cautiously. Besides, she reminded herself as she felt the white-hot heat of her own initial anger cool ever so slightly, he had a point. She'd examined Kalatha's documents; she had a moral obligation to examine his, as well, and to listen to his magistrate's construction of the language involved. The chance that she'd misunderstood or misinterpreted the originals was minuscule, but it did exist, and it was her responsibility to be absolutely positive she had not.

"Milord," she said finally, keeping her voice very level, "you've assured me that your own opinions—or prejudices—are not the basis for your disagreements with Kalatha and the war maids. I, in turn, assure *you*, that any 'differences of opinion' I may hold have not been and will not be permitted to influence my reading of the law or of the evidentiary documents. I will examine them again, if you so desire. And I will discuss them with your magistrate. In the end, however, my interpretation of them will be based upon *my* reading of them, not yours. And if I come to the conclusion that they support my original belief that Mayor Yalith's reading of them is correct, then I will so rule as Champion of Tomanāk."

Trisu's gray eyes glittered. There was anger in them, but not nearly so much as she'd expected. Indeed, that hard light seemed born of confidence, not temper. Which only increased her sense of confusion.

If she ruled formally in this case as Tomanāk's champion, her decision was final. That was one reason champions so seldom made formal rulings. Most of them, like Kaeritha herself, preferred simply to investigate and then to recommend rulings to the appropriate local authorities. It prevented bruised feelings, and it allowed for local compromises, which any champion knew were often a truer path to justice than cold, unparsed legalism. Yet Trisu seemed unfazed by the possibility of an adverse decision which would absolutely and permanently foreclose any revisiting of the dispute. Indeed, he seemed to welcome the possibility of a ruling from her, and she wondered if he had deliberately set out to goad her into exactly this course of action.

"The ruling of Scale Balancer's champion must, of course, be final," he said at length. "And, to be honest, Milady Champion, even if you should rule against me, simply having the entire matter laid to rest once and for all will be a relief of sorts. Not that I believe you will."

"We'll see, Milord," Kaeritha said. "We'll see."

"Here it is, Dame Kaeritha."

Salthan Pickaxe was some sort of distant cousin of Trisu, although he was at least twice Trisu's age. That sort of relationship between a lord and his chief magistrate was scarcely unheard of, but Kaeritha had been more than a bit surprised by Salthan. He was much more like Sir Altharn then his liege, with a lively sense of humor hiding behind bright blue-gray eyes and a thick, neatly trimmed beard of white-shot auburn. He was also, she'd been amused to note, much more gallant then his cousin. Indeed, he seemed quite taken by the combination of Kaeritha's dark black hair and sapphire eyes. Which, to be fair, was such an unusual combination among Sothōii that she'd become accustomed to their reaction to her exotic attractiveness.

But Salthan was also at least as intelligent as Trisu, and he seemed just as mystifyingly confident as his cousin.

Now he took a heavy wooden scroll case from its pigeonhole and eased its contents out into his hand. He was obviously well accustomed to dealing with documents which were no longer in their first youth, but it was unhappily apparent that not all of the keepers of Lorham's records had been. Kalatha's documents were, by and large, in much better shape than Lorham's, and it showed in the care Salthan took as he slowly and gently unrolled the scroll.

Age-fragile parchment crackled, and Kaeritha felt a tingle of that unease any archivist feels when her examination of ancient materials threatens them with destruction. But Salthan got it open without inflicting major additional damage. He laid it out on the library table, then adjusted the oil lamp's wick and chimney to provide her with the best possible light.

It was as well he had, Kaeritha thought, leaning forward and squinting at the document before her. It was, as Trisu had said, a duplicate copy of Lord Kellos' original grant to the war maids, and it was even more faded and difficult to read than the original. No doubt because of the indifferent care it had received, she thought. Still, she could make out the large numeral "3" in the margin, which indicated that it was the third copy made, and she recognized the crabbed, archaic penmanship of the same scribe who had written out the original.

She ran her eyes down the section which set forth the boundaries of the grant, looking for the language which defined the specific landmarks around the river and the disputed gristmill. It was the least ambiguous and archaic of the entire document, and she might as well start with the parts that were easiest to follow. Besides, the exact boundaries were at the heart of the issue, so—

Ah! Here they were. She bent closer, reading carefully, then stiffened.

That can't be right, she thought, and reread the section. The words remained stubbornly unchanged, and she frowned in puzzlement. Then she opened the document pouch she'd brought with her and extracted the notes she'd written out so meticulously in Kalatha's library. She opened them and laid the neatly written pages on the table beside the scroll, comparing the passage she'd copied with the document before her on a word-for-word basis. It was absolutely clear and unambiguous.

" . . . and the aforesaid boundary shall run from the east side of Stelham's Rock to the corner of Haymar's holding, where it shall turn south at the boundary stone and run two thousand yards across the River Renha to the boundary stone of Thaman Bridlemaker, which shall be the marker for the boundary of the Lord of Lorham."

That was the exact language from the original grant at Kalatha. But the language in the document Salthan had just laid before her said—

" . . . and the aforesaid boundary shall run from the east side of Stelham's Rock to the corner of Haymar's holding, where it shall turn south at the boundary stone and run one thousand yards to the north side of the River Renha, the agreed-upon boundary of the Lord of Lorham."

It wasn't a minor ambiguity after all, she thought. It was a flat contradiction. If the document before her was accurate, then Trisu was completely correct—the disputed gristmill on the southern bank of the Renha was on his property and always had been. For that matter, Kalatha's claim to undisputed control of the river's water rights was also nonexistent, since the river would lie entirely within Trisu's boundaries. But how *could* it be accurate? Surely the original grant must supersede any copy in the event of differences between them, and the one before her could only represent a bizarre mistake.

Yet that was preposterous. True, it was a copy, not the original, yet it was scarcely likely that the same scribe who had written out both documents would have made such a mistake. And it was even less likely that such an error could have been missed in the intense scrutiny all copies of the original grant must have received by those party to it.

Unless one copy was a deliberate forgery, of course . . .

But how could *that* be the case? If this was a counterfeit, it was a remarkably good one. Indeed, it was so good she couldn't believe anyone in the Lorham could have produced it in the first place. However good Salthan might be as a librarian, turning out such a flawless false copy of a document over two centuries old must be well beyond his capabilities. So if a forgery had been produced, who had produced it, and when?

She carefully hid a grimace at the thought, wondering how in the world anyone would ever be able to answer those questions. But answering them could wait at least until she'd determined that they were the only ones which required answers.

She considered her options for a few more seconds, then looked up at Salthan with a painstakingly neutral expression.

"Thank you," she said, tapping the scroll very carefully with a fingertip. "This is exactly the section of Lord Kellos' grant I wanted to see. Now, if you please, Lord Trisu also mentioned that you have a copy of King Gartha's proclamation, as well."

"Yes, we do, Lady," Salthan replied. "In fact, it's in rather more readable condition than Kellos' grant. Let me get it for you."

"If you would," she requested, and leafed through her other notes for the sections of the war maid charter relevant to the other points in dispute between Trisu and his neighbors that she'd copied in Kalatha.

Salthan opened the proper case and unrolled a second scroll, just as carefully as he'd unrolled the first one. He was right; this document was much more legible than the Kalatha land grant, and Kaeritha bent over it, eyes searching for the sections she needed.

She read through them one by one, comparing the language before her to that she had copied in Kalatha, and despite all of her formidable self-control, her frown grew more and more intense as she worked her way through them. Then she sat back and rubbed the tip of her nose, wondering if she looked as perplexed as she thought she did.

Well, she thought, *it just may be that I'm beginning to understand yet another reason He sent me to deal with this instead of Bahzell or Vaijon. He does have a way of choosing His tools to fit the problem . . . even when we poor tools don't have a clue why it has to be us. Or exactly where we're supposed to go next.*

"I appreciate your assistance, Sir Salthan," she said after a moment. "And I think I may be beginning to understand why your and your lord's interpretation of the documents is so fundamentally different from that of Mayor Yalith. There does seem to be a degree of . . . discrepancy now that I've had a chance to lay my notes side by side with your copy. I don't pretend to understand where it came from, but it's obvious that until it's resolved, it will be impossible for anyone to rule definitively in this case."

"I couldn't agree more, Milady," Salthan said soberly. Trisu's magistrate was sitting across the table from her now, his blue-gray eyes intent . . . and troubled. "Unlike you, I haven't had the opportunity to compare the documents to one another, but I *know* these copies have been here in this library from the day they were first penned. Under the circumstances, I think My Lord and I have no alternative but to believe they're accurate, and, unlike his late father, Lord Trisu is not the sort of man to tolerate the infringement of his rights or prerogatives. Which is why, after he'd asked me to research the language and had seen the relevant passages for himself, he began to press Kalatha over these matters."

"No doubt you're right," Kaeritha said. "On the other hand, Sir Salthan, I can't quite escape the suspicion that he's a little more irritated over the apparent violation of his rights or prerogatives when the suspected violators are war maids."

"Probably—no, certainly—you're right, Dame Kaeritha. And he's not alone in that regard, either. But does that truly have any bearing on whether or not our interpretation is correct in the eyes of the law?"

"No," she said, although she was guiltily aware that part of her wished it did. On the other hand, champions of Tomanāk were still mere mortals. They had their prejudices and opinions, just like anyone else. But they also had a unique responsibility to recognize that they did and to set those prejudices aside rather than allow them to influence their decisions or actions.

"Are you familiar, Sir Salthan," she continued after a moment, "with the sorts of abilities Tomanāk bestows upon His champions when he accepts Sword Oath from them?"

"I beg your pardon?" Salthan blinked, clearly surprised by the apparent *non sequitur*. Then he shrugged.

"I'm scarcely 'familiar' with them, Milady. I doubt that very many people are, really. I've done some reading, of course. And to be honest, I did a little more research when Lord Trisu told me a champion had come to visit us. Our library, unfortunately, isn't especially well stocked with the research books I needed. The best anything I had could do was to tell me that Tomanāk is less . . . consistent from champion to champion than many of the Gods of Light are."

" 'Less consistent,' " Kaeritha murmured, and smiled. "That may be as concisely as I've ever heard it put, Sir Salthan. There are times when I wish He was more like, oh, Toragan or Torframos. Or

Lillinara, for that matter. *Their* champions all seem to get approximately the same abilities, in greater or lesser measure. But Tomanāk prefers to gift each of His champions with individual abilities. For the most part, they seem to mesh with abilities or talents we already had before we heard His call, but sometimes no one has any idea why a particular champion received a specific ability. Until, of course, the day comes when he—or she—*needs* that ability."

"And is this such an occasion, Milady?" Salthan asked, his eyes more intent than ever.

"Yes and no." Kaeritha shrugged. "I've had the need for almost all of the abilities He's granted me at one time or another already. But I have to admit that I should have begun to suspect there was a specific reason He'd sent me to deal with this problem. Especially when Lord Trisu reminded me that the controlling language itself is in dispute."

"I wish I'd had the opportunity to examine the Kalathan originals," Salthan said a bit wistfully. "It's been obvious from the beginning that there was a fundamental contradiction between what I was reading here and the language Mayor Yalith and her magistrates were citing. But without the chance to see the originals for myself, there was no way for me to judge how accurate—or, for that matter, honest—their citations were."

"Well, I have had the opportunity to examine them," Kaeritha told him. As she spoke, she stood and crossed to a another table, under the library window, where she had placed her sheathed swords when she and Salthan entered. No champion of Tomanāk ever left the sword—or swords—which was the emblem of her authority behind when engaged upon official duties. Now she unbuttoned the retaining strap on the sword she normally wore at her left hip and drew the glittering, two-foot blade.

Salthan raised an eyebrow in surprise as she drew steel, and then she smiled, despite the gravity of the moment, as his other eyebrow rose to match it when her sword suddenly began to glow with a blue nimbus bright enough to be clearly visible even in the well-lit library.

"As I say," she continued in a deliberately blasé tone, "I have had the opportunity to examine them. Unfortunately, it didn't occur to me then just how *thoroughly* I should have 'examined' them."

She sat back down, facing him over the original table once more, and laid the sword flat before her, its glittering blade across both the scrolls Salthan had located for her.

"And now, Sir Salthan," she said in a far more formal voice, "I have a request to make of you as Champion of the Keeper of the Scales."

"Of course, Milady," the Sothōii said quickly, and Kaeritha noted his tone and manner carefully. She was gratified by his prompt acquiescence, but she was even more gratified when she was unable to detect any sign of hesitation or indecision. Clearly he felt no more hesitation about accepting her authority than he would have felt accepting the authority of any male champion.

"This is primarily for the record," she told him, "because you are the primary custodian of these documents." She turned her sword slightly, angling the hilt in his direction. "Please place your hand on the hilt of my sword."

He obeyed, although she felt dryly amused by the fact that this time he did hesitate ever so slightly. Not that she blamed him. This was undoubtedly the first time anyone had ever invited him to lay hold of a sword wrapped in the corona of a god's power.

She waited until his initial gingerly touch settled into something a bit more confident when no lightning bolt sizzled down from the rafters to incinerate him where he sat. Then she nodded.

"Thank you," she said, as encouragingly as she could without stepping out of her own magisterial role. "And now, Sir Salthan, will you attest for me, in the presence of the God of Justice, that to the best of your personal knowledge, these are the original copies of the proclamation of King Gartha and the Kalathan land grant of Lord Kellos which were originally placed in the custody of the Lords of Lorham?"

"To the best of my personal knowledge, they are, Milady," Salthan said in a calm, formal voice, his eyes never wavering under her intent regard. The blue light clinging to her sword never wavered, either, she noted. In fact, it grew stronger.

"And also to the best of your personal knowledge, they are authentic and unchanged. There have been no additions, no deletions, and no alterations?"

"None, Milady," Salthan said firmly.

"Thank you," she repeated, and nodded for him to remove his hand. He did so, and if he sat back in his chair with a bit more alacrity than he had leaned forward, Kaeritha didn't blame him a bit.

She looked down at the documents before her, then lifted her sword across her open palms, holding it between her and the scrolls.

All right, she thought, closing her eyes while she reached out to that ever-present link connecting her to the blazing power of Tomanāk's presence. *It took me a while to get the hint. I'm sorry about that, although I suppose I could point out that having Leeana along was enough to distract anyone. But now that I'm here and You've more or less used Salthan to rub my nose in it, suppose You tell me whether or not these documents are forgeries.*

She sensed a distant, delighted rumble of divine laughter . . . and approval. Then she opened her eyes again and looked down at her sword.

Which, she was no longer the least bit surprised to see, continued to glow a bright, steady blue.

Kaeritha Seldansdaughter sat in the chamber Lord Trisu had assigned to her in Thalar Keep and gazed out the window at a cloudless sky of midnight blue spangled with the glitter and glow of Silendros' stars. It was a clearer sky then she'd seen any night since arriving on the Wind Plain, and she had never seen the stars brighter or larger than they looked tonight. A crescent nail-paring moon glowed purest silver in the eastern sky, and she studied it with an intent frown, wondering what Lillinara thought She was doing to let this situation get so out of hand.

Well, she told herself scoldingly, *that's probably not entirely fair. It's not as if She were the only god with an interest in this affair. But what in the world is She thinking about? And why hasn't She spoken to Her Voice at Quaysar about it?*

That was the heart of the entire question. Of course, it would have helped if it had occurred to Kaeritha to test the authenticity—or, at least, the accuracy—of the documents at Kalatha. She should have, if only in the name of thoroughness, although to be fair to herself, she'd had absolutely no reason to doubt them. And even now she was certain that Yalith and her council saw no reason to question them. And why should they? They knew they had the original, controlling documents in their possession.

Unfortunately, Tomanāk Himself had seen fit to assure Kaeritha that the copies in Trisu's possession were most definitely not forgeries. One of those special abilities she'd mentioned to Salthan was that no one could lie successfully to her while touching her sword, and that no false or misleading document or planted evidence could evade her detection when she held the blade and called upon Tomanāk. Which meant Trisu's documents were not simply genuine, but that they accurately set forth the original language and *true intent* of both Gartha and Kellos. Kaeritha had seen enough in other investigations she'd conducted to be unwilling to rule very many things categorically out of consideration, but she was not prepared to question His personal assurances.

Which meant that somehow, impossible as it manifestly must be, the *original* documents at Kalatha were the forgeries.

So far, Kaeritha had not shared that conclusion with Trisu. And she had invoked her champion's authority to extract Sword Oath from Salthan to keep the results of this afternoon's examination and investigation to himself. Which meant that effectively no one but she realized where the unpalatable chain of evidence was leading her. Nor did she intend to share that with anyone else until she saw a clearer path through the maze before her.

She let her mind wander back an hour or two to this evening's after-dinner conversation with Trisu.

"And has your investigation thrown any fresh light on my differences with Mayor Yalith?" Trisu asked as he toyed with his glass. Like many Sothōii nobles, he was particularly fond of the expensive liqueurs distilled in Dwarvenhame and the Empire of the Axe. Kaeritha liked them just fine herself, but she also entertained a lively respect for their potency. Which was why she had contented herself with wine rather than the brandy Trisu had offered her.

"Some, Milord," she said.

He leaned back, cocking an eyebrow, and regarded her thoughtfully.

"May I take it that whatever you and Salthan discovered—or discussed, at least—this afternoon has at least not inspired you to immediately rule against me?"

"It was never my intent to 'immediately rule' for or against anyone, Milord," she said mildly. "I would prefer, at this point, not to be a great deal more specific than that, although honesty and simple justice do compel me to admit that, so far at least, the situation is considerably less cut and dried than I had assumed initially."

"Well," he said with a slight smile, "I suppose I must consider that an improvement, given your original comments to me." Kaeritha's temper stirred, but she suppressed it firmly, and he continued. "And I must admit," he went on, "that I'm gratified to see exactly the sort of impartiality and willingness to consider all the evidence which I would have expected out of a Champion of Tomanāk. The more so because I have something of a reputation for stubbornness myself. I know how difficult it is for anyone, however honest or however good his—or her—intentions, to truly consider fresh evidence which appears to contradict evidence he's already accepted as valid."

For a moment, Kaeritha wondered if somehow Salthan's oath had slipped. But even as the thought crossed her mind, she dismissed it out of hand. She didn't believe the magistrate would have knowingly or intentionally violated it under any circumstances. More than that, even if he'd been inclined to do so, he couldn't have been able to break an oath sworn on a champion's sword, which, in the moment of swearing, actually *was* the very Sword of Tomanāk. It was simply a fresh warning to her never to underestimate Trisu's intelligence simply because she detested his opinions and attitudes.

"It's not always easy, no," she agreed. "But it *is* a trick any of Tomanāk's champions has to master. I imagine the lord of any domain has to be able to do much the same thing if he's going to administer justice fairly. "

She smiled affably, hiding her amusement—mostly—as his eyes flashed when her shot went home.

"On the other hand, Milord," she continued more briskly, "I feel I'm definitely making progress where the documents and their interpretations are concerned. At the moment, I have at least as many questions as I have answers, but at least I believe I've figured out what the questions themselves are. And I feel confident Tomanāk will lead me to their answers in the end.

"But there is one other matter which doesn't relate to the documents or, actually, officially to Kalatha itself in any way."

"Indeed?" he said coolly when she paused.

"Yes, Milord. When I spoke with Mayor Yalith, it was clear to me that more was involved than the simple legalities of your disagreement explained. There was, quite frankly, a great deal of anger on the war maids' part. And, to be equally frank, it became quite apparent in speaking with you that the same is true from your perspective."

Trisu's gray eyes were hard, and she raised one hand in a slight throwing away gesture.

"Milord, that's almost always the case when a dispute reaches the point this one has. It's not necessarily because either side is inherently evil, either. It's because the people on both sides are just that—people. And people, Milord, get angry with other people they feel are wrong or, even worse, out to cheat them in some way.

It's a fact of life which any judge—or champion of Tomanāk—simply has to take into consideration. Just as you have to take it into consideration, I'm sure, when you're forced to adjudicate between the conflicting claims of two of your tenants."

It would have been too much to say that Trisu's anger dissipated, but at least he nodded grudgingly in an admission that she'd made her point.

"Quite often," she continued, "there are additional causes for anger and resentment. When people are already unhappy with one another, they're seldom as interested as they might otherwise be in extending the benefit of the doubt to the people they're unhappy with."

"I understand that you're attempting to prepare me for some point you intend to raise and think I'll find objectionable, Lady Champion," Trisu said with a thin smile which actually held a trace of genuine amusement. "Shall we simply agree that you've done that now and get on with it?"

"Well, yes, I suppose we could." Kaeritha gave him an answering smile and nodded her head in acknowledgment.

"Where I was going, Milord, is that the mayor's share of the ... intransigence in this dispute seems to be fueled in no small part by her belief that you've shown insufficient respect for the Voice of Lillinara at Quaysar."

"What you truly mean, Milady," Trisu responded in a flat, hard voice, "is that she believes I have shown *no* respect for the Voice. And, while we're on the subject, that she bitterly resents my failure to solve the disappearance—or murder—of the Voice's handmaidens."

Once again, Kaeritha was surprised by his blunt, head-on attitude. Not that she should have been, perhaps, she reflected. Trisu was in many ways the quintessential Sothōii. He might be capable of tactical subtlety on the battlefield, but he disdained anything that smacked of the indirect approach in his own life.

She felt a fresh flicker of anger at the confrontational light in his eyes, but she reminded herself once more never to underestimate this intolerable young man's native intelligence. Nor was she about to forget that the evidence she herself had turned up that afternoon strongly suggested that there was more than a little merit to his interpretation of the actual legal disputes.

"I suppose that is what I mean," she conceded after a moment, "although that's considerably more ... pointed than the manner in which I would have chosen to express it."

He looked at her long and steadily, then dipped his head in a small bob of acknowledgment. He even had to the grace to blush ever so slightly, she thought. But one thing he didn't do was retreat from the point he'd just made.

"No doubt it was more confrontational than one as courteous as you've already proven yourself to be would have phrased it to her host, Milady. For that, I apologize. But that was essentially what she said, was it not?"

"Essentially," she acknowledged.

"I thought it would be," he said and gazed at her speculatively for a few more seconds. "Given your willingness to consider and examine the evidence Salthan and I offered you, I would assume you've raised this point in order to hear my side of it directly."

His tone made the statement a question, and she nodded.

"Dame Kaeritha," he began after a moment, "I won't attempt to pretend that I'm not more uncomfortable dealing with Lillinara and Her followers than I am with other gods and their worshipers. I don't understand Lillinara. And I don't much care for many of the things Her followers justify on the basis of things She's supposed to have told them. To be perfectly honest, there are times I wonder just how much of what She's supposed to have said was actually invented by people who would have found it convenient for Her to tell them what they wanted to hear in the first place."

Kaeritha arched her eyebrows.

"That's a . . . surprisingly frank admission, Milord," she observed.

"No sane man doubts the existence of the gods, Milady," he replied. "But no *intelligent* man doubts that charlatans and tricksters are fully capable of using the gods and the religious faith of others for their own manipulative ends. Surely you wouldn't expect someone charged with the governance of any domain to close his eyes to that possibility?"

"No, Milord, I wouldn't," she said, and felt a brief flicker of something very like affection for this hard-edged, opinionated youngster. "In fact, that sort of manipulation is one of the things champions spend a lot of their time undoing and repairing."

"I thought it probably would be." Trisu sipped brandy, then set down his glass, and his nostrils flared.

"I brought up my . . . discomfort with Lillinara intentionally, Milady. I wanted you to be aware that *I* was aware of it. And because I am aware of it, I reminded myself when I met Lillinara's newest Voice that the fact that I don't like what someone tells me She wants me to do doesn't *necessarily* make that someone a liar.

But in this instance, I've come to the conclusion that the so-called 'Voice' at Quaysar is one of those manipulators."

"That's an extremely serious charge, Lord Trisu." Kaeritha's voice was low, her expression grim, yet she wasn't remotely as surprised to hear it as she should have been.

"I'm aware of that," he replied with unwonted somberness. "It's also one which I haven't previously made to anyone in so many words. I would suspect, however, that Mayor Yalith, who—despite our many and lively differences—is an intelligent woman, knows that it's what I think."

"And why do you think it, Milord?"

"First and foremost, I'm sure, is the fact that I don't much care for this particular Voice. In fact, the day I first met her, when she arrived to take up her post at Quaysar, she and I took one another in immediate and intense dislike."

"Took *one another* in immediate dislike?" Kaeritha repeated, and Trisu chuckled sourly.

"Milady, I couldn't possibly dislike her as much as I do without her disliking me right back! I don't care how saintly a Voice of Lillinara is supposed to be."

Despite herself, Kaeritha laughed, and he shrugged and continued.

"It's not unusual, I imagine, for the lord of any domain to have differences of opinion with the priests and priestesses whose spheres of authority and responsibility overlap with his. Each of us would like to be master in his own house, and when we have conflicting views or objectives, that natural resentment can only grow stronger.

"But in this case, it went further than that."

He paused, and Kaeritha watched his face. It was as hard, as uncompromising, as ever, yet there was something else behind his expression now. She didn't know quite what the emotion was, but she knew it was there.

"How so, Milord?" she asked after the silence had stretched out for several breaths.

"I don't—" he began, then stopped. "No, Dame Kaeritha," he said, "that's not true. I started to say that I don't really know how to answer your question, but I do. I suppose I hesitated because I was afraid honesty might alienate you."

"Honesty may anger me, Milord," she said with the seriousness his tone and manner deserved. "It shouldn't, but I'm only the champion of a god, not a god myself. But this much I will promise you, on my sword and His. So long as you give me honesty, I will give you an open ear and an open mind." She smiled without humor. "As you've been honest with me, I'll be honest with you. You hold certain beliefs and opinions with which I am as uncomfortable as I'm sure you are with the war maids. No doubt you'd already realized that. But whether or not I agree with you in those matters has nothing to do with whether or not I trust your honesty."

"That was well said, Milady," Trisu said with the first completely ungrudging warmth he'd displayed. Then he drew a deep breath.

"As I'm sure Mayor Yalith told you, the original town of Quaysar has effectively been absorbed by the temple there. In the process, the office of the Voice of the temple has merged with the office of the mayor of Quaysar, as well. By tradition, the same person has held both of them for the past seventy-odd years. Which means that the Voice isn't simply the priestess of the temple, but also the secular head of the community. In that role, she is one of my vassals, which has occasionally created uncomfortable strains between the various Voices of the temple and my own father and grandfather. Inevitably, I suppose, given the unavoidable difficulties the Voices must have faced in juggling their secular obligations to the Lord of Lorham with their spiritual obligations to his subjects. And, of course, to the war maids over whom my house has no actual jurisdiction.

"My father had seen to it that I would be aware that such difficulties were only to be expected from time to time. I think he was afraid that without such an awareness I would be unwilling to consider the sorts of compromises which situations like that might require. Even as a child, I'm afraid, I wasn't exactly noted for *cheerful* compromises." He snorted a sudden laugh of his own and shook his head when Kaeritha looked a question at him. "Your pardon, Milady. I was just thinking about how fervently my tutors and arms instructors would have endorsed that last statement of mine."

Kaeritha nodded. At least he was able to laugh at himself sometimes, she thought.

"At any rate," he continued, "I was prepared for the possibility that the new Voice and I might not exactly take to one another on sight. What I wasn't prepared for was the . . . well, the wave of *wrongness* that poured off of her."

" 'Wrongness'?" Kaeritha repeated very carefully.

"I don't know a better word for it," Trisu said. "It was as if every word she said rang false. *Every* word, Milady. I've met other people

I simply didn't like, and I'm sure other people have had that reaction to me. But this was like a dog and a cat closed into the same cage—or perhaps a snake and a ferret. It was there between us from the instant she opened her mouth, and although it shames me to admit it, something about her frightened me."

He looked squarely at Kaeritha, and his gray eyes were dark.

"If you want the full truth of it, Milady," he said very quietly, "I wasn't at all sure which of us was the ferret . . . and which the serpent."

Kaeritha stared up at the glowing heavens, remembering Trisu's expression and the sound of his voice, and a chill ran down her spine like the tip of an icicle. Trisu of Lorham might be a pain in the arse. He might be opinionated, and he was certainly stubborn. But one thing she did not believe he was was a coward. For that matter, no true coward would have been prepared to admit to a champion of Tomanāk that he'd been frightened by anyone. Especially not if he was also a thorough conservative of Trisu's stripe admitting he'd been frightened by a woman.

But Yalith had shown no sign of any similar feelings towards the Voice of Quaysar. It was tempting, dreadfully so, for Kaeritha to put the difference down to all of the other differences between Kalatha and the Lord of Lorham. Yet tempting or not, she knew that simple answer was insufficient.

Which was why she knew she had to travel to Quaysar herself. And why she felt an icy edge of fear of her own at the thought.

"Welcome back to Kalatha, Dame Kaeritha." Mayor Yalith's voice was much warmer than it had been the first time Kaeritha entered her office, and her smile was broad. "How may we serve you this time?"

"Actually, I'm more or less just passing through on my way to Quaysar," Kaeritha replied, watching the mayor's expression with carefully hidden attentiveness. "I've spoken to you, and to Lord Trisu. Now I think it would be just as well for me to speak to the Voice and get her perspective on the disputes between your town and Trisu, not to mention her temple's own . . . difficulties with him." It seemed to her watchful eyes that Yalith's quick nod of approval was automatic, almost unconscious. "I hadn't realized from our previous discussion that she was also the secular head of the Quaysar community. The fact that she is means she's probably had much more direct contact with him than I'd previously assumed."

"I'm sure she has," Yalith said a bit sourly. "I doubt that she's enjoyed it any more than I have, though." The mayor shook her head. "I realize that the Voice is Lillinara's personal servant, but it would take a saint, not merely a priestess, to endure that man as her liege."

"He can certainly be one of the most irritating people I've ever met," Kaeritha acknowledged even as she mentally filed away Yalith's tone and body language. Clearly, the mayor, at least, had no reservations about the Voice. Kaeritha wished the same were true for her.

"If he's irritating to a visiting champion of Tomanāk, you can probably begin to imagine how 'irritating' he can be as a permanent, inescapable neighbor!" The mayor shook her head again, with a grimace.

"I doubt that proximity makes him any *easier* to deal with, anyway," Kaeritha agreed. The mayor snorted a laugh and waved for Kaeritha to take one of the chairs facing her desk.

The knight seated herself in the indicated chair and leaned back, crossing her legs.

"Before I move on to Quaysar," she said in a tone which was as everyday sounding as she could keep it, "I wonder if you could tell me a little more about the Voice." Yalith's eyebrows rose, and Kaeritha shrugged. "I understand that she's almost as new to her office as Trisu is to his lordship," she explained, "and I'd like to have a little bit better feel for her position and personality before I walk into her temple and start asking questions which some priestesses might consider impertinent or even insulting. Especially coming from a champion of someone else's god."

"I see." Yalith rested her elbows on the arms of her chair, steepling her fingers under her chin. She pursed her lips for several seconds, clearly marshaling her thoughts, but Kaeritha saw no evidence of any uneasiness or misgivings.

"The present Voice is younger than the last one," the mayor said finally. "To be honest, when I first met her, I thought she might be *too* young for the post, but I was wrong. Actually, I think she may seem to be younger than she truly is."

"You do? Why?" Kaeritha asked.

"She's an extraordinarily attractive woman, Dame Kaeritha, but she has one of those faces that will look young until she's at least eighty." The mayor smiled. "When I was younger myself, I would have cheerfully traded two or three fingers from my left hand for her bone structure and coloring. Now I just envy them."

"Oh." Kaeritha smiled back. "One of *those.*"

"Definitely one of those," Yalith agreed. Then she shook her head. "But she doesn't really seem aware of it herself," the mayor continued more seriously. "I sometimes wonder if her appearance was an obstacle for her in her pursuit of her calling, but her vocation is obvious once you've spent even a very few minutes with her. There's a . . . a presence to her that I've never experienced with any other Voice. Once you've met her, I think you'll understand why the Church assigned her to Quaysar."

"I'm sure I will," Kaeritha replied. "At the same time, Mayor, a spiritual vocation doesn't always translate into effectiveness when it comes to managing the more mundane affairs of a temple. I'd imagine that would be even more the case for a priestess who's also a mayor. How would you evaluate her in that regard?"

"I've only been to Quaysar myself once since she became Voice there," Yalith said. "She's visited us here four times since then, but most of the contact between us has been through her handmaidens. So my impressions of her abilities as an administrator are all secondhand, as it were."

She arched an eyebrow, and Kaeritha nodded her understanding of the qualifier.

"Well, having said that," the mayor continued, "I would have to say she seems to be at least as efficient and effective as her predecessor was, which is pretty high praise all by itself. I certainly haven't heard about any internal problems, at any rate. And given my own experiences, I can't say that the difficulties she's apparently had with Trisu of Lorham give me any cause to question her ability to work comfortably with an unprejudiced secular superior."

"I see." Kaeritha considered that for a moment, then cocked her head to one side. "Given what you've said about how relatively little direct contact you've had with her, I suppose that's probably as definitive an opinion as anyone could expect you to have formed. Did you know the previous Voice better than that?"

"Oh, yes!" Yalith smiled. It was a broad smile, warm, yet touched with sadness. "The old Voice came from Kalatha herself, actually. I knew her long before she heard Lillinara's calling. In fact, we grew up together."

"You did? Somehow, I had the impression she was older than that."

"*Old?* Shandra?" Yalith snorted, then grimaced. "I suppose I shouldn't call her that. I know any Voice gives up her old name and takes a new one in religion. But she was actually a year or two younger than I was, and I'll always think of her as the blond-haired kid who insisted on tagging along when I went fishing in the river."

"So she was actually *younger* than you," Kaeritha mused. "And from your manner and tone, she sounds as if she were an extraordinary person."

"Indeed she was," Yalith said softly.

"How did she come to die?" Kaeritha asked. "Because I thought she was older than she was, I'd simply assumed it was old age, or perhaps some illness she was unable to fight off because of her age. But if she was as young as you are . . ."

"No one is really sure," Yalith sighed. "Oh, it *was* an illness, but it came on extraordinarily suddenly, and I think it took her and her physicians by surprise because she'd always been so healthy. The constitution of a courser, she always used to joke with me when we were girls." She shook her head sadly. "But that wasn't enough this time. She became ill one day, and she was gone less than three days later. I didn't even realize she was seriously ill in time to get to Quaysar to tell her goodbye."

"I'm sorry for your loss," Kaeritha said softly. *Even sorrier than you can guess, given what I'm beginning to suspect*, she added silently to herself. "But you'd say you're pleased with the job the new Voice is doing as her successor?"

"As pleased as anyone could be after losing someone like Shandra," Yalith agreed firmly. "We were extremely lucky to have two such strong Voices in succession. In fact, I think possibly our present Voice may even be better suited to the . . . less pleasant aspects of our disputes with Trisu than Shandra would have been. Her faith is obviously just as deep, but Shandra always shied away from confrontation. She wasn't *weak*, or anything like that, but she preferred finding a consensus or arriving at compromises. Which is fine, as long as the person on the other side of the dispute is equally willing to be reasonable. Our present Voice is a bit more willing to remember that she speaks as the *Mother's* Voice when it comes to rebuking Her children's misbehavior."

"So she's been supportive of Kalatha's position against Trisu, not simply concerned by his failure to adequately investigate the deaths of her handmaidens?"

"Oh, yes." Yalith nodded emphatically. "She hasn't made any secret of her feelings in that regard, and she's a strong supporter of our decision to stand fast, at least until we get some sort of reasonable offsetting concessions from Trisu in any compromise settlement. Although she did insist on reviewing the original documents herself before she took any official position."

"She did examine them? Here?"

"No, not here. She was unable to leave Quaysar at the moment, so she sent two of her handmaidens to fetch them back to the temple."

"Just two handmaidens to transport them?" Kaeritha sounded surprised, and Yalith chuckled in harsh understanding.

"We're just as aware as you are of how . . . convenient some people might find it for those documents to disappear, Dame Kaeritha. I sent along an escort of ten war maids, and Lanitha went along to care for the records themselves." She shrugged. "But there weren't any problems. That time, at least."

"I see." Kaeritha frowned thoughtfully. "I'm glad you did send an escort, though," she said. "Just from a purely historical perspective, those documents are priceless. I imagine the war maids have always seen to it that they were properly looked after whenever they left Kalatha."

"That was the only time they ever did leave Kalatha," Yalith replied. "But I'm sure any of my predecessors would have been just as careful about protecting them."

"Oh, I'm sure they would," Kaeritha agreed. "I'm sure they would."

"Hello, Dame Kaeritha."

Leeana Bowmaster had changed a great deal during Kaeritha's absence. Or, no, Kaeritha decided. That conclusion might still be a bit premature. Her *appearance* had certainly changed a great deal; it remained to be seen how much the young woman under that appearance had changed.

"Hello, Leeana," the knight replied. "You're looking good."

"Different, you mean," Leeana corrected with a smile, almost as if she'd read Kaeritha's mind.

"Well, yes. But in your case, I think, 'different' and 'good' may mean the same thing. And, no, I'm not talking just about outward appearances, young lady. The last time I saw you, you weren't exactly the happiest young woman I'd ever seen."

"Oh." Leeana looked down at her bare toes and actually wiggled. "I guess maybe you have a point," she admitted after a moment.

The two of them stood on one of the main training salle's covered porches. The porch's plank flooring was rough and unfinished under Kaeritha's boots, and must have felt even more so to Leeana's bare feet. But the girl didn't seem to notice that. Nor did she appear aware of how the fine garments, rich embroidery, and semi-precious stones of a great baron's daughter had vanished forever.

Kaeritha was. She'd anticipated changes, and she hadn't expected to find Leeana lounging about in the sorts of gowns her mother would have approved. But the leather breeches and smocks Leeana had favored as casual, get-your-hands-dirty clothing back home at Hill Guard Castle when her mother wasn't looking had also disappeared. Instead, she wore the garments the war maids called the chari and yathu, which together, Kaeritha had discovered, were the standard costume of the actual *war* maids.

Kaeritha wondered what Leeana's parents would have had to say if they'd seen her at the moment. The chari was bad enough—a short, green kilt which fell barely halfway to her knees and would have been unutterably shocking to any properly reared Sothōii noblewoman. But the tightly laced yathu above it would have reduced that same properly reared Sothōii noblewoman to near hysteria.

"There *do* seem to have been some changes in your appearance, though," she acknowledged with a smile. She cocked her head. "Are you comfortable with them?"

" 'Comfortable' is such a . . . flexible word," Leeana said with a grimace. She reached up and slid an index finger under the shoulder strap of her yathu. "I've seen heavy draft harnesses that were probably more 'comfortable' for the horses wearing them! Besides," she grimaced again and withdrew her finger to indicate her bosom with a wave of her hand, "it's not as if *I* really need it."

"*Ha!* You may think that now, girl, but I think your opinion will change in a year or two." She eyed the girl consideringly for a moment, then chuckled. "As a matter of fact, and bearing your height in mind, I expect you'll end up appreciating it even more than I would. And it probably won't take any 'year or two,' either, now that I think about it!"

"Really?" Leeana looked at her quickly, then blushed and looked back down at her toes. But she also grinned, and Kaeritha shook her head.

"I'd say the odds are in favor of it," she said judiciously. "I was never particularly . . . well endowed myself. I doubt I ever would have been, even if Mistress Sherath hadn't started working my backside off in the Morfintan mage academy's exercise salle when I was a year younger than you are now. But you're already taller than I am, and you're not done growing. I'd say you've still got a bit of filling out to do, and it looks to me like you're probably going to be built a lot like your mother. So wait a few years before you start complaining about the yathu."

"If you say so, Dame Kaeritha," Leeana murmured obediently, and Kaeritha suppressed another chuckle.

She didn't doubt that, at the moment, Leeana did find the yathu confining. For her own part, however, and speaking from personal experience, Kaeritha thoroughly appreciated and approved of that firm support for any reasonably endowed female human being expected to engage in brisk physical exercise. At the same time, she rather suspected that the war maids had chosen that particular form of support at least partly for its shock effect. A way to thumb their collective nose at the standards of feminine "propriety" which they had rejected.

Under different circumstances, the yathu might almost have been described as a short, abbreviated—*very* abbreviated—bodice, but it wasn't boned and happened to be made out of fabric-lined, glove-supple leather. Whereas the main support of a regular bodice came from below, with little or no weight actually bearing on the shoulders, the yathu was equipped with shoulder straps which crossed on the wearer's shoulder blades. It was shorter, snugger, and stronger than any conventional "bodice" Kaeritha had ever seen, and it was short enough to allow its wearer to do things like crawling lithely and unobtrusively through the bushes without encumbrance. Which also made it ideal as standard wear when it was time for calisthenics or any other form of strenuous physical exercise.

Whether the war maids' intentions had been solely to provide proper support or to combine that with a poke in respectable Sothōii society's eye, however, Kaeritha rather doubted that Baron Tellian—or Baroness Hanatha—would have approved of the yathu's undeniable brevity and snug fit . . . or of the way that their daughter's shapely form (and navel) were exposed for all the world to see.

"Don't go fishing for compliments, young lady," she said now, her tone severe, and Leeana produced a sound suspiciously like a giggle.

That giggle, and the girl's entire body language, did a great deal to reassure Kaeritha. Leeana had been called away from her morning calisthenics to speak with Kaeritha, and the war maids' physical training regimen was as demanding as any Kaeritha herself had ever experienced. It was certainly more rigorous than anything *Leeana* had ever experienced before leaving Balthar. Not that the girl had ever been indolent or lazy. But the war maids believed in pushing their new recruits—especially the probationary ones— hard. Partly, Kaeritha supposed, that was part of the training intended to make the difference between their old lives and their new ones clear on an emotional as well as an intellectual level. But it was also a testing process designed to identify the young women with the potential and mindset to become *war* maids.

The great majority of those who went on to become the war maid community's warriors would serve as the light infantry, scouts, and guerrillas most Sothōii thought of whenever they thought about war maids at all. That combat style required speed and stamina more than sheer size or brute strength, and the physical training required to provide those qualities was demanding and unremitting. It had been Kaeritha's observation that most people—including most men, she thought sardonically—didn't much care to invest the focus and sweat required to maintain that high pitch of physical conditioning.

From what she could see so far, it looked as if Leeana was actually enjoying it.

"Are you happy, Leeana?" she asked quietly after a moment, and Leeana looked up quickly. Her smile disappeared, but she met Kaeritha's eyes steadily.

"I don't know," she said frankly. "I've cried myself to sleep a night or two, if that's what you're asking." Her shoulders moved in what could have been called a shrug if it had been a little stronger. "I can't say I didn't expect that, though. And it's not because life here in Kalatha is so hard or because I'm not a baron's daughter anymore. It's because I'm not legally *Father and Mother's* daughter anymore. Does that make sense?"

"Oh, yes, girl," Kaeritha said softly, and Leeana drew a deep breath.

"But aside from missing Mother and Father—and being mis- erably homesick from time to time—I'm actually enjoying myself. So far, at least." Her smile returned. "Erlis—she's the Hundred in charge of physical training here in Kalatha—has been running me hard ever since I got here. Sometimes I just want to stop running long enough to drop dead from exhaustion, but I'm learning things about myself that I never knew before. And at least until she gets me brought up to a physical standard *she* finds acceptable, I'm excused from attending more 'traditional' classes."

"Traditional classes?" Kaeritha repeated.

"Oh, yes." Leeana's smile turned into a wry grin. "I have to admit that I'd hoped running away to the war maids would at least rescue me from the clutches of my tutors. Unfortunately, it turns out that the war maids require all of their members to be literate, and they 'strongly encourage' us to continue with additional education."

"I see," Kaeritha said, hiding a smile of her own as she recalled the team of strong horses it had required to drag *her* into a classroom when she'd been Leeana's age.

"What matters most, though," Leeana continued quietly, "is that by coming here I've done the most important thing. Father's enemies can't use me against him anymore, and I have the chance to be something besides an obedient little broodmare making babies for some fine stallion who completely controls my life."

"Then I'm glad you have the opportunity," Kaeritha said.

"So am I. Really." Leeana nodded firmly as if to emphasize the mere words.

"Good." Kaeritha rested one hand lightly on the girl's shoulder for a moment. "That was what I wanted to know before I leave for Quaysar."

"Quaysar? You're going to visit the Voice?"

There was something about the way Leeana asked the question that narrowed Kaeritha's eyes.

"Yes. Why do you ask?"

"No reason," Leeana said, just a bit too quickly. "It's just—" She broke off, hesitated, then shook her head. "It's just that I have this . . . uncomfortable feeling."

"About what?" Kaeritha was careful to keep any suggestiveness out of her own tone.

"About the Voice," Leeana said in a small voice, as if she were admitting to some heinous fault.

"What sort of feeling? For that matter, why do you have any 'feelings' about her at all? I didn't think you'd even met her."

"I haven't met her," Leeana admitted. "I guess you could say that what I've got is a 'secondhand feeling.' But I've talked to some of the other war maids about her. A lot."

"You have?" Kaeritha's eyes narrowed. Her discussion with Yalith hadn't suggested that the Kalatha community was as heavily focused on the Voice as Leeana seemed to be implying.

"Yes," the girl said. "And to be honest, Dame Kaeritha, it's the way they've been talking to me about her that worries me most."

"Suppose you explain that," Kaeritha suggested. She stepped back and settled her posterior onto the porch's railing, leaning back against one of the upright roof supports and folding her arms across her chest. The morning sunlight was warm across her shoulders as she cocked her head.

"You know I'm the most 'nobly born' person in Kalatha right now, right?" Leeana asked after a moment, and Kaeritha raised one eyebrow. The girl saw it and grimaced. "That's not an 'oh what a wonderful person I am' comment, Dame Kaeritha. What I meant to say is that even though I was only Father's daughter, not his real heir, I've seen a lot more sorts of political and aristocratic backbiting and maneuvering than most of the people here have."

"All right," Kaeritha said slowly, nodding as Leeana paused. "I'll grant you that—on an aristocratic level, at least. Don't make the mistake of assuming that peasants can't be just as contentious. Or just as subtle about the way they go about biting each other's backs."

"I won't. Or, at least, I don't *think* I will," Leeana replied. "But the thing is, Dame Kaeritha, that the way people here are talking about the Voice strikes me as, well, peculiar."

"Why?"

"First," Leeana said very seriously, her expression intent, "there's exactly which of the war maids seem to be doing most of the talking. It isn't the older ones, or the ones in the most senior positions—not people like Mayor Yalith, or Erlis, for example. And it isn't the very youngest ones, except in a sort of echoing kind of way."

"What do you mean, 'echoing'?"

"It's almost like there's an organized pattern," Leeana said, obviously choosing her words with care. "I think that's what drew my attention to it in the first place, really. There've been enough whispering campaigns organized against Father over the years for me to be automatically suspicious when I seem to be seeing the same thing somewhere else."

"And you think that's what you're seeing here?"

"I think it *may* be," Leeana said, nodding slowly. "It took a day or two for my suspicions to kick in, and the thing that made me start wondering in the first place was that I seemed to be hearing exactly the same sorts of things, in almost exactly the same sorts of words, from half a dozen or more people."

Kaeritha's blue eyes narrowed even further, and Leeana nodded again.

"It wasn't just a matter of people expressing the same general opinions, Dame Kaeritha. They were making the same *arguments*. And the way they were doing it—the way they were choosing their words, and who they were talking to—makes me think that it's an organized effort, not something that's happening spontaneously."

It was an enormous loss to the Kingdom of the Sothōii in general that its invincible cultural bias against the possibility of female rulers had deprived the Barony of Balthar of Leeana Bowmaster as its liege, Kaeritha thought. She'd known from the outset that Leeana was keenly intelligent, but the brain behind those jade-green eyes was even better than she'd suspected. How many young women Leeana's age, the knight wondered, thrown into a world and facing a future so radically different from anything they had ever experienced before, would have had enough energy to spare to think analytically about what people around them were saying about anything, far less about someone as distant from her own immediate—and exhausting—experiences as the Voice of Quaysar?

"Tell me more," she invited, still keeping her own voice as neutral as she could.

"The thing that struck me most about what the war maids talking about the Voice were saying," Leeana continued obediently, "was that they all agreed that the new Voice had changed the policies of the old Voice. Changed them for the better, in the opinion of whoever was doing the talking, that was. I know you never actually discussed with me what took you to Kalatha in the first place, Dame Kaeritha, but I knew the sorts of research you'd asked Lord Brandark to do before you left. And—" she glanced away for a moment "—I heard Prince Bahzell and Father discussing it a little. So I know you're really concerned about the disputes between Lord Trisu and the war maids."

Kaeritha frowned, and Leeana shook her head quickly.

"I haven't discussed it with anyone here, Dame Kaeritha! I know you and Mayor Yalith talked about it—or talked about something, anyway—and if Tomanāk sent you here, then it's certainly not my place to be blabbering away about it. But that's part of why what I was hearing bothered me, I think, because the same people who were talking about how much they approved of the Voice were talking about Trisu. And what they were saying was that the new Voice, unlike the *old* Voice, understood that the war maids couldn't put up with the way lords like Trisu were trying to turn the clock back. She understood that it was time the war maids stood up to people like him. That when someone pushed the war maids, the war maids had to push back—hard. Maybe even harder than they'd been pushed in the first place, since they had so little ground they could afford to surrender.

"That was enough to get me started listening to the *way* they were saying things, not just *what* they were saying. And when I did, I realized they were suggesting, or even saying outright, in some cases, that it was the Voice, not Mayor Yalith or her Council, who'd really pulled Trisu up short."

"They may believe that," Kaeritha said, forbearing any attempt to pretend Leeana hadn't accurately deduced her purpose in traveling to Kalatha, "but I've spoken to both the mayor and Lord Trisu. From the way both of them speak about the disputes—and about each other—the Voice has definitely played a secondary role, at most."

She watched the girl carefully. There were some thoughts—and suspicions—which she wasn't prepared to share with anyone just yet. Besides, she was curious as to how closely this acute young woman's analysis would parallel her own.

"That's just it," Leeana said. "From what they were saying, the Voice didn't charge right in and begin speaking in Lillinara's voice or anything like that. Instead, they were saying—bragging, almost—that she was too subtle and wise to be that openly 'confrontational' herself. They said it was because she had to maintain the 'neutrality' of her office as Voice. But I've seen and heard about too many 'subtle and wise' noblemen who adopted the same sort of tactics. As far as I can tell, most of them were only avoiding open confrontations so they could hide in the shadows better when it came time to plant a dagger in someone else's back. Either that, or they were setting someone else up to do what they wanted done for them. Preferably someone gullible enough that they could convince him the idea had been his own in the first place."

"Are you suggesting that a Voice of Lillinara is doing that in this case?"

"I'm suggesting that it's possible," Leeana said, undeterred by the slight chill frosting Kaeritha's tone. "And that's not the only thing I think is possible. The way the war maids who seem to approve of the Voice are talking is also undercutting the authority of Mayor Yalith and the Town Council. Not directly, and not openly, maybe, but that's the effect it's having, and I don't think that's an accident. Every time they talk approvingly about how insightful the Voice is, and how clearly she sees what needs to be done, the implication is that *without* the Voice, Mayor Yalith and the Council *wouldn't* have seen how important it was to stand up to Trisu. I've seen that before, too. Not personally, but I did pay attention to my history lessons, Dame Kaeritha. I think this is an attempt to undermine the authority of the people who are supposed to be governing Kalatha. And I think the Voice is either actively involved in it herself, for some reason, or else that some third party is using her, as well."

"I see." Kaeritha contemplated Leeana for several more moments, then shrugged. "Is there anything else?" she asked.

"Well," Leeana said, and looked away again. She seemed uncomfortable for some reason, almost a bit flustered. "There's the fact that the ones I'm worried about seem to be actively recruiting from among the younger war maids. I think that's one reason I've heard so much about it in the relatively short time I've been here. The fact that I used to be Father's daughter—still am, really, until my probationary period is over—might make me more valuable in their eyes, and they might figure I'd be young and new enough to be easily impressed and convinced.

"And," she turned to look back at Kaeritha, "some of the other things they've been saying about the Voice make me . . . uncomfortable."

"Like what?" Kaeritha asked.

"It's just . . . well, I suppose—" A faint flush of color brushed Leeana's cheeks. "I never expected to hear someone suggesting that a Voice of Lillinara would be so . . . promiscuous."

"Promiscuous?" Kaeritha fought successfully not to grin, but Leeana's blush darkened anyway.

"I'm not all *that* innocent, Dame Kaeritha," she said just a touch huffily. "For that matter, I grew up on one of the Kingdom's biggest stud farms, for goodness' sake! So I'm quite familiar with what goes on between men and women, thank you. Well," she added hastily as Kaeritha chuckled despite herself, "as familiar as I can be without actually— That is, as— Oh, you know what I mean!"

"Yes, Leeana," Kaeritha said, her tone just a bit contrite. "I do know what you mean."

"Well," Leeana went on in a slightly mollified voice, "what bothers me I guess is that the people who seem so fond of the Voice's political views are also talking about how 'liberated' her views are on . . . other things."

"Leeana," Kaeritha said carefully, "Lillinara doesn't require celibacy of any of Her Voices. Some of them take individual vows of celibacy when they decide they have a vocation to serve Her, but that's different. A personal decision to free them from other needs and desires in order to concentrate solely on Her, and there's actually some disagreement as to whether or not She really approves of it even then. In fact, her High Voices *can't* be virgins. She is the Goddess of Women, you know—*all* women, not just the patron of maidens—and She feels that Her church, and Her priestesses, need to have experienced the things they're going to be counseling Her worshipers about."

"Really?" Leeana considered that for several seconds, her expression intent, then nodded. "That makes sense," she pronounced with the definitiveness of the young.

"I'm glad you approve," Kaeritha murmured, and the girl blushed again. Then she grinned.

"On the other hand," Kaeritha continued, "it sounded to me like you were talking about something you feel goes a bit far even bearing that in mind."

"Well, yes," Leeana agreed, but her expression remained thoughtful, and she cocked her head at Kaeritha. "Can I ask *you* a question, Dame Kaeritha?"

"Of course you may," Kaeritha assured her, but the girl hesitated a moment, despite the reassurance.

"I was wondering," she said finally, slowly, "about how the other gods feel about that." She looked away, gazing out over the training salle's grounds. "For example, you're a Champion of Tomanāk. How does *He* feel about it?"

"About celibacy?" Kaeritha chuckled. "Let's just say that as the God of Justice, He wouldn't exactly think it was 'just' to require His followers to forswear something that fundamental to the mortal condition. Like Lillinara, He expects us not to be *casual* about it, and He expects us to recognize and meet any responsibilities which might arise out of it. But all of the Gods of Light celebrate life, Leeana, and I can't think of anything much more 'life-affirming' than the embracing of a loving, shared physical relationship."

"Really?" There was something about that single word which made Kaeritha wonder exactly what the girl was thinking. But then Leeana shook herself, and turned back towards her.

"That makes sense, too," she said. "But it doesn't sound like what the people who worry me are saying, either."

"What do you mean?" Kaeritha asked intently.

"The loving and sharing part seems to get left out a lot," Leeana said simply. "And so does the part about responsibility." Kaeritha frowned, but she didn't interrupt, and the young woman continued. "There were a couple of other parts that surprised me a little, just at first. They shouldn't have, but I guess that despite everything, I've got a lot more 'conventional' leftovers in my attitudes then I realized I did. I mean, the war maids are a community of women who've chosen not to live in a society run by men. Under the circumstances, I should have been surprised if many of them *hadn't* chosen other women as their partners, not the other way around.

"But even if that surprised me, at first, it didn't take me long to understand it. And what *bothered* me, Dame Kaeritha, wasn't who someone chose to fall in love with. It was the way these particular war maids were talking about the what the Voice thought about the proper 'freedom' when it comes to choosing lovers, whether they're men or women."

She didn't seem a bit flustered by her subject matter now, Kaeritha noted. It was as if her concentration on explaining what she meant had banished such mundane concerns.

"Why?"

"Because the sort of commitment and responsibility you're talking about doesn't seem very important to them. They talk about it as if it were, well, *only* physical. As if it's all about selfish pleasure, or just a momentary fling. Like . . . like the other person doesn't really matter, or isn't really real. Just a *convenience*. I'm not naive enough to think there aren't a lot of people in the world who feel that way anyway, Dame Kaeritha. But these women were laughing—almost snickering—about it, like they knew what they were suggesting was wrong and that only made it better, somehow. And every time I heard one of them saying something like that, I thought about all of the people who *already* believe that all war maids think that way."

Kaeritha frowned, and her thoughts were grim. It was possible Leeana was overreacting to a few chance words. As she herself had said, she was the product of a Sothōii upbringing herself. Perhaps not quite as conventional as most, but even an 'unconventional' Sothōii rearing was bound to leave a few footprints.

Yet Kaeritha didn't think that was the case. Not only was Leeana keenly intelligent and observant, but the situation she described fitted only too well into the pattern *Kaeritha* had begun to discern. Or that she was afraid she had, at any rate.

"Do you think I'm imagining things?" Leeana asked, once again almost as if she could read Kaeritha's mind, and the knight shook her head.

"No. I'm certain you're not imagining things, Leeana. It's possible you're reading more into what you've heard than was actually intended, but I don't believe you've imagined anything."

"Oh," Leeana said in a voice which was suddenly so tiny that Kaeritha looked at her in surprise.

"I'd hoped I was," the young woman said softly.

Kaeritha left Kalatha seven days later.

She hadn't intended to stay that long, but her conversation with Leeana had suggested to her that there might be more that needed looking into at Kalatha than she'd thought. Conducting her own discreet investigations took more time than she'd allowed for. But that was all right . . . it also took her longer than she'd expected to secure another opportunity to examine the original charter and land grant.

Mayor Yalith's assistant, Sharral, was as helpful and efficient as ever, but it turned out to be extraordinarily difficult to arrange the visit to the town's archives this time around. Lanitha, Kalatha's librarian and archivist, was relatively new to her position, and more than a bit young for responsibilities of such magnitude. She was, however, attentive and determined to discharge those responsibilities to the very best of her ability. Which, Kaeritha knew from her previous visits to the town archives, was quite high.

This time, though, Lanitha, although she made it obvious she was trying her very best, found it difficult to schedule an opportunity for Kaeritha to consult the required documents. Given their importance to the town of Kalatha itself, and to all war maids in general, Kaeritha wasn't surprised that the young woman responsible for their security and proper care wanted to be present whenever they were consulted. If their positions had been reversed, Kaeritha would have felt exactly the same way. Not only that, but Lanitha had been a great help to her and Yalith when she first examined them. Still, she could have wished for it to take less than three days for Lanitha to clear her schedule sufficiently to allow her to offer Kaeritha the degree of personal assistance the champion of any god, and especially of the God of War and Justice, deserved. And then, on the fourth day, when Kaeritha arrived at the archives, she was surprised (although probably less so than she should have been) to discover that Lanitha had been called away by an unanticipated personal emergency. She'd left her profound apologies and promised she would be available the next day—or the day after that, at the very latest—but it had been simply impossible for her to keep her scheduled appointment.

Despite the undeniable frustration she felt at the delays, Kaeritha had put the time she found on her hands to efficient use. Most casual observers might have been excused for not noticing that, but Kaeritha had been a champion of Tomanāk for quite a few years. And one thing champions of Tomanāk learned—*well*, most *of His champions, at any rate*, Kaeritha had corrected herself with a smile—was how to conduct an unobtrusive investigation. It helped that most people expected a champion's methods to be flashy and dramatic. As, indeed, some of the tools in Kaeritha's arsenal were, she cheerfully admitted. But there were times when it was far better to be discreet, and this seemed to be one of them. Which was why none of the war maids of Kalatha noticed that the visiting champion of Tomanāk sharing their meals, working out with them in the exercise salle, or training in weapons craft with them, managed to pick up an amazing amount of information.

Some of it was entirely open and aboveboard, and no less valuable because it was. Kaeritha's own two-sword technique was one she had evolved almost entirely on her own. The fact that she'd been born ambidextrous helped explain why it had occurred to her, but there'd been few weapons masters (or mistresses) in the Empire of the Axe who taught a combat technique which used a primary weapon in each hand. Many of them taught sword and dagger, or sword and dirk, and even more of them taught techniques for fighting with one's off hand, since it was always possible for one's normal weapon hand or arm to be wounded. But all of that was quite different from fighting with matched short swords in both hands simultaneously.

Quite a few of the war maids, however, used a technique which, despite many differences in detail, was very similar overall. Erlis, the Commander of One Hundred in charge of Leeana's physical training class, was one of them, and Kaeritha looked forward to her opportunities to match her own skills against the Hundred's. Erlis appeared to enjoy their training matches just as much as Kaeritha did, although it quickly became apparent to both of them that for all her own experience and skills, the war maid was thoroughly outclassed. But that, as Erlis pointed out herself, was as it ought to be when the person she was measuring her own abilities against was a chosen champion of the God of War.

But in addition to adding some new wrinkles to her own combat repertoire, Kaeritha found the opportunity to spend time with Kalatha's war maids in informal surroundings invaluable. It wasn't so much what they said to her, as what they said to one another . . . or *didn't* say to her when she asked carefully casual questions. Kaeritha's natural hearing was more acute than that of most humans, although it fell far short of the sensitivity of a hradani like Bahzell. But one of her abilities as Tomanāk's champion was to "listen" to conversations she couldn't possibly have overheard otherwise. It wasn't like the telepathy many magi possessed, and she could only "listen" to conversations she knew about and could see with her own eyes. But it meant that even across a crowded ballroom—or a noisy training yard—she could sit in unobtrusively while other people spoke.

It was an ability she used sparingly, because it would have been so easy to misuse. But it was also one which was extraordinarily helpful to any investigator, and she employed it to good effect during her extended stay in Kalatha.

And what she heard confirmed her unhappy suspicion that Leeana had not been an alarmist young woman seeing shadows where none existed. In fact, if anything, the girl had underestimated what was happening.

There was nothing overt enough that Kaeritha could have taken it to a magistrate, but the pattern was clear. There were at least three factions in Kalatha.

One was Mayor Yalith's, which—for the moment, at least—was the most numerous and the most important and influential one. As Yalith herself, its members were angry with Trisu and determined to force him to admit his transgressions. They were gratified by the Quaysar Voice's strong support, but they were still essentially prepared to allow the system to work. Partly because they were convinced of the rectitude of their own positions and believed that, ultimately, the courts must decide in their favor. But also partly because they accepted that it was incumbent upon them to *prove* that they and their demands had been reasonable from the outset. It wasn't because they were any less angry than anyone else, but they were only too well aware that the subjects of the Kingdom of the Sothōii were predisposed to view all war maids with disapproval. They were determined not to provide that prejudice with any fresh ammunition to use against them.

The second faction Kaeritha had identified consisted of most of the townsfolk who weren't firmly behind their mayor. Their view of the disputes was that the mayor and her council were pushing too hard. It wasn't that they doubted Yalith's arguments or her judgment of the technical legalities of the situation; they simply didn't feel the confrontation with Trisu was ultimately worth what it was likely to cost. Whatever else they might think of him, he was the most powerful noble in the vicinity, and they were going to have to deal with him—and his sons—for years to come, regardless of what any judge in a court might decide. Very few people in that faction, however, were upset enough to actively oppose Yalith. They simply didn't *support* her, except with a certain disgruntled sense of civic responsibility, and there appeared to be significantly fewer of them than there were of the mayor's strong partisans.

But it was the third faction which worried Kaeritha. The smallest of the three, it was also the angriest. It consisted primarily, although not exclusively, of younger war maids and those too junior in Kalatha's hierarchy to force their own opinions upon the Town Council. The most senior of them whom Kaeritha had identified so far was a mere Commander of Fifty—the equivalent of an infantry captain in the Royal and Imperial Army—but that didn't necessarily mean they weren't influential. They were the ones who were most furious with Trisu, most militant in their insistence that their rights, and those of all war maids, must be defended. They were impatient with any argument which suggested they must be cautious, or appear reasonable. It was time for someone *else* to be reasonable, as far as they were concerned, and in all honesty, Kaeritha found it easy to sympathize with them in that view.

But many of the conversations she overheard went beyond that. There were no more than ten or fifteen women whom Kaeritha would have considered "ringleaders." The vast majority were no more or less than understandably outraged and angry women reacting to endless years of prejudice and bigotry. But those ten or fifteen Kaeritha had picked out clearly had an organized agenda. They weren't simply angry; they were *manipulating* the anger of others and using it to subtly undermine the traditional figures of authority in the Kalathan war maid community. That was bad enough, but Leeana had also been correct about the rest of what they were saying. Whether they were actually taking their cue directly from the Voice at Quaysar or not—and at this point, whatever her suspicions, Kaeritha had no way of knowing whether they were—they were using the Voice's supposed statements and views to assert that Lillinara Herself supported self-centered, narcissistic life choices which appalled Kaeritha. And which she was grimly certain would be equally appalling to Lillinara. It wasn't just the denial of responsibility, or the notion that it was morally acceptable to *use* someone else for one's own advantage or pleasure. It was the fact that they justified that denial and notion at least in part on the basis that it was time the war maids "got even" for all the indignities and oppression they had ever suffered.

Kaeritha knew, from bitter personal experience, the difference between vengeance and justice, and she knew what bitter tang she tasted in the low-voiced, bitter conversations she listened to about her.

Unfortunately, all she had were suspicions. It was nothing she could really take to Yalith, and even if it had been, Yalith was angry enough herself that she might not have listened. Besides, there was something about the mayor's own position that bothered Kaeritha. Yalith's tenure as mayor of Kalatha predated the beginnings of the current confrontation with Trisu. If, as Kaeritha had come to suspect, the original documents at Kalatha had been tampered with somehow, Yalith ought to have been aware of it. Which suggested, logically, that if something nefarious was going on in Kalatha, Yalith was a part of it. Kaeritha didn't think she was, and she'd done a little subtle probing of the mayor's honesty—enough to be as certain as she could without the same sort of examination she'd given Salthan that Yalith honestly and sincerely believed she was in the right.

Which suggested to Kaeritha that something more than mere documents might have been tampered with in Kalatha.

"I am *so* sorry about the delay, Dame Kaeritha," Lanitha of Kalatha said as she ushered Kaeritha into the main Records Room. "I know your time is valuable, to Tomanāk as well as to yourself, and I hate it that you sat around cooling your heels waiting for me for almost an entire week."

She shook her head, her expression simultaneously harassed, irritated, and apologetic.

"It's like there was some sort of curse on my week," she continued, bustling around the Records Room to open the heavy curtains which normally protected its contents and let the daylight in. "Every time I thought I was going to get over here and pull the documents for you, some fresh disaster came rolling out of nowhere."

"That's perfectly all right, Lanitha," Kaeritha reassured her. "I imagine everyone's had weeks like that, you know. I certainly have!"

"Thank you." Lanitha paused to smile gratefully at her. "I'm relieved that you're so understanding. Not that your sympathy makes me look any more efficient and organized!"

Kaeritha only returned her smile and waited, her expression pleasant, while the archivist finished drawing back the curtains and unlocked the large cabinet which contained the most important of Kalatha's official documents.

"Mayor Yalith—or, rather, Sharral—didn't tell me exactly which sections you're particularly interested in this time," she said over her shoulder as she opened the heavy, iron-reinforced door.

"I need to reexamine the section of Kellos' grant where the boundary by the grist mill is established," Kaeritha said casually.

"I see," Lanitha said. She found the proper document case, withdrew it from the cabinet, and set it carefully on the desk before the Records Room's largest eastern window. Her tone was no more than absently courteous. But Kaeritha was watching her as carefully and unobtrusively as she'd ever watched anyone in her life, and something about the set of the archivist's shoulders suggested Lanitha was less calm than she wanted to appear. It wasn't that Kaeritha detected any indication that Lanitha was anything but the honest, hard-working young woman she seemed to be. Yet there was still that *something* . . . almost as if Lanitha had some inner sense that her own loyalties were at odds with one another.

The archivist opened the document case and laid the original copy of Lord Kellos' grant to the war maids of Kalatha on the desktop. Kaeritha had done enough research among fragile documents to stand patiently, hands clasped behind her, while Lanitha carefully opened the old-fashioned scroll and sought the section Kaeritha had described.

"Here it is," the archivist said finally, and stepped back out of the way so that Kaeritha could examine the document for herself.

"Thank you," Kaeritha said courteously. She moved closer to the desk and bent over the faded, crabbed handwriting. The document's age was only too apparent, and its authenticity was obvious. But the authenticity of Trisu's copy had been equally obvious, she reminded herself, and rested the heel of her hand lightly on the pommel of her left-hand sword.

It was a natural enough pose, if rather more overly dramatic than Kaeritha preferred. The last time she'd been in this room, she'd taken both swords off and laid them to one side, and she hoped Lanitha wasn't wondering why she hadn't done the same thing this time. If the librarian asked, Kaeritha was prepared to point out that last time, she'd been sitting here for hours while she studied the documents and took notes. This time, she only wanted to make a quick recheck of a single section. And, as Lanitha's own profuse apologies had underscored, she was behind schedule and running late.

There it was. She leaned forward, studying the stilted phrases more intently, and ran the index finger of her right hand lightly along the relevant lines. Only a far more casual archivist than Lanitha could have avoided cringing when anyone, even someone who'd already demonstrated her respect for the fragility of the documents in her care, touched one of them that way. The other woman moved a half-step closer, watching Kaeritha's right hand with anxious attentiveness . . . exactly as the knight had intended.

Because she was so focused on Kaeritha's right hand, she failed to notice the faint flicker of blue fire which danced around the *left* hand resting on the champion's sword hilt. It wasn't very bright, anyway—Tomanāk knew how to be unobtrusive when it was necessary, too—but it was enough for Kaeritha's purposes.

"Thank you, Lanitha," she said again, and stepped back. She took her hand from her sword as she did so, and the blue flicker disappeared entirely. "That was all I needed to see."

"Are you certain, Milady?" Lanitha's tone and expression were earnest, and Kaeritha nodded.

"I just wanted to check my memory of the words," she assured the archivist.

"Might I ask why, Milady?" Lanitha asked.

"I'm still in the middle of an investigation, Lanitha," Kaeritha reminded her, and the other woman bent her head in acknowledgment of the gentle rebuke. Kaeritha gazed at her for a moment, then shrugged. "On the other hand," the knight continued, "it's not as if it's not going to come out in the end, anyway, I suppose."

"Not as if what isn't going to come out?" Lanitha asked, emboldened by Kaeritha's last sentence.

"There's a definite discrepancy between the original documents here and Trisu's so-called copies," Kaeritha told her. "I have to say that when I first saw his copy, I was astonished. It didn't seem possible that anyone could have produced such a perfect-looking forgery. But, obviously, the only way his copies could be that different from the originals has to involve a deliberate substitution or forgery."

"Lillinara!" Lanitha said softly, signing the Mother's full moon. "I knew Trisu hated all war maids, but I never imagined he'd try something like that, Milady! How could he possibly expect it to pass muster? He must know that sooner or later someone would do what you've just done and compare the forgery to the original!"

"One thing I learned years ago, Lanitha," Kaeritha said wearily as she watched the archivist carefully returning the land grant to its case, "is that criminals *always* think they can 'get away with it.' If their minds didn't work that way, they wouldn't be criminals in the first place!"

"I suppose not." Lanitha sighed and shook her head. "It just seems so silly—and sad—when you come down to it."

"You're wrong, you know," Kaeritha said quietly, her voice so flat that Lanitha looked quickly back over her shoulder at her.

"Wrong, Milady?"

"It isn't silly, or sad," Kaeritha told her. "Whatever the original motivation may have been, this sort of conflict between the documents here and those at Thalar is going to play right into the hands of everyone else like Trisu. It isn't the sort of minor discrepancy that can be explained away as clerical error. It's a deliberate forgery, and there are altogether too many people out there who are already prepared to think the worst about you war maids. It won't matter to them that you have the originals, while he has only copies. What will matter is that they'll assume *you* must have made the alterations."

"Then I suppose it's a good thing a Champion of Tomanāk is on the spot, isn't it, Milady? Even the most prejudiced person would have to take *your* word for it that Trisu or someone working for him is the forger."

"Yes, Lanitha," Kaeritha said grimly. "They certainly would."

The road to Quaysar ran almost due east from Kalatha, and the morning sun shone brightly into Kaeritha's face two days later as Cloudy trotted briskly along. Birds soared and dipped overhead, calling to one another against the impossibly blue sky as they rode the brawny wind gusting out of the northwest, and the endless sea of young grass rippled and hissed musically as the stiff gusts pushed waves across it. The morning was still cool, but there was a sense of life and energy wrapped up in the wind and the high, beautiful cries of the birds, and Kaeritha drew that energy deep into her lungs.

It was tempting to abandon herself to the sensual enjoyment of the new day, but the dark suspicion which had first whispered to her in Trisu's library had hardened into something even darker which cast its own ominous shadow across the morning.

She still had altogether too many questions and far too few answers, she reminded herself. Yet even as she conscientiously bore that in mind, she knew which way the facts she had been able to test all pointed. What she didn't begin to know was how all this could have happened, or why Lillinara and Tomanāk seemed to have agreed that it was *her* job to deal with it.

Not that she was tempted even for a moment to pretend that it *wasn't* her job. This was exactly the sort of task which had attracted her to Tomanāk's service in the first place. The fact that she wished with all her heart that someone like the war maids had been available to her mother—or to her—when she was a child only stiffened her resolve still further. She had no clear idea exactly what she was going to encounter at Quaysar, yet there was a stink of Darkness about this entire business. It was only too probable that she was riding directly into that Dark, but it was one of a Champion of Tomanāk's functions to carry Light into even the deepest Darkness.

Of course, sometimes the Light failed.

Dame Kaeritha Seldansdaughter knew that, just as she knew how few of Tomanāk's champions ever died in bed. But if that was the price to hold off the Dark which had claimed fallen Kontovar, it was one she would pay. And if worse came to worst, the letter she had dispatched to Bahzell under Sword Seal contained all of her suspicions, discoveries, and deductions. If it should happen that this time she was fated to fail, she knew with absolute certainty that her brother would avenge her and complete her task as surely as she would have done that for him.

She smiled warmly at the thought, then shook off her dark musings and raised her head, turning her face more fully to the sun and luxuriating in its warmth.

Quaysar was impressive.

The temple's original architects had found one of the few genuine hilltops the Wind Plain offered. It was obvious as Kaeritha approached that the upthrust knob upon which the temple and the town which supported it stood was basically a solid plug or dome of granite. It was nowhere near as towering as it had seemed at first glance, she realized as she drew closer. But it didn't have to be, either. The low, slightly rolling flatlands of the Wind Plain stretched away in every direction, as far as the eye could see, and even Quaysar's relatively low perch allowed it to command its surroundings effortlessly.

The old town of Quaysar, which had been folded into the temple community, was surrounded by a low but defensible wall. Newer buildings and outlying farms spread out from the old town along the arms of the crossroads which met beside the sizable pond or small lake at the base of the granite pedestal which supported the temple, and Kaeritha saw workers laboring in the fields as Cloudy trotted past them.

The temple itself had its own wall, which was actually higher than that of the old town and rose sheer from the very lip of the temple's stony perch. That sort of security feature was no part of the temples of Lillinara in the Empire of the Axe, but the Empire was the oldest, most settled realm of Norfressa. Things had been far less orderly on the Wind Plain when Quaysar was first constructed. For that matter, they still were, she supposed. At any rate, she didn't blame the original builders for seeing to it that their temple was not simply located in the most defensible position available but well fortified, to boot.

She couldn't see much of the temple buildings with the wall in the way, but the three traditional towers of any temple of Lillinara rose above them. The Tower of the Mother, with its round, alabaster full moon, was flanked by the slightly lower crescent moon-crowned Tower of the Maiden and the Tower of the Crone, with its matching globe of obsidian. The added height of the prominence upon which the entire temple stood lifted them even higher against the blue sky and high-piled, snow-white clouds to the south, and Kaeritha felt her imagination stir as she realized how they must look against the night heavens when the silver-white glow of Lillinara touched their stonework. Quaysar was far from the largest temple of Lillinara Kaeritha had ever seen, but its location and special significance gave it a majesty and a sense of presence she had seldom seen equaled.

Yet as she drew closer still, the imagined image of towers, burning with cool, radiant light against the star-strewn heavens faded, and an icy chill touched her heart. No silver Lady's Light clung to those towers or those walls under the warm sunlight of early afternoon. But Kaeritha's eyes weren't like those of other mortals. They Saw what others didn't, and her mouth tightened as an ominous, poison-green light flickered at the corner of her vision.

She knew that stomach-churning green. She'd Seen it before, and her mind went back to a rainy day in Baron Tellian's library when she'd told him how unhappily familiar with the presence of the Dark champions of Tomanāk were.

She inhaled deeply and gazed up at the temple, trying to isolate those elusive flickers of green. She couldn't, and her jaw clenched as she failed. Each of Tomanāk's champions perceived evil and the handiwork of the Dark Gods in his or her own, unique fashion. Bahzell, she knew, received what he called "feelings"—an impression of things not yet fully perceived, yet somehow known. Another champion she had known heard music which guided him. But Kaeritha, like some magi to whom she had spoken, Saw. For her, it was the interplay of light and shadow—or of Light and Dark. That inner perception had never yet failed or deceived her, and yet today, the meaning of what she Saw was ... unclear. She couldn't pin it down, couldn't even be positive that the green light-devils dancing at the edges of her vision were coming from the temple, and not the town clustered below it.

That shouldn't have happened. Especially not when she'd come already primed by her suspicions and earlier investigations. The revealing glare of evil should have been obvious to her ... unless someone—or some*thing*—with enormous power was deliberately concealing it.

She made herself exhale and shook herself. The concealment wasn't necessarily directed specifically against *her*, she told herself. Whatever was happening in Quaysar was clearly part of a years-long effort, and the very thing which would make Quaysar such a prize in the eyes of the Dark was its importance to Lillinara and, specifically, to the Sothōii war maids. But that also meant Quaysar was more prominent, and more likely to draw pilgrims and visitors, than most other temples of its relatively modest size. And with pilgrims came those besides Kaeritha whose eyes might See what the Dark preferred to keep hidden.

Yet logical as that conclusion was, the fact remained that it required tremendous power to so thoroughly obscure the inner sight of a champion of Tomanāk. Indeed, such power must have completely blinded the perceptions—whether of sight, or hearing, or sensing—of anyone less intimately bound to the service of her god.

Which meant that somewhere atop that timeworn tooth of granite waited a servant of the Greater Dark.

Yes, she told herself grimly. *And it's probably the "Voice" herself. In fact, it would almost have to be. There's no way anything this Dark and powerful could hide itself from an uncorrupted Voice. But whatever it is, it doesn't have complete control. Not even a Dark God himself could keep me from Seeing if that were the case. Great!* She snorted in harsh laughter. *It's not* everyone *in Quaysar. Marvelous. All I have to do is assume that anyone I meet serves the Dark until she proves differently!*

She closed her eyes and drew another deep breath.

All right, Tomanāk, she thought. *You never promised it would be easy. And I suppose I'd be riding off in search of reinforcements instead of riding in all by my fool self, if my skull wasn't just as thick as Bahzell's. But it is. So, if You don't have anything else to do this afternoon, why don't You and I go call on the Voice?*

"Of course, Dame Kaeritha! Come in, come in! We've been expecting you."

The officer in command of the temple's largely ceremonial gate guard bowed deeply and swept his arm at the open gate in a welcoming gesture. He straightened to find Kaeritha gazing down at him from Cloudy's saddle with a quizzical expression and frowned ever so slightly, as if surprised that she hadn't ridden straight past at his invitation.

"Expecting me?" she said, and he cleared his throat.

"Uh, yes, Milady." He shook himself. "The Voice warned us several days ago that you would be coming to visit us," he said in a less flustered tone.

"I see." Kaeritha filed that information away along with the officer's strong Sothōii accent and the warmth which had infused his own voice as he mentioned the Voice. It was uncommon for a temple of Lillinara in the Empire of the Axe to have its gate guard commanded by a man. It was scarcely unheard of, even there, however, given the small percentage of Axewomen who followed the profession of arms, and she supposed it made even more sense here in the Kingdom of the Sothōii, where even fewer women were warriors. Yet she also saw two war maids in chari and yathu standing behind him, with swords at their hips, crossed bandoliers of throwing stars, and the traditional war maid garrottes wound around their heads like leather headbands. Given the special significance Quaysar held for all war maids, she found it . . . interesting that the temple's entire guard force didn't consist solely of them.

The way the guard commander had spoken of the Voice was almost equally interesting, especially from a native Sothōii. He seemed completely comfortable in the service of a temple not simply dedicated to the goddess of women but intimately associated with the creation of all those "unnatural" war maids. Undoubtedly, anyone who would have accepted the position in the first place must be more enlightened than most of his fellow Sothōii males, but there was more than simple acceptance or even approval in his tone. It came far closer to something which might almost have been called . . . obeisance. For that matter, Kaeritha didn't much care for the look in his eyes, although she would have been hard put to pin down what it was about it that bothered her.

"Yes, Milady," the officer continued. "She knew you'd visited Kalatha and Lord Trisu, and she told us almost a week ago that you would be visiting us, as well." He smiled. "And, of course, she made it abundantly clear that we were to greet you with all of the courtesy due to a champion of the War God."

Kaeritha glanced at the rest of his guard force: the two war maids she'd already noticed and three more men in the traditional Sothōii breastplate and leather. They were too well trained to abandon their stance of professional watchfulness, but their body language and expressions matched the warmth in their commander's voice.

"That was very considerate of the Voice," she said after a moment. "I appreciate it. And she was quite correct; I have come to Quaysar to meet with her. Since she was courteous enough to warn you I was coming, did she also indicate whether or not she would be able to grant me an audience?"

"My instructions were to pass you straight in, and I believe you'll find Major Paratha, the commander of the Voice's personal guards, waiting to escort you directly to her."

"I see the Voice is as foresightful as she is courteous," Kaeritha said with a smile. "As are those who serve her and the Goddess here in Quaysar."

"Thank you for those kind words, Milady." The officer bowed again, less deeply, and waved at the open gateway once more. "But we all know only serious matters could have brought you this far from the Empire, and the Voice is eager for Major Paratha to bring you to her."

"Of course," Kaeritha agreed, inclining her head in a small, answering bow. "I hope we meet again before I leave Quaysar," she added, and touched Cloudy gently with her heel.

The mare trotted through the open gate. The tunnel beyond it was longer than Kaeritha had expected. The temple's defensive wall was clearly thicker than it had appeared from a distance, and the disk of sunlight waiting to welcome her at its farther end seemed tiny and far away. Her shoulders were tight, tension sang in her belly, and she was acutely conscious of the silent menace of the murder holes in the tunnel ceiling as she passed under them. This wasn't the first time she'd ridden knowingly into what she suspected was an ambush, and she knew she appeared outwardly calm and unconcerned. It just didn't feel that way from her side.

Major Paratha was waiting for her, and Kaeritha raised a mental eyebrow as she realized the major was accompanied only by a groom who was obviously there to take care of Cloudy for her. Apparently, whatever the Voice had in mind included nothing so crude as swords in the temple courtyard.

"Milady Champion," Paratha murmured, bending her head in greeting. The major had a pronounced Sothōii accent, and stood an inch or so taller than Kaeritha herself, but she wore combination plate and chain armor much like Kaeritha's own and carried a cavalry saber. If she was a war maid, she was obviously one of the minority who'd trained with more "standard" weapons.

That much was apparent the instant Kaeritha glanced at her, just as it would have been to anyone else. But that was all "anyone else" might have seen. The additional armor Paratha wore was visible only to Kaeritha, and she tensed inside like a cat suddenly faced by a cobra as she Saw the corona of sickly, yellow-green light which outlined the major's body. The sensation of "wrongness" radiating from her was like a punch in the belly to Kaeritha, a taste so vile she almost gagged physically and wondered for a moment how anyone could possibly fail to perceive it as clearly as she did.

"Quaysar is honored by your visit," the tall woman continued, smiling, her voice so bizarrely normal sounding after what Kaeritha had Seen that it required all of Kaeritha's hard-trained self-control not to stare at her in disbelief.

"Major Paratha, I presume," she replied pleasantly, instead, after she'd dismounted, and smiled as if she'd noticed nothing at all.

"I am," Paratha confirmed. "And our Voice has bidden me welcome you in her name and assure you that she and the entire temple stand ready to assist you in any way we may."

"Her graciousness and generosity are no less than I would expect from a Voice of the Mother," Kaeritha said. "And they are most welcome."

"Welcome, perhaps," Paratha responded, "yet they're also the very least the Mother's servants can offer a Servant of Tomanāk who rides in search of justice. And since you come to us upon that errand, may I guide you directly to the Voice? Or would you prefer to wash and refresh yourself after your ride, first?"

"As you say, Major, I come in search of justice. If the Voice is prepared to see me so quickly, I would prefer to go directly to her."

"Of course, Milady," Paratha said, with another pleasant smile. "If you'll follow me."

Well, Kaeritha thought as she followed Paratha into the temple complex, *at least I can be sure where to find* one *of my enemies.*

It took a physical act of will to keep her hands away from the hilts of her weapons while she trailed along behind the major. Paratha seemed to glow in the temple's hushed, reverent dimness, and tendrils of the sickly radiance which clung to her reached out to embrace others as they passed. There was something nauseating about the slow, lascivious way those dully glowing light serpents caressed and stroked those they touched. Most of them gave no indication that they realized anything had touched them, but as Kaeritha walked past them behind Paratha, she Saw tiny, ugly spots, like a leprosy of evil, upon them. They were so small, those spots—hardly visible, only a tiny bit more intense than any normal, fallible mortal might be expected to bear. Yet there were scores of them on most of the acolytes and handmaidens she and Paratha passed, and they blazed briefly stronger and uglier as the major's corona reached out to them. Then they faded, sinking inward, until not even Kaeritha could See them.

That was bad enough, but those who *did* feel something when Paratha's vile web brushed over them were worse. However hard they tried to conceal it, they felt the caress of the Darkness draped about Paratha, and a flicker of pleasure—almost a twisted ecstasy— danced ever so briefly across their faces.

Kaeritha's pulse thudded harder and faster as they moved deeper and deeper into the temple. They'd entered through the Chapel of the Crone, which was not the avenue of approach Kaeritha would have chosen in Paratha's place. Whatever crawling evil had infested Quaysar, this was still a temple of Lillinara. To defile its buildings and, even more, its inhabitants and servitors might be an enormous triumph for the Dark, but the stones themselves must remember to whose honor and reverence they had been raised. However great the triumph, it could not pass undetected forever, and of all of Lillinara's aspects, it was the Crone, the Avenger, whose fury Kaeritha would have least liked to face.

And yet, there was also a sort of fitness, almost a logic, to

Paratha's chosen course, for the Crone *was* the Avenger. She was the aspect of the goddess most steeped in blood and vengeance. Her Third Face, most apt to merciless destruction. There were those, including one Kaeritha Seldansdaughter, who felt that the Crone all too often verged upon the Dark Herself, and so perhaps there was a certain resonance between this chapel and the shadowy web which rode Paratha's shoulders and soul.

"Tell me, Major," she asked casually, "have you been in Lillinara's service long?"

"Almost twelve years, Milady," Paratha replied.

"And how long have you commanded the Voice's guards?"

"Only since she arrived here," Paratha said, glancing back over her shoulder at Kaeritha with another smile. "I was assigned to the Quaysar Guard almost eight years ago, and I commanded the previous Voice's guards for almost a year and a half before her death."

"I see," Kaeritha murmured, and the major returned her attention to leading the way through the temple.

They passed through the chapel, and Kaeritha felt the accumulation of Darkness pressing against her shoulders, like a physical presence at her back, as she moved deeper and deeper into the miasma of corruption which had invaded the temple. She was afraid, more afraid than she'd believed she could be even after she'd deduced that Quaysar must be the center of it all. Whatever evil was at work here, it was subtle and terrifyingly powerful, and it must have worked its weavings even longer than she had believed possible. The outer precincts of the temple, and those members of the temple community furthest from the centers of power, like the gate guards who'd greeted her upon her arrival, were least affected. She wondered if that was deliberate. Had they been left alone, aside from just enough tampering to keep them from noticing what was happening at Quaysar's core, as a part of the corruption's mask? Or had whatever power of the Dark was at work here simply left them for later, after it had fully secured its grasp on the inner temple?

Not that it mattered much either way at the moment. What mattered were the barriers she sensed going up behind her. The waiting strands of power, snapping up, no longer threads but cables. The fly had entered the web of its own volition, arrogant in its own self-confidence, and now it was too late for escape.

She glanced casually over her shoulder and saw more than a dozen other women, the ones who had reacted most strongly to the touch of Paratha's Darkness, following behind. They looked as if they were merely continuing whatever errands had been theirs before Kaeritha's arrival, but she knew better. She could See the latticework of diseased radiance which bound them together, and the shroud about Paratha was growing stronger, as if it were less and less concerned about even attempting to conceal its presence.

They passed rooms and chambers whose functions Kaeritha could only guess at, and then they entered what was obviously a more residential area of the temple. She had a vague impression of beautiful works of art, religious artifacts, mosaics and magnificent fabrics. Fountains sang sweetly, water splashed and trickled through ornate channels where huge golden fish swam lazily, and a cool, hushed splendor lay welcomingly all about her.

She noticed all of it . . . and none of it. It was unimportant, peripheral, brushed aside by the tempest of Darkness she felt gathering all about her, sweeping towards her from all directions. It was a subtler and less barbaric Darkness than she and Bahzell and Vaijon had confronted in the Navahkan temple of Sharnā, and yet it was just as strong. Possibly even stronger, and edged with a malice and a sense of endless, cunning patience far beyond that of Sharnā and his tools.

And she faced it alone.

Paratha opened a final pair of double doors of polished ebony inlaid with alabaster moons, and bowed deeply to Kaeritha. The major's smile was as deep and apparently sincere as the one with which she'd first greeted Kaeritha, but the mask had grown increasingly threadbare. Kaeritha Saw the same green-yellow glow at the backs of Paratha's eyes, and she wondered what the other woman Saw when she looked at *her*.

"The Voice awaits you, Milady Champion," Paratha said graciously, and Kaeritha nodded and stepped past her through the ebony doors.

The outsized chamber beyond was obviously intended for formal audiences, yet it was equally obviously part of someone's personal living quarters. Pieces of art, statues, and furniture—much of it comfortably worn, for all its splendor—formed an inviting focus for the vaguely throne-like chair at the chamber's center.

A woman in the glowing white robes of a Voice of Lillinara sat in that chair. She was young, and quite beautiful, with long hair almost as black as Kaeritha's own and huge brown eyes in an oval face. Or Kaeritha thought so, anyway. It was hard to be certain when the poison-green glare radiating from the Voice blinded her so.

"Greetings, Champion of Tomanāk," a silvery soprano, sweeter and more melodious than Kaeritha's, said. "I have longed for longer than you may believe to greet a champion of one of Lillinara's brothers in this temple."

"Have you, indeed, Milady?" Kaeritha replied, and no one else needed to know how much effort it took to keep her own voice. conversational and no more than pleasant. "I'm pleased to hear that, because I've found myself equally eager to make *your* acquaintance."

"Then it would seem to be a fortunate thing that both of our desires have been satisfied this same day," the Voice said.

Kaeritha nodded and bent her head in the slightest of bows. She straightened, rested the heel of her right hand lightly on the hilt of one of her swords, and opened her mouth to speak again.

But before she could say a word, she felt a vast, powerful presence strike out at her. It slammed over her like a tidal wave, crushing as an earthquake, liquid and yet thicker and stronger than mortar or cement. It wrapped a crushing cocoon about her, reaching out to seize her and hold her motionless, and her eyes snapped wide.

"I don't know what you intended to say, Champion," that soprano voice said, and now it was colder than Vonderland ice and sibilant menace seemed to hiss in its depths. "It doesn't matter, though." The Voice laughed, the sound like fragments of glass shattering on a stone floor, and shook her head. "The arrogance of you 'champions'! Each of you so confident he or she will be protected and guided and warded from harm! Until, of course, the time comes for someone like your master to discard you."

Kaeritha felt the power behind the Voice pressing upon her own vocal cords to silence her, and said nothing. She only gazed at the Voice, standing motionless in the clinging web of Dark power, and the Voice laughed again and stood.

"I suppose it's possible that you truly have found a way to interfere with my plans here, little champion. If so, that will be more than a mere inconvenience. You see? I admit it. Yet it isn't something I haven't planned against and allowed for all along. The time had to come when someone would begin to suspect my Mistress was playing Her little games here in Quaysar. But, oh, *Dame Kaeritha*, the damage I've done to your precious war maids and their kingdom first! But perhaps you'd care to dispute that with me?"

She made a small gesture, and Kaeritha felt pressure on her vocal cords vanish.

"You had something you'd care to say?" the Voice mocked her.

"They aren't *my* 'precious war maids,'" Kaeritha said after a moment, and even she was vaguely surprised by how calm and steady her voice sounded. "And you're scarcely the first to try to do them ill. Some of the damage you've inflicted will stick, no doubt. I admit that. But damage can be healed, and Tomanāk—" it seemed to her that the Voice flinched ever so slightly at that name "—is the God of Truth, as well as Justice and War. And the truth is always the bane of the Dark, is it not, O 'Voice'?"

"So you truly think these stone-skulled Sothōii will actually believe a word of it? Or that the war maids *themselves* will believe it?" The Voice laughed yet again. "I think not, little champion. My plans go too deep and my web is too broad for that. I've touched and . . . convinced too many people—like that pathetic little puppet Lanitha, who believes Lillinara Herself commanded her to help safeguard my minor alterations so the war maids get what should have been theirs to begin with. Or your darling Yalith and her council, who don't even remember that they used to say anything else. As you yourself told their fool of an archivist, those who already hate and despise the war maids—those like Trisu—will never believe that *they* didn't forge the 'original documents' at Kalatha. And the war maids won't believe they're forgeries either. Not after all my careful spadework. And not without a champion of Tomanāk to attest to the legitimacy of Trisu's copies . . . and to explain how *Kalatha's* come to have been altered without the connivance of Yalith and her Council. And I'm very much afraid that you won't be around to tell them."

"Perhaps not," Kaeritha said calmly. "There are, however, other champions of Tomanāk, and one of them will shortly know all I know and everything I've deduced. I think I could safely rely upon him to accomplish my task for me if it were necessary."

The Voice's brown eyes narrowed and she frowned. But then she forced her expression to smooth once again, and shrugged.

"Perhaps you're correct, little champion," she said lightly. "Personally, I think the damage will linger. I've found such fertile ground on both sides—the lords who hate and loath everything the war maids stand for, and the war maids whose resentment of all the insults and injustices they and their sisters have endured over the years burns equally hot and bitter. Oh, yes, those will listen to *me*, not your precious fellow champion. They will believe what suits their prejudices and hatreds, and I will send my handmaidens forth to spread the word among them. *My* handmaidens, little champion, not those of that stupid, gutless bitch this place was built for!"

She glared at Kaeritha, and the knight felt the exultant hatred pouring off of her like smoke and acid.

"And to fan the flames properly," the false Voice continued, her soprano suddenly soft and vicious . . . and hungry, "Trisu is about to take matters into his own hands."

Kaeritha said nothing, but the other woman saw the question in her eyes and laughed coldly.

"There are already those who believe he connived at—or possibly even personally ordered—the murder of two handmaidens of Lillinara. He didn't, of course. For all his bigotry, he's proven irritatingly resistant to suggestions which might have led him to that sort of direct action. But that isn't what the war maids think. And it won't be what they think when men in his colors attack Quaysar itself. When they ride in through the gates of the town and the temple under his banner, coming as envoys to the Voice, and then butcher every citizen of Quaysar and every servant of the temple they can catch."

Despite herself, Kaeritha couldn't keep the horror of the images the false Voice's words evoked out of her eyes, and the other woman's smile belonged on something from the depths of Krahana's darkest hell.

"There will be survivors, of course. There always are, aren't there? And I'll see to it that none of the survivors anyone knows about were ever part of my own little web. The most attentive examination by one of your own *infallible* champions of Tomanāk will only demonstrate that they're telling the truth about what they saw and who they saw doing it. And one of the things they will see, little champion, will be myself and my personal guards and the most senior priestesses, barricading ourselves into the Chapel of the Crone to make our final stand. Trisu's men will attempt to break into it after us, of course. And I will call down the Lady's Wrath to utterly destroy the chapel's attackers . . . and everyone inside it. Which will neatly explain why there are no bodies. Or, at least, none of *our* bodies."

She shook her head in mock sorrow.

"No doubt some of Trisu's fellows will be horrified. Others will be charitable enough to believe he simply ran mad, but some of them will feel he was justified in burning out this nest of perversions, especially when the question of forged documents comes to the fore. And whatever Tellian and the Crown may do, little champion, the damage will be done. If Trisu is punished while protesting his innocence and flourishing his proof of forgery, then his fellow lords will blame his liege and the King for a miscarriage of justice. And if he isn't punished—if, for example, some interfering busybody champion of Tomanāk should examine him and find he's telling the truth and had nothing to do with the attack—then the *war maids* will be convinced it's all part of a cover-up and that he's *escaped* justice. And so will be many within the Church of Lillinara."

"Was that your plan all along?" Kaeritha asked. "To sow dissension and hatred and distrust?"

"Well, that and to enjoy the pretty fires and all the lovely killing, of course," the false Voice agreed, pouting as she studied her polished fingernails.

"I see." Kaeritha considered that for a moment, then cocked an eyebrow at the other woman. "I imagine it wasn't too difficult to assassinate the old Voice once Paratha became the commander of her bodyguards. I don't know whether you used poison or a spell, and I don't suppose it matters much, either way. But I would like to know what you did with the Voice who was supposed to replace her."

The false Voice froze, staring at her for just a moment. It was only an instant, almost too brief to be noticed, and then she smiled.

"What makes you think anyone did anything 'with' me? There was no need. It's not as if I were the first oh-so-perfect, straight and narrow priest or priestess to realize the truth, you know. Or would you pretend that no others have ever joined me in transferring my allegiance to a goddess more worthy of my worship?"

"No," Kaeritha acknowledged. "But it's not as if it happens very often, either. And it's never happened at all in the case of a *true* Voice. Nor has it in your case. You were never a priestess of the Mother— or did you truly think you could fool a Champion of Tomanāk about that?" She grimaced. "I knew the moment I Saw you that you were no priestess of Lillinara. In fact, I'm not entirely certain you were ever even human in the first place. But the one thing I'm positive of is that whoever—or whatever—you may be or look like, you are not the Voice the Church assigned here."

"Very clever," the false Voice hissed. She glared at Kaeritha for several seconds, then shook herself. "I'm afraid that sweet little girl suffered a mischief before she could take up her duties here," she said with pious sorrow. "I know how dreadfully it disappointed her—in fact, she told me so herself, just before I cut her heart out and Paratha and I ate it in front of her." She smiled viciously. "And since it bothered her so, and since I was in some small way responsible for her failure, I thought it incumbent upon me to come and discharge those responsibilities for her. A duty which I am now about to complete."

"Ah." Kaeritha nodded. "And just where do *I* fit into these plans of yours?" she inquired.

"Why, you *die*, of course," the false Voice told her. "Oh, not immediately—not *physically*, that is. I'm afraid we'll have to settle for just destroying your soul, for the moment. Then I'll replace it with a little demon whose essence I happen to have handy. He'll keep the flesh alive until 'Trisu' gets around to attacking. Who knows?" She smiled terribly. "Perhaps he'll enjoy experimenting with some of my guards. I'm afraid you won't be around anymore to observe the way he broadens your sexual horizons, but no doubt *he'll* be amused. And then, when Trisu attacks, you'll die gallantly, fighting to defend the temple against its desecrators. I think that will add a certain artistic finish to the entire affair, don't you? And whether it does or not, the opportunity to treat one of Tomanāk's little pets to the experience she so amply deserves would make this entire investment of effort worth while in its own right."

"I see," Kaeritha repeated. "And you believe that you can do all of this to me because—?"

"I don't *believe* anything," the false Voice told her flatly. "You've been mine to do with as I chose from the instant you stepped into this chamber, you stupid bitch. Why do you think you haven't been able to so much as move your head, or shift your feet?"

"A good question," Kaeritha conceded. "But there's a better one."

"What '*better* one'?" the false Voice sneered disdainfully.

"Why do *you* think I haven't been able to?" Kaeritha asked calmly, and both swords hissed from their sheaths as she catapulted towards the other woman.

The sudden eruption of movement took the false Voice completely by surprise. She'd never even suspected that Kaeritha had simply *chosen* not to move or speak when she became aware of the power crushing down upon her. Whoever—or whatever—the "Voice" might be, she had never before tried to control a champion of Tomanāk. If she had, she would have realized that no coercion, no spell of control or compulsion, even backed by the power of another god's avatar, could hold the will or mind of one who had sworn herself to the War God's service and touched His soul as He had touched hers. And because the false Voice hadn't realized that, she was still staring at Kaeritha—gawking in disbelief—as two matched short swords wrapped in coronas of brilliant blue fire drove through her heart and lungs.

A scream of agony cored with fury ripped through the audience chamber as the creature masquerading as a Voice of Lillinara fell back in a scalding gush of blood. Kaeritha twisted her wrists before the swords slid free, and even as she did, she went forward on the ball of her left foot while her right foot flashed up behind her. The heel of her heavy riding boot smashed into the person she'd sensed charging up behind her. It wasn't the clean, central strike she'd hoped for, but it was enough to deflect the attack and send the attacker crashing to the floor with a whooping cry of anguish.

Kaeritha let the force of her kick pivot her on her left foot so that she faced Major Paratha and the Voice's other servitors. The crackling blue aura of a champion of a God of Light roared up like a volcano of light, blasting through the audience chamber like a silent hurricane. It clung to her, flickering between her and the rest of the world like a thin canopy of lightning. But she could see through it clearly, and her eyes found Paratha with unerring speed. The major's saber was still coming out of its scabbard, and at least half of the others seemed stunned into momentary paralysis. But that paralysis wouldn't hold them for long, and Kaeritha knew it.

Every champion of Tomanāk had his or her own preferred combat style. Kaeritha's was totally unlike Bahzell's, except for one thing; neither of them was ever prepared to stand on the defensive if they had any choice. And since there was no one to watch her back or coordinate with, Kaeritha Seldansdaughter decided to make a virtue of the fact that there was only one of her.

She charged.

There was no doubt in her mind that Paratha was the most dangerous of her remaining opponents. Unfortunately, Paratha seemed disinclined to face her in personal combat. The major dodged swiftly, darting behind one of the corrupted priestesses, who shook herself and then charged to meet Kaeritha with no weapon besides a dagger and the naked fury blazing in her eyes.

Kaeritha's right blade came down with lightning speed and all the elegance of a cleaver. It lopped off her opponent's right hand like a pruning hook removing a limb. The woman shrieked as blood spouted from the stump of her wrist, and then Kaeritha's *left* blade went through the front of her throat from right to left in a backhanded fan of blood. Some of the blood splashed across Kaeritha's face, painting it like a barbarian Wakūo raider's.

"Tomanāk! *Tomanāk!*"

Kaeritha's war cry echoed in the chamber as another dagger grated on her breastplate, and a short, vicious thrust put one of her swords through her attacker's belly. The mortally wounded priestess fell back, writhing and screaming, and Kaeritha's champion's healing sense cringed as she realized all of the daggers coming at her were coated in deadly poison.

She slashed a third priestess to the floor with her right hand even as her left sword darted out to engage and parry yet another dagger. She twisted between two opponents, killing one and wounding the other as she passed, and then she was behind them all and spun on her toes like a dancer to charge once more.

"*Tomanāk!*"

Her foes seemed less eager to engage her this time, and she smiled like a direcat, teeth white through the blood on her face, as she slammed into them once more. Two more priestesses went down, then another, and finally Kaeritha heard alarm bells ringing throughout the temple complex.

Her jaw tightened. She had no doubt at all that the Voice and Paratha had drawn upon their patron's power to make certain Quaysar's guard force was loyal to them, whether or not those guards knew what they truly served. And even if there'd been no tampering at all, any guardsman who entered this audience chamber and saw the Voice and half a dozen or more of her priestesses dead on the floor was unlikely to assume that the person who'd killed them was the intended victim of an ambush by the Dark. She had no more than seconds before a veritable flood of guardsmen and war maids came pouring in upon her, and her swords flashed like lethal scythes as she slashed her way through the dagger-armed priestesses towards Major Paratha.

The bodies between them flew aside, screaming or already dead, and Paratha was no longer falling back. The major still declined to rush forward, watching with no more apparent emotion than a serpent as her allies fell like so much dead meat before Kaeritha's blades. But she made no effort to flee, either, and as Kaeritha looked at her, she Saw something she had never Seen before.

A cable of vile yellow-green energy linked Paratha to the corpse of the false Voice, and even as Kaeritha watched, something flowed along that cable. Something coming from the dead Voice to the living Paratha. And there were other cables, reaching out to the

fallen priestesses, as well. The web of sickening luminescence centered on Paratha, sucking greedily at whatever flowed along it.
Kaeritha didn't know what it was, but the corona which had clung
to Paratha from the outset suddenly blazed up, fierce and bright
as a forest fire to Kaeritha's Vision. And as it did, Kaeritha knew
at last which of the Dark Gods she faced, for a huge, hideous spider
wrapped in flame arose behind Paratha.

The spider of Shīgū, the Queen of Hell and Mother of Madness. Wife of Phrobus and mother of all his dark children. Far more
powerful than her son Sharnā, with a foul and twisted malice none
of her offspring could equal, and Lillinara's most bitter enemy for
the way in which her parody of womanhood perverted and fouled
all that Lillinara stood for.

The flame-wrapped creature towered up, compound eyes ablaze
with hatred and madness. Its mandibles clashed, dripping with
venom that flamed and hissed, bubbling on the polished stone floor
as it burned its way into it. Claws scraped and grated, and the
vilest stench Kaeritha had ever imagined filled the audience chamber. The hideous apparition loomed over her, reaching for her with
more than mere claws and pincers, and a black tide of terror lapped
out before it.

Even as Kaeritha recognized the spider, Paratha seemed to grow
taller. The false Voice hadn't been Shīgū's true tool, Kaeritha realized; *Paratha* had. The Voice might even have believed that she was
Shīgū's chosen, but in truth, it had always been Paratha, and now
the major no longer hid behind the camouflage of the Voice. She
was drinking in the life energy—probably even the very souls—of
her fallen followers, and something more was coming with it. Potent
as all that energy might be, it was only a focus, a burning glass which
reached out for something even stronger and more vile and focused
it all upon the major.

Paratha's face was transfigured, and her entire body seemed to
quiver and vibrate as Shīgū poured energy into her chosen. Kaeritha
remembered Bahzell's description of the night he had faced an
avatar of Sharnā, and she knew this was worse. Harnak of Navahk
had carried a cursed blade which had served as Sharnā's key to
the universe of mortals. Paratha carried no key; she *was* the key,
and Kaeritha's mind cringed away from the insane risk Shīgū had
chosen to run.

No wonder she'd been able to penetrate Lillinara's church, kill
Lillinara's priestesses and Voices and replace them with her own
tools! For all the endless ages since Phrobus' fall into evil, no god

of Dark or Light had dared to contend openly with one of his or her divine enemies on the mortal plane. They were simply too powerful. If they clashed directly, they might all too easily destroy the very universe for whose dominion they contended. And so there were limits, checks set upon their power and how they might intervene in the world of mortals. It was why there were champions of Light and their Dark equivalents.

Yet Shīgū *had* intervened directly. She had moved beyond the agreed upon limits and stepped fully into the world of mortals. Paratha was no champion. She was Shīgū's focus, her anchor in this universe. She wasn't touched by the power of Shīgū—in that moment, she *was* the power of Shīgū, and Kaeritha felt a terrifying surge of answering power pouring into her from Tomanāk.

"So, little champion," Paratha hissed. "You would contend with *Me*, would you?"

She laughed, and the web of her power reached out to her living minions, as well as the dead. Kaeritha heard their shrieks of agony—agony mingled with a horrible, defiled ecstasy—as Shīgū's avatar seized them. They didn't die, not right away, but that was no mercy. Instead, they became secondary nodes of the web centered upon Paratha. They blazed like human torches to Kaeritha's Sight as the same power crashed through them, and the will which animated Paratha—a will Kaeritha realized was no longer mortal, if it ever had been—fastened upon them like pincers. All nine of the remaining priestesses moved as one, closing in to form a deadly circle about Kaeritha with Paratha.

"So tasty your soul will be," Paratha crooned. "I'll treasure it like fine brandy."

"I think not," Kaeritha told her, and Paratha's eyes flickered as she heard another timbre in Kaeritha's soprano. A deeper timbre, like the basso rumble of cavalry gathering speed for a charge. The blue corona flickering around Kaeritha blazed higher and hotter, towering over her as the luminously translucent form of Tomanāk Orfro, God of War and Justice, Captain General of the Gods of Light, took form to confront the spider of Shīgū. The priestesses caught up in Shīgū's web froze as if stilled by some wizard's spell, but although Paratha drew back ever so slightly, her hesitation was only brief and her mouth twisted like the snarl of some rabid beast.

"Not this time, *Scale Balancer*," she—or someone else, using her voice—hissed venomously. "This one is *mine!*"

Her body seemed to tense, and, on the last word, a deadly blast of power ripped from her. It screamed across the audience chamber like a battering ram of yellow-green hunger, and the entire temple seemed to quiver on its foundations as it slammed into Kaeritha. Or, rather, into the blue nimbus blazing about her. The nimbus which deflected its deadly strength in a score of shattered streamers of vicious lightning that cracked and flared like whips of flame. Small explosions laced the chamber's walls, shattered fountains, and incinerated two of the living priestesses where they stood, and Kaeritha felt the staggering violence of the impact in her very bones. But that was all she felt, and she smiled thinly at her foe.

"Yours, am I?" she asked, and a strange sense of duality swept through her on the tide of Tomanāk's presence. "I think not," she repeated, and Paratha's face twisted in mingled fury and disbelief as Tomanāk's power shed the fury of her attack.

Kaeritha's smile was hard and cold, and she felt the call to battle throbbing in her veins. She was herself, as she had always been, and the will and courage which kept her on her feet in the face of Shīgū's hideous manifestation were her own. But behind her will, supporting it and bolstering her courage like a tried and trusted battlefield commander, was Tomanāk Himself. His presence filled her as Shīgū's filled Paratha, but without submerging her. Without requiring her subservience, or making her no more than his tool. She was who she had always been—Kaeritha Seldansdaughter, Champion of Tomanāk—and she laughed through the choking stench of Shīgū's perversion.

Paratha's entire face knotted with livid rage at the sound of that bright, almost joyous laugh, and the spider snarled behind her. But Kaeritha only laughed again.

"Your reach exceeds your grasp, Paratha. Or should I say Shīgū?" She shook her head. "If you think you want me, come and take me!"

"You may threaten and murder my tools," that voice hissed again, "but you'll find *Me* a different matter, little *champion*. No mortal can stand against My power!"

"But she does not stand alone," a voice deeper than a mountain rumbled from the air all about Kaeritha, and Paratha's face lost all expression as she and the power using her flesh heard it.

"If we two contend openly, power-to-power, this world will be destroyed, and you with it!" Paratha's mouth snarled the words, but the entire audience chamber shook with the grim, rumbling laugh which answered.

"This world might perish," Tomanāk agreed after a moment, "but you know as well as I which of us would be destroyed with it,

Shīgū." Paratha's lips drew back, baring her teeth like a wolf's, but Tomanāk spoke again before she could. "Yet it will not come to that. I will not permit it to."

"And how will you stop it, fool?!" Paratha's voice demanded with a sneer. "This is My place now, and *My* power fills it!"

"But you will bring no more power to it," Tomanāk said flatly. "What you have already poured into your tools you may use; all else is blocked against you. If you doubt me, see for yourself."

Paratha's eyes glared madly, but Kaeritha's heart leapt as she realized it was true. She had never faced such a terrifying concentration of evil, yet that concentration was no longer growing.

"If I am blocked, then so also are *you*," Paratha grated. "You can lend no more power to your tool, either!"

"My Swords are not my tools," Tomanāk replied softly. "They are my champions—my battle companions. And my champion is equal to anything such as you might bring against her."

"Is she *indeed*?" Paratha laughed wildly. "I think not."

Her saber seemed to writhe and twist. The blade grew longer, broader, and burned with the same sick, green radiance as the giant spider and its web.

"Come to me, *Champion*," she crooned. "Come and die!"

She leapt forward with the words, and even as she did, the remaining priestesses charged with her. They came at Kaeritha from all sides, a wave of deadly blades, all animated and wielded by the same malign presence.

Unlike the priestesses, Kaeritha was armored. But there was only one of her, and she dared not let them swarm over her with those envenomed daggers. Nor did she care to face whatever unnatural power had been poured into Paratha's blade while the priestesses came at her back. And so she spun to her left, away from Paratha, and her twin blades struck like serpents trailing tails of blue fire as she ripped open the belly and throat of the nearest priestess. She vaulted the body, lashing out with her right-hand sword, and another priestess staggered away as the backhand stroke slashed the tendons behind her knee.

Paratha—or Shīgū, if there was any difference—shrieked in wordless, enraged fury. Her remaining tools pursued Kaeritha, charging after her madly, and Kaeritha laughed coldly, deliberately goading Paratha with the sound.

She supposed some idiots who'd paid too much attention to bad bard's tales might have thought it cowardly, or unchivalrous, to concentrate on her unarmored, dagger-armed foes rather than go directly for the opponent who was also armored and armed. But although Kaeritha might be a knight, she'd been born a peasant, with all a peasant's pragmatism, and Tomanāk's Order believed in honor and justice, not stupidity. She turned again, once she was clear of the closing perimeter, and two more of Paratha's priest-esses caught up with her . . . and died.

Paratha's shriek was even wilder than before, but the two sur-viving priestesses fell back. The sole unwounded one bent over and seized the crippled one's arm and dragged her to one side, and Kaeritha turned once again—slowly, calmly, with a direcat's preda-tory grace—to face Paratha and the flaming spider form of Shīgū.

The glaring light web still connected Paratha's body to those of the false Voice and all of the others except Kaeritha herself, living or dead, in the audience chamber. But there was a difference now. The strands connected to the dead women glared with a brighter, fiercer radiance that flared high, then faded and died. And as they died, the nimbus about Paratha blazed more brilliantly still. The bodies themselves changed, as well. They went in an instant from freshly slain corpses to dried and withered husks. Like flies in a true spider's web, Kaeritha thought, sucked dry of all life and vitality.

Tomanāk had blocked Shīgū from pouring still more strength into her avatar, and so she had ripped everything from her dead servants, devouring even their immortal souls and concentrating that power in Paratha.

"Come on, 'Major Paratha,'" Kaeritha invited softly. "Let's dance."

Paratha screamed wordlessly and charged.

Whatever else Paratha might have been, she was an experienced warrior. She had the advantage of reach, and her armor was every bit as good as Kaeritha's. But she also realized she had only one weapon to Kaeritha's two, and for all her shrieking fury, she was anything but berserk.

Kaeritha discovered that almost too late, when Paratha's head-long charge suddenly transmuted into a spinning whirl to her left. The demented shriek had very nearly deceived Kaeritha into think-ing her foe truly was maddened by rage, attacking in a mindless fury. But Paratha was far from mindless, and she pivoted just beyond Kaeritha's own reach, while her longer, glowing saber came twisting in in a corkscrew thrust at Kaeritha's face.

Kaeritha's right hand parried the thrust wide, and their blades met in a fountaining eruption of fire. Blue and green lightning crackled and hissed, exploding against the chamber's walls and ceiling, blasting divots out of the marble floors like handfuls of thrown gravel. She gasped, staggered by the sheer ferocity of what should have been an oblique, sliding kiss of steel on steel. No doubt Paratha had felt the same terrible shock, but if she had, it didn't interrupt her movement. She was gone again, fading back before Kaeritha could even begin a riposte.

Kaeritha's entire right arm ached and throbbed, and sweat streaked her face as she turned, facing Paratha, swords at the ready, while alarm bells continued to clangor throughout the temple complex.

"And what will you do when the other guards come, little champion?" Paratha's voice mocked. "All *they* will see is you and me, surrounded by the butchered bodies of their precious priestesses. Will you slay them, as well, when I order them to take you for the murderer you are?"

Kaeritha didn't reply. She only moved forward, lightly, poised on the balls of her feet. Paratha backed away from her, eyes lit with the glitter of hell light watching cautiously, alertly, seeking any opening as intently as Kaeritha's own.

Kaeritha's gaze never wavered from Paratha, yet a corner of her attention stood guard. She'd always had what her first arms instructor had called good "situational awareness," and she had honed that awareness for years. And so, although she never looked away from her opponent, she was aware of the remaining unwounded priestess creeping ever so cautiously around behind her.

Paratha gave no sign that *she* was aware of anything except Kaeritha, but Kaeritha had almost allowed herself to be fooled once. Now she knew better. And she also knew she had only one opportunity to end this fight before the guards Paratha had spoken of arrived.

Paratha slowed, letting Kaeritha close gradually with her. Her saber danced and wove before her, its deadly, glowing tip leaving a twisting crawl of ugly yellow-green light in its wake, and Kaeritha's nerves tightened. The priestess with her poisoned dagger was close behind her, now, and Paratha's glittering eyes narrowed ever so slightly. If it was going to happen, Kaeritha thought, then it would happen—

Now!

The priestess sprang forward, teeth bared in a silent, snarling rictus, dagger thrusting viciously at Kaeritha's unguarded back. And in the same sliver of infinity, with the perfect coordination possible only when a single entity controlled both bodies, Paratha executed her own, deadly attack in a full-extension lunge.

It almost worked. It *should* have worked. But as Tomanāk had told Shīgū, his champion was the equal of anything the Spider might bring against her. Kaeritha had known what was coming, and she'd spent half her life honing the skills she called upon that day. Perfectly as Paratha—or Shīgū—had orchestrated the attack, Kaeritha's response was equally perfect . . . and began a tiny fraction of a second *before* Paratha's.

She twisted lithely, turning her torso through ninety degrees, and lunged at Paratha in a consummately executed stop-thrust. Her left-hand blade met the longer saber, twisting it aside in another of those terrible explosions of light and fury, then slid down its glaring length in a deadly extension that punched the blue-caparisoned short sword through Paratha's breastplate as if its tempered steel had been so much cobweb. And even as she lunged towards Paratha, her right-hand sword snapped out *behind* her, and the priestess who had flung herself at Kaeritha's back shrieked as her own charge impaled her upon that lethal blade.

For one instant, Kaeritha stood between her opponents, both arms at full extension in opposite directions, her sapphire eyes locked with Paratha's hell-lit eyes of brown. The other woman's mouth opened in shocked disbelief, and her saber wavered, then fell to the floor with a crackling explosion. Her left hand groped towards the cross guard of the sword buried in her chest and blood poured from her mouth.

And then the instant passed. Kaeritha twisted both wrists in unison, then straightened, withdrawing both her blades in one, crisp movement, and the bodies of both her opponents crumpled to the floor.

The alarm bells continued to sound, and Kaeritha turned from her fallen enemies to face the audience chamber's double doors. Foul-smelling smoke drifted and eddied, and small fires burned where the reflected bursts of contending powers had set furniture and wall hangings alight. The walls, ceilings, and polished floors were pitted and scorched, and the windows along the eastern wall had been shattered and blown out of their frames. Bodies—several as seared as the chamber's furnishings—sprawled everywhere amid pools of blood and the sewer stench of ruptured organs.

The blue corona of Tomanāk continued to envelop her, and she knew that any priestess who saw it—and who was prepared to think about it—would recognize it for what it was. Unfortunately, it was unlikely that most of the temple's regular guards would do

the same. Worse, she knew that although Shīgū's avatar had been
vanquished, the Spider Goddess' residual evil remained. Shīgū might
have been considerate enough to concentrate most of her more
powerful Servants here in the Voice's chambers for the attack on
Kaeritha. But she hadn't concentrated *all* of them, and even if her
remaining Servants hadn't hungered for revenge, they must know
that their only chance of escaping retribution lay in killing or at
least diverting Kaeritha.

Her jaw tightened. She knew what she'd do, if she'd been one
of Shīgū's tools faced by a champion of Tomanāk. She would feed
the uncorrupted members of Quaysar's guard force straight into
the champion's blades, and the chaos and confusion and the fact
that none of the innocents knew what was really happening would
let them do exactly that. Any champion would do all she could
to avoid slaying men and women who were only doing their sworn
duty, with no trace of corruption upon their souls. And if, despite
all she could do, that champion found herself forced to kill those
men and women in self-defense, the Dark would count that a far
from minor victory in its own right.

But Kaeritha had plans of her own, and her sapphire eyes were
grim as she kicked the chamber's doors wide and stalked through
them, swords blazing blue in her hands.

The bells were louder in the corridor outside the Voice's quarters, and Kaeritha heard sharp shouts of command and the clatter of booted feet. The first group of guards—a dozen war maids
and half that many guardsmen in Lillinara's moon-badged livery—
came around the bend at a run, and Kaeritha gathered her will.
She reached out, in a way she could never have described to
someone who was not also a champion, and seized a portion of
the power Tomanāk had poured into her. She shaped it to suit
her needs, then threw it out before her in a fan-shaped battering
ram.

Shouted orders turned into shouts of confusion as Kaeritha's
god-reinforced will swept down the corridor like some immense,
unseen broom. It gathered up those who were responding to what
they thought was an unprovoked attack upon the temple and its
Voice and simply pushed them out of the way. Under other circumstances, Kaeritha might have found the sight amusing as their
feet slid across the temple's floor as if its stone were polished ice.
Some of them beat at the invisible wall shoving them out of
Kaeritha's path with their fists. A few actually hewed at it with
their weapons. But however they sought to resist, it was useless.

They were shunted aside, roughly enough to leave bruises and contusions in some cases, but remarkably gently under the circumstances.

Yet some of the responding guards were *not* pushed out of Kaeritha's way. It took them precious seconds to realize that they hadn't been, and even that fleeting a delay proved fatal. Kaeritha was upon them, her blue eyes blazing with another, brighter blue, before they could react, for there was a reason her bow wave hadn't shunted them aside. Unlike the other guards, these were no innocent dupes of the corruption which had poisoned and befouled their temple. They knew who—or what—they truly served, and their faces twisted with panic as they found themselves singled out from their innocent fellows . . . within blade's reach of a champion of Tomanāk.

"*Tomanāk!*" Kaeritha hurled her war cry into their teeth, and her swords were right behind it. There was no way to avoid her in the corridor's confines, nor was there room or time for finesse. Kaeritha crunched into them, blazing swords moving with the merciless precision of some dwarvish killing machine made of wires and wheels.

Those trapped in front of the others lashed out with the fury of despair as they saw death come for them in the pitiless glitter of her eyes. It did them no good. No more than three of them could face her simultaneously, and all of them together would have been no match for her.

Those in the rear realized it. They tried to turn and flee, only to discover that the same energy which had pushed aside their fellows caught *them* like a tide of glue. They couldn't run; which meant all they could do was face her and die.

Kaeritha cut them down and stepped across their bodies. She continued her steady progress through the temple's corridors, retracing her path towards the Chapel of the Crone, and sweat beaded her brow. Another group of guards came charging down an intersecting passageway from her left, and once more her battering ram broom reached out. Most of the newcomers gawked in disbelief and confusion as they were shunted firmly aside . . . and those who were not gawked in terror as Kaeritha stalked into their midst like death incarnate, brushing aside their efforts to defend themselves and visiting Tomanāk's judgment upon them in the flash of glowing blades and the spatter of traitors' blood.

She resumed her progress towards the chapel, and felt a fatigue which was far more than merely physical gathering within her.

Forming and shaping raw power the way that she was was only marginally less demanding than channeling Tomanāk's presence to heal wounds or sickness. It required immense concentration, and the drain upon her own energy was enormous. She couldn't keep it up long, and every innocent she pushed out of her way only increased her growing exhaustion. But she couldn't stop, either. Not unless she wanted to slaughter—or to be slaughtered by—those same innocents.

Her advance slowed as her fatigue grew. Every ounce of will-power was focused on the next section of hall or waiting arch-way between her and her destination. She was vaguely aware of other bells—deeper, louder bells, even more urgent than the ones which had summoned the guards to the false Voice's defense—but she dared not spare the attention to wonder why they were sound-ing or what they signified. She could only continue, fighting her way through the seemingly endless members of Quaysar's Guard who had been corrupted.

And then, suddenly, she entered the Chapel of the Crone, and there were no more enemies. Even the innocent guards she had been pushing out of her way had disappeared, and the clangor of alarm bells had been cut short as though by a knife. There was only stillness, and the abrupt, shocking cessation of combat.

She stopped, suddenly aware that she was soaked with sweat and gasping for breath. She lowered her blades slowly, wondering what had happened, where her enemies had gone. The sounds of her own boots seemed deafening as she made her way slowly, cautiously, down the chapel's center aisle. And then, without warning, the chapel's huge doors swung wide just as she reached them.

The bright morning sunlight beyond was almost blinding after the interior dimness through which she had clawed and fought her way, and she blinked. Then her vision cleared, and her eyes wid-ened as she saw a sight she was quite certain no one had ever seen before.

She watched the immense wind rider dismount from the blue roan courser. He wore the same green surcoat she wore, and the huge sword in his right hand blazed with the same blue light. She stared at him, her battle-numbed mind trying to come to grips with his sudden, totally unanticipated appearance, and his left hand swept off his helmet. Foxlike ears shifted gently, cocking themselves in her direction, and a deep voice rumbled like welcome thunder.

"So, Kerry, is this after being only for those with formal invi-tations, or can just anyone be dropping in?"

She shook her head, unable to make herself quite believe what she was seeing, and stepped out through the chapel doors two of the Quaysar war maids had swung wide. The temple courtyard seemed impossibly crowded by the score or so of coursers and wind riders behind Bahzell. Most of the wind riders were still mounted, interposing with their coursers between the remainder of the Quaysar Guards and the chapel. Two of them weren't. Baron Tellian of Balthar and his wind-brother Hathan had dismounted behind Bahzell, and Kaeritha shook her head in disbelief.

"Bahzell," she said in a voice which even she recognized was far too calm and remote from the carnage behind her, "what are *you* doing here? And what are you—or any hradani—doing with a *courser*, for Tomanāk's sake?"

"Well," he replied, brown eyes gleaming with wicked amusement, "it's all after being the letter's fault."

"Letter?" She shook her head again. "That's ridiculous. My letter won't even arrive at Balthar for another day or two!"

"And who," he asked amiably, "said a thing at all, at all, about *your* letter?" It was his turn to shake his head, ears tilted impudently. "It wasn't from you, being as how it's clear as the nose on Brandark's face that you've not got the sense to be asking for help *before* you need it. No, this one was after coming from Leeana."

"Leeana?" Kaeritha parroted.

"Aye," Bahzell said a bit more somberly. "She'd suspicions enough all on her own before ever you came back to Kalatha from Thalar. She'd written a bit about them to her mother, but it was only after you and she spoke that she was sending the lot of her worries to Tellian and me. As soon as ever I read her letter, it was pike-staff clear as how I'd best be on my way to Quaysar. I'm hoping you won't be taking this wrongly, Kerry, but charging in here all alone, without so much as me or Brandark to watch your back, was a damned-fool hradani sort of thing to be doing."

"It was my job," she said, looking around for something to wipe her blades on. Tellian silently extended what looked like it had once been part of a temple guard's surcoat. She decided not to ask what had happened to its owner. Instead, she simply nodded her thanks and used it to clean her swords while she continued to gaze up at Bahzell.

"And I never once said as how it wasn't," he replied. "But I'm thinking you'd be carving bits and pieces off of my hide if I'd gone off to deal with such as this without asking if you'd care to be coming along. Now wouldn't you just?"

"That's different," she began, and broke off, recognizing the weakness of her own tone as Bahzell and Tellian both began to laugh.

"And just *how* is it different, Kerry?" another, even deeper voice inquired, and Kaeritha turned to face the speaker.

Tomanāk Himself stood in the courtyard, and all around her people were going to their knees as His presence washed over them. Wind riders slid from their saddles to join them, and even the coursers bent their proud heads. Only Kaeritha and Bahzell remained standing, facing their God, and He smiled upon them.

"I'm still waiting to hear how it's different," He reminded her in gently teasing tones, and she drew a deep breath as His power withdrew from her. It left quickly, yet gently, flowing back through her like a caress or the shoulder slap of a war captain for a warrior who had done all that was expected of her and more. There was a moment of regret, a sense of loss, as that glorious tide flowed back to the One from Whom it had come, yet her contact with Him was not severed. It remained, glowing between them, and as He reclaimed the power He had lent her, she found herself refreshed, filled with energy and life, as if she had just arisen on a fresh day and not come from a deadly battle for her very life and soul.

"Well, maybe it's not," she said after a moment or two and with a fulminating sideways glower for Bahzell. "But it still wasn't *Leeana's* place to be telling you that I needed help!"

"No more did she," Bahzell said. "All she wrote was what she suspected—not that it was after taking any geniuses to know what such as you were likely to be doing about it if it should happen as how she was right." He shrugged.

"All right," Kaeritha said after another pregnant moment. "But that still leaves my other question."

"And which other question would that be?" Tomanāk asked.

"The one about him and *him*," she snapped, jabbing an index finger first at Bahzell and then at the huge stallion who stood regarding her over her fellow champion's shoulder with what could only be described as an expression of mild interest. "What's a hradani—*any* hradani, but especially a *Horse Stealer* hradani—doing with a courser? I thought they, um, didn't like one another very much."

"Ah, now, I don't think it's my business to be telling that particular tale," Tomanāk told her with a slow smile. He chuckled at the disgusted look she gave Him, then turned his head, gazing about the temple courtyard. There were dozens of bodies lying about, Kaeritha realized—all that was left of the corrupted members of the Quaysar Guard who had tried to prevent Bahzell and his wind brothers from fighting their way to her aid. Tomanak gazed at them for several seconds, then shook His head with a sad sigh.

"You've done well, Kaeritha. You and Bahzell alike, as I knew you would. I believe this temple will recover from Shīgū's interference, although you'll still have your work cut out for you in Kalatha. My Sister will be sending two or three of her Servants to aid you in that work, but this is still a matter of Justice, and so falls under your responsibility."

"I understand," she said quietly, and he nodded.

"I know you do. And I know I can count upon you and Bahzell to complete all the tasks you've been called to assume. But for today, my Blades, enjoy your victory. Celebrate the triumph of the Light you've brought to pass. And while you do," He began to fade from their sight, His face wreathed in a huge smile, "perhaps you can get Bahzell to tell you how a Horse Stealer became a wind rider. It's well worth hearing!" He finished, and then He was gone.

"Well?" Kaeritha turned to her towering sword brother and folded her arms.

"Well what?" he asked innocently.

"Well you know perfectly *well* what!"

"Oh," Bahzell said. "That 'well.' " He grinned toothily at her. "Now that's after being a mite of a long story. For now, let's just leave it that while you've been off enjoying your little vacation in Kalatha and Thalar, there's some of us as have been doing some honest work a bit closer to home."

"Work?" Kaeritha repeated. "*Work?* Why, you hairy-eared, overgrown, under-brained, miserable excuse for a champion! I'll give you *work*, Milord Champion! And when I'm done with you, you'll wish you'd never—"

She advanced upon him with fell intent, and Bahzell Bahnakson demonstrated once again the sagacity and tactical wisdom which were the hallmarks of any champion of Tomanāk.

He took to his heels instantly, and despite the carnage all about them, Baron Tellian and the other wind riders burst into laughter as Kaeritha paused beside a planter only long enough to snatch out a handful of ornamental river stones suitable for throwing at him before she went speeding off in pursuit.